HomEfront

portal wars III

Jay Allan

Also by Jay Allan

Marines (Crimson Worlds I)
The Cost of Victory (Crimson Worlds II)
A Little Rebellion (Crimson Worlds III)
The First Imperium (Crimson Worlds IV)
The Line Must Hold (Crimson Worlds V)
To Hell's Heart (Crimson Worlds VI)
The Shadow Legions (Crimson Worlds VII)
Even Legends Die (Crimson Worlds VIII)
The Fall (Crimson Worlds IX)
Tombstone (A Crimson Worlds Prequel)
Bitter Glory (A Crimson Worlds Prequel)
The Gates of Hell (A Crimson Worlds Prequel)

MERCS (Successors I)
The Prisoner of Eldaron (Successors II)
The Black Flag (Successors III) – June 2016

Into the Darkness (Refugees I)
Shadows of the Gods (Refugees II)
Revenge of the Ancients (Refugees III) – March

Gehenna Dawn (Portal Worlds I)
The Ten Thousand (Portal Wars II)

The Dragon's Banner (Pendragon Chronicles I)

HOMEFRONT

Homefront is a work of fiction. All names, characters, incidents, and locations are fictitious. Any resemblance to actual persons, living or dead, events or places is entirely coincidental.

ISBN: 978-0692582343

It is fatal to enter any war without the will to win it.

- Douglas MacArthur

Part One
Return

Chapter 1

From the Journal of Jake Taylor:

I sit here writing this on the eve of our return. Soon we will go through the Portal, step from the steaming jungles of Ghasara, and onto the frozen steppes of Siberia. It is an undiscovered Portal on Earth, or at least it appears to be, and though we will emerge in a deserted wasteland far from our objectives, we shall have time to bring our forces through unopposed. Then the war for Earth will begin.

Earth. My home. Home to all of us. And yet now, to my mind, barely the fading sinews of a dream almost faded from re-membrance. We have spent years in hell, my soldiers and I, the lives we once knew sacrificed on the pyre of aggrandizement and power for the corrupt politicians who rule Earth. I know where I was born, where I lived before I was sent to Erastus. But I'm not sure I even have a home anymore. Looking at a whole world is one thing, but the thought of walking through the New Hampshire woods and back to that house, so full of memories of childhood and family, is terrifying. I don't know what has become of my family, if they are still there—or indeed, still alive—but the thought of truly going home terrifies me more than any battle. I left a boy, gentle in nature and bookish, and I return a warrior, a killer, part machine and so far from that mild-mannered kid I must remind myself that he was indeed once me. What will they think of me? Will they know me? Will they fear me?

But there is more of concern than my own possible homecoming. We have much to reckon with, the men of UN Force Erastus, and the other soldiers who have rallied to our cause. For years we fought an unjust war, feeding our own brethren into the fires even as we slaughtered thousands of the Machines, the disrespectful name we created for the Tegeri's genetically engineered allies. We cursed the Tegeri, called them murderers, aggressors, and yet it was we who filled those roles, and though the soldiers of Earth sent to war were lied to and deceived, it is yet our hands awash with the blood of the innocent. I shall carry that to my grave, the fading, partial recollections of the Machines I killed, the stench of death on the battlefield, the feeling in my stomach when I first learned the truth...all of it.

I have sworn vengeance on those who caused this tragedy—all of us have—and we shall have it, or none of us will survive. We shall spill the blood of our enemies, watch as the life slips from their eyes and they breathe their last painful, gasping breaths. And we shall never cease, not until all responsible are dead, and all who aided them and are stained with their guilt.

Our ranks have swelled, and we now number almost 60,000, a vastly greater force than escaped the terrible battle on Juno against the Black Corps. My officers have used the Tegeri knowledge of the Portal network to travel to other embattled worlds, to seek out the commanders of each Earth force, to rally our brothers to our side. And on each planet, as they told the Earth soldiers the terrible truth, the Tegeri and their Machine allies disengaged and began to withdraw through the Portals. Whether the warriors on those worlds joined us or not, their wars were over. They would lose no more men to the ravages of battle. They would slaughter no more of the Machines, the creatures they had reviled but who were only defending themselves.

Not all believed us. Our story is a difficult one to accept, and these men had spent years fighting the Machines, watching their own friends and comrades die at the hands of the Tegeri's manufactured soldiers. The hatred spawned on the battlefield grips deeply, and it takes long to fade. Still, thousands flocked to our banners, swelling our ranks.

Now it is almost time. Time for our return. Time to take the

war to our true enemies, and bring this nightmare to its final conclusion. There is just one more battle. One more front.
   Homefront.

"We're at 50% strength, sir. I need evac now…our medic got hit and I've got six seriously wounded." Lieutenant Lyle Webster was crouched behind a rock outcropping. His platoon had been on the line for three straight days of nonstop combat, and only twenty-one of the forty-three men who'd marched out of Firebase Sigma with him were still standing. His six wounded were lying in a row, in the most protected spot he could find, and Private Haas was doing his best to keep them alive, despite his complete lack of medical training or equipment.

"I'll get a bird out there as soon as I can, Lieutenant. We've got units in the same shape all along the line, so you might be on your own a while."

That's just great, Webster thought grimly, glancing back at his makeshift aid station and completely unqualified medic. "Yes, sir," he replied simply. There was no point in arguing. He knew Major Tomms would do whatever he could for his soldiers. "Sir, we're running low on ammo too…"

"Logistics are backed up now too, Webster." A pause. "I'll see if I can get you something in the next couple hours. Can you hold until then?"

Webster swallowed hard. The answer to that question depended on a lot of things, not the least of which was what the Machines did next. "Yes, sir. We'll hold." Webster wasn't sure bravado was much of a substitute for reality, but it was all he had right now. Besides, if his men didn't hold they'd get run over by the Tegeri. Their position was strong, but the ground behind was wide open—a perfect killing ground for pursuing a broken force.

Webster had no idea what had prompted the all-out attack orders from UNGov. The war on Samar had been proceeding satisfactorily, with progress almost a year ahead of schedule. But the new offensive threw all of that out of whack. Casualties were through the roof, and as far as Webster knew, no reinforcements had been sent in months. It felt like an act of desperation, but why? Nothing happening on Samar certainly. So what?

"Rizzo, I want you to move to the left. Grab a good spot with decent cover. Just in case they decide to hit us." The Machines had been standing on the defensive all along the line, retiring from one covered position to the next, yielding ground but taking a terrible toll from the attackers in return. But Webster wasn't going to get careless. The enemy had to know how battered his people were. If they chose to counterattack now, he was far from sure his savaged platoon could hold. He damned sure wanted his only surviving sniper ready for them.

"Got it, Lieutenant. Maybe up on that small ridge." Rizzo pointed upward to a jagged line of rock about fifty yards north.

Webster nodded. "Looks good to me, but it's your call. Just be ready in case those bastards decide to come at us."

"Yes, sir." Rizzo grabbed the heavy sniper's rifle from where he'd leaned it against a rock, and he slipped around the nearest outcropping, crouching low and heading for the spot he'd chosen.

Webster slid down and sat behind the rock, reaching behind him into his pack. His hands rooted around for a few seconds and came out with a small nutrition bar. He hated the things... they were dry and mealy, and they tasted like shit. But it was all he had left, and even with his stomach twisted in knots, he was too hungry to ignore it any longer. He knew the thing would sit in his gut like a rock, but he couldn't afford to let his energy levels slip. Not now. He tore off the wrapping and took a small bite, making a face as he began to chew.

"Lieutenant, we've got activity along the enemy line!" It was Barofsky, the scout, on the comlink. His voice was pitched with excitement. Webster had sent him forward to reconnoiter along a narrow defile that offered cover at least halfway to the enemy position.

Webster shoved the rest of the food bar into one of his pockets, and reached out for his rifle, spinning around and looking cautiously over the rock. The enemy line was at extreme range, but that didn't mean a bullet couldn't find your forehead if you got careless.

He expected to see Machines climbing out of their cover and moving toward his line, and his body tensed, reacting to thoughts of incoming enemy shells that might begin falling any second. But nothing was coming his way. He reached down to his belt and pulled up his scanning goggles, setting them for Mag 10 and slipping them on his head.

The Machines were retreating! At least that's damned sure what it looked like.

He tapped the com unit on his shoulder, flipping it to the battalion command line. "Major, the…"

"The Machines are retreating," Tomms replied before Webster could finish. "I know, Lieutenant…we're getting reports of the same thing all across the line."

Webster felt his stomach clench slightly, half expecting the major to order his people to attack immediately. But exhausted, low on ammunition, and with half a dozen wounded comrades to worry about, an attack was the last thing his people needed. And if his soldiers went forward and it wasn't a real retreat…if it was a ruse…

"I want your people to stay put until further notice, Lieutenant," Tomms said over the com. "At least until we can figure out what's going on."

Webster felt a wave of relief. "Yes, sir. Understood." He flipped his com to the platoon line. "Everybody stay put. Nobody gets careless, nobody does anything stupid, got it?"

He peered again over the top of the small outcropping, eyes looking through his scanner. No doubt…the enemy was pulling back, abandoning the strong defensive line that had essentially stopped the human offensive. Webster was grateful for any break, but still there was one question looming large in his head.

What the hell is going on?

*   *   *

"My God, it's as hot as the sun here." Captain Lars Hampton

stood in front of the Portal, the shimmering dance of lights still visible from the passage. He rubbed his hand across his face, wiping away the beads of sweat that had already begun forming.

Hank Daniels let out a deep laugh. "You, my friend, have never been on Erastus." Daniels stepped out on a thick ledge of rock and looked out over the yellow, sandy desert lying before him. Samar's sun was huge in the morning sky, and its rays beat down remorselessly on the blasted landscape below. The Portal was built into the side of a small desert mountain, perhaps fifty meters above the seemingly endless expanse of flat sand. "This is like a bracing blast of refreshing air." Daniels turned and smiled, but despite his words, he too was sweating profusely.

The veteran colonel was one of Jake Taylor's inner circle, one of the men who had been with the legendary leader since the beginning. Though he didn't want to admit it, to himself or anyone else, he'd been off Erastus for years now, and he'd marched and fought across worlds with cool breezes and stinging rains...and even snow. Erastus, the world he and his brethren had called Gehenna, was indeed hotter than Samar, its two suns denying it any real night, providing only a pair of brief twilight periods, when only one was in the sky. It was the hottest world men had ever lived upon, and while Daniels wore his service there as a badge of honor, deep down he knew he was no longer as adapted to the hellish climate as he had once been.

Many of the men in the Army of Liberation, most now in fact, had flocked to the colors once the crusade had already begun, and they looked up to Taylor almost as if he were somehow divine, an avatar sent to lead them to destroy those responsible for the terrible injustice they had suffered. But Hank Daniels had known Taylor when he was a mere corporal, blissfully unaware of the fraudulent nature of the war he and his fellow-soldiers were fighting. Daniels was a Supersoldier, just like Taylor, just like the other surviving Erastus veterans. And that made the troops from the other Portal worlds view him almost as they did Taylor, with a sort of nervous deference. But Hank Daniels wasn't the quiet, philosophical warrior Taylor was, and his easily provoked and often foul mouthed diatribes were known and feared throughout the army.

"It's not refreshing me, sir. I feel like I'm going to pass out."

"You won't." Daniels turned and looked at the rest of the half dozen soldiers who'd come through the Portal with him. "None of you will. I thought I was going to die when I first stepped out into the heat of Erastus. But you're more durable than you think, your bodies more adaptable." Daniels paused. "I'm not saying you'll be comfortable, but you'll survive well enough."

Unless the troops of Force Samar don't listen to our entreaties and decide to shoot us instead. He decided not to share that last dark thought with his comrades.

"So, let's go. The sooner we get the airship assembled and find the Samar HQ, the faster we can get out of here." Daniels fully intended to complete his mission, to rally Force Samar to the Army of Liberation's banner. But he knew he didn't have time to waste. The army would be moving on Earth soon...and the idea of missing the final invasion was more than he cared to contemplate. Daniels had been with Taylor from the start, and he was determined to be at his friend's side when they stepped foot on the green grass of Earth.

*   *   *

"Start with that crate." Captain Yantz pointed toward one of the large boxes they had brought through the Portal, glancing at his two assistants. Yantz was one of the AOL's tech officers, and he and his comrades had worked wonders keeping the army's vehicles and equipment working using a combination of parts cannibalized from wrecked units and some bits and pieces provided by the Tegeri. Hank Daniels was on Samar to convince as many of the members of its planetary army as he could to come over to the AOL, but first Yantz had to get him more than two thousand kilometers to the coordinates T'arza had provided marking Force Samar's nearest major concentration.

Daniels turned and watched as Yantz' people worked. He knew they wouldn't have a single transport or airship still functional without the supply line from their former enemies. It had taken Daniels a bit longer that Taylor to trust T'arza and the other Tegeri, but he'd eventually come around, and now he felt the same guilt Taylor did, relived the hundreds of times he'd killed Machines, and the satisfaction he'd felt gunning them down, feeling as though he was wiping out alien monsters, creatures who would come to Earth and spread death and destruction if they got past him and his comrades.

What fools we were, he thought, feeling the usual surge of rage deep inside. Taylor was the heart and soul of the AOL, and his commitment to destroying those responsible for the war was like steel. But Daniels was the one man in the army whose anger burned even hotter. If Taylor's determination ever failed, if the suffering and cost of the crusade ever became more than he could bear, Daniels knew it would fall to him to push his friend forward, to do whatever it took to win the final victory. Hank Daniels would never forget what UNGov had done, and he would let nothing interfere with his vengeance. Humanity had allowed itself to be fooled, to let tyrants exploit its fears to gain its meek surrender. And now it would have to pay whatever price the universe demanded, wash away the sins of its foolishness with blood.

"We'll have the airship ready in two hours, sir." Yantz was pulling structural supports out of one of the crates as he spoke, lining them up in piles organized by size.

"Two hours?" Daniels knew Yantz was good, but two hours was fast, even for the gifted engineer.

"Yes, sir," Yantz snapped back. "We've assembled and disassembled this thing a dozen times over the last year. Sooner or later we had to get good at it."

"Two hours is good, alright, Captain. "You manage that, and I'll personally ask General Taylor to give you a commendation."

"Thank you, sir!"

Daniels smiled at the energy in Yantz' voice. Jake Taylor was his friend, more than a brother. But he was always amazed at the near-worship so many of the soldiers in the army felt for their commander. He'd have never imagined his old comrade, Corporal Taylor could inspire men this way. Taylor had always been a good man, a friend you wanted at your back in a tight spot. But he'd become...something else. And Daniels knew it was that power inside his old comrade that gave them all hope.

"Very well, Captain. If you're going to be done in two hours, I better think about what I want to say to the officers of Force Samar."

* * *

"General Simmons, we have a report from the outer pickets in blue sector." There was a strange tone to the communications officer's voice, not shock quite, but profound surprise at least. "They report a party requesting a...parlay."

"A parlay?" Simmons turned abruptly, his voice harsh and raw. "The Machines want to talk? After twelve years of bloody war they want to talk?" His words were heavy with anger, but also surprise. He'd come to Samar with the first expeditionary force, and as long as there had been a Force Samar in the field, Tyrell Simmons had been a part of it, and for the last six years, its commander. And in all that time he'd never received a communication of any sort from the enemy.

"No, sir, not the Machines...they're humans, sir. They say they are from the Army of Liberation, whatever that is, and they request an immediate meeting with you."

"Humans? How is that possible?"

"I don't know, sir, but Captain Tillis seems quite certain. They are human, he reports, though there is something...different...about their leader."

"Different?" Simmons' gut tightened. Could it be a trick? Some kind of ploy? A suicide force sent to destroy army headquarters? "Different how?" he snapped back.

"For one thing, Captain Tillis says his eyes are silver...like metal."

Simmons stared back at the comm officer. Silver eyes? Some kind of construct? Perhaps it is a trick. But...

"Tell, Captain Tillis he is to keep them at his checkpoint. I will meet with them there as soon as possible."

"Yes, General." A few seconds later: "Captain Tillis acknowledges, sir. He will detain the visitors and await further instructions." Another pause. "Are you sure you should go, sir? You are the army commander, and your death would be a major victory for the enemy. Perhaps Major..."

"No." Simmons' voice was hard, decisive. "I will go. Perhaps it is unwise, but if I fall victim to an enemy ruse, so be it. The army will remain intact, and Colonel Posca will take command. Besides, if this is not an enemy trick, if these are really human beings...I must know who they are and why they have come."

"Yes, sir." The officer sounded less than convinced. But arguing with generals wasn't in his job description.

"Have my transport ready in five minutes, Lieutenant."

"Yes, sir." The officer punched a few keys and turned back to acknowledge. But Simmons was already out the door.

* * *

"I know this is difficult to accept, General, but I must ask you to review all the evidence again. In all your time on Samar, have any of your people ever returned home? Gone back through the Portal to Earth? Anyone besides the UNGov staffers?" Hank Daniels sat at the makeshift table, just outside the firebase where his airship had landed. The sun was searing hot, but there was no shade save for a small canopy a group of soldiers had hastily erected. The heat was still getting to him, but not as badly as it had at first. There was still a soldier of Erastus inside him, and it was clawing its way out, shaking a shadowy fist at Samar's massive sun as if to shout, "Is that all you've got?"

Simmons looked across the table, trying not to stare at Daniels' eyes. "All a lie? Everything? But we fought the Machines for twelve years. They killed thousands of my men."

"Because we invaded their worlds, we attacked them on sight. You said you came to Samar in the first wave, General. Did the Tegeri or the Machines attack you at the Portal? Did they wipe out your lead elements before you could gain a foothold? Or did they only start fighting when you attacked them?"

Simmons had a blank expression on his face, a look of uncertainty and confusion. Daniels knew his new acquaintance was thinking back, his mind peeling the pages to those fateful first days when he'd arrived on Samar. And he knew whatever recollection remained to the general would support what he had said. Daniels hadn't been there in the first days of the Erastus campaign, but T'arza had told him the Machines had never been the first to fire, not on any contested Portal world. And he had come to believe the Tegeri representative, and even to trust him.

"But the slaughters...they attacked the first colonies. They killed all those people. I saw the vids, we all did." Simmons' normally gruff voice was soft, uncertain.

"Those videos were doctored, General. They were fakes. Intended to work us up to fight, to get us to accept our postings and to feel like we were going off to defend Earth from a pack of alien monsters." Daniels reached into his pocket and pulled out a data chip, setting it down on the table. "Here is the real footage, but I have to warn you...you may find it upsetting."

Simmons looked up at one of the aides standing next to the table and gestured. The officer saluted and ran off, returning a moment later with a large tablet. He set the device on the table in front of the general.

Simmons picked up the chip and slipped it into the tablet. The screen lit up with a view of a colonial settlement, a series of semi-portable shelters lined up in a rectangular grid, with the old American flag flapping the in the breeze in a small center square. It was a peaceful image, but that changed in a few seconds. Explosions lit up the dusk sky, and shadowy figures moved forward, coming at the village from beyond a low ridge. The attackers held assault rifles, and as they cleared the ridge, they opened fire. The colonists were rushing out of their homes and into the makeshift streets of the settlement...right into the assault weapon fire.

The images were similar to the ones Simmons and Daniels had seen in training camp...but then they focused on the attackers as they moved steadily, relentlessly forward. They weren't

Machines, as they had been in the videos Simmons had seen before. Nor were they Tegeri. They were men, UN special forces, and they maintained their fire as they closed, killing everyone in sight. Simmons stared at the screen, watching in horror as the soldiers chased the few survivors, running them down, killing them all. Men, women, children…it didn't matter. By the time the shooting stopped, every colonist was dead.

Simmons looked up from the screen, but he didn't say anything, not for a long while. Finally, he said, "How do I know these are real? Perhaps they are the ones that have been modified."

"The truth is, you don't know. You will have to decide for yourself." Daniels' voice was calm, rational. He was a zealot, a man obsessed with defeating UNGov, but there was no trace of that as he sat at the table and spoke to the commander of Force Samar. He was reason itself. "You will have to consider everything, General. You will find the Machines are gone, within another day, two at most, the last of them will have transited offworld."

Daniels saw the confusion in Simmons' face, the frustration as he tried to make sense of the situation. "Whatever you decide to do, the war on Samar is over. The Machines will not come back. The left because we came here, because we asked them to. They are not your enemy. The Tegeri are not your enemy. They fought you for so long only because they were attacked, because they knew if human forces reached the Tegeri homeworld they would invade.

"As I said, the war here is over…but none of you will be allowed to return to Earth. UNGov expected your struggle to continue for another decade at least. If things had gone on according to their plan, your replacements would have been steadily reduced, leaving as few soldiers in the field as possible when the planet was finally conquered. But we have upset their planning. You still have a large force deployed, one far beyond any reasonable garrison. Yet, still, you will remain here, all of you, for as long as you live. Go ahead…report the situation. Request permission for your people to begin to return to Earth. See what response you receive."

Daniels knew the whole truth, that UNGov never allowed its soldiers to return from the Portal worlds where they fought. The last thing the politicians wanted was a population of veteran troops running around on Earth, a constant threat to their authority. And that was especially true now that the AOL was rampaging across the Portal worlds constituting the worst threat to UN control since the takeover forty years before. Daniels knew UNGov would never allow 15,000 veterans to come back from Samar...and their refusal would make his case. He felt an uncomfortable feeling in his stomach, a coldness. What would UNGov do with the planetary armies now that the Tegeri were pulling back from all the contested worlds? According to T'arza, there were fifty-three such planets, and the Tegeri estimate of total deployed human strength was 680,000.

That is a lot of men, deceived or forced outright to abandon their lives, to leave Earth forever for a life of unending war...

What will they do? Will they call them back now, hoping they will fight us? Or will they leave them where they are, strand them...or worse?

"I already reported that the Machines are withdrawing. I was told to prepare to survey the formerly-Machine held areas of the planet, and to locate as many Portals as possible. And to ready my forces to conduct exploratory missions through any such transit points we locate." Simmons hesitated. "I requested authorization to send my wounded back to Earth at least...but permission was denied." Another pause. "I was told UNGov wanted to maintain full strength on Samar, that the withdrawal was likely a ruse, that they expected the Machines to return."

"And how would they know that?" Daniels had managed to keep his words civil and calm, but now his anger toward UNGov was showing itself. "How would they have any idea what the Tegeri were planning?" He looked down at the table for a moment and then back up at Simmons. "There is something else I must tell you, something my experience on Erastus, and the other worlds we've visited has taught me. You have spies in your army, General. Even if you do not have any operating in the open, such as an Inquisitor team, you can be certain some of your officers and men are reporting to Geneva. Indeed, any of your personnel who have had return privileges to Earth must be suspect. And others too. It is unlikely you will be able to identify them all, no matter what you do."

"I do not doubt what you say, Colonel, but does that not make your mission here fraught with danger? Would it not be the safer course for me to have you arrested and turn you over to UNGov officials?"

"Indeed, General, that would be the safer alternative, assuming they don't simply decide to do away with you to contain the contamination. If that is the course you choose, I would suggest you waste no time. The longer we parlay, the more suspect you will become."

"Why would you tell me all of this? Why would you come here and risk what I may choose to do?"

"As to why I am here, the simple answer is because General Taylor ordered me to come. We seek to reach as many of our compatriots, human soldiers consigned to fight UNGov's dirty war. I am here because I could reach Samar in the time I had available, and because we will not let our brothers continue to fight and die in bondage when we have the ability to bring them the truth."

Daniels paused and looked across the table. "And, as for the risk…I have been at war my entire adult life, General, and I have never let the danger interfere with my actions. I have come asking a great deal of you, and if I am to ask so much of your people, it is only reasonable that I prove my intentions, that I put myself at risk in coming here. If you choose to ignore all I have said and shown you then so be it." He sat silently for a few second then added, "Though I warn you to position as many of your soldiers as possible before you make a move. I cannot express strongly enough how formidable my enhancements make me in combat." There was no anger in Daniels' voice, no animosity. Yet his words dripped with unintentional menace.

"So," Simmons said, hesitating before continuing. "…suppose I am persuaded. What would you have me do?"

"First, you must secure the Portal…with men you absolutely

trust. You must allow nothing to leave Samar. Not even the crews ferrying in supplies. You must detain everyone who transits in, and you must keep all but your chosen guards from the Portal. You are three transits from Earth, and that should slow UNGov's response time."

Simmons nodded. "Yes, that makes sense. Go on."

"You must redouble security on all vital installations...supplies, communications, that kind of thing. And also yourself and your top officers, at least the ones you know you can trust. You may have UN operatives in your ranks who will attempt to assassinate you if they are unable to report back to Geneva."

"Assassination? Is that really a risk?"

"It is. We learned that the hard way, on Bellemonte. General Cho was murdered in his sleep by one of his own officers." Daniels face turned somber. "It was a tremendous recruiting tool for us—practically the entire army joined us, and the killer...didn't escape." He leaned forward, staring at Simmons. "But recruiting tool or not, it is not something I care to repeat. The image of General Cho lying on his cot covered in his own blood is still with me. I have no desire to add another such nightmare to the list of those that already plague my sleep."

Simmons leaned back and sighed, his face twisted in a confused frown. Daniels knew what he was thinking, and he understood. It wasn't easy to imagine one of your own murdering you in the night. A good commander breathed his every breath for his soldiers, and Daniels' impression was that Simmons was one of the best. War, deprivation, despair...they were all difficult to endure, waking nightmares that tore away at one's spirit, but disloyalty was the worst. Simmons had likely long realized he had UNGov informers in his ranks. But Daniels knew Force Samar's commander was now thinking about that fact in ways he never had...and imagining which of his soldiers were really UNGov assassins, waiting to murder him in the night.

"Very well," Simmons finally answered. "What else? Would you have me order the army to prepare to march? To move to whatever Portal you came through and go to join your...Army of Liberation?"

"No." Daniels could see the surprise in Simmons' face at his response. "We want you to join us, General, all of you. But General Taylor has one requirement. Your soldiers must each decide for themselves. This is not an order going down the chain of command...it is rebellion, a capital offense. We will be invading Earth, striking at the heart of the government and fighting any forces it deploys against us. We will be outnumbered, outgunned...in every way, our crusade is a desperate endeavor. We will face enormous danger...and we may be forced to make difficult choices, to cause terrible hardship and loss, even among the innocent on Earth. Every man, even the lowliest private must be a volunteer. He must be there because he shares our commitment, and our outrage at what has been done to us. Not because he was ordered to come."

"And what of the others?"

"Assuming you choose to join us, General, those who elect to stay will be placed under the command of the highest-ranking officer who remains behind."

"That is all?"

"We would disable their heavy weapons, and we would take most of the transport vehicles so they couldn't easily follow us. But otherwise, yes. That is all." Daniels took a deep breath. "I can hear the question in your mind, General. Yes, there is risk in that, especially as there is a chance the ranking officer that remains behind will be a UNGov operative. We would be safer if we did more, certainly, if we took them with us as prisoners or...worse. But then we would be what we fight against...and we will not do that. I will not. Jake Taylor would not." He stared at Simmons. "And we hope you would not either."

"I would not, Colonel. Certainly not. Though it is clearly a risk, especially if you are right about UNGov operatives planted in my army."

"There are risks we must take, General, dangers we must endure because we are men of honor, because we will not become like those who now rule Earth. Perhaps we will fail because of that, but if we did not act in such a manner, even victory would become defeat, for we would become the same thing we had replaced."

Simmons leaned back, turning his head and staring off into the distance. Daniels sat quietly. He understood how difficult this was for the general, how sudden, shocking.

"Very well, Colonel," Simmons said, his tone grave, somber. "You have convinced me. Too much of what you say makes sense…and now I begin to think for myself, more perhaps than I have before. And as I think, I begin to realize how little time we have. I will see to garrisoning the Portal immediately. And tomorrow we will address the army together…and put this choice to them. Though I fear many will be overwhelmed and elect to stay behind, only to regret that choice later."

"No doubt you are correct, General. But that cannot be avoided. No man can come with us, save by his own free will." Daniels leaned back in his chair. "Perhaps we should get some rest now, General. Tomorrow will be a big day."

Simmons nodded, but a troubled look came upon his face. "But…" his voice trailed off.

"But what, General? Please speak freely."

"If there are UNGov operatives in my army, how can we be sure none of them come with us?"

"We can't." Daniels' voice was somber. "No doubt some have already infiltrated the Army of Liberation. But they have no way to communicate with Earth…and General Taylor is a wise commander. He will handle any problems that arise. All we can do here is refuse anyone you suspect."

It wasn't a satisfying answer, but it was all he had.

Chapter 2

From the Journal of Jake Taylor:

It is one thing to decide on a momentous course of action, a long quest where completion lies far in the future, to plan it and move steadily toward its conclusion. But it is quite different to stand at the precipice, ready to take the last step, to begin the final, terrible battle.

For years now, ever since the fateful day I discovered that all I had believed was false, that I had been lied to and sent to die by those I had called my leaders, I have moved forward coldly, relentlessly. I watched my soldiers suffer and die, listened over a com line as my best friend slipped away, far from me and beyond my help. I saw my closest companions change slowly, becoming instead mindless followers or recoiling from the reptilian monster I had become. But through all the pain, the darkness, the terrible unending loss, my devotion never wavered. Until now.

Our ranks have been swelled by men from the other planetary armies, and I now have almost 60,000 soldiers under my command. The Tegeri have supplied us, enabling my army to remain combat effective, though we have no factories, no significant civilian population to support us. My veterans from Erastus, cybernetically-enhanced for almost a decade now, are few, their numbers have dwindled to less than four thousand. But they are the greatest warriors mankind has ever known. And the others, the vast majority of my force, though they are no match for the Supersoldiers, are veterans of years of war against the Machines, against the superior technology of the Tegeri, and they are more than a match man for man against anything UNGov has to throw at us.

Still, though my forces have never been stronger, it is now I pause, at this moment for which I have so long struggled and pushed forward. Before I saw only that which drove me on, the outrage of what had been done to us, and to mankind as a whole. The innocent Machines killed in our unjust war, the guilt for that horror that clings to every one of my soldiers. I strove forward, driven by the insatiable need for vengeance. I swore to free a world, whatever it takes. I spoke softly into the darkness, to the shades of those lost in our battles, promising savage justice to ease their tormented spirits.

But now I see other things. Thousands of my men dead already, on battlefields far from Earth...and thousands more killed by them, in combats that should not have happened but did. And looking ahead, I see my 60,000 fighting the final battle for Earth...and dying in their thousands. My army is the largest it has ever been, but it is a laughably small force to invade a world.

I have long sworn that we would free Earth from tyranny, whatever the price. But now that cost is clearer in my mind, mounds of the dead lying unburied, burning and ruined cities, the suffering of millions. UNGov is responsible for the war against the Tegeri, and for usurping what had remained of humanity's freedom. But it is I who will unleash this new nightmare on the world, my soldiers who will march through the Portal and begin this war. My cause may be worthy, but that will be cold comfort to the thousands—millions?—who will die. And even those who survive will never be the same, for some horrors change men, even in victory.

I have been sure of the justice of my crusade, and so I remain. But now I see the horrors in my mind too, the terrible cost. I know my next order will unleash hell on mankind. We have no more steps forward in the trail back to Earth. The next march will be home...and our return may very well destroy that home.

We wait now for the last parties sent out to rally support, but when they return, my excuses will be gone. Then will come the true test of my strength, for I must stand before my army and send them forth. And the orders will be clear and brutal...the destruction of UNGov, at all costs.

At all costs...words of great clarity, yet it is so easy to overlook their true meaning, the horror they can unleash. And yet I must give just that command.

And I will give it. Even if it destroys me.

Jake Taylor stood outside the portable shelter, the oval-shaped bit of hyper-plas that had served as his office and quarters for the past four years. It had been bright white once, he supposed, when it was new, but it had already become yellowed under the relentless light and heat of Erastus when he'd taken it for his use, and now it was a dull gray, the caked on dirt and relentless rains of a dozen worlds leaving their marks. He had no idea what the structure had been used for back on Erastus, before Hank Daniels had found it and had it set up as an office for the nascent AOL's commander. Perhaps it had been a comm center or a small aid station, but none of that really mattered anymore. Now it was his, and soon it would be disassembled yet again and hauled through the Portal in pieces, as it had been through each transit point along the march of the army, from planet to planet as his soldiers moved ever closer to home. To the final battle.

The Army of Liberation had been on Ghasara for more than twelve Earth months, though the planet revolved so slowly around its sun there had been no noticeable changes in season over that time. Taylor had halted his battered army next to the Portal that led to Earth...and used the Tegeri's knowledge of the Portal network to send parties out to other worlds, to rally other human forces to join the crusade. It was a difficult mission, he knew, for a handful of men to move through a series of Portals, sometimes with thousands of kilometers to travel on each world through varied conditions, to reach the next transit point. But he had realized the army needed reinforcements before it could hope to make the final transit and take on all the power of UNGov Earthside. And the only source of new recruits were the various UN Forces fighting on the other Portal worlds.

The strategy had been a success, with Taylor's handpicked officers proving extremely persuasive. Not every Earth soldier agreed to return with them, to join the AOL and commit to the destruction of the only government they had known. But many did. First hundreds, then thousands of soldiers had trickled back. Tens of thousands.

The Army of Liberation had almost been destroyed in the cataclysmic campaign on Juno. Thousands had been killed, including almost two thirds of Taylor's irreplaceable Supersoldiers. And numbered among the dead was Tony Black, Taylor's oldest and best friend. Taylor had thought he was beyond feeling pain and emotional loss, that he'd truly become the cold-blooded avenger his soldiers thought he was. But Black's death had hit him like a punch to the gut, and the pain still endured, more than a year later. Taylor still found himself looking for Black when he was uncertain, his impulse to seek his friend's guidance proving slow to die.

He wondered what he would do the next time circumstances compelled him to put a friend at risk. Would he send another of his oldest comrades into the heart of danger if that's what victory demanded? He'd been certain he would do anything to complete the quest, but now the shade of his dead friend haunted him, and he wasn't so sure. He knew he wouldn't have the answer, not until he was forced to make such a fateful decision.

His eyes paused on the two flags hanging outside his shelter, the sight of the fabric flapping in the wind bringing him out of his daydreams. One had been designed by his own support personnel and, understanding his people's need for a standard to rally behind, he had declared it the official flag of the Army of Liberation. The other was a battle standard, ragged and worn, but far better made than the army's flag, sewn on fine hyper-nylon. The banner of the Black Corps had come to stand next to that of the AOL by Jake Taylor's personal command. It was a strange choice in many ways. No force had killed more of his people, come closer to stopping the crusade before it reached Earth, than the enhanced warriors of the Black Corps. They had been the army's most terrible adversary. But Taylor knew those men had not been his enemies, not really. The terrible fighting on Juno had been engineered by UNGov, by their lies and the atrocities they had inflicted on their own soldiers. The men of the Black Corps had been subjected to the same invasive surgeries and cybernetic enhancements as the Erastus veterans, and then they'd been sent after Taylor's soldiers under the belief the AOL had sold Earth out to the Tegeri, and murdered thousands of their fellow human soldiers in the furtherance of their treason.

Taylor sighed, his thoughts drifting back to Major Evans. It was great men and women, Taylor knew, who sometimes stopped the worst tragedies, as often as not by pure force of will, and Evans had been such a man. The commander of the Black Corps eventually discovered the truth, and when he realized Taylor's men were liberators and not monsters, he switched sides. But neither he nor Taylor had any inkling of the darkest truth about what UNGov had done to the soldiers of the Black Corps. For they had been subjected to far more than just the cybernetic enhancements that made them such formidable warriors...they were conditioned as well, deeply and irreversibly, and they had no power to resist the commands of their designated superiors. They attacked Taylor's troops again, by surprise and against their will. But after the initial cries of treachery, Taylor realized the terrible truth. The men of Black Corps couldn't join his army. They would only be turned against their new allies the moment one of their UNGov masters was able to transmit the code words. No, Taylor had known at that moment he had to go on without Evans and his people.

But the major had other thoughts, darker ones. The rage against what had been done to him and to his soldiers burned hot within him, and his pride and honor waxed greatly. He would not be a slave, he declared, nor would he allow himself to again become the tool of an evil and oppressive government.

He would not raise a weapon against Taylor or the AOL. Never again. And his men listened to his final speech with rapt attention, and then they followed his lead, to the last man. Taylor had already left Juno, but he knew what had happened there, the ultimate end of that terrible tragic campaign. Four thousand men of the Black Corps stood at attention, watching as their commander paused for a moment...and then pulled a pistol from his holster and took his own life. And then, first in small groups and then by the hundreds, his soldiers followed his lead, choosing death over servitude...over a life as a slave.

Taylor had found the Black Corps flag in the hands of some of his soldiers just after the AOL left Juno, a spoil of war a squad had found at the end of the campaign and brought with them through the Portal. When Taylor found it, he took it and immediately declared it would be displayed outside his headquarters, as a tribute to the courage of the Black Corps, and as a reminder of the evil his people were going to Earth to destroy. And there it had remained, for the almost eighteen Earth months that had passed since then.

Bear Samuels slipped around the side of the shelter, making hardly a sound despite his massive size. Taylor's electronic ears had heard the big man coming, but he suspected an unaltered soldier would have been taken completely by surprise.

"Bear," he said without turning around. He didn't want to give his hulking friend the impression he'd sneaked up undetected. "What can I do for you?"

"Jake, Hank and his people have transited back," the towering officer said with his usual southern drawl.

Taylor felt a wave of excitement...and something else. Was it fear? Hank Daniels' group was the last one. Whatever reinforcements they had managed to recruit on Samar, Taylor's final reason for delay was gone. It was time. Years of struggle had brought them all to this point. It was time to invade Earth, to win or die. And for all the certainty and resolution he'd communicated to the army over the past four years, Taylor was plagued with doubts.

"How did he do?"

Bear reached over and put an arm on Taylor's shoulder. "He did great, Jake. Looks like he got maybe half of Force Samar. About 8,000 give or take. Puts us close to 70,000 effectives. And he says more may follow."

Taylor nodded. Hank Daniels was a hothead, the last person most people would expect to succeed at explaining the crusade and rallying forces to the cause. But Taylor knew Daniels was a believer too, a man who felt, perhaps even more fervently than Taylor, that those who had seized Earth's future must be made to pay for their actions. And it turned out that enthusiasm was contagious. Daniels had led two expeditions, and he'd brought back more followers than anyone else, by a considerable margin.

Taylor looked out over the camp, allowing himself a moment of amazement at its size. He'd left Erastus with a force just over thirteen thousand strong, almost ten thousand of them enhanced Supersoldiers. Now, despite the losses incurred since then, he had over five times the manpower he began with… though the road the army had traveled had cost him almost two-thirds of his oldest comrades, mostly lost in the deadly struggle with the Black Corps.

Taylor felt the urge to delay, to order another round of recruiting expeditions. But he knew he couldn't. The nearest contested Portal Worlds were many transits away. It would take months, possibly years for his people to reach them. And he'd waited as long as he could. UNGov knew he was out here… and there was little doubt they were well aware his forces would eventually return to Earth. He'd given them enough time to prepare, too much. Time served them, not him. They had the resources of a world to draw upon. No, he couldn't wait. It was time.

"Okay Bear…it begins. Tell Frantic to get his people ready. They transit tomorrow." Karl "Frantic" Young was another of Taylor's original comrades, a soldier who had served at his side since the early days on Gehenna…and the man he had chosen to lead the advance guard, three hundred soldiers who would go through the Portal…who would secure the area and spread out, gathering intelligence before the main army followed.

"Yes, Jake." Bear was always informal with his commander, and it was something Taylor appreciated, somewhere deep down. So many of his soldiers believed in the crusade, and they looked at him as something beyond just another man. The unquestioning loyalty was useful, no doubt, but Bear—and Frantic and Hank Daniels—kept Taylor grounded. They were his link to the past, to the days when he wore stripes on his sleeve and crawled around the blast furnace that was Gehenna. He'd hated his service there, they all had. They'd spent hours talking of other places, of where they'd come from on Earth, playfully taunting each other with tales of cool breezes and refreshing spring rains—and in Taylor's case, snow-covered New Hampshire hills. But now Taylor realized that in some way, in spite of all that, Erastus had become his home too, and his memories of that blasted hell had taken on a sentimental aspect. Some part of him longed to shed the responsibilities of an army commander, to go back to the days when he was in charge of only the handful of men around him, friends and comrades he knew well... and trusted with his life.

Bear turned and began to walk away, but Taylor stepped after him. "Bear," he called to his friend.

Samuels stopped and turned around. "Yeah, Jake?"

"Tell Frantic we'll have dinner in my tent tonight. And find Hank and tell him too. I want the old crew, Bear...all of us who are left." Taylor's voice was soft, distracted. "One more night together before the final battle, eh?" He forced a grin. "We can talk about old times."

Bear Samuels returned the smile. "Yeah, Jake," the giant replied. "Old times. I'd like that. I think all the guys will." Then he turned and walked down the camp's main road.

* * *

The Army of Liberation had grown massively, and its camp had expanded along with its troop roster. Hundreds of shelters were lined up in neat rows, clustered around mess halls and other support structures. And next to one mess hall, in the wet clay just outside the door, lay a line of rocks. To the soldiers walking past before and after the evening meal, it was nothing out of the ordinary. But for a select few, it was a signal, a prearranged pattern they had been waiting for, and they took note as they entered. The message was a simple one. There would be a meeting, an hour after sunset, just outside the camp.

Mitchell Klein walked past the mess shelter, his eyes darting toward the line of stones. He knew what the signal meant... indeed, he'd placed the rocks there himself. Klein had been a soldier in Force Phillos, a lieutenant and a communications specialist, and he'd spent most of his time working like the other soldiers, first in Force Phillos and now in the AOL. But Klein wasn't a draftee like the others, he hadn't been conscripted or blackmailed into enlisting. He'd come voluntarily. And unlike the soldiers of Force Phillos, he'd always expected to return to Earth one day...not only return, but to receive a rich reward for his years of service on a shithole like Phillos. Klein was a spy, one sent to Phillos by UNGov, to monitor his comrades and seek out any signs of disloyalty.

UNGov kept watch over the population closely, seeking to cut off any dissent or rebellion before it had the chance to grow into something dangerous. Schools encouraged children to report any suspicious behavior by their parents, neighbors were recruited to spy on those who live around them. And when armies were sent to the Portal worlds to fight the Tegeri, they carried in their own ranks UNGov agents who fought alongside their comrades, but watched them closely too.

For several years, he'd thought his posting was a waste of time and resources. There were few opportunities for UNGov's stranded soldiers to do anything but fight the Machines. He'd seen plenty of despair and demoralization, and even grumbling about UNGov, words that would get people sent to reeducation camps back home. But he wasn't back home, and UNGov wanted as little disruption in its planetary armies as possible. So Klein allowed the mildly seditious behavior to go by without intervention. He was there just in case something major ever occurred, widespread mutiny or the like.

Then Jake Taylor and the Army of Liberation arrived. They told their story of UNGov perfidy, and they rallied the warriors of Force Phillos to join them. Klein hadn't been sure what to do. His directives covered a wide array of potential acts of disloyalty, but none of them addressed an invasion by another Earth force, one in open rebellion against UNGov. His first instinct was to stay behind—Taylor had announced that anyone who didn't wish to join his crusade would be allowed to remain on Phillos, unmolested by his forces. But Klein, thoroughly indoctrinated in UNGov's way of doing things, couldn't believe that Taylor would leave those who didn't join him. He suspected a force of Taylor's loyalists would remain behind, that they would attack and kill the soldiers who had stayed. So he joined those flocking to the AOL's banners.

Klein had even considered truly committing himself to Taylor's cause. He had to admit, the AOL's commander was a charismatic individual who had an almost hypnotic effect when he addressed soldiers. It would be easy to accept what Taylor said, allow himself to be swept up in the same wave of enthusiasm that embraced the other men around him. But Klein was a pragmatist. For all the roaring of the troops, even for the steadily swelling ranks of the army, he knew they didn't have a chance. UNGov didn't have much of an army on Earth—the lack of quarreling nation states made that need obsolete. But it did have extensive internal security forces and the resources of an entire world to deploy. Even with Taylor's skill, and the experience of 70,000 hardened veterans, he couldn't see how they could win in the end.

No, Klein decided to retain his allegiance to UNGov, to continue in his role as a spy, now monitoring the AOL as it made its way closer to Earth. He had no way to report anything to his superiors on Earth, not yet, at least. But he'd had some success at finding his fellow agents, his counterparts who had been deployed to the other armies that had supplied recruits for the AOL. His clandestine signals had been answered, and now he had half a dozen operatives in his nascent cell.

They operated slowly, cautiously. The small number of agents he'd found was proof of how effective Taylor was at rooting out treacherous elements in the army. UNGov had deployed dozens of agents to each planetary force, yet only a few appeared to remain. To what extent the others had decided to remain behind with their respective forces...or whether Taylor and his people had discovered and killed them, he didn't know.

Klein had exercised caution up to now, and his handful of agents had done little but have the occasional clandestine meeting. But now the army was about to move back to Earth. If he was going to accomplish anything, now was the time. He thought of the rewards UNGov would shower on its agents if they managed to help defeat the AOL...promotions, cash donatives, power. His greed pushed back against his fear, driving him to make a move now, to reach for the chance to advance himself, and his small group, to the upper ranks of Earth's privileged class.

He would meet with his people tonight, at the spot they had chosen outside the camp. They would all have missions. Most would try to contact UNGov as soon as the army began transiting to Earth. The Portal led to a very remote location, and Klein was certain Taylor would try to get as much of his army through and in place before they were discovered. The sooner UNGov knew where the invasion was coming from, the quicker they could crush it...and reward their loyal agents.

But Klein had set his own sites higher. He had a plan, one that would ensure him not just rewards, but a route to the highest levels of government and power, possibly even a seat on the Secretariat one day. It was the stuff of dreams, power and luxury unimaginable. And all he had to do was complete the mission he'd set for himself.

All he had to do was assassinate Jake Taylor.

* * *

"This reminds me of old times, of simpler times." Taylor never thought he'd refer to his days on Erastus with anything like fondness, yet something of the sort had managed to work its way into his mindset. "Back with the 213th at firebase Delta." His thoughts drifted across the years, his general's stars fading away, replaced by a non-com's stripes. There had been six of them among those stationed at base Delta, men who were more than friends, closer than brothers. Four of them were gathered now, poking at the last scraps of the closest thing to a celebratory dinner possible using Tegeri-supplied field rations.

Two other chairs sat at the table, placed there at Taylor's command, but empty. The first paid homage to Tom Warner, a sniper Jake and his closest friends had called 'Longbow.' Warner had been dead many years, killed in action long before Taylor's rebellion. But his comrades still remembered him, still missed him. He was still one of them, as he would always be, as long as even one of them remained. They spoke of him often, of his adventures, of how his often-extreme cockiness somehow never rendered him unlikable. Longbow Warner had never served a day with the Army of Liberation, yet to Taylor and his comrades, he was as woven into its history as any of them.

The second chair was Tony Black's. The former street tough from the Philadelphia slums had fought under the AOL's banner. Indeed, he had been Taylor's second in command since the day they'd raised the flag of revolt. He hadn't always agreed with Taylor's decisions, and the two had sometimes clashed over how to proceed, but Jake had considered Black his best friend. He still did.

Black had been killed on Juno, in the final stages of the campaign. He'd been far from Taylor as he lay dying, and their final words were via the com unit. Taylor still ached for his friend, and he regretted that he hadn't been there to comfort Black at least, if he couldn't save him. But he'd become used to loss. War was all he knew now, and in war men died. Even old comrades. Even best friends.

"They were simpler times, Jake." Hank Daniels sighed and pushed back his plate. "We've seen a lot of things since then none of us could have imagined, friends, but I'd wager not one of us could have foreseen sitting around the table reminiscing about Erastus. We called the place Gehenna…hell! Now, I'll be damned if part of me doesn't wish we were back there. I used to say some pretty nasty stuff about senior officers back then, but now I understand. The responsibility is crushing, it wears you down. There was a certain freedom in just following orders. We faced danger on the field, certainly, but at least when we got back to base we had a break. Yeah, the food was lousy…" He poked at his plate. "…not that it's all that much better now…but we could drop down on our bunks and just sleep. I haven't had a decent night's rest in years."

Taylor nodded. "Nor I. I used to think it was miserable rolling around in the heat, trying to get to sleep. But there are worse things than physical discomfort, aren't there? Soldiers fight, they die and they watch friends die. But now the fate of an entire world rests in our hands. It's a burden, a heavy one."

"You have done well, Jake. Whatever happens in the days and weeks to come, what you have accomplished is remarkable." Karl Young looked across the table at Taylor. "Our road has been a difficult one, and we have not come this far without loss, certainly. But we are here, and tomorrow the first boots will pass through the Portal…and the final chapter will begin. You should take some time, a few moments even, and reflect on all you have accomplished.

"Thank you, Karl…but I—we—set out with a single purpose, and that purpose still lies before us. When we stand in Geneva, when the worldwide apparatus that enslaves mankind lies in ruins, the men and women responsible dead at our feet… then I will do as you say. Though no victory, no success will erase the price we have paid, will continue to pay. Is there joy in such a victory? Or merely relief, grim satisfaction that a great evil has been vanquished.

Taylor's thoughts were darker still. He knew destroying UNGov would be enormously difficult, but even if his people were successful, what would follow? UNGov had exploited mankind's fear to seize control of the world—but men and nations had yielded their freedom voluntarily. For all UNGov's evils, hardly a shot had been fired on Earth in its rise to power.

What would follow its destruction? He suspected there

would be cries for him to take power, to create a new government to replace UNGov. But Taylor was a soldier, not a politician. He understood war, fighting against an enemy, battling for the comrades at his side. But he had no idea how to govern a world, and even less desire to try. What would he do? If he simply walked away, disbanded his army, would a disordered world find its way to some kind of just government? He might have convinced himself to believe that at one time, but no longer. He suspected if he didn't take power he would just leave the way open for a new UNGov to fill the void. But if he stepped into the place of those he deposed, would he be anything different? Or would he just become what he'd hated, what he'd fought to destroy?

He forced the thoughts from his mind, the same way he usually did, by reminding himself he should focus on the battle at hand, which had to be won before the future of Earth would even become a factor. But it still loomed heavily, closing in on him...the realization that even victory against overwhelming odds would only bring him to a new crisis.

"Well," Taylor said, looking around the table at his three closest friends, "I do have some official business while we are here."

The other three men looked back at him, with the rapt attention—the almost hero worship he'd come to so despise. Taylor, more than anything, just wanted to be one of them, like he'd been years before. But he knew he wasn't anymore, not really. Even those closest to him had fallen under the spell of the great leader. They called him Jake, they joked around, with him at the dinner table...but he knew they saw him differently than they had back on Erastus. When they'd fought in that desert hell, he knew any of these men would have risked their lives to save him...but now he suspected any of them would walk off a cliff if he ordered it. Tony Black had been the only who really resisted Taylor's transformation to larger than life commander, and even he had repented as he lay dying.

"Something for each of you, before we begin the final war." He reached down to a small sack at his feet, pulling out three tiny boxes. He tossed one to each of his friends, and leaned back. "Well," he said a few seconds later, waving his hand as he did. "Open them."

The three men paused another few seconds and then, almost as one, they opened the packages. Each one of them contained a small silver insignia, the two bright stars of a major general. It was a rank that hadn't existed for forty years, not since UNGov had taken control of Earth and dissolved the national armies. The planetary forces in the war against the Tegeri had each been commanded by one general, who wore a single brigadier's star, and the AOL had followed the same custom. But as various planetary armies had rallied to the cause, several former theater commanders had joined the AOL, confusing the chain of command with additional one-star generals.

"The three of you are my executive officers, and your rank should make that clear. I cannot lead this army alone, and though we have added some excellent officers to our ranks, there should be no doubt that the three of you are my most trusted companions."

He looked around the table, and he could see his friends had become a bit emotional. Bear Samuels, the gentle giant, looked as if he might throw the table aside and rush to embrace Taylor...and Young and Daniels seemed like they just might do the same.

"You deserve it...but there is more than just friendship and appreciation to this." Taylor paused. "We face a titanic struggle, and we all know the vagaries of war. If I am killed, there can be no doubt. The three of you are in command after me."

"Jake..." Young's voice trailed off, as if the words he'd expected had failed to come.

"I am just a man, Karl," Taylor said. "If I die, the three of you will keep the army together, and continue the quest. What we do is more important than any of us, and as long as one man remains in the army, it must continue."

The room fell silent as Taylor's comrades stared down at the bright metal stars in their hands. Finally, he said, "Okay, that's the business of the evening. We all know what to do tomorrow...and in the days to come. So, let us set aside duty...for just a few moments. Let us just be soldiers, gathered together on the eve of battle. Let us sit and tell stories, and if our exploits are a bit exaggerated, we will forgive each other the embellishments!"

Taylor forced a smile. He knew this might be the last time he spent with these three good friends. Tomorrow, Karl Young would lead the vanguard through the Portal. And the others would follow. They would be scattered, possibly around the world...and some of them, all of them, could die in battle. So if this was to be the last night, he was determined to make it one worthy of the designation.

"I will start," he said, scooping up his glass from the table and taking a deep drink. "Do you guys remember that skinny little corporal from the 207th? You know, the one who thought he was such a good card player..."

Chapter 3

From the Office of the Secretary-General:

It is hereby **ORDERED** that All UNGov internal security units undergo a program of supplemental military training, commencing immediately. Each unit will detach one-half its strength to its designated training facility within 72 hours. The program will take six weeks, after which the remaining half of each unit will report.

All units are further advised that no relaxation in internal security objectives and standards will be tolerated, and personnel remaining on duty will be held fully accountable for any lapses that occur. Security staff should be prepared for extended work periods and suspension of all leaves.

This action is deemed necessary in the interests of planetary security, and all UNGov personnel are expected to make whatever efforts are necessary to maintain order and stability planetwide. –Anton Samovich, Secretary-General, UNGov.

Anton Samovich stared out the floor-to-ceiling windows of his massive office. The view from the top of UNGov's kilometer-high headquarters was magnificent, and Samovich could look out north, over the sparkling blue of the lake or southeast, to the snow peaked magnificence of Mont Blanc. But the Secretary-General, the most powerful man in the world saw none of it. His vision was directed inward, his thoughts not on Earth's capital nor the beauty and splendor of its surroundings. Earth's effective ruler saw other images, blasted deserts crisscrossed with trenches, thick sweltering jungles with massive trees and strange, alien-looking vines. He saw the Portal worlds men had discovered, and the armies UNGov had sent to each of them. But now many of those armies weren't fighting the Machine enemy. No, they were on the march, moving steadily through the Portals, one world at a time…back to Earth. And at their head was a single man, a soldier with metallic gray eyes and an old, worn uniform.

Jake Taylor. The name had become a curse to Samovich. Taylor had somehow taken control of UN Force Erastus, and then he defeated the army the Secretariat had sent to destroy him, a force that outnumbered his own by three to one. Fifty thousand men had marched through the Portal to Erastus…and not one had returned. Not a single survivor, not even a message.

It had been months before the Secretariat managed to gather a new force large enough to send to Erastus, and when they arrived on that sunbaked world they found nothing…nothing save debris and the burnt out remains of Taylor's abandoned camp. His army was gone. They had marched through some other Portal, one unknown to the UN forces. That had been four years before…and Taylor's army was still at large, somewhere out there, on an unknown Portal world. His people had invaded half a dozen other planets, rallying the conscripts of the local forces to their side…and defeating any who opposed them. Even the Black Corps, the invincible army UNGov had sent to destroy Taylor's rebels on the planet Juno.

Samovich reached into his desk and pulled out a small canister, tipping it over and dumping two pills in his hand. His stomach was on fire, the constant stress turning his indigestion into a swirling vortex of pain. He popped the pills in his mouth, washing them down with a gulp of water.

He leaned back and closed his eyes, feeling relief almost immediately. The drug was attuned to his own DNA, a customized treatment that had been created by the Secretariat's medical staff after he'd complained of the ineffectiveness of the other drugs they'd prescribed. The cost had been astronomical no doubt, but the notion that millions of creds shouldn't be squandered treating the heartburn of one man while most of the people in the world received grossly inadequate medical care was utterly lost on him. Samovich had clawed his way to the pinnacle of the government, and while he was once focused on the power and privilege rank would give him, now he simply considered it his due. As for those dying in ghettoes and decaying towns and suburbs…he rarely gave them any thought at all, save perhaps how to keep them in line and suppress any riots or protests that occurred from time to time.

"Taylor," he whispered under his breath, his tone dripping with hatred. Samovich had no tolerance for rebels. In his view, the government was to be obeyed. He and his fellow officials certainly knew better how to run the world than the seething masses, and their constant whining over rations and housing and medical care. If only they would accept their place in the scheme of things, so many resources would be freed for more productive pursuits.

For decades his internal security forces had pursued just that goal, rooting out groups opposing the government…and sending their members to the "reeducation camps," where most of them were terminated as "hopeless" cases. But still, dissent had refused to die, and now, after forty years, the threat of alien invasion, for so long a shadow UNGov used to keep the people in line, was losing its potency. The wars still went on, but after so many years, the belief that the monstrous Tegeri were on the verge of bursting through the Portals slaughtering—and in the most shamelessly excessive UN propaganda, eating—people wherever they went had faded. Fear was a powerful weapon, indeed it was the tool the original Secretariat had used to gain world domination. But now that had faded. The Tegeri were still thought of as bloodthirsty aliens, but most people considered the threat contained, a position supported by UNGov's own propaganda touting its successes in chasing the enemy from numerous Portal worlds.

Had he not had greater concerns, Samovich suspected he would be spending most of his time cracking down on cells of resistance and the proto-rebel groups he knew were forming all around the world. But he had more pressing matters. Jake Taylor was more than just a rebel, more than some insurgent plotting impotently in a dark hole somewhere. He was a trained warrior, an experienced officer...and a Supersoldier, a cyborg created by UNGov itself. He had defeated every force sent against him, including the Black Corps, a unit composed of cybernetically-enhanced soldiers like himself. The few reports trickling back suggested that many men of the UN planetary armies had defected to his cause, replacing his losses and swelling his ranks.

And worse, Samovich knew, it appeared that the Tegeri were helping Taylor. Indeed, that was almost a certainty. How else could the rogue have kept his army supplied and replaced the ordnance they had expended in battle? That connection spelled trouble, not only because it gave Taylor a supply source, but also because the Tegeri weren't truly the monsters UNGov had made them out to be. Samovich was party to the dark secret, one few people on Earth knew. UNGov had orchestrated the war with the Tegeri, even going so far as to kill their own operatives who had actually conducted the assaults the aliens were blamed for. Anything to keep the secret. The Tegeri lie was incredibly useful propaganda. The truth, should it ever get out, would light a match on the fuse of rebellion. The secret had to be preserved...at all costs. But Samovich suspected Taylor's army knew the truth, from the mysterious commander himself down to the lowliest private.

How can we keep the secret? How?

"No," he said softly to himself. "There is no way." He breathed deeply as he attacked the problem, trying to decide on his best strategy to counter Taylor. Training the security forces was a step...defeating Taylor's army, killing his traitorous followers, that was certainly necessary. But crushing the invaders when they finally came would be only a partial solution. He'd never manage to destroy Taylor, to chase down all of his followers, even the scattered survivors who fled the battlefield... not before the word spread. Samovich knew Taylor would do everything possible to tell the people of Earth the truth, to rally them to his cause. And that could cause disaster, even after Taylor himself was dead.

Samovich got up and walked over to the window wall behind his massive desk, a small smile slipping on his face as he did. He stared out over the magnificent vista, for the first time in days taking a moment to appreciate what was laid out before him. Forty years of rule by UNGov had made Geneva and its environs the capital of the world, and the Secretariat members who ruled the planet had turned their enclave into a virtual paradise. If there were slums in other areas of the world, if once-great cities had deteriorated into ghastly nightmares where those with no place else to go picked through the ruins and tried to survive, them men and women entrusted to rule—and protect—Earth had little concern for any of it. They lived in luxury that shamed dukes and kings of old.

Protect, Samovich thought, as his smile grew. Of course. That is the answer. The same answer they came to forty years ago...

He suddenly knew what he had to do to defeat Taylor, and he cursed himself for not realizing it sooner. The answer was the same as it always was, as it had been decades past when UNGov had become the sole government on Earth.

They are the same gullible sheep they've always been. I had forgotten the lesson taught us by the original Secretariat.

He would devote whatever resources it took to defeat Taylor in the field, to hunt down and kill every last man who followed him. But even before that he would launch a full scale propaganda war, one that would turn all humanity against the rebel commander. Jake Taylor, the tool of the Tegeri, the man who slaughtered his fellow soldiers. The human being the Tegeri had suborned when they were incapable of defeating UNGov in the field. Images were racing through his mind, lies after lies...the things he would see repeated a million times, until the name Jake Taylor was synonymous with treachery, with evil. Taylor, the man who'd agreed to provide millions of humans as slaves, even as food sources for the Tegeri young...all in exchange for the aliens' assistance in making him mankind's absolute ruler.

Samovich felt a wave of excitement. Yes, this was the answer. It was the way. He'd already set the wheels in motion to prepare his forces to fight Taylor's army. Now it was time to begin another war, one fought with words and broadcasts and information networks. It was a struggle he was uniquely prepared to fight. And win.

*   *   *

"Something is definitely going on. I don't know what, but there have been too many sudden changes. They're up to something for sure." Carson Jones stood in the middle of the small circle, turning as he spoke to look at his companions in the flickering light of a dozen candles.

The meeting was in the basement of an abandoned building, a damp, musty space with a low-hanging ceiling of half-rotten wood. Jones was tall enough that he had to crouch, and he'd banged his head twice already. It was far from an ideal meeting place, but UNGov's intelligence agencies were extremely efficient, and more than willing to dangle large sums in front of desperately poor citizens to coax them to inform on those around them. Jones wanted to hate people who took government payoffs, who helped to send their neighbors to the reeducation camps. But he knew deprivation wore down a person's strength and their morality. Most people would do things they were ashamed of to put food in their children's stomachs, and Carson Jones didn't feel completely comfortable condemning them out of hand.

The Resistance had been close to wiped out over the nearly forty years of UNGov rule. Jones had known calling the meeting was a huge risk, but if there was an opportunity, a chance to launch a truly credible challenge to the Earth's totalitarian rulers, he knew they had to take it. He'd almost sent out the signal, the call to other cells worldwide. But he didn't know enough yet to take such a dangerous step.

"Well, they've definitely increased troop recruitment quotas. They're blackmailing everybody under thirty who gets in any petty trouble or falls a credit behind on their taxes to enlist. I've also heard that they've been expanding the training camps, increasing their capacity to handle the increased flow of recruits." Enrique Delacorte was sitting on an old crate, one that looked a bit wobbly but so far had held him up. Delacorte was a precious resource to the Resistance, a UNGov employee. He wasn't privy to any secrets, just part of the cleanup crew, but any government job was far more lucrative than work anything in the private sector, and Delacorte had every reason to support UNGov, save for one thing. He detested the oppression, the complete lack of freedom, though he'd never known anything else.

He was thirty years old, and UNGov had ruled the world since before he was born. But then he'd found a stash of old books, history texts, mostly, all of them on the banned list. He'd almost panicked when he found them, unsure if he should run or if he should turn them in, and possibly risk suspicion that they were his. But instead he opened one up and read a few pages. Then he flipped through another…and another. The books were full of lies…that's what UNGov's propaganda said. But something rang true as he read, and it prompted him to continue. He took the books and found a new hiding place. One at a time, he snuck them home, reading every word five times before he went back to get another.

What he learned shocked him profoundly. He read of a world where people chose their jobs, where they went about their business more or less as they chose…where they could move about the streets without papers, travel without a special approval. A place where the population elected leaders…where the people voted, not just a small group like the Secretariat, but everyone.

He'd heard of such things before, when he was young and mostly from older people, the ones who'd been adults before the Tegeri attacked and UNGov took control. But such talk was forbidden, and people learned to keep their mouths shut… or they vanished in the night, taken to reeducation camps for "reorientation."

"Are you sure, Enrique? About the quotas?" Jones' words

shook Delacorte from his daydreams.

"Ah…yes, Carson. I'm sure. It's all classified, but they act like I'm not even there when I'm cleaning. I suspect if anyone high up in Intelligence saw how careless they are he'd have a fit.

Jones nodded. "So what does that mean? Maybe the Tegeri are winning the war." UNGov broadcast a steady diet of news reports profiling military heroes and great victories pushing the Tegeri and Machines steadily back. But Jones didn't believe a word UNGov said or published.

He stared down at the floor for a few seconds. "If that's the case, perhaps there is nothing we can do now. UNGov is evil, but if the war is going badly…"

"That's not it."

Jones turned, along with everyone in the room, looking at the shadowy figure carefully climbing down the rickety stairs. Devon Bell was the newest member of the cell. He'd been excluded for a long time, mostly because no one else had trusted him. Bell was a UNGov employee just like Delacorte, but he was ranked considerably higher. He was a genuine beneficiary of the largess UNGov showered on its own, and he lived in the gated sector, in a home none of the others could even imagine.

He'd insisted he sincerely wanted to help overthrown UNGov, but none of the others, scared to death that he seemed to know who they were, believed him. Not until he told them the identity of a genuine double agent who was on the verge of infiltrating their cell. His warning got them out just in time… and it got him a long awaited invitation to join the group. There were those who still didn't trust him, who thought he was just infiltrating, hoping to identity some of the other cells the group dealt with…but Jones had decided to trust him. And Bell had never given him cause for regret.

"Devon…how do you know that?"

Bell stepped into the dank cellar. "Sorry I'm late, by the way. I didn't want to take any chances, and I had a hard time getting away." He looked over at Jones. "I know because no reinforcements have been sent to any Portal world. Not in over a year."

The room fell silent, save for the occasional sound of rats

scurrying across the floor above. Finally, Jones spoke. "Are you certain about this?" He looked around the room, and he could see the expressions of his comrades. Clearly, some of them doubted Bell's report.

"Yes, Carson. I'm absolutely sure." Bell paused, everyone in the room staring back at him. "You—all of you—know I have...access...to UNGov's information systems." Bell's work was in encryption, helping to develop the encoding systems that kept sensitive data secret. Upon occasion it also allowed him to—very carefully—decode messages he wasn't supposed to see. It was deadly dangerous, and one slip up was enough to get him buried in a ditch somewhere, but he'd done his best to provide the Resistance with useful information. That had made him both more and less suspect, depending on the member of the cell making the determination. "I have seen three different communiqués. All troops coming out of the training program are being diverted somewhere...I don't know where. But UNGov is trying to put together an army on Earth, there is no doubt of that."

"But that could support the idea that the Tegeri are breaking through. UNGov is preparing for a last ditch defense...here on Earth." Delacorte's voice was shaky, tenuous. He'd grown up on propaganda about the Tegeri, about how they had attacked and destroyed the first colonies. He had come to despise UNGov as well, and to believe that a more open and just government could also lead mankind against the alien menace. But if Earth was about to be invaded...

"No," Bell said, his voice stern. "Taken alone, I can understand that interpretation, but I have additional information. No troops have been withdrawn from any of the Portal worlds. None. The new recruits are completely inexperienced...if UNGov was truly preparing to face an imminent invasion, they would pull back veterans from the Portal worlds. Even if the Tegeri are winning, our forces could retreat, and the experienced soldiers would be spread out through the new units."

"Perhaps things are worse than we thought. The Portal armies could have been wiped out already. Maybe the Tegeri are massing now, building their forces before following up with an invasion." Jones began with an assured tone, but by the time he finished, he sounded doubtful. It just didn't feel right. After forty years, what could have happened to utterly destroy the Earth armies? And could the war being going the same way on every world?

"I thought of that too, Carson. Which is why I checked the logistics reports for last month." His tone was odd, and Jones got an impression how great a risk Bell had taken to get the information. "We are still sending supplies to the various armies." He paused. "It's strange. Food shipments have remained normal, but weapons and ammunition flows are sharply off for a number of worlds."

"They wouldn't be sending provisions if there weren't troops left there…and if the armies were being pushed back, making a desperate stand, they would need ordnance, wouldn't they?"

"Yes…they would. Even more than if they were conducting operations normally." Bell took a look around the room, finally taking a seat on a pile of boxes. "What's even more difficult to understand is that some worlds have been receiving military supplies while other haven't. So if we've got some armies still there, eating food but using no weaponry, what are they doing? It sounds more like a scenario where they have driven the enemy offworld…or where the Tegeri chose to withdraw."

"So what does that mean?" Jones asked the question, to no one in particular. "Fighting on some worlds, but not on others…and UNGov building a secret army on Earth?" He took a deep breath and ran his hand over his head, brushing his hair out of his eyes. "It doesn't make sense…"

"Perhaps it does." The voice came from the far end of the room, from an old man who had been silently watching until now.

Everyone in the room turned, almost as one, and they stared in rapt attention at the gray haired man in the corner. Stan Wickes was tall, but his body was hunched over, likely the result of years of poor nutrition. His face was worn and wrinkled, and he looked every day of his seventy years and then some. His clothes were soiled and ragged, and he looked like the homeless wanderer he was. All except for his eyes. There was a brightness there, an unmistakable intensity. And something else too. Defiance, burning brightly.

"What if it is the Tegeri who are close to defeat? What if the UNGov is preparing for the day they must control Earth without the fear of alien invasion to keep the people in line?" Wickes' voice was far stronger and louder than one would expect looking at him. His tone was commanding, decisive.

No one answered right away. Finally, Jones spoke, his tone heavy with respect, "You may be right, Captain. That makes considerable sense." He turned toward Bell. "Anything you've seen to suggest this may be possible?"

"Nothing specific," Bell replied. "But it certainly fits with the reduction in ordnance shipments. If the planetary armies have defeated the Tegeri and driven them off planet, there's no need for ammunition, certainly not in wartime quantities."

Jones turned back to Wickes. "So, if that is the case, what do we do, Captain?"

Wickes stood up and walked to the center of the cellar. He had a pronounced limp, the result of age and more than one beating by UNGov goons. He moved slowly but steadily, and he turned around and looked at each of his comrades in turn. "We can't know, Carson…and I don't know if we should try to find out. Sending people like Devon to try and spy more aggressively is extremely dangerous. Whatever is going on, it won't be easy data to reach."

The old man turned slowly as he spoke, his eyes panning over each of the revolutionaries sitting around him. "Sometimes we must make decisions with less information than we might want…we must rely on gut instinct. And my gut tells me it is time to make our move."

He stopped and faced Jones. "Give the word, Carson. Contact the other cells. If they agree, then we go." He slapped a fist down in his palm. "By God, yes…we shall strike. And after forty years of crawling in the dirt we will strike a blow for our freedom.

He appeared more energetic than he had just minutes before, as though the promise of action rejuvenated him. He walked over and took Jones' hand, pulling him up from his seat. Then Bell...and the others one at a time. "Stand with me my friends, my comrades, and remember, we are brothers in arms."

"Yes, Captain," Jones said, his own voice feeding off the older man's enthusiasm. "We are all brothers in arms." He looked at Wickes, his eyes settling on the small pocket on the old man's tattered jacket, and the black letters printed there, barely visible after so many years. USMC.

*　　*　　*

"Nine hundred on Juno, thirty-four hundred on Alantris, just under two thousand on Helios..." Anton Samovich stared down at the tablet, his finger scrolling slowly as he read the figures. He'd known the approximate numbers, of course, but these were the results of the census he'd ordered, and they were exact.

They'd better be exact...

"So, just over twenty thousand total on the worlds Taylor's army have marched through."

"Yes, Secretary-General. Our best estimate of those killed in action on these worlds is 29,500, excluding of course, the Black Corps, which was completely wiped out, the last 4,000 apparently by their own..."

"Yes," Samovich snapped back at the aide. "I am well aware of the fate of the Black Corps." His face darkened. He'd thought that plan had been foolproof, an army far larger than Taylor's, with the same cybernetic enhancements...and conditioned to obey orders no matter what. But Taylors' army had fought them like banshees, inflicting at least a 3-1 ratio of casualties. Still, it wasn't the military loss that most troubled Samovich. Somehow, the Black Corps, or Taylor's people, had discovered the conditioning...and the blasted soldiers who had survived the fighting killed themselves so they couldn't be ordered to fight against their will. Samovich was used to dealing with compliant citizens, easily cowed with threats and empty promises. The thought of people strong enough, defiant enough, to choose defiance and death over government control was unsettling to say the least.

"So, there are twenty-thousand soldiers on these worlds who survived the fighting with Taylor, but chose not to join him."

"That is correct, Secretary-General. Twenty thousand, four hundred sixteen to be exact. As per orders, we have ceased shipments of weapons and ammunition, but we continue to supply food and other basic sustenance. We have received multiple requests for authorization to transit back to Earth now that hostilities have ceased on the subject worlds, and we have responded in all cases with orders to stand by and assume defensive positions in case the Tegeri return."

Samovich sat unmoving, his mind deep in thought. Twenty-thousand veterans...they would be enormously valuable in supplementing the raw recruits and hastily-reassigned internal security units he had available to face Taylor's army if it came. When it came...Samovich had no doubt that the rebel leader would return to Earth, with a goal no less audacious than destroying UNGov outright. Dealing with a true zealot with large forces behind him was something new to Samovich, and UNGov overall. His security forces had done an excellent job of seeking out and terminating potential extremists among the population, preventing any from achieving dangerous levels of power. But now he faced a true revolutionary leader, one with an army behind him...the best, most experienced army in existence. All Samovich could do was wait...and see what Taylor did next. And prepare for the greatest test he had ever faced.

He thought of the troops stationed on the Portal worlds, idle, the Tegeri gone, Taylor's forces long moved on. God, he needed those soldiers. The pragmatist in him wanted to recall them all, divide them up, use them to leaven his raw units. But the autocrat screamed back. No, they may not have joined Taylor, but they are still suspect. There were good reasons for UNGov's policy against allowing veterans to return to Earth, and they applied doubly to forces that had encountered Taylor and his army, soldiers who knew thousands of their former comrades marched with Taylor. No, he couldn't take the risk, couldn't allow his forces to be infiltrated by thousands of men who could be rebel sympathizers.

He stared down at his desk for a moment, an idea beginning to form, a very dark one. Yes, he thought, of course. I can't take the risk of bringing those men home, but that doesn't mean they can't be useful, very useful indeed.

"Get me Alexi Drogov...immediately. I have a very important mission for him."

Chapter 4

From the Writings of T'arza, Elder of House Setai:

The humans' great tragedy is almost upon them. Taylor has rallied many of his people to his banner, and his army stands now on the brink of returning to their homeworld, to fight the final battle with the masters who rule mankind. Though I cherish peace above all things, the warrior blood of my ancestors burns hot now, calling to me the battle, to stand at my friend's side during his great test. But alas, I cannot. As a Tegeri, I would only damage Taylor's cause, fuel his enemy's propaganda. To the vast majority of his people, I am a bloodthirsty murderer, a monster from an alien world, come to bring death and destruction to humanity. It is a lie, of course, a vicious fabrication, but the truth can only spread with Taylor's victory, and there is little I can do to influence that. All that could be done has been. We have supplied his forces, though we have provided them only weaponry at or near their technology level, nothing that would appear out of place, or fuel suspicions of my peoples' involvement.

The war with the humans is over, at least for the Tegeri. We have pulled back from every contested Portal world, withdrawn all of our forces from any point of contact. This action was not without risk, as it opens the way for the human forces to advance ever farther into the Portal network, even to threaten Homeworld itself. But this danger is not the worst we face, nor is Taylor's advance the only reason for our withdrawal. For the Darkness, the enemy spoken of in the texts left behind by the Ancients, is again coming, and it brings death and destruction in its wake. It is the true enemy, the foe the humans and Tegeri were meant to face together, save for the terrible historical tragedy that forced us to war with the beings we should call brothers.

We withdrew our armies from their blood-soaked battle-fields, taking advantage of the confusion caused by Taylor's rebellion, but for the New Ones and Tegeri who fought on those worlds there will be little rest, little peace. For they must prepare to face the Darkness, and somehow defeat the great evil that long ago destroyed the Ancients, the wise and mighty race that built the Portals so long ago.

The fate of the humans lies in Taylor's hands, as does our ultimate victory or defeat against the Darkness. For if he fails, we will have no choice but to destroy Earth, lest we face enemies on two fronts and fall, as the Ancients did ages ago. And yet, even the monstrous crime of destroying our own human brethren is unlikely to save us. The Ancients foretold that our two races together could stand where they had fallen and defeat the great enemy. But alone my people have little chance. What power have we ourselves to face that which destroyed our forefathers, the Ancients, beings who strode across the stars almost as gods?

Indeed, it is not only the fate of his own people that lies in Taylor's hands...it is ours as well, and that of all the Other Races the Ancients planted, our young brethren only now grasping weakly toward civilization. To them we are the elders, and even as our race wanes and slips away, we are all that stands between them and utter doom. If we are to be destroyed, so then so shall they be. And in all the galaxy there shall be naught but silence and death.

"The troop withdrawals will be complete in five more cycles of the sun. By the next solar phase, all forces previously deployed against the humans will be massed on Alantria, awaiting orders to move to the frontier and deploy against the Darkness. The forces withdrawn from the struggles on the

Portal worlds have been reequipped with high tech weaponry. Combined with the newest reserves, there are over two million New Ones now under arms, awaiting the command to depart." T'arza spoke softly, but his voice carried solemn authority. He was the elder of a great house, a member of the Council...and the Tegeri elder selected as liaison with the Chosen, the human selected by the Council to lead the rebellion against the Earth government. The Council had long debated how to end the war with the humans, to obtain peace and reunite with their brother race and prepare to face the Darkness. It was T'arza of the Setai who suggested they seek out a single contact, a human with the strength of character and intelligence to lead a rebellion.

Since the day T'arza approached Jake Taylor on the world Taylor's people called Erastus, he had spent much of his time among humans, and he was now the Tegeri who best knew his peoples' enigmatic brother race. He had been a Tegeri of noble rank, and the patriarch of his house, but now T'arza was the most important member of his race and, in many ways, he carried on his shoulders the fate not only of the Tegeri, but of all the legacy of the Ancients.

"And," T'arza continued, "on Ghasara, Taylor and his soldiers stand beside the Portal leading back to Earth. The final campaign to liberate the humans homeworld is about to begin."

"We thank you for your words, T'arza, and for your tireless efforts. Your wisdom and dedication are an example for all." The First of the Council spoke slowly, gravely. He was ancient, even by the long-lived standards of the Tegeri, and he was frail and weak. Still, he rose slowly, clearly with tremendous effort, and he looked down the great council table. "I rise, T'arza of the Setai, in tribute to you, and I bid all of the Council to follow me. You have acquitted yourself with the honor and wisdom we have all come to expect from you. What hope we have, it flows from your work. I now name you Oritai, honored of your people. Henceforth, you shall wear the white robe, that all who see you might know of your deeds."

The others had risen at the behest of the First, and now they gazed upon T'arza, and as one they slapped their hands on the table, signaling their agreement by acclamation.

T'arza nodded somberly. He was not one to seek praise and, in truth, though he appreciated the One's words, the attention being lavished upon him made him uncomfortable. But the designation as Oritai was one of his peoples' greatest honors, one he knew he must accept with grace and humility.

"I thank you all for that that you have given me this day. You humble me, my brethren. I can answer only with my most solemn promise that I shall continue to do what must be done, whatever that may be."

The Tegeri nobles continued pounding on the table for another moment. Then the First sat down, followed by the others. When all had taken their seats, T'arza then sat, as custom demanded. Then he spoke, "Again, my thanks to you, First, and to all of you." A short pause. "But now I propose we return to the business at hand. We have much to discuss, much to decide."

"You speak truth, T'arza. Where would you have us begin?" The First looked at T'arza with hazy, clouded eyes.

"I would look first to Taylor. I would have us consider one final time if there is any way we can support his cause, any effort we have not made?"

"I believe we have done all for Taylor and his people that we can." C'tar spoke from the far end of the table, his ancient voice still strong as he spoke from the far end of the table. The Grandmaster of the Seminary was the oldest of his race, and his wisdom was respected and heeded by all Tegeri. He had been the first to speak out, to declare that if Taylor's quest failed, the Tegeri would have to destroy the humans. And he had backed T'arza when the leader of House Setai proposed launching an attack on Oceania to interdict the human supply lines when Taylor's forces were heavily engaged on Juno. Indeed, the respite that action created had been key to Taylor's victory, and the Tegeri intervention had not been connected to the human dispute.

"We have provided weapons and ammunition, all copied from their own technology, with what enhancements we could make. We have also supplied shelters, food, medicines. Indeed, we have risked as much as we dare, for even what we have given

Taylor is beyond anything his people could have provided for themselves. Our support is clear, though not in an obvious way that would feed the Earth government's propaganda efforts. Were we to go any further, for example to supply weapons clearly beyond Earth technology, it is likely we would do more harm than good to Taylor. However well supplied he may be, he must win the hearts and support of a large number of his people. Were we to allow the Earth government any proof of our involvement, we would give them the tools to turn all mankind against Taylor. We cannot take such a chance."

C'tar turned toward T'arza. "You know this, Oritai, master of the Setai, yet your concern for Taylor keeps you from true acceptance. It does you credit, yet now you must allow your friend to play his role in this great drama...and trust to his abilities. And it is time for us to turn our full attention to the approaching Darkness, before it is too late."

T'arza paused, returning the Grandmaster's gaze. Finally, he simply nodded and said, "You speak truth, wise C'tar, as always." He paused briefly, turning to look down the table at his fellow Council members. "We have done all we can for Taylor. His path is now his own. C'tar speaks wisdom. We must look to our preparations against the Darkness, prepare for the great struggle to come."

He hesitated again, his gaze dropping to the table. Finally, he looked up again and said, "And we must place our faith in Taylor, trust in his resolve and his abilities. We must believe he will free mankind...and that he will lead them to our aid. Before it is too late."

Chapter 5

From Jake Taylor's Address to the Army of Liberation:

Soldiers! Men of the Army of Liberation! We have come far. Some of you have marched with me from the beginning, others have joined us along the way. But none of that matters now. For now we stand on the brink of our final struggle. It is time to liberate our homeworld, time to erase the terrible stain the horror of UNGov has left on human history. And in this battle to come we are all brothers, comrades in arms...no longer men of Force Erastus or Force Juno or Force Phillos. We are the Army of Liberation, each of us sworn to do whatever must be done to destroy the great evil that rules Earth.

I envisioned this moment years ago, when I first left the blasted hell of Erastus, but even then, determined as I was, I could not foresee this gathering, so many noble soldiers, 70,000 warriors ready to take on a world! We cannot know what will happen after we march through that Portal. We may be divided into different groups, scattered around the globe. But whatever missions await us, whatever battles and struggles you may be called upon to face, know that I am with each of you. Always.

Go forth, my soldiers. Face the foe with the honor and strength you have shown in all things. Know always that our cause is just, that we fight to destroy a great evil...and restore freedom to our families and people. I will not lie and tell you our task is easy, nor that it will not be costly. Many will die, perhaps most of us. But we will prevail. Whatever it takes.

It was cold. Damned cold.

Karl Young had served more than ten years on Erastus, and in that time his body had thoroughly adapted to the brutal conditions there. The soldiers who'd left the planet they called Gehenna along with Jake Taylor took with them that conditioning, the lower hydration and wiry, muscular frames of men who'd marched thousands of kilometers in the blow torch heat of that nightmare world. It had been years now, and Young and his comrades had adapted yet again. When he'd first left Erastus, even a cool breeze on a temperate world cut through him like a knife. He remembered lying on his cot, wrapped in as many coverings as he could find yet still shivering uncontrollably. But he'd gradually adapted to cooler temperatures, and even to the cold, stinging rains they'd encountered on more than one planet. He'd seen worlds where a brief shower dropped more precipitation than Gehenna's deserts saw in a year. But none of that had prepared him for the icy blasts of the Siberian winter.

"My God," he said, struggling to control the shivering long enough to get his words out clearly. "What frozen hell is this?"

"It's a Russian winter, sir. It's thwarted more than one invasion before. Napoleon, Hitler…my grandfather used to tell me the stories when I was young." There was something in the statement, the slightest flash of patriotic pride, perhaps. The terminus from Ghasara was located in the northern wastes of eastern Russia, an almost uninhabited wasteland of deep frozen lakes and endless snow-covered steppes. Ivan Stokaya was Russian, like over half the troops that had come through the Portal with Young. Or at least his parents had been born Russian—technically, Stokaya had been a citizen of UNGov's universal state his entire life. But for all UNGov's efforts to eradicate connections to the old nation states and their varied cultures and histories, vestiges stubbornly remained.

The few people that had lived in the area had long been rounded up by UNGov and moved to more centralized areas. Earth's government preferred to have its citizens living where they were more easily watched, and few of the planet's wastes were more remote and inaccessible than the frozen tundra of northeastern Russia. But UNGov didn't know there was a Portal terminus in this frozen waste, and their efforts to depopulate the region had inadvertently created an ideal entry point for Taylor's army, one overlooked even by UNGov's network of spy satellites.

Indeed, the Portal was in a perfect location to transit without being detected, which was one reason why the army had gone to Ghasara. The Tegeri maps of the Portal network had offered other opportunities—there were many Portals on Earth that UNGov had yet to discover—but this northern wasteland was preferable to an exit point buried deep below the Earth or at the bottom of an ocean.

Young fastened the hook at the top of his parka, and then he reached down and slid his hands into the heavy gloves that had been hooked to his belt. The Tegeri had supplied Taylor's people with cold weather gear, and now Young knew why.

"Well, let's hope we don't add to that list, Captain." Young stamped his feet, moving around trying to get warm, but all he could feel was wave after wave of biting cold. He looked up at Stokaya, his eyes tearing from the bitter wind, lashes sparkling as the moisture froze almost immediately. "Is everyone through?"

"Yes, sir. All troops have transited. They are awaiting your orders."

Young just nodded. His orders from Taylor were clear. First, scout out the area and confirm it was safe for the army to follow. And then he was to send out the infiltration teams, small groups of soldiers from various areas of the Earth who would spread out, hide, blend in...find their ways by whatever means they could back to their homes. Once there, they would spread the word, rally the people from the bottom up. The strategy was a gamble—no one really knew how deep UNGov's control ran, whether or not the people still had the capacity to rise up, to resist and destroy their oppressors. But there was no other option. No 70,000 men every made could conquer an entire world unaided. The AOL would fight to the last, Young was sure of that. But they needed help too.

Young longed to go with the teams, to see the lands of his

childhood after so many years…but covert ops were out of the question for him. Most of the Supersoldier mods weren't terribly obvious, at least if he wasn't wearing his exos and the fittings where they attached to his body were covered by clothing. But the metallic eyes were a dead giveaway. The average person wouldn't know what he was at a distance, but his very gaze would bring attention to him. And on Earth ruled by UNGov, there was almost always someone watching, an internal security operative or a citizen paid to spy on his neighbors. And when word got to the proper authorities, UNGov would understand immediately. They would know there were Erastus veterans back on Earth.

"All right, Captain. Deploy the scouting parties. As soon as we confirm we are here undetected, we'll release the infiltration teams…and we'll send word back to the army and set up a perimeter around the Portal."

"Yes, General," Stokaya snapped back. The officer saluted, and then he turned and trotted into the cluster of troops milling around the Portal.

Young watched his aide go, trying to think of anything but the cold. He didn't relish the picket duty, protecting the Portal while the army came through, not the least of which because there would be no portable heaters, no fires…nothing that might be detected. He shivered as his eyes darted upward, toward the clear blue sky. What is this frigid hell like at night, he thought, shivering slightly as he did.

*   *   *

Li Wong pulled the hood of his heavy coat over his head as he stared off across the snowy steppe. The cold was brutal, though he had to admit, the Tegeri-supplied gear was doing a credible job of keeping him something not too far from warm, even in the frozen Russian wasteland around the Portal.

Li had volunteered for sentry duty on the perimeter around the terminus. Not only guard duty, but night guard duty. He could only imagine how cold it would get when the sun set in another hour. By the end of his shift, it would be a few hours before dawn. But by then, Li Wong would be gone.

He wore the insignia of a sergeant, the rank he had held in Force Alantris, but his true allegiance was to UNGov. He was an intelligence officer, originally sent to spy on the soldiers fighting the Machines on Alantris. He'd volunteered for the five year term of service, one that offered considerable compensation and a cushy government posting upon return. But instead of finishing his last year and going back to receive his rewards, he'd been swept up, first into the battle against the mysterious human army that had invaded Alantris...and then joining that force, following Jake Taylor and his Erastus veterans on their crusade against UNGov.

Li had gone along, at first because his whole unit had defected, and he feared what would happen if he didn't go with them. But then he began plotting, on his own at first, and later with other UNGov operatives he found in the ranks of the AOL. They began to meet, very cautiously at first, and to plot. But there had been little they could do...until now.

The time for action had come. There weren't a lot of UNGov agents left in the army. Jake Taylor had a remarkable talent for sniffing out disloyalty, and more than a hundred men with allegiance to Geneva had been rooted out and executed as spies. But Wong had managed to survive, as much because he'd been too afraid to do anything but act like a normal soldier. Beyond a few clandestine meetings, Wong had played the role of a sergeant in the AOL, not daring to vary from that in any meaningful way.

Until now. Things were coming to a head, and despite his firsthand knowledge of Taylor's skill and ability, he had to believe UNGov on Earth would prevail...and his survival and prosperity depended on what he did now. He could fight in the ranks, and probably end up dead along with all the fools who'd sworn their allegiance to Taylor...or he could strike a blow, alert UNGov to the presence of the Portal and the coming of the AOL. Then he would be a hero, and the rewards would be unimaginable.

He looked out at the setting sun, its reddish rays providing the last bits of the day's light. Soon it would be night... and he would run for it. He was afraid, and he could hear his heart pounding in his ears. But there was no choice. If he didn't make his move now, the chance would be lost. Slowly, with great effort, he pushed back the fear, shoving rationality into the forefront of his mind. It was almost time, and he had to be at his best. Success meant a life of comfort and privilege. Anything else meant frozen death.

*   *   *

"We have a soldier missing, General." Ivan Stokaya stood at the doorway of Young's small shelter, the frigid dawn wind whipping around him.

"Come in, Captain. And close the door." Without any artificial heat source, the shelter was cold, but it was well-insulated, and however uncomfortable, it was a damned sight warmer than it was outside, from Young's trapped body heat if nothing else.

Young was lying on his field cot, covered in a massive pile of blankets, some miscellaneous hunks of fabric, and something that looked a lot like a tarp of some kind. He'd been awake for the last hour, but the great warrior, who had fought through more than ten years in the legendary cauldron of Erastus and then served alongside Taylor as the AOL fought its way across a dozen worlds, had been steeling his courage to face the bitter cold.

Young took a deep breath and swung his legs over the cot, sitting up to face Stokaya. "Missing?"

"Yes, sir. Sergeant Li. He was on picket duty last night, sector H. He didn't answer the 4am check in, so Lieutenant Hammond sent two men to check his position. When they got there, he was gone."

Young stood up, wrapping a large blanket around his shoulders as he did. "Gone?" His voice turned somber. "Is it possible the cold got to him? Could he have frozen to death? Wandered off and gotten lost in the darkness?"

"They searched everywhere, sir. After the initial report, the lieutenant sent a dozen men to search. They found footsteps about a kilometers out, sir. It appears he must have covered his tracks until he was that far away from the camp."

"Could he have gone mad? The cold maybe?" But Young knew that wasn't the case…he knew it as well as his aide did, and the realization made his stomach clench. "Or something else…"

He dropped the blanket and moved across the tiny interior of the shelter, reaching for his parka. "I want a platoon sent after him, Captain. Immediately. They are to find him at all costs and bring him back."

"Yes, sir," Stokaya snapped back. He turned back toward the door.

"And, Captain…"

"Yes, sir?"

"They are to bring him back at all costs. Dead or alive."

"Yes, sir."

Young sighed and watched his aide slip back out through the door. He shoved his arms into the coat and zipped it up to the top. Then he took a step to follow, pausing for an instant.

Fuck, he thought. This is just what we need…

Young hesitated for perhaps half a minute, thinking…and readying himself for the early morning blast of frozen wind. Then he shoved the door open and strode out into the hazy dawn light. At least he didn't feel the cold as much as he had been…his mind was elsewhere. His force had been sent to lead the way for the army, but now the entire operation was in jeopardy.

He had a UNGov spy in his ranks, and even now the man was on the loose. If Li got word to the government…

Young tapped the small communicator pinned on his jacket. "Captain Carrington," he said, instructing the small AI to connect him with the specified officer.

"Yes, sir?" Carrington's response was almost immediate.

"Chris, I need you to get your men together right away. I've got a special mission for you, and it's urgent."

"Yes, General. Where do you want us?"

"Meet me at sector H as soon as you can…I'm on my way there now."

"We'll be right there, sir."

Young tapped the com unit again, cutting the link. His faced was twisted with frustration, and rage. This was serious. If UNGov got word of the invasion before the army had even transited…

No, he could not allow that to happen. He'd sworn his devotion to the crusade, and he wouldn't let himself fail his comrades so badly. If the AOL had to fight its way out of the Portal, even against a small, hastily-gathered UN force, the casualties would be enormous. He fought back against the frustration he felt inside, the boiling anger trying to force its way out. His friends called him Frantic, a handle he'd picked up on Erastus, one that poked fun at his frequent outbursts. But this time he was determined to keep control.

Jake trusted me with this mission…

Carrington was an Erastus veteran, a Supersoldier just like Young…and so were all his men. The enhanced warriors were only five percent of the army's numbers, but Young knew they were a vastly higher portion of its fighting power. One Supersoldier was a match for five regular men, perhaps even more. Even more importantly right now, they would have the advantage over Li Wong…if they managed to pick up his trail, they should be able to catch him. And when they did…

Young hastened his pace, practically jogging as he moved out toward the position where Li had been posted. He'd been entrusted to lead the first force through the Portal, and the idea of failure was anathema to him. If he failed in his mission, he would have failed Taylor too. And Jake Taylor was his longtime commander…and his friend. He would die for Jake Taylor… and he wasn't about to let his leader down now. Whatever it took.

*   *   *

Li stopped and dropped to his knees. He'd been running for

hours, and his legs just gave out. He gasped hard, still shudder-
ing from the frigid air as it filled his lungs. He had no idea where
he was, no clue how to reach a settlement or some other place
he could contact UNGov. He was pretty sure his com unit didn't
have the range he'd need, at least not unless he got closer to
some kind of government post somewhere. He'd been tempted
to try, to see if he got lucky, picked up some rogue station that
could connect him with Geneva, but he'd held back. The AOL
advance guard was as likely to pick up any transmission he made,
likelier in fact, since they were closer and no doubt looking for
him by now.

He felt a pang of regret for taking the risk he had. If he'd
just stayed behind, he could have played his role as a sergeant
in the army, as he'd done for so long. Then, at least, he'd be in
camp, instead of out here in the wilderness running God knows
where and panicking that every tree rustling in the wind was his
pursuers finally catching up to him.

Instead, he'd seduced himself with dreams of rewards…
high government postings, a villa in Geneva, all the trappings
UNGov showered on its truest servants. And the man who had
warned them of the AOL's arrival, gotten the word out in time
to resist as the thousands of soldiers on Ghasara begin moving
through the Portal one or two abreast? He didn't have the slightest doubt…he'd be a hero. And he didn't have political ambition,
just a desire to live the rest of his life in comfort and privilege.
That made him the perfect tool for the rapacious politicians
who ran UNGov.

Still, he'd taken a wild gamble. Or had he? Staying with the
army wasn't a much better option. Li knew Taylor and his band
of zealots didn't have a chance, not against the combined might
of all UNGov. And if he got caught in their ranks he could easily find himself as dead as the rest of them. No, making a run
for it was the right choice.

He told himself he had surprise on his side, and a big head
start. The advance guard hadn't brought any vehicles through
the Portal, no transports, no airships. And even if they rushed
any through now, they would take time to reassemble. Li had

been through half a dozen transits, and he was well aware how much work was required to take apart large pieces of equipment so they would fit through the small Portal openings. No, there would be no vehicles. General Young would almost certainly send people after him, but at least they'd be on foot, like he was.

But he does have Supersoldiers...

That was the thought that scared him. The Erastus veterans with their cybernetic enhancements. They weren't like normal men. They had surgically-implanted artificial fibers in their arm and leg muscles, making them stronger and faster. Their enhanced systems included expanded glycogen storage, giving them endurance far beyond that of normal men. Their lungs were modified, increasing the efficiency of their respiration. They were superior in virtually every physical ability.

If one of them caught him...he tried to put the thought out of his head. There were only twenty of them with the advance guard, and there was a lot of ground to cover. He'd changed his direction multiple times, and he'd done the best he could to clear his tracks leading away from his post. He told himself he had enough of a lead, that the area was just too vast for his pursuers to cover. But he wasn't sure he believed it. The Erastus men were Taylor's oldest and most loyal troops. Li knew they would follow him, without rest, without food...that they would keep coming until they dropped from exhaustion and died.

And I will drop long before they do...

He looked all around, his mind racing, trying to decide which way to go. Then he saw it, off in the distance. A hill. More than a hill...a great surging elevation, almost a small mountain. It was so far ahead, he could barely see it as a shadow against the afternoon sky. But it was his best chance.

Some UNGov facility should pick up my transmission from up there...

They could send a flyer to get me...before the Supersoldiers get here...

He took another deep breath, and he forced himself back to his feet. He had ten kilometers to go, he guessed. Maybe twelve. And a lot of that would be uphill. But it was his best chance.

He looked behind himself nervously but there was nothing he could see.

Yes, my best chance. My only chance.

*   *   *

"He must have his com unit off, sir. We're not getting any signal at all. I don't care how quick the bastard is, we'd be reading something if he was still on the net."

Carrington listened to Lieutenant James' reporting over the unitwide channel. He'd considered keeping his people on radio silence, but he'd decided that just couldn't work. They had too much ground to cover, and they had to be able to share anything the found. There were twenty of them, and they'd moved out from camp, each with an eighteen degree slice of the circle to cover. That wasn't a lot of ground at the beginning, but now they were fifteen kilometers from base, and each one of those swaths of ground was almost five klicks wide, and getting bigger with every meter. They all had the cybernetic eyes of a Supersoldier, but that didn't mean they could see through hills or clumps of trees.

Besides, it didn't matter. Li couldn't listen unless he switched his com unit on, and if he did, one of Carrington's people would almost certainly pick up his signal...and get a direct feed on his location.

"I want you all to keep scanning," Carrington snapped back, "...for anything. Even the slightest reading. I'm sure he does have his com off, but you can be certain he'll try to signal someone eventually. He's not going to walk all the way across Siberia. He'll be looking for some good ground to get a sig..." He paused, his eyes settling on a shadow in the distance. It was a hill, a big one, rising above the horizon. It was far away...he doubted he would even have seen it yet had it not been for his enhanced vision. But there it was. The highest ground he or any of his people had yet seen.

"Sir? Are you okay, Captain?"

"Yes, Lieutenant. I'm fine. I've got some high ground coming up in front of me. It's where I would go if I was trying to get a signal out. I'm going to check it out. The rest of you, keep your eyes open…any big hills, ridges, check them out. Got it?"

A chorus of 'yes sirs' rattled from his earpiece. "And keep everybody informed. Anybody sees anything, even if it's just a wild hunch…you get on the com and report it."

He took a deep breath. The more he looked at the distant gray of the hillside, the more he had a feeling that was where Li Wong was headed. It was the wildest guess, he knew. Wong could have gone in any direction, and no doubt there was high ground all around. But something told him this was the way.

He pulled his rifle off his back, checking it carefully as he walked, pulling out the cartridge and slamming it back into place. He'd loaded it and checked it when he'd left camp, but fifteen years of war had taught him to be cautious, meticulous. He heard Jake Taylor's voice in his head, the great commander's constant harangue to his troops, 'Carelessness gets soldiers killed.'

If Li Wong was out there, he'd be on the high ground…hard to see, and maybe lying in wait, ready to bushwhack any pursuers. Carrington hurried his pace. If Li was out there, the sooner he could catch him the better. He didn't know if anyone would pick up a signal from Li on that peak, but he wasn't going to take any chances…not if he could do anything about it.

*   *   *

"Attention, any UNGov personnel who receive this message, attention. I have a report of the utmost importance. General Taylor's army is transiting into a previously unknown Portal situated in northern Siberia. I am transmitting coordinates of the Portal, and also of my current location. Please relay this communique without delay to UNGov Intelligence headquarters in Geneva. I need immediate assistance, I repeat, I need immediate assistance. I am being pursued, and I must get to UNGov headquarters with the intelligence I possess."

Li looked down at the com unit. He had no idea if there was

anyone in range…except for the AOL, of course. He'd caught a glimpse of at least one pursuer when he'd been about halfway up the hillside. He didn't know who it was, but he'd decided to find a good place and set up an ambush. But then he saw the speed of his adversary, and he got a cold feeling in his stomach. One word went through his head. Supersoldier.

He started to panic, and he could feel his heart pounding wildly, sweat dripping down his neck despite the frigid cold. He almost took off and ran, but after a few minutes he managed to get ahold of himself. This was life and death, and he realized if he lost control, he was as good as dead.

I'll never outrun him, he thought, struggling to hold back the hopelessness. And trying to ambush him is a risky proposition. His eyes, his ears—if I move, if I breathe too hard…he'll be on me in an instant. And I don't stand a chance in hand to hand combat, not with one of them…

He'd looked up the steep hillside and realized his best chance—his only chance—was getting to the top and trying to signal for help. He was still in the middle of the wilderness, but the elevation would help. Maybe he could pick up a UNGov airship passing by, or some kind of exploratory party. Something…anything. It was a better risk than trying to outrun a man who could run three times the speed of a normal human, and whose bloodstream would be flooded with adrenalin long after Li himself had collapsed from exhaustion.

And so that's what he'd done. It had taken another fifteen minutes to reach the top, or close to it anyway. Then he'd flipped on the com unit at maximum power and started talking.

He turned about forty-five degrees, facing southeast instead of due east. The com unit transmitted 360 degrees, but he was directing all its extra power to push the signal farther in the designated direction. He needed every edge he could get.

"Attention all UNGov personnel," he began again, "this is a report of the utmost…"

He saw the motion, almost too late, but he reacted, ducking just as the figure leapt around a row of boulders and into view, and a series of bullets slammed into the rock wall behind him.

He threw himself to the side, bringing around his own weapon as he did. He looked up, and he got a glimpse of his attacker...just before he felt the impact, bullets slamming into his body. He didn't feel pain...he didn't feel much, in fact. Just a strange floating sensation, and weakness...such weakness.

He felt the com unit slip out of his hand. The cold of the pistol was still in his other, but he had no strength to wield it. He tried to lift his arm, bring it around to fire at his attacker, but... nothing. It fell to his side, the weapon slipping slowly from his grip.

He lay on the ground, his eyes looking up at the darkening pre-dusk sky. The cold was gone, even the fear. Even the urgency to call for help. He knew it was too late for that.

A shadow blocked his view of the sky. His assailant, standing above him, looking down.

My killer, he thought with the last bits of lucidity left to him. You won, Supersoldier.

He had a passing thought. Perhaps someone received his message. But he didn't really care. It was too late for him. It no longer mattered who won the war. He took a last breath, deep, painful. And then the darkness came.

Chapter 6

UNGov Communique GR-201374:

All UNGov installations are hereby instructed to activate class one alert protocols and to report all unidentified contacts or communications signals immediately to the Department of Internal Security, Geneva. Further, any suspicious individuals are to be detained immediately and held for questioning. All regional directors are responsible for supervising the terms of this edict, and all personnel will be held responsible for any failure to comply. This status is in effect until further notice.

"Mr. Bouvaire…" Raj Singh peered around the half open door to his supervisor's office, looking nervous as he did. "I am sorry to interrupt you, sir, but I think I have something to report."

Pierre Bouvaire looked up from the tablet he'd been reading. "You think you have something to report?" Bouvaire's voice was arrogant, impatient. He was a career UNGov bureaucrat, one extremely dissatisfied with his posting…and it showed in his attitude and behavior. "What exactly does that mean?"

Bouvaire was the director of the Salekhard Federal facility. It was far from one of the best posts available for a UN bureaucrat. Indeed, Bouvaire often suspected it was fairly close to the worst. At least on Earth. It was cold, not far from the Arctic Circle, in fact, and essentially a deserted wasteland. Still, Bouvaire would take his position any day over some administrative posting to one of the Portal worlds.

"Ah…well, sir, I picked up…something. It wasn't a message exactly, it was…"

Bouvaire glared at his subordinate. "Unless you want a transfer to a worse shithole than this, Specialist Singh, you had better start making sense."

"Yes, Administrator." Singh struggled to focus. Bouvaire had a reputation for being arbitrary, and sometimes downright abusive to his subordinates, to the point where they only approached him on matters they couldn't avoid. Singh had almost ignored the small signal he'd detected rather than bring it to his volatile supervisor. But all Federal facilities had been placed on alert and ordered to report anything abnormal. And failing to report something that turned out to be important would carry far more terrible consequences than enduring one of Bouvaire's tirades.

"I detected something at my station, sir. I believe it was a communication of some kind, a transmission at the extreme edge of detectable range, but I was not able to read anything intelligible. Just a fleeting signal, and a bunch of static…" He paused. "…and something that might be a voice, but barely audible." He reached into his pocket, pulling out a small handheld device. He pressed a button and played the twelve second clip.

Bouvaire listened quietly. Then he leaned back and sighed. "That could have been anything. Solar activity. Weather. Your 'voice' could just be some interference that happens to sound like speaking. Or maybe it's some com traffic from one of the mining operations." There were several major concerns working in the area. The Urals were a rich source of precious minerals, and UNGov-sanctioned mining groups continued to exploit that wealth. Indeed, that was the only reason Bouvaire and his people were here in this forsaken hinterland. The rest of the inhabitants who had called this frozen nightmare home had been relocated decades earlier, as part of UNGov's efforts to move population into more concentrated, manageable locations. Bouvaire wasn't sure if he should curse the mines for his frigid near-arctic posting…or thank them for keeping him on Earth instead of on some wretched Portal world. His opinion varied depending on the day, and just how annoying things got. But Singh and his scrap of a signal were pushing him toward cursing the blasted place.

"Yes, sir, but…" Singh paused again, but he caught himself and continued before Bouvaire reacted.

"…it didn't seem like any kind of natural phenomenon. And I don't think it was from one of the mines either. For one thing, the direction was all wrong. It was coming from the east, not the north or south."

"From the east?" Bouvaire shook his head. "You must have made some kind of mistake. There's nothing to the east for thousands of kilometers. Just frozen tundra."

"There was no mistake, sir." Singh's tone showed defiance, certainty in his work. But he caught himself and pulled the attitude back. Nothing good could come from upsetting Bouvaire any more than necessary. "I definitely picked up a signal, sir. There is something out there. Some kind of transmitter."

Bouvaire sighed. Singh could have picked up anything. Perhaps there was some kind of government party out there, exploring for resources or on some mapping expedition. He almost told Singh to forget about it, but then he paused, glancing down at his desk. He'd gotten a reminder about the alert status just the day before. He fished around on his desk, finally finding the tablet with the communique, panning his eyes quickly over it. He had no idea what was going on, what UNGov was looking for. But there was no point in taking a risk, whatever minuscule chance there was that Singh had found anything important. At least if he kicked it upstairs, he could get it off his desk…and cover his ass too.

"Alright, Singh. Get back to your station and clean up that signal the best you can. See what the main AI can do to filter out some of that interference. Then I'll send it to Geneva."

"Yes, sir," Singh replied. Then he nodded and backed out of the door, heading toward his desk.

Bouvaire shook his head. It was nothing important. He was almost sure of it.

But what the hell, at least it will look like I'm taking the alert seriously.

* * *

Drogov stood next to the Portal, looking back over the long line of troops waiting for his order to advance. They looked particularly sinister in their heavy radiation suits, like something from an old comic book or science fiction serial. But they'd need the suits. Drogov couldn't have imagined the chaos and destruction on the other side of the Portal...if he hadn't seen it on three other worlds already.

Alexi Drogov was a killer, a cold-blooded practitioner of his trade, but even he'd been shocked by the pure evil genius of Samovich's plan. He'd always thought UNGov's policy of never allowing veterans to return from the Portal worlds was a bit harsh. Drogov wasn't a soldier certainly, but he considered himself somewhat of a fighting man. And be found the idea of abandoning men who'd fought for years, who'd followed orders and won their wars, to be a bit...distasteful. If he hadn't been so skilled at removing emotions from the equation, he might have even had some reservations about being involved. But what Samovich had sent him to do was an order of magnitude worse than simply denying the warriors a trip home, and he owed his ability to comply to the frozen blood that circulated through his veins.

Samovich knew he couldn't make an exception and allow the soldiers to return to Earth. As much as he needed the veterans to leaven his hurriedly-assembled forces, he just couldn't trust their loyalty...not after Taylor had gotten to them. Even these men who had refused to follow Taylor's army knew that many of their comrades had. Putting them in the line on the other side would be asking for trouble, and it was a gamble the mercurial Samovich hadn't even seriously considered.

But the Secretary-General had a streak of paranoia to match his brilliance. He worried about leaving these men for too long with no enemy to fight. He'd imagined all kinds of ways they could pose a threat, not the least of which would be forcing their way through the Portals to return home without permission…and once on Earth, if they found Taylor's army battling UNGov forces, what would they do? It was too great a risk.

Then it had come to him. A way to eliminate any risk from the stranded forces…and to help him defeat Taylor as well. He thought back to UNGov's original plan to seize power, the deception that had allowed his predecessors to conquer a world, with just a few murders and a series of skillful lies, and he devised his own version. Then he charged his most trusted aide to see to its execution.

UNGov had destroyed most of the weaponry in the arsenals of the nation states decades ago. It had been a self-serving act, driven by fear that one or more of the old governments, or some rebellious splinter group from the disenfranchised military establishments, might use them to challenge the newly-established order. But some weapons still remained, even forty years later. Much of it was non-functional after so many years of neglect, but Samovich had remembered an old report, back in his days as an aide to the Secretariat. Something about salted bombs, cobalt-cased nuclear weapons designed to maximize radiation release, to kill as much population as possible, while leaving buildings and infrastructure more or less intact. They were terrible weapons, ones all the nation-states of Earth had sworn never to build. And yet UNGov inspectors had founds stockpiles of the weapons in at least four national arsenals.

And now, decades after the fearsome bombs had been produced, they had found a purpose. Samovich had planned the entire operation, and Drogov, the loyal henchman, had seen it done. A dozen bombs were sent to each Portal world, hidden in the crates and boxes carrying the normal supplies. And the cleverest, the most wickedly evil part of the plan was the order that preceded it all, the directive to concentrate all forces in base…to prepare to evac back to Earth. An order that kept each the full strength of each army within the lethal zone of the warheads.

Drogov imagined the celebrations, the joy of the soldiers at receiving word they would be going home, that their war was over and they would soon return to families and friends they thought they'd never see again. He was both appalled—and impressed—at the cold ruthlessness of it all.

On each planet, when the devices detonated, more than 99% of the soldiers present died, some almost instantly, from doses of radiation so enormous they simply dropped in place, and others slower, in an hour or two…or five, amid scenes of vomiting and seizures and terrible pain. Some of them would still be alive when Drogov's troops came through the Portal, but almost all of these would be incapacitated, unable to resist and already condemned to death by the mortal doses they had received. All, perhaps, save a few who were out on guard duty or in some sort of protective structure. And that was what Drogov's team of security troops was for. Samovich's command had been clear. No one was to survive. No one.

Drogov's people had already been to three worlds, and now they prepared to transit to Oceania. The bombs there had been set to detonate an hour earlier, and the small robot scanner Drogov had just sent through confirmed that fact. The paradise world, by far the most magnificent planet men had yet discovered now had a deep wound on its rocky waterfront, a deadly cloud of radiation that would poison streams and rivers, contaminate a large stretch of coastline, and kill everything within a thirty-kilometer radius of the main basecamp, including the human soldiers stationed there. In another few minutes, Drogov would give the order, and his soldiers would begin moving through. They would search the base and its surroundings, and they would shoot down anyone still alive. Then, when they were certain no one was left, not a guard who had run off into the hills, not a wounded man hiding in a shelter somewhere, they would move on to the next world. And when they were done, not a soldier would remain on any of the planets Taylor's soldiers had visited. There would be nothing left but bodies, and silent ruins of the camps that had once housed armies.

But the warriors of the planetary armies would not have finished their service to UNGov. These dead soldiers were to serve the government's propaganda needs, become the props in another monstrous lie, one designed to turn the people of Earth against Taylor and their would-be liberators. Samovich and Drogov might have been responsible for the horrifying genocide, but as far as the inhabitants of Earth were concerned, their soldiers were killed by Jake Taylor and his rebels, as retribution for their refusal to join his crazed rampage. Once Drogov had completed his mission of death, Samovich would take to the airwaves, the information networks, even the streets. His propagandists would spread the word about Jake Taylor, the traitor to his race, the human who had gone over to the Tegeri with his murderous comrades…and massacred thousands of loyal Earth soldiers. And Samovich would give his address surrounded by flag-draped coffins, his somber voice, choked with emotion as he eulogized the dead…and promised retribution against the monsters responsible for the heinous act.

Even Drogov's dark mind had been surprised at the evil brilliance of the plan, and for a moment he felt a strange chill, almost a fear of his longtime associate. What mind could conceive such a plan?

Then he glanced at his chronometer and turned toward the first unit in line. "Advance," he yelled, with all the authority he could muster. And he watched as his men moved steadily forward, one rank at a time disappearing into the swirling lights of the Portal. On to another world, to another terrible graveyard, like Death himself, to run his scythe through the heaps of dead and dying men.

Chapter 7

Communiqué Issued from Resistance Headquarters in New York:

> I say, while yet from that tower's base afar,
> We saw two flames of sudden signal rise,
> And further, like a small and distant star,
> A beacon answered.

"Well, it is done. The message is sent." Carson Jones sat on a chunk of broken concrete, looking across the room at the old man he'd known so long. Stan Wickes was standing, and Jones would swear his companion seemed ten years younger than he had a few days before, that some new fire raged within him. The old Marine was clearly ready for a fight.

For all Jones had sworn himself to the struggle against UNGov, now that they had lit the fuse he felt a tidal wave of emotions. Tension, anxiety...fear. Yes, fear, more than he'd ever felt before. He'd always considered himself a courageous man, one ready to fight for what he believed...to die for it if need be. But now he could barely keep himself from shaking as he sat in the abandoned cellar.

"It's okay, Carson." Wickes' voice was odd, soothing in a way Jones couldn't quite explain, though he felt it quite strongly. "It's normal. We all feel it."

"What?" Jones asked, trying as hard as he could to maintain his composure.

"The fear, Carson. The fear before going into battle. You are questioning your courage now, wondering if you are truly ready for what is coming." Wickes stared at his companion, who looked back, silent, a stunned expression on his face. "Don't worry, Carson…you will do what you must. We all feel what you are feeling. Any man who says he isn't scared in battle is lying… or mad."

Jones looked up, his eye's meeting his comrade's. "You mean you're scared too?"

"Of course I'm scared. I'm only human like you. But I have less to lose. I am old, my life lies mostly behind me. My friends from youth, my loved ones…they are gone already. It is easier for me to think only of duty, of striking a blow against those who would see mankind in bondage forever. You are still young, my friend, with the promise of a life yet ahead of you, as I was when I first heard shots fired in anger."

Stan Wickes had been a Marine, and a combat veteran. He'd fought in the Pacific War, when the U.S. and its Japanese allies battled against the Russian-backed Chinese Hegemony. It was the last major war the nations of Earth had fought among themselves…and it had fizzled out before it became a true world war. But it lasted long enough for Wickes to see combat, and to learn what it was like to watch friends die.

He'd been young then, with a girlfriend back home and a family sending him letters every day. He had certainly felt fear then, wave after wave of panic, pushing at him to run, to flee for his life, forsake his comrades, and hide in the jungle. He'd resisted it, and he'd done his duty, but years later it had all faded a bit in memory. He recalled the basics, of course, but the feeling of that primal fear, and the strength he'd somehow managed to summon to resist it…it all felt a bit unreal almost fifty years later.

"Do you think we have a chance, Stan? I mean a real chance?" Jones' voice had none of its usual confidence and strength.

Wickes paused. He knew the answer to that question. Without some external event, the Resistance was likely to fail. He'd almost counseled caution, but then he realized that whatever small chance there was, it was the best they were likely to get. UNGov's internal security was relentless, and the Resistance had grown weaker, not stronger over the past forty years. He'd seen friends disappear...and waited for days and weeks after, his stomach clenched, his back soaked with sweat, to see if his colleagues had given the interrogators some clue, some bit of trivial information that led them to him.

He'd been about to tell Carson not to send the communique, to wait for another day, another opportunity. But then he realized that day would, more than likely, never come...certainly not while he still lived. He hesitated, but then he told himself that even a small chance was better than none at all, and he remembered life before UNGov's takeover, when men and women, at least in some nations, could speak more or less freely, without fear of undue prosecution. It was more like a dream now, fading slowly in the old man's mind. But it still remained, and while it did, Wickes would do anything for the slightest chance to bring those days back, to know when he died that Jones and Bell, and the others, would taste liberty in their own lives, as he once had.

"Yes, Carson...we have a chance. A good one as long as we stay focused and do what we must." He felt a twinge of guilt. He knew he was lying to his friend, or at least twisting the truth beyond recognition. He'd always believed anyone going into battle deserved honesty, but he also knew that whatever chance they had could be lost if there was no hope. And he wouldn't let that happen, no matter what it took.

He looked over at Jones, flipping a coin mentally to decide if he'd been convincing enough. "Let's go, Carson," he said. "We don't have a lot of time. The other cells will all commence operations at midnight, GMT. And we've got to be ready."

And you'll be better off if you're busy...right up until the balloon goes up.

*　*　*

The UNGov Building in New York was an impressive structure, a skyscraper dating from another time, when America had been a true superpower...the superpower. That golden age of dominance had been long past even before UNGov seized worldwide dominance, and it had been a greatly weakened America that had yielded its sovereignty to the Geneva government. Now, New York was a backwater, a city mostly fallen into poverty and despair. It was still home to millions, though its great media and financial industries were mostly gone, both functions having long ago moved to European capitals closer to UN Headquarters in Geneva. Indeed, New York had once been the home of the original United Nations itself, the precursor institution to UNGov, though the fading metropolis had lost that distinction twenty years before the first Portal was discovered.

The city still retained much of its population, though most of those of means had long ago fled and now there were only teeming masses, workers employed in low-paying government-owned industries or those on relief, barely feeding themselves on the modest benefits they received. Crime was rampant, and people rarely left their homes, huddling instead in fear when they didn't have to be out for work or to buy food. They lived in mostly crumbling apartment buildings, slowly deteriorating without maintenance, and the surrounding infrastructure had fallen almost into ruin as what little funding the government allocated had been stolen and misdirected by those with influence. It was an urban hell, sucked dry of its resources and left to rot, one of many that dotted UNGov's Earth.

Despite the rhetoric and the speeches about the war, about programs to alleviate the suffering of poor citizens around the world, UNGov was at its heart an institution run for itself, to benefit those who held its highest positions. From the top to the bottom it was riddled with greedy, grasping bureaucrats, seeking only to ensure their own comfort and to claw their way to more power. It was a toxic culture, the ultimate manifestation of the ills of the governments that had come before. The people, in all their wallowing, downtrodden misery, were at best a necessary evil in the eyes of those living in the perverse luxury of Geneva.

The rebel groups around the globe, operating in the shadows

for forty years, knew that, but they spent most of their time avoiding detection, seeking to survive as the security forces of totalitarianism hunted down so many of their comrades. There was little doubt millions of others understood the evil of their government as well, though fear kept them quiet. It wasn't spoken of, certainly not in public, but most people had seen someone—a friend, an acquaintance, a neighbor—dragged away in the night for 'reeducation.' Few ever returned.

It was understandable. Even those with the courage to speak out were stopped by the futility of it all. It was bravery, perhaps, to risk one's life to strike a blow for freedom, but to die for nothing, to throw oneself on a sword in an act of utter futility? Even the greatest stalwart lost heart when facing such a reality.

But the revolutionaries would be silent no more. They would cower in fear no more. They had planned for forty years, passed the torch from those who remembered freedom to a generation that had never tasted it. They had paid a steady price in blood, as thousands of their numbers were interrogated and executed. But that was over now. Tonight they would strike a blow for freedom. And once begun, their war would not stop, not while a single one of them still drew breath.

"The guards are dead." Bell looked around as he walked toward Carson Jones. There was an eerie satisfaction in his voice that suggested he'd enjoyed killing the two sentries. UNGov's internal security forces were far from gentle, and most of the members of the Resistance harbored deep resentments. But Bell was a UNGov employee himself, one highly ranked enough to avoid the worst abuses of the enforcers. But he had his own reasons for hating UNGov, and though he'd kept them to himself, they were as potent as those of anyone else in the Resistance. More so even, and a fire burned inside him, pulling from the darkest part of his mind a savage burning hatred. There was nothing Devon Bell wouldn't do to destroy UNGov. Nothing.

"Good." Jones gestured with his hand, urging Bell to hurry, to duck into the alley along with the rest of the team. "Okay," he said, turning toward the men and women stacked up behind him in the narrow passageway. "It's time. In…" He glanced down at the old, scuffed watch on his wrist. "...six minutes, we will strike our first blow. At the same time, all around the world, our brothers and sisters will be doing the same. In London, Paris, Tokyo, Moscow, Hong Kong, Nairobi...everywhere. We have been hunted like animals, our comrades have been captured and killed...but now we strike back with the fury of righteousness. And once this begins, it will not—it cannot—end. From this moment, we hide no more. No, by God, we fight. Every moment, with every gram of strength that remains to us. The future of mankind rides with us, the dying spark of liberty is in our hands. Go, now, each of you. You all know what to do...and though many of us will die, and perhaps none of us shall meet again, never forget that you are all heroes, and with you goes the best that mankind can be."

There were perhaps twenty men and women in that alley, and as one they thrust their fists into the air, suppressing the wild shouts they all wanted to scream. Jones knew they were afraid, as he himself was. But he had faith in these people, a firm belief they would do what they must. Whatever chance they—all the rebels worldwide—had, they would give it their best. He tried to push away the doubt, the sober assessments of UNGov's resources, of the brutal intensity of the internal security agents. Hopelessness would serve nothing, and now was the time to believe...and to think of nothing but victory.

And something is going on, something out of the ordinary...if UNGov has another problem, if they are distracted enough, perhaps we have a chance...

"Go," he repeated, waving his hands. "There is no time. We have less than four minutes."

The revolutionaries began to disperse, sneaking away through the maze of alleys and small back streets. They slipped into old buildings, down into abandoned cellars, into the crumbling tunnels of the old subway system. Jones ran too, with Bell right behind. They looked out into the street, and seeing nothing they raced across, ducking into a small service road. They stopped about twenty meters down in, right in front of a gray-haired man in a worn olive-green coat.

"Captain," Jones said, "you shouldn't be here. We have to get away."

"Not yet, Carson," Wickes said, an almost hypnotic sound to his voice. "After forty years we strike at last...this is the first shot of the war to come. I will stay and see it before I leave. I will stay here for all my comrades who are gone, who didn't live to see this day for themselves."

Bell sighed. "Carson, we don't have time for this...if we get caught here it just weakens the rebellion. We have to go...get into hiding and prepare for the next blow." Bell respected the old Marine, but he didn't share the almost limitless adoration his comrade did. He knew Jones' father had been in the service too, another Marine, though one who'd died years before. The elder Jones had been wounded in action before the UNGov takeover, and when the new government downgraded the medical ratings of the old veterans, his health steadily deteriorated. He'd been dead for more than twenty years now.

Bell understood his friend's attitude toward Wickes, but in his mind all things were subordinate to destroying UNGov. There was no place for sentiment, no room for pointless gestures. He stripped the veneer away and saw their goal as he knew it truly was. To destroy UNGov, to kill its people, to grind it into the dust of history, without mercy, without pity. He was ready to do that, but he sometimes doubted his comrades were committed enough to become what they would have to become. Monsters savage enough to destroy another monster.

The images in his head fueled his hatred, the face of a woman, young pretty. Lydia had been his lover, though she'd always insisted they keep the relationship a secret. He found out why a year later. She had been a member of the Resistance, one whose luck eventually failed her. As far as Bell had known, she just disappeared, and it took him almost a year to discover what had happened to her, how she had died on the concrete floor of an interrogation room in such torment as he could hardly imagine. He died that day, at least every part of him that was human. All that remained was a shadowy revenant, living only for vengeance.

"Just a minute more, Devon," Carson said, humoring the old man as Bell knew he would. He opened his mouth, ready to argue, but he stopped himself. It was pointless. And if he had to stay here he might as well watch too. He turned and looked down the long alley out into the street. It wasn't much of a view, but if they were any closer they'd almost certainly be injured by the debris or picked up almost immediately by the UNGov response teams. Bell didn't like the delay, but he was still pretty sure they could get away after the blast, unless they got closer.

"Twenty seconds," Jones said softly.

Bell's eyes shifted, falling on the old Marine for a moment. Wickes was a bit more prone to fits of remembrance and nostalgia, but Bell admired the old man nevertheless. He knew Wickes had his own grievances against UNGov. Earth's masters had treated the veterans of the old nation states shamefully, refusing to honor any of the promises they'd been made. And for years, the internal security teams had focused heavily on the retired soldiers and Marines as suspects, imprisoning them for the slightest signs of resistance.

Yes, we all have our reasons for revenge, the fire that drives us…that will allow us to do what we must, whatever it takes. Bell's thoughts drifted, back to a blue sky, a sunny day…and a woman with auburn hair, wild, blowing in the breeze.

Then the ground shook and the sound of the explosion pulled him back to reality. He looked out, just before he and his companions were engulfed by a massive cloud of dust…and in the distance, he heard the rumbling sound of the great building coming down. He was still looking, but his sight was blocked by the dust clouds. He coughed and rasped for air, and then he felt a tug on his arm. It was Captain Wickes, grabbing his sleeve and pulling him back, down into a large cellar door…closing it.

He followed, gasping at the air, still heavy with debris, but breathable once the door was closed. Then he felt Wickes pulling again, leading him down into the old subway station…and to the long-abandoned tunnel that would lead them to safety. Or whatever passed for safety for a group of rebels, outnumbered and on the run.

Part Two
A World at War

Chapter 8

Jake Taylor's First Words as He Stepped from the Portal onto Earth:

I have returned. After eighteen years, I have returned. And I wield the bloody sword of vengeance against the wicked.

John MacArthur gripped the airship's controls tightly, his eyes locked on the scanning display. He was looking at a small dot, a UNGov flyer, one that was heading directly for the AOL's positions. MacArthur was the army's overall air commander, and he knew he had no place in the cockpit of a single Dragonfire attack craft. But one ship was all he had, all the army had...at least until the engineers managed to reassemble more. It had been somewhat of a miracle that they'd managed to get even one bird up in less than two days. The Dragonfire was a fiendishly complex piece of machinery, and it had to be completely disassembled to get it through the Portal. But Taylor had urged his technicians on, imploring them to get him some air power as soon as possible. And they'd responded by doing virtually the impossible. By all accounts the second ship would be airborne tomorrow, and another half dozen a day after that.

But tomorrow isn't the problem, MacArthur thought, staring at the icon on his scanner. The army had been in an uproar when he'd transited through the Portal, with rumors of some spy who'd managed to get off a transmission to UNGov, warning them of the AOL's arrival. MacArthur was a colonel, part of the army's command structure and privy to the most confidential information. He knew very well the rumors were far more than that. Though various versions of the story were circulating, it was true that a UNGov operative had snuck away from the advance guard...and managed to send a brief signal before he'd been caught and killed. He'd only had his field com, and it was unlikely there had been anyone in range to receive the fleeting transmission. But Jake Taylor was not a man to take unnecessary chances. The army had been ordered to accelerate the pace of the transit, and the whole thing had turned into an example of barely managed chaos.

For two days the army had labored day and night, units moving into defensive positions, widely-separated from each other as a precaution against nuclear attack. The soldiers had dug and cut trees and erected heavy weapons, as even more of their comrades streamed through the Portal. And for every moment of those two days, MacArthur and the other senior officers had waited each minute, expecting an enemy strike that hadn't come. Until now.

One flyer wasn't a strike, not exactly. But it was enough to confirm to UNGov that the AOL was here. MacArthur was jamming the airwaves with every watt of power he could spare, but he knew that didn't matter. Even if he shot the thing down before it could get off a signal, its failure to return would be its own message. And his jamming would cut off the bird's homing signal back to base...which meant UNGov already knew something was wrong.

He moved his arm, angling the throttle and bringing the airship around on a direct course for the enemy bird. "Arm air-to-air missiles," he snapped. "And I want all defensive systems on full." He knew he had a crack crew, a one-time assembly of airship commanders gathered for this mission, the most experienced personnel he had. Still, he believed in seeing to every detail himself.

"All defensive systems active and under AI control, sir." A short pause. "Air-to-air missiles one and two armed and ready to launch."

MacArthur stared at the display, watching the crosshairs move slowly together as the ship's AI worked on acquiring a target lock.

That ship's got a good pilot, he thought grimly. I hope all their crews Earthside aren't that good.

He nudged the thrust again, trying to improve the ship's position, help the AI get a lock. Then he heard the familiar whine… the lock signal. Fire, he thought to himself as he depressed the trigger, feeling the ship buck slightly as it released the ordnance.

"Reload," he said, angling the throttle again, closing the distance. He had two missiles in the air, but he was going to fire two more. He had to get that ship.

"Missiles three and four, armed and loaded." A short pause. "Ready to fire, sir."

MacArthur flashed back briefly to some of the battles he'd fought with the AOL. They'd been perpetually low on supply then, and he'd had to ration every missile like it was his last scrap of food or drop of water. But now the Tegeri had resupplied the entire army, delivering vast quantities of virtually exact copies of all weapons systems…missiles, autocannon rounds, even three dozen brand new airships, indistinguishable from the Dragonfires he already had save that they were new and not patched back together half a dozen times.

He tapped the throttle slightly to the left, and an instant later he heard he the tone again. Locked. He pulled his finger tight, firing again. Now he had four missiles in the air.

"Autocannons ready," he ordered. The four missiles were more than enough to take down the enemy craft, but MacArthur wasn't taking any chances.

"Autocannons loaded and ready, Colonel."

"Very well," he replied as he shoved the stick forward, pushing the thrust to maximum. His screen displayed the UNGov ship trying to escape with the four missiles closing on its tail. And behind that, MacArthur's airship, moving steadily closer.

He took a deep breath and locked his eyes on the targeting screen. His focus was almost total, but there were thoughts floating in his head, around the edges of the intense concentration, realizations of what was happening now.

He was back on Earth. They all were. And the final war had begun.

*   *   *

"Let's go…we need to get you on your way." Bear Samuels stood next to the row of newly-assembled trucks, watching as his people handed out packs and directed the three to six member teams to their designated vehicles. There was noise in the background, and bustling activity as "Frantic" Young directed the troops along the front line as they dug trenches and set up rows of heavy weapons around the perimeter of the army's position. There were more than six thousand men deployed on the forward lines, stretched out in an extended order designed to limit potential damage from nuclear or chemical attack. There was an attitude of grim determination in the ranks of those men, a sense that they were outnumbered and outgunned, but that they would still prevail somehow.

But the small groups now mounting up and driving away in the transports had an even more dangerous job, and possibly one upon which the true chance for victory depended. These men would leave the camp, they would drive as far as they could before they ran out of fuel or had to abandon the trucks to hide from enemy patrols. Then they would walk, moving through woods or brush when possible, doing everything they could to hide from the enemy as they made their way to their old homes.

The infiltration teams had two missions. First, to avoid being killed or captured while they made their way, however they could, back to the cities and towns where they'd lived before they were drafted. And second, to seek out family, old friends, teachers… anyone who'd known them, who could identify them and would listen to what they had to say. They were the vanguard of the battle of hearts and minds, a desperate struggle that would be fought in cities and towns across the world.

Jake Taylor was a gifted leader, victorious in battle and loved by the men under his command. But he was also perhaps the only man in the AOL who recognized the true evil his army faced, the levels to which the politicians of UNGov would go to preserve their power and privilege. His troops were, for the most part, simple soldiers, men who'd come into the military without much in the way of advanced education and who had learned the way of the warrior...devotion to duty, loyalty to comrades. But Taylor knew how different his adversaries were from the straightforward fighting men he commanded.

He'd spent as much time in the months and years leading up to this moment thinking about the information war his people would face as he had the actual fighting. He knew his soldiers expected to be greeted as liberators, or at least welcomed by throngs of curious townspeople who would listen to their rallying cries, and welcome them home as heroes. But Taylor was far less optimistic. For four years his forces had advanced across the Portal wars, fought a dozen battles...and for all that time, he suspected, the UNGov propaganda machine had been in full swing.

The Tegeri had been insistent that their connection to Taylor be a secret, lest UNGov be given the chance to link his people to the terrible alien enemy men had feared for four decades. But Taylor knew even the gifted aliens didn't understand what men like those who ran UNGov were capable of. He expected not only caution, but fear from the people his troops encountered... even hatred. His worst fears were that his army would be compelled to open fire on civilians, normal people they had come to liberate, turned into misguided partisans by UNGov's unceasing lies and deceit.

He was determined to do whatever was possible to prevent such tragedies, but his options were limited. The yells and shouts of his soldiers wouldn't carry far, and they wouldn't be very convincing to civilians conditioned on UNGov propaganda. Taylor had a few tools that might help him, technological marvels given to him by the Tegeri. But he knew he had to exert tremendous care in their use. And they were far from enough to win the support of a world.

But the connections between mothers and sons, fathers and

sons. The joy of seeing a brother, long thought lost forever. Childhood friends, embracing for the first time in years. These were the kinds of things that could stand up to government lies, and Taylor was determined to utilize this great power for all it was worth.

His army had soldiers from every corner of the globe, from what had once been Russia and China…and Japan and Poland and Germany. He would send these men out, to their homes, in those places and more. To France and England. To the rugged Highlands of Scotland and the warm, sunny coasts of Spain. And even across the oceans…to the remnants of the United States, Canada. Mexico. And South America.

He would send them home, selected groups, veterans with the skill and ability to make a long journey behind enemy lines… with some chance of success. He knew for many it would be a suicide mission. Thousands of kilometers lay between most of them and home, a long way to journey behind enemy lines. They would be found, and when they were they would be killed…or worse. UNGov had many skilled interrogators in its ranks, and Taylor had no doubts the horrors his captured men would face.

But some would get through. He believed that, though he wasn't sure if that belief was born of knowledge or simply from his need to have some kind of faith. And those who did would spread the word, not to terrified civilians facing phalanxes of armed troops but one on one, to friends and loved ones. People who would believe them, who would burn hot with anger when they understood what had happened to their sons and brothers and husbands.

Samuels moved down the column of transports, stopping at each and shaking the hands of the team members. Bear's shoulder bore the two stars of a major general, but the giant hadn't forgotten his roots as an enlisted man. These soldiers were going into extreme danger, running a gauntlet by themselves, with only a few fellows at their sides. Samuels knew the entire army was in grave danger, that they faced a terrible struggle that would claim many of them. But there was something different about facing danger surrounded by thousands of comrades. The infiltration teams would be alone…alone on the world that had once been their home. And General Chuck Samuels figured the least he could do is wish them each well before they departed.

"Good luck, boys." Bear grasped the hand of a soldier standing just outside the next transport in line. "Where you guys headed?" He knew they were going to Warsaw…he knew where all the transports were going. But he wanted to let the soldier talk about home, even for a few seconds.

"Thank you, sir. I'm from Otwock, sir. It's a town just outside Warsaw." He gestured toward the three others standing by the transport. "The rest of the guys are from the same area."

"Any family back in Otwock?" Bear almost didn't ask. Most of the soldiers had left friends and family behind when they'd gone to war…but they'd fought for years with no contact with home, no real hope of ever returning. He knew they were all thinking the same things…what has changed, who is still there, still alive? And how will they see me? As what I was before…or as the creature war made me?

Bear himself had those same thoughts. He'd left a mother and a father behind, and two sisters as well. Were they still alive eighteen years later? If they were, they no doubt mourned him as dead, not daring to hope he'd managed to survive so long. If he made it back there, his arrival would be a shock…and he would bring with him the fire of rebellion in his wake. Certainly, UNGov was a cancerous government, but Taylor and Bear and the soldiers of the AOL would plunge the world into war. People would have to choose sides. Men like Bear, inured to hardship and violence, had an easier time casting themselves into battle. But he had come from simple folk, and he wondered, will they embrace this rebellion? Or will they fear it…and curse it for engulfing their world in fire.

"Yes, General…my father. And a brother. My mother got sick a few years before I got drafted. Her medical rating was too low, and we didn't have the money to buy drugs on the black market. She hung on for a while, a month…a bit more. But then she passed." Bear had drifted off into thoughts of his own family, but he pulled himself back, catching the last of the soldier's words…and feeling a surge of strength from them. It was out-rages like the man had described that made the army's crusade a noble one…and he would follow it through to the very end.

"I'm sorry about your mother…but that's why we're here, isn't it soldier? To make sure things like that don't happen to anyone else." Bear patted the man on the shoulder and looked over his comrades. "I'll keep a good thought for your father and brother, son. For all your fathers and brothers…and mothers and sisters and friends. Remember, boys, we're all with you. To the very end."

He held his gaze for a few seconds, and he could see the animation on their faces as they boarded the transport. Bear was always amazed how a few words could drive men to face hell-ish danger with a determined stare. But then he realized, Taylor could do the same to him.

Perhaps that's how we do the things we do.

He walked up to the next vehicle, and he smiled again. "Hello, soldiers…where you guys headed?" His eyes glanced down the line of trucks, stretching almost out of sight. Bear was tired, but he was also determined. None of these men would go, not until he wished them well personally. He didn't know if it would make a difference, if his little rallying cries would save lives, keep the men focused on their objectives. But as long as there was a chance, Bear Samuels was going to see it done.

* * *

"Colonel MacArthur shot down the flyer, sir, and he says he is almost certain our jamming prevented it from sending any kind of warning. So it is unlikely UNGov has received any reports on our dispositions." Hank Daniels was following after Taylor, matching his commander's swift pace. Taylor was edgy…even more than he had been since the army began to transit back to Earth. Daniels was trying to reassure Taylor, but he didn't even sound like he'd convinced himself.

"Come on, Hank, you know better than that." Taylor's voice suggested he appreciated his friend's efforts, but also that he wasn't buying a word of it. "The damned thing's disappearance is its own signal. What do you think is going to happen when it doesn't come back? What would you do if MacArthur's bird hadn't returned from a scouting run?"

Daniels exhaled loudly, a signal that one of the AOL's grimmest realists was done trying to find the silver lining. "Okay, okay, I agree. So what do we do now?"

"We get ready, that's what. First, I want those anti-air vehicles reassembled...they have priority over everything except the Dragonfires. When UNGov realizes we're here, they're going to be able to hit us by air long before they can get appreciable land forces here."

Daniels nodded. "I agree. The Reapers will be a big surprise to the UNGov forces."

Taylor nodded, even allowing himself a brief grin. "Yes, I'm inclined to agree." Reaper wasn't an official name, just something that had caught on somehow. The new weapons system didn't have any name, and certainly not one Taylor or his people were likely to pronounce. The Tegeri had given them the forty vehicles, basically armored half-tracks mounted with an array of anti-aircraft weaponry. They were built to fit in alongside the human-designed ordnance, to not give away the fact that the Tegeri were supporting Taylor and his people...at least not in any way that offered propaganda opportunities to UNGov. Taylor had no doubt the Secretariat was well aware of his Tegeri connection, but as long as he didn't offer them alien-looking equipment they could capture and plaster all over the information nets he figured it was okay deploying whatever he could.

"I think we'll be in good shape if we can get them in place in time. MacArthur should have a full squadron up before they can hit us, and if he's got the ground support network backing him up we should be able give them a hell of a bloody nose."

Taylor knew UNGov didn't have a large air force to throw at his people. Earth's only government didn't maintain an army of any substance outside of the disputed Portal worlds, only internal security forces designed to spy on the people and put down riots and rebellions. He suspected some gear originally intended for the armies on the Portal planets had been diverted to whatever defensive forces his enemies had managed to assemble to face his people. But he also knew, for all the resources at its disposal, UNGov couldn't match the battle experience of his warriors. And they had spent a fortune creating the Black Corps, resources that did not go into raising earthbound armies. That investment was now lost, not a single soldier left. Taylor's people had an uphill fight, no doubt. But the more he thought about it, the more a small spark of a thought formed deep in his mind. They had a chance...a real chance.

"So it's a race then? Can we get our vehicles and airships built in time...or will the enemy get a shot at all of it while it's still sitting around in crates?" Daniels had a way of keeping things brutally succinct.

Taylor was used to his friend's blunt mannerisms, but he couldn't hold back a wince as he thought of his priceless Tegeri technology being blown to bits before it was even assembled. "Hank, I want you to go over there. They've really got to pick up the pace and get these things in the field."

"You got it, Jake." There was a twinge to his voice that made Taylor smile. He couldn't imagine a better kick in the ass to get things done than having Hank Daniels hovering around scowling.

Chapter 9

UNGov Worldwide Media Broadcast:

I have just received word in the studio that Secretary-General Samovich himself will address the world in the aftermath of these terrible attacks. The Secretary-General will be live in just a moment, but before we cut to him, I would like to take the chance to recap for viewers just tuning in. Over an approximate twelve-hour period, eighteen government installations around the world were attacked by terrorist groups acting in an apparently coordinated manner. The attackers targeted major institutions in the world's largest cities, and they appear to have timed their strikes to cause maximum casualties, not only to UNGov staff, but to citizens conducting business at the facilities. The death toll exceeds 41,000, mostly clerical workers and others employed at the various sites...as well as over 1,000 children in a special school at the London UNGov building.

The Secretariat has been in emergency session formulating a response to these wonton acts of destruction, and around the world, UNGov field teams have been working around the clock, tending to the wounded and counseling the loved ones of those lost. It is indeed a black day for the entire world, one which causes us all to imagine just what kind of evil exists among us, the terrible monsters who lash out at our noble experiment in world government, heedless of the death and suffering caused by their unbridled extremism.

And now, Secretary-General Anton Samovich, live from UNGov headquarters in Geneva...

Anton Samovich walked into the massive studio, his eyes darting back and forth, watching the staff run around in a barely controlled frenzy. They were shocked, certainly…and scared too. In forty years of UNGov rule there had never been a domestic crisis like the one that had unfolded over the past sixteen hours. The media was just another tentacle in UNGov's massive machine, and now it was in full operation, making certain the billions of people in the world came to the 'correct' conclusions about the Resistance's attacks.

Samovich was still a little shaken himself, though he'd been a master politician long enough to hide whatever he was feeling, and to any who looked at him, he appeared totally in control. He'd been worried enough about Taylor and his army, focused on that danger almost to the point of obsession, but now he realized he had another problem, a domestic one. He'd been shocked enough when he'd gotten word of the first attack, but a few minutes later his aides returned with word of a second, and then a third. Within twelve hours, reports had streamed in from around the world, and by the time it was over, there had been no fewer than eighteen incidents. UNGov facilities all around the world had been targeted by coordinated groups, and for the most part, obliterated.

His first reaction had been rage. For years he'd driven his internal security units hard, giving them more and more power—searches, seizures, field judgments, summary executions…anything to maintain control, to prevent exactly the sort of thing that had just happened. He knew there was still an active underground, but he'd considered them to be a few holdouts, able to gather occasionally and complain about UNGov, but without any real capabilities. But in a few hours that theory had been proven completely wrong. The rebels had access to powerful explosives, and enough intelligence to gain entry to sensitive facilities. He still doubted the traitors had the power to threaten the government in any real way, but they'd certainly had enough to create a worldwide incident. One they expected would draw attention to their cause. But the Secretary-General had no intention of allowing their actions to increase their support. Quite the contrary, he had every intention of turning it all against them…and he didn't have a doubt the masses would buy everything he told them…and 'showed' them.

Samovich walked slowly, solemnly toward the lectern. His demeanor was perfect, his expression carefully deliberate, sadness, yet strength too…intended to empathize with the people, but to reassure them as well. The perfect message. Their leader was human, emotional…but he was strong too, ready to protect them from the danger. He was a master at what he did, but deep inside he still couldn't quite believe how gullible people were, how easy to lead and deceive.

He listened to the news reports as they were broadcast, nodding his head slowly in approval as he watched the footage, the video of the perfectly staged disaster sites. The 'facts' of the terrorist attacks were perfect, and he'd made sure his teams had provided plenty of footage of very normal looking people being carried out of the rubble. By the time his teams had finished with it, the footage looked extremely authentic. The incidents had taken him completely by surprise—and he swore someone was going to pay for that fact—but he'd responded quickly, always a believer that no crisis was to be wasted and that with enough lies anything could be turned to an advantage.

And so it had, so far at least. The rebels might have weapons and explosives, but UNGov controlled the information nets… and with that, Samovich could make the people believe anything he wanted. The Resistance groups had exercised great care in their timing and choice of targets, clearly attempting to minimize casualties. For all the physical damage they had caused, fewer than 800 people had been killed, the 41,000 figure the newscasters were reporting being purely the creation of Samovich's propagandists…as was most of the footage of charred bodies being removed from the smoking ruins.

The bit about the children was his favorite part, probably because it had been his idea, a way to inflame opinion even further and to generate greater support for the government's efforts to bring the culprits to justice. It hadn't even been that difficult to come up with the required bodies. There were always orphans from those who were liquidated in the reeducation camps. They were usually raised on government orphanage farms and typically put to work in the fields at around ten years of age—and frequently drafted into the planetary armies when they reached adulthood. But a few dozen had just served a far greater purpose…even if they'd been killed and half-incinerated to do it.

Samovich turned when he got to the podium, and he looked out for a moment. He stood, as if he was marshaling the strength to address the terrible events of the last day, to put aside his heartbreak and lead his people through this tragedy. Then he cleared his throat and began.

"My fellow citizens of United Earth, it is with a heavy heart that I have come to speak to you this day. We have faced challenges together, struggles the generations who preceded us could hardly have imagined. First contact with an alien race, a historical milestone gone horribly wrong…and a forty-year war for survival against a savage and technologically advanced enemy, a desperate struggle that has absorbed resources and caused widespread suffering and shortages." There was no harm in reminding the population of the Tegeri threat, and to reinforce their thinking that UNGov was the shield protecting them from bloodthirsty aliens. To focus their blame for the squalor and conditions many of them endured.

"But today we are reminded that human beings, men and women just like us, are also capable of almost unspeakable evil. We see it here, in the images of these destroyed buildings, in the bodies pulled from the wreckage…" He paused an instant, as if emotion was overwhelming him. "…in the children, massacred while they attended school."

He stared into the camera, silent for a moment, giving his global audience a chance to absorb his carefully chosen words.

"Nothing I can say will take away the pain we all feel, the outrage at such a dastardly series of terrorist attacks. There are no words, no explanations that can make decent people understand what inspires such hideous evil in some. All we can do is see to those injured…and aid the loved ones of the lost in any way possible. And to that end we have dispatched counselors and crisis management teams to each of the stricken areas."

His face hardened, and his voice deepened as he gradually fed anger into his meticulously constructed demeanor. "And we shall find and apprehend those responsible. Have no doubt, my fellow citizens, that your government will spare no effort or expense, leave no stone unturned in our relentless effort to bring those who perpetrated this heinous act to justice. And all who aided or abetted them. There will be no place to hide, no dark hole deep enough for the villains to hide. We will destroy them utterly and without remorse, whatever the cost. And we will take whatever steps are necessary to ensure that nothing like this can ever happen again. This, I promise each and every one of you."

With my sincere thanks to these rebels for giving me an excuse to tighten security worldwide…and for the support I will gain when you are found and brought to the scaffold. Or, if you prove too elusive, when some other convict stands there in your place.

"And now, let us have a moment of silence, a tribute to those we lost this day, and a display for all to see of our solidarity as a people, and our never ending quest for justice and peace." He bowed his head, staring at the top of the lectern while a single thought went through his mind.

My God, a minute can feel like a long time…

*   *   *

"Secretary-General, sir…" Pete Rogers' voice was shaky, and he struggled to return Samovich's gaze." The aide had served the Secretary-General for years, long before Samovich had secured the top job, and he knew how to handle his sometimes unpredictable and volatile boss. But he was nervous this time, clearly worried about how Samovich would react to what he had to report.

"Yes, yes, what is it? I haven't got all day, man." Samovich's tone was edgy, impatient. He wasn't in the mood to waste time. He had enough to worry about already.

"Sir, several days ago the administrative center at Salekhard sent in a signal they had received. It was...well, sir...it was very garbled, mostly static, and they weren't even sure if it was artificial or some kind of natural phenomenon. So...it ended up in a low-priority queue..." The aide paused, his eyes carefully probing the Secretary-General's expression.

"Get to the point," Samovich said, his voice growing thick with menace. "Unless you want a transfer to the Antarctic research station, where slow, stammering bullshit might be tolerated more than it is here in my office."

"Yes, sir." Rogers tried to get control over his nerves, with very limited success. He was used to Samovich's impatience, and he'd survived it before. But he knew things were different now. The boss was already upset, worried about the rebel army on the Portal worlds...and angry that his security staff had been caught flatfooted by the Resistance's massive strike. And the news he had to give Samovich was even worse.

"When the message was finally analyzed," he continued, "it was determined that it was likely an artificial transmission...a probability greater than eighty percent. There are no known expeditions in the range of areas where the signal originated, so the file was upgraded to..."

Samovich stared at the aide with a withering gaze. "Skip to the end of this...now."

Rogers' eyes were wide with fear, but he swallowed hard and continued. "Sir, we dispatched a flyer to investigate the projected origin of the transmission. It is deep within the Siberian Wilderness Zone, outside of normal satellite surveillance arcs. And..."

"And?" Samovich was out of patience.

"And it disappeared, sir. The flyer. We lost contact with it. Communications reports that they had picked up something that could have been jamming before they lost all trace of the ship...but they can't be sure it..."

"Send an entire wing to scout the area," Samovich snapped, "and a second wing in support two hundred kilometers behind... with full scanners engaged. And order all satellites in position to be retasked immediately for a full sweep of those coordinates."

"Yes, Secretary-General, immediately sir." The aide look surprised, stunned even at the precision of Samovich's response. He bowed his head slightly and turned to go and relay the orders.

"And Rogers…"

The aide stopped and turned back toward Samovich. "Sir?"

"Tell them I'll be down to Communications in ten minutes… and somebody down there better have a damned good answer as to why it took them several days to analyze this transmission." There was a coldness in Samovich's voice that left little doubt how seriously he took the matter. "Understood?"

"Yes, sir."

Samovich paused, only for an instant. Then he said, "And place all UNGov installations on full alert. I want Blue and Green divisions to mobilize immediately and prepare to ship out to Siberia in six hours. And all other AOE units are to be ready to go on a day's notice." Samovich had named his nascent defense force the Army of Earth. It wasn't terribly imaginative, perhaps, but it was something, an identity that would pull his soldiers together, make them feel like part of a greater whole, the army tasked with no less sacred a task than defending mother Earth against a mob of bloodthirsty traitors.

"Yes, Secretary-General." It was clear from the sound of his voice the aide didn't understand.

But Anton Samovich had no such doubts. He wouldn't know for sure of course, not until the flyers and satellite scans confirmed it, but there wasn't really any question in his mind. He had never been more certain of anything.

Taylor's people were back on Earth.

Chapter 10

Communications Clip Captured in New York City:

Raven this is Viper. Raven this is Viper. We are pinned down, south of Canal, with UNGov forces in close pursuit. I am taking the chance to send this to warn you...there are Inquisitor teams all over New York, and all first level refuges appear to be blown. Multiple Resistance teams have been eliminated or captured. Repeat, multiple Inquisitor teams, backed up with regular security forces...with extensive intelligence about our organization. We have lost half our personnel, at least two captured. We're going to risk making a run for it in a few...wait, what is...No! Go! Get...(transmission ends)

"Come on, Captain...we have to get to one of the backup safe houses. We've had too many people captured already... we've got to assume some of them have broken by now, and all our other locations are compromised." Jones knew his people all had suicide doses, but he also knew it was one thing to plan to kill yourself in the event of capture and quite another to swallow that clear liquid, knowing that single brief action would end your life in a matter of seconds. Even the knowledge of almost certain torture if captured was sometimes inadequate to override the human urge for survival. Besides, the Inquisitor teams were using heavy stun cannons, clearly attempting to take prisoners for interrogation.

Wickes simply nodded. He was calm, a touch of sadness in

his eyes perhaps, mourning for those lost in the fighting, but otherwise totally in control. Jones, so strong, so anxious just a few days earlier to strike a blow, was clearly shaken. The younger man was experiencing a baptism of fire that Wickes had gone through decades before. The New York team had lost at least a dozen of their group, friends, comrades, familiar faces now gone. Jones was having trouble dealing with it all, but Wickes was a veteran, and he knew well the cost of war.

"Yes, Carson," the old Marine said. "It is time for us to go. We must consider any second level refuge compromised as well if anyone aware of its location has been captured or is missing." Unlike his friend, Stan Wickes had seen battle before, though when he'd been in the line with his fellow Marines almost half a century before they'd been as well armed and equipped as their enemies. Now, Wickes was a rebel, running, hunted, waiting for the opportunity to leap out of the shadows and strike again.

He knew his comrades were all in shock to a certain extent. They'd known, of course, that UNGov would strike back, but Wickes realized that awareness had not prepared them for the true reality of what they had begun. An image passed through his mind, a kid, barely in his twenties, crawling through a burning city somewhere in Asia, throngs of terrified civilians streaming by as he and his unit pushed forward. Wickes had gone through Marine training, but even that grueling routine had left him ill-prepared for the realities of combat. The memories were old now, but still strong, and he could remember exactly how scared he was, how it felt, every second a struggle not to throw down his weapons and run...a test of will he won each time by the barest of margins, only to face it again an instant later. He knew his fellow rebels were feeling now their own version of what he himself had endured in those first days in the field so long ago. And he knew it was a battle they had to face on their own, that there was little he could do to help.

"The Bronx location," Jones said. "It's one of the newest. Only a few of us know about it...and no one who's been captured, at least not yet."

"Good call," Wickes snapped back, nodding. "We can probably get there underground..." He paused. His instinct told him the old subway tunnels were a better way to go than through the streets. UNGov troops were everywhere above ground. With martial law in effect, street traffic had been outlawed save for those going to and from work...and with the documents to prove it. It would be hard to avoid the checkpoints and patrols to get far enough north without being caught...and more difficult still crossing one of the bridges to the Bronx. But he had doubts about his chosen route as well. The security forces weren't stupid...they would know about the old train tunnels, and they'd have at least some presence down there. And a subway tube was a closed in place, a hard spot to escape from if they ran into a UNGov force down there.

He walked over an old wooden chest sitting against the wall and opened it, pulling out an assault rifle. He stared at it for a second and then handed it to Jones. "We'll have to fight anyone we find down there...there won't be any place to run. And it will be nasty, fast. If we run into UNGov troops down there, you just start shooting...and you don't stop until they're all down. Got it?" He looked over at the others, gesturing with his head for them to come over and take the weapons he was pulling out of the case.

Once everyone was armed, he started pulling out sacks of extra cartridges, tossing one to each of the rebels standing in a rough line behind him. He could see the hints of surprise in some of their eyes. They all knew him as 'the captain," the ex-Marine who was the leader of their cell. But most of them also knew him as the quiet old man, the one prone to sit off to the side, only occasionally offering an opinion. But now that things had hit the fan, he seemed a different person. His energy level had soared, and the years had seemed to drain away from his careworn face. Stan Wickes was a Marine, and as grimly realistic as he was about his peoples' chances, he still preferred an almost hopeless fight to sitting around hiding, skulking in the darkness.

He took two more rifles from the chest, strapping one around his shoulder and gripping the other tightly as he pulled out a pack of extra clips, and threw it around his other shoulder.

His eyes dropped down. There were half a dozen rifles left, and he felt a wave of regret at abandoning them...especially after they'd been so difficult to get. But he already had one spare slung across his back, and he didn't want to load down the others. They would have enough to handle, controlling their fear, staying focused when it came to a fight.

He took a last fleeting look at the precious rifles, and then he closed the chest gently. Maybe they'll still be here, he thought, not believing that for an instant. He knew the UNGov forces would find this spot, as they would those across the river. Indeed, they could find it any moment—it was time to go.

Wickes turned to face the other six men in the room. "I want everybody's eyes wide open down in those tubes. If we run into a security patrol, it's a fight to the death, understood? There's no way to run down there, no place to escape...so don't even try. And don't waste an instant. If you give the other guy a second, he's going to use it to blow your brains out, understood?" He knew he was repeating himself, but he wanted to burn it into their heads.

Wickes could see Jones out of the corner of his eye, nodding. It took the others a few seconds more to process what he had said, but they too signaled their understanding. "Okay, let's go." Wickes moved to the door, opening it slowly and peering out of the building. He looked both ways. The dark street seemed quiet, abandoned. There were no visible patrols, but he knew there were surveillance devices everywhere...and also UNGov security forces hiding in key spots, watching and waiting to catch rebel groups on the move. He looked up, half expecting to see the sky full of airships, flying back and forth and scanning the roads. But there was nothing.

Don't forget the regular people, he thought grimly, his eyes pausing briefly on the windows of buildings lining the avenue. He knew his compatriots assumed the population was all on their side, cheering in their homes for the brave resistance fighters, but Wickes knew better. Downtrodden people lost their will to resist, and their thoughts went instead to survival, to living their lives quietly and avoiding the attention of their masters.

It was always a small group that led rebellion…and most people only followed when they saw success, a chance of victory. The population would stream out of their homes, shouting and throwing flowers at the victory parade, but unless that day came, most of them would view the Resistance as little more than a group of dangerous lunatics.

Right now, the citizens of New York were as likely to blame the revolutionaries for bringing the UNGov forces down upon them as they were to root for the rebels. The government troops had been far from gentle, and Wickes could only guess how many hundreds of innocent civilians had been killed in the strife, and how many thousands rounded up for interrogation. No, the rebels couldn't count on anyone but themselves. And there were a lot fewer of them than there had been a week before.

"Okay, let's go," he said firmly, with an authority he hoped would help his rookie soldiers, "right across the street and down the alley. We can get into the cellar of that building, and there's a passage to the old subway station there." He looked over the five men and two women behind him, all of them nodding with various levels of commitment. Even Carson looks like he's ready to puke, he thought, realizing with black amusement that he'd switched places with his energetic colleague. Carson Jones had been the driving force of the peacetime resistance, urging the group to take action. But now, after a few days of hiding and fighting, the young rebel was beginning to understand just what 'action' meant.

He'll be okay…he's a good kid. Just give him time…if I can keep him alive that long…

"Go!" he snapped, leaping through the door and running across the empty street, pausing only for an instant to look north then south, his rifle at the ready. Then he dashed the rest of the way and slipped between the two buildings, heading for the basement door just up ahead.

*   *   *

"We've taken eleven rebel refuges, sir. Most of them were

deserted, but three were not. We killed thirty-one revolutionaries...and captured three." Captain Jergen paused. The Inquisitor had been clear that he wanted as many prisoners as possible for interrogation. But the insurgents weren't stupid...they knew what awaited them if they surrendered, and across the city, they were choosing to fight to the death rather than face UNGov's torture chambers.

"We require more captives than that, Captain." The Inquisitor didn't raise his voice, nor was there any significant emotion in his tone. But Jergen still felt a chill. UN Inquisitors had a fearsome reputation, even among their own underlings. Indeed, that was their entire purpose, and the very mention of an Inquisitor spread fear and despair among UNGov's enemies. Often the mere suggestion that one of these terrible agents might be dispatched was enough to quell any disorder. Judge, jury, and executioner by government mandate, all an Inquisitor had to do to pass a death sentence was point at the victim.

"Yes, Inquisitor." Jergen answered as firmly as he could manage. "We've issued stun cannons, but it's hard to get the troops to use non-lethal ordnance when the enemy is firing at them with assault rifles.

"Yes, Captain. I understand. Perhaps you had best remind them that I am expecting them to take at least fifty percent of these rebels captive."

The Inquisitor stood before the officer with the arrogant bearing of a man born to power, but Jergen knew that his commander, so diligently embracing his role as a fearsome hammer of UNGov power, had only held his rank for a few months. Michael Poole had been a colonel in the security forces before that, and he owed his promotion to the mysterious losses the Inquisitor corps had suffered over the past several years. There were rumors everywhere that at least a dozen had been killed in action out on Portal planets, presumably by the Tegeri.

That seemed strange to Jergen...Inquisitors were usually used to maintain order among the populace. The soldiers on the Portal worlds were trapped there, fighting for their lives against the enemy, and their obedience was usually secured with a somewhat lighter touch.

And I suspect combat veterans are a little more difficult to intimidate than terrified civilians...

So, what would Inquisitors be doing out there?

He put such thoughts out of his mind. They had no bearing on what was happening in New York, and in the world's other big cities. And he also knew that recently-promoted Inquisitors tended to be the most dangerous, especially to their own subordinates, more prone than those with longer experience to careless use of the awesome powers they had relentlessly pursued for so long. Poole seemed to be handling his new authority fairly well, but Jergen wasn't going to take any chances.

"I will see to it personally, Inquisitor." Jergen hesitated. "I also have reports on our own losses, sir. They are...somewhat higher than we'd anticipated...ten dead, twelve wounded."

Poole stared down at his subordinate. "Perhaps if our troops could capture more of these rebels, we would benefit from better intel and cut our losses." The Inquisitor didn't sound like he cared at all how many of his troops were lost, as long as the rebels were crushed. UNGov was always prepared to expend a few lives for its version of the public good, and Jergen knew the Inquisitor's rewards would be based on destroying the resistance movement in New York and not on keeping his casualties low.

"Yes, Inquisitor. With you permission I will see to it."

Poole nodded silently.

Jergen snapped back, "Sir!" Then he turned and trotted down the street, feeling his stomach unclench a little with each step he took from the Inquisitor.

*   *   *

Wickes moved cautiously forward, staring ahead into the darkness. He had a portable lamp, all his people did. But using it would simply advertise the presence of the rebel group. It was dark, but there were a few spots where light from outside made its way in through partially-open accessways or cracks in the street above. It wasn't much, but it was something.

It still got dark as hell between the old stations, and Wickes had flicked his lamp on a few times, looking around to get his bearings, to make certain they were heading in the right direction. But for most of the way he had moved slowly, checking the way with his foot before taking another step. The tunnels were damp, and in places the filthy water came up to his knees. Twice he'd stopped and whispered to those behind him to take care, to move as quietly as possible and to keep the sloshing sounds to a minimum.

He felt a little claustrophobic in the tunnels. Wickes had endured a few bad experiences during the Pacific War. The battles around Seoul had been brutal, and his unit had fought more than one action against the enemy's infiltration teams, often pursuing them into their tunnels. The remembrance of combat in such close quarters had stuck with him his entire life, as had the feeling of shoving past and climbing over his dead comrades. The ancient images included more than soldiers who'd been killed…the twisted faces of the dead civilians were even more vivid, men and women—and children—who had sought refuge in the tunnels only to get caught in the most savage fighting.

He tried, with limited success, to put old nightmares out of his mind, but he could still feel the sweat dripping down his back, and a bit of nausea in his stomach. Focus, Wickes, focus, he thought to himself. He knew if his people encountered a group of UNGov troops, it was likely whichever side saw their opponents first would win. The UN troops sent to put down risings in cities were not the combat veterans fighting on the Portal worlds. They were trained bullies, used to intimidating unarmed civilians. He knew the men and women at his back weren't veterans either, but they were courageous, and committed. And they knew their alternative to victory was death. That was a potent motivator.

Wickes stopped suddenly, stretching his arms out, reaching back to signal his people. "Stop," he whispered, holding his rifle out at the ready. He stood still, listening carefully. The men and women behind him froze in place…he'd told them at least half a dozen times he wanted them silent when he signaled, and they had listened.

He held his breath, trying to hear something, anything, up ahead. He'd thought he heard a splash, but now there was nothing. You must be hearing things, old man, he thought to himself. But something held him in place, his boots bolted to the submerged floor, legs rigid lest he send ripples across the knee deep water.

He didn't hear anything, but there was a something, a feeling he hadn't felt in a long time, but one he remembered well. He didn't know what to call it—combat instinct?—but he knew what it was. He knew it was real. And he knew it was telling him there was trouble ahead.

He'd been frozen in place for two minutes, perhaps three. Then everything happened all at once. He heard the sound again, a soft splash just up ahead in the darkness. Boots in the water!

"Against the walls," he said, as the sounds of his rifle echoed loudly through the confines of the tunnel. "Fire...everybody fire."

His people responded quickly, and in an instant they were all shooting down the tunnel, the sounds of half a dozen assault rifles on full auto almost deafening in the confined space. Wickes had told them all to make sure they knew where their comrades were in the dark, and he'd promised to skin anyone who shot one of their own.

His instincts had served him. His people had gotten off the first shot. But it was only an instant, a second perhaps, before the return fire came. Wickes' combat experience had saved the lives of his people, his command for them to move toward the walls saving them from the initial enemy volley as the inexperienced UNGov troops fired right down the center of the tunnel.

"Keep firing," he shouted, as he reached down and grabbed another clip, ejecting the spent one and jamming the replacement home with barely a pause to his fire. The enemy shooting was definitely lighter than it had been, but there was nothing to do but stand in the open and fire into the darkness until one side was wiped out. He was focused on the enemy, and he could hardly hear anything but the fire. Still, somehow he knew his people had taken losses as well as the enemy. Their fire had also diminished, if less so than the enemy's had. And he just knew. Maybe a splash as one of his comrades fell into the murky water. Or some kind of sixth sense, a battlefield presence. But there was no time for that now. There was nothing in the world, no concern at all save hosing down the enemy position with fire.

He was still shooting thirty seconds later when he realized there was no return fire. "Cease fire," he snapped. "Cease fire," he repeated more forcefully when half his people kept shooting.

He reached back behind him, pulling a flare from where he'd hooked it to his shoulder strap. He twisted it and threw it down the corridor. The light was almost blinding to his dark-sensitized eyes, but he resisted the urge to look away. He moved his head quickly, checking everything before the flare sank in the murky water and went out. His body tensed, and he snapped up his rifle, firing three times as he saw movement in the pile of bodies. One of the UNGov troops twisted and pitched forward, face down into the water.

"Let's go...now. You find anybody moving, breathing, you kill them, you got it?" Wickes' voice was harsh, almost brutal. He knew some of his people might find it difficult to gun down a wounded trooper, to put two rounds into the head of an injured man, gurgling on his own blood. Wickes didn't like it either, but he knew even a dying man could pull around a pistol, and one sudden, unexpected move was enough to kill one of his people. If he had to choose between the UNGov troops and one of his own...that was no choice at all.

Besides, you have to kill them all anyway. You can't let anyone survive and report your location. Bad enough someone will come looking for them when they don't return to base.

He ran up toward the enemy, splashing wildly through the water he'd so recently moved through with great caution. The flare had sunken into the water, and he had pulled out his flashlight, aiming its focused beam straight ahead. He reached the enemy position, the others just behind him, and he moved the flashlight around taking a look at the whole area.

Eight, he counted to as he looked all around. "Nine," he

whispered to himself as he shoved one of the bodies with his foot, uncovering another, mostly-submerged trooper below. He took another few seconds, satisfying himself there were no more enemies around. Then he turned. Two men and a woman stood behind him. Jones' faced was twisted into a painful grimace, his right hand holding his left arm, with blood oozing through his fingers. Wickes could see right away it wasn't mortal, but he was damned sure it hurt like hell.

He felt a pit in his stomach. Had only three of his people survived? Then he saw another, Lees, hobbling forward through the murky water. "Hall and DeVito are dead," she said, her voice heavy with pain.

Wickes' eyes snapped down to her thigh, to the massive—and spreading—slick of wetness. She was bleeding...badly. His mind raced back to his training, to his experience on the battle-field. If they didn't get a tourniquet on that leg, Lees wasn't going to make it. But they'd just had a firefight, and the sounds would have carried far down these tunnels. If there was another UNGov force behind them, and he paused here...

"Alright, Lees," he said, sliding his rifle over his shoulder and pulling his knife from its sheath. "I'm not gonna lie to you, Emily...this is going to hurt like a motherfucker. But I need you to stay quiet, okay? We have to get you patched up and get out of here." He leaned forward, looking into her eyes. "You with me?"

"Yeah," she said, her voice a mix of fear and feigned tough-ness. "I'm with you, Cap."

Wickes nodded, taking his knife and cutting a long strip from his jacket. Then he moved toward Lees. "Okay, Emily...I need you to hang on for me. I know this is going to hurt."

She nodded, and he leaned forward, moving the knife toward the wound and slipping it under the torn fabric of her pants. She squirmed, and her face went pale, but the only sound she made was a barely audible squeal. "That's good, Emily. Stay with me...it's going to get worse, I'm afraid." He cut off a section of the cloth strip, folding it up a few times and putting it over the wound. Lees recoiled a little, and then, when he pushed down hard, she lurched wildly. She struggled to stay silent, but she cried out despite her best efforts. Then she gasped for a deep breath and gritted her teeth without another sound.

"You're doing great, Emily," Wickes said, his voice as soothing as he could manage with adrenalin coursing through his veins. He tied off the cloth with a knot and took a breath. Then he sliced another section from the jacket.

"Okay, Emily. Almost done. I've got you bandaged up…now I've just got to get this tourniquet above the wound…to stop the bleeding. I gotta get it tight, so I'm going to have Bilby hold you down. You follow me?"

She stared back, her face hair soaked with sweat. "Yeah, Cap," she said miserably.

Wickes nodded moving his hand slowly, sliding the cloth to the top of her thigh. He wrapped it around three times, and then he looped the two ends around, tying a knot. "Okay, Emily… this is it…the last part. I need you to be tough for me." He turned his eyes toward Bilby, and the message they held was clear. This is going to be bad…

Bilby moved forward, putting his arms around Lees' torso. He gripped her hard, looking back and nodding to Wickes as he locked his hands behind her.

Wickes returned the gesture. Then he took a deep breath and pulled the strips of cloth. Tight.

Lees howled loudly, tears streaming down her face. But Bilby was more than half again her weight, and he held her in place as Wickes pulled hard, and tied the makeshift tourniquet off.

"Okay, Emily…it's done." She looked barely conscious as she stared back up at him. Her hair was matted against the side of her head, and her face was wet with tears. Her eyes were dull and sad. But she managed to return his gaze and say, "Thanks, Cap."

"Okay," he replied with a thin smile. He was pretty sure the round had missed her femoral artery, and even with all the bleeding he figured she'd make it. If they got her to the safe house soon. He knew she couldn't have much left in her. None of them did.

He aimed the flashlight at the wall of the tunnel, looking for faded signage or some clue as to where they were. Then he caught it in the corner of his eye, stepping forward to get a better look. It was an old station just ahead, and a wall of broken tile, half the dark pieces that had been formed into words gone. But there was some left, enough.

"Yankee Stadium," he whispered under his breath. And then louder, "We're almost there."

"Alright, Jack," he said to Bilby. "You help Lees."

The big man nodded. "I got her, Cap."

"You good, Carson?"

"Yeah, Cap. I'm fine."

"Alright then…let's get the hell out of here."

It's time. I'm sick of crawling around like a rat. I'm ready to strike again.

Chapter 11

Colonel John MacArthur to Black Lightning Squadron:

Don't let the guys in the ground batteries have all the fun, boys. We've got Dragonfires, the enemy's got Dragonfires. Let's show them the difference between veteran pilots fighting for freedom and a bunch of rookies, enslaved and struggling to keep themselves in bondage. Never forget that justice is on our side, and the future of mankind rides on our victory. On me, men, follow...straight up the center. And the crew who takes down the most enemies gets a barrel of beer to celebrate, courtesy of General Taylor. On me!

"All batteries, keep firing." Taylor issued the command, barely listening as his aide repeated it into the communications unit. The general, the man who was the architect of all that had now begun, stood rigidly in the middle of his headquarters, watching on the display as the AOL's forces engaged the UNGov airships all around the army's perimeter.

"And tell General Young to get down to the supply dump... we need to get ammo moving to those ground units faster." The Tegeri-built vehicles had an awesome rate of fire, and they were death itself to the enemy air squadrons. But they were ripping through rounds as fast as Taylor's people could get resupply to them. Faster. Even now, there were units cutting back on their fire, guns laying idle in the middle of the battle for lack of ammunition.

At least we've got the ammo, even if we're short of transports to move it up to the front quickly enough.

It was a strange difference from the parsimony Taylor had been forced to employ for most of the last four years, but the Tegeri had provided him with enough ordnance to supply his army for months, and he'd be damned if he'd trade lives to save ammo, as he'd been forced to do so many times before.

"Yes, General!" The officer's voice was sharp, filled with reverent respect for the army's commander.

Taylor suppressed a sigh. *If only they knew the burden their adoration has become...*

The AOL's commander mourned for every soldier he lost, but there was a difference between those fighting at his side for freedom...and the thousands he knew had made him the focus of their loyalty, who were out there dying for him. He found that upsetting, the cult of personality that took his crushing responsibilities and made them ever heavier. Taylor was as determined as ever to see quest fulfilled and Earth freed from tyranny. But there was a thought, deep in his mind...an uncertainty. Taylor would do anything to see his army to victory, but there was part of him at least, that wasn't sure he wanted to survive the battle.

It had taken more than a day for UNGov to send a follow up mission to search for the downed scout flyer...twenty-six hours Taylor's people had put to good use, twenty-six hours during which Hank Daniels had not moved from his position at the center of the activity. As far as Taylor had heard, Daniels had not departed from his post long enough to eat, to drink, to go to the bathroom. He suspected that was a slight exaggeration. Taylor was a veteran warrior, and he knew it was of such tales that legends were made. But he knew Hank Daniels too, and he suspected the embellished stories were not all that far from the truth.

Whatever Daniels had done, he'd certainly pushed the technicians beyond even Taylor's wildest expectations. By the time a new flight of UNGov scouts arrived, there were a dozen ground craft active...and a full squadron of Dragonfires under MacArthur. The battle lasted only a few minutes...and Taylor was stunned at the effectiveness of his Tegeri-provided anti-air batteries. By the time the Dragonfires were engaged there was nothing left but a couple damaged craft…and MacArthur and his people made short work of those.

But UNGov had been more careful this time. MacArthur's airships picked up another UNGov squadron, one positioned two hundred kilometers behind the first one…and by the time his forces pursued, the enemy flyers had already made a run for it. The AOL's air commander had pushed his craft to the limits, and he'd almost caught up with the enemy. He'd even taken two of their ships down as they fled. But the rest got away, broadcasting a warning that the Army of Liberation was back on Earth.

The response had come quickly, as Taylor knew it would, and now UNGov was throwing every air asset it could muster against the AOL's still deploying forces. Taylor understood. He would have done the same thing. If they could pen in his forces, push them back against the Portal, they would have the war half won. Taylor knew there was one thing he could never allow himself to forget…UNGov could replace its losses. His people could not.

The battle had gone well so far. MacArthur had lost one of his Dragonfires, but the crew managed to bring their damaged bird down with only a single fatality. The early word was 50/50 the craft could be repaired and return to duty. Some of the other airships had also taken damage, but they were all still in the fight.

The UNGov forces had lost over a dozen flyers, mostly to the deadly ground batteries. Their formations were scattered and disordered, and MacArthur's outnumbered birds were taking full advantage, weaving around and gaining advantageous position. Still, Taylor knew numbers would begin to tell soon. MacArthur would lose more ships…and if the enemy got past them…

"Get me a com link with Colonel MacArthur's ships, Lieutenant." Taylor stared at the displays, his eyes darting from the location of the air battle back a few kilometers to the workshops and supply dumps of the army. He didn't have a doubt the UNGov forces had been ordered to bomb and strafe his support positions. It was the obvious strategy. His people had just come through, and a Portal crossing was a difficult enterprise for a large force, necessitating considerable reassembly of equipment to bring an army back to combat readiness. His ground forces were mostly there, at least the 40,000 or so who'd come through so far. But MacArthur only had a third of the army's Dragonfires in the air, and even with the withering fire of the ground batteries, it was only the greater skill and experience of the pilots holding back the enemy.

"You are connected, sir."

"This is General Taylor, men. I have watched with great amazement as you have met the enemy...and sent so many of them crashing to the cold ground. I can only wish I was up there, beside you all, striking the first blow for freedom. But alas, I am not, so all I can do is thank each of you...and remind you that we are all counting on you to hold back the enemy as long as possible, to keep them from breaking through and bombing our supply depots, destroying the rest of the Dragonfires on the ground, before they are even uncrated and assembled. We are all there with you, men, in spirit if not body, and I urge you forward, to give all you have, to meet the enemy and hold them back, despite the numbers. You make my heart swell with pride, my brave warriors."

Taylor cut the channel...there was a fine line between boosting morale and distracting men in battle. He felt a wave of guilt, as he always did after addressing the soldiers. He'd meant everything he'd said, and he knew his words would drive them on. But it felt like manipulation too, like he was pulling on puppet strings, pushing his people to fight more fiercely, to take greater and greater chances lest they let him down. He tried to push back on the feeling, but he knew in his heart that men would die because of his speech, that they would throw themselves into the maelstrom, rallied by their commander's urgings...and ignoring all caution.

But that is war, Jake...it is what you signed on for when you launched this crusade. It is your soldiers' lot to throw themselves on the enemy, to die by the thousands if need be to gain the victory.

And it is your part to carry the burden…and endure the guilt for all of it.

Chapter 12

Alexi Drogov's Speech to Shadow Company Recruits:

You have been selected to join this company because you are among the most experienced operatives and security officers in UNGov service. You have, in all cases, displayed the resolve and the ruthlessness necessary to maintain our form of government and to suppress pointless and destructive dissent among the population. But that is no less than the duty of any member of UNGov. You have all displayed more. An understanding of loyalty, a willingness to do whatever must be done...to place the successful completion of a mission above all things. You have all shown an ability to cast aside petty moral concerns and to focus on the larger goal of preserving and defending our noble experiment in world government.

We face a crisis now, one we could not have imagined even a few years ago, a threat rising not from the streets, not from the lower classes or those clamoring for liberties they would only abuse if they had them. No, nothing so simple, so easy to face. We are threatened by a force of soldiers from our noble planetary armies, seasoned veterans, trained killers armed with the most advanced weaponry known to our science. These traitors have aligned themselves with our enemies, the murderous Tegeri, and even now they have returned to Earth through a previously undiscovered Portal. They seek nothing less than the destruction of UNGov, to establish themselves and their tyrant commander as the government of Earth.

You shall serve to prevent this. You will infiltrate the enemy positions. You will assassinate their officers and commanders. You will show no mercy, no hesitancy to do what it needed. It is imperative that we cast a light on the atrocities these invaders commit as they advance. Where such cannot be obtain, you will create incidents. If you must terminate a group of civilians so the invaders can be blamed for it, so be it. Nothing is more important than victory. Our comrades in the field armies will face this enemy frontally, seeking to destroy them in battle. But you will be behind the lines, damaging the enemy, causing disorder in their ranks.

You all understand the ways of UNGov, and our commitment to reward those who devote themselves to the prosperity and preservation of our great government. Those of you who serve well will see advancement, wealth, power. You will be recognized as heroes by a grateful world.

And those who do not serve well, who lack the strength, the determination, the courage for this great fight...they will die, likely at the hands of the bloodthirsty enemy. And if not by the foe, then by me. I am Alexi Drogov, and I have been doing the dirty work to make UNGov prosper since before most of you were born. If you fail me, if you betray me, I promise you, the last thing you will see is my eyes, staring into yours as the light of your life drains away.

"My fellow citizens, it is with the most profound regret and revulsion that I must address you this evening. There are some things that have happened that are so terrible, so utterly horrific, that I could not allow you to hear of them through a normal newscast. No, it is my responsibility to announce this nightmare...and to speak to each of you, to ask for your support and courage as we face this challenge together."

Samovich stood behind the lectern, the same one he'd used days before, when he'd addressed the world about the Resistance terrorist attacks. Now he was back again, and determined to deliver a performance that put that one to shame.

"Your brave soldiers, those who stand in the breech and hold off the alien menace, have achieved victory on over a dozen Portal worlds, driving the Tegeri and their murderous Machines back...back to whatever hellish world bred them. Yet there is no joy in this announcement, no call for parades and joyous celebrations. For, instead of victorious soldiers returning to the appreciation of a grateful world, on this day the Portals shimmer as something very different returns."

He paused, knowing the screens of a billion displays had just cut to scenes of flag-draped coffins, hundreds of them, thousands, streaming through the Portals, while military bands stood by, playing a mournful accompaniment.

"On each of these worlds, a force more terrible even than the Tegeri, blacker, more fearsome, has descended. For from the Portal world of Erastus has risen a rebellion, an army of human soldiers—human monsters—who have joined the enemy, sworn their loyalty to bloodthirsty aliens over their fellow soldiers, over the Earth and its legitimate government...over all of you."

Samovich took a deep breath, carefully modulating between outrage and sadness as he spoke. "Using the Tegeri knowledge of the Portals they fell upon the human armies there, the ruthless aliens stepping aside while these traitors attacked without warning. They massacred our soldiers, fell on them with all manner of dread weapons given to them by the Tegeri. They refused all attempts to negotiate...and they continued their attacks until they had slain all before them. And then they moved on, along with their alien allies."

He looked down at the lectern, pausing for the twelve seconds he had deemed the optimum time. He knew the shot on the screens of his viewers had cut back to him and that it was now going back to the scene of coffins being carried through the Portal. And pulling back, he knew, to show the images of civilians crying, mostly women—mothers and wives he suspected those watching would assume...wrongly. Now that is efficiency, he thought to himself...recycling video of the families of reeducation camp victims to put some power behind his propaganda. He knew there was a particular scene coming any second, a woman who looked like everyone's idea of a grandmother, doubling over in near-hysteria. He remembered it because he had picked it out himself from the library of selections. It would serve well...

"More than twenty-thousand dead," he said softly. "Murdered not by an alien enemy but by human traitors, creatures so utterly detestable, words do them no justice." He paused again. He preferred speaking to live crowds—actually he'd rather avoid most people altogether, but it was easier to read reactions from an audience right there, to adjust tone and pacing to maximize the manipulation. Still, he was confident his address was having the desired effect...and now he was going to drop the real bomb on them all. And if everything went well, he would turn the people of Earth into one massive force of partisans, fighting in the streets to preserve UNGov.

"And this is not the worst of it, my fellow citizens. No, not even close. These traitors are not content with murdering other soldiers...now they have returned to Earth, through a previously undiscovered Portal. Even now they have begun their march, across the snowy steppes of eastern Russia, bringing death and destruction with them every step they take.

"They have come to conquer, to destroy...as the advance guard for their Tegeri allies. They are well armed and equipped, and they bring death to all who stand in their way. Already, I have dispatched our air forces to meet them, all the flyers that could be put into the sky. Our brave pilots and crews will fight them...indeed even as I speak the battle rages. And while our brave air forces battle in the skies above, all the troops we were able to raise are moving even now, on their way to face this enemy...and to destroy them utterly."

Samovich paused again, letting the angry rage of his last comments fade into a more somber tone. "Yet our brave soldiers need your help, all of you. UNGov does not field great armies, not on Earth. We do not rule by coercion, as the nation-states that preceded us did. We field no massive conscript forces, numbering in the millions and equipped with weapons of mass destruction. No...instead, our ranks are filled with civilian security forces, police trained to protect and serve civilians...

and trainees originally bound for the planetary armies. They will fight bravely…they will fight for all of you. But I must ask that all of you fight for them as well. If elements of this army of traitors get past our brave soldiers, it is every citizen's duty to scorn them, to strike against them in any way possible, with sticks and stones if necessary. For have no doubt…these monsters will burn your cities, and rape and pillage their way across our beloved world."

Samovich gasped loudly for air. "We are together, all of us…the men and women of a united Earth, and here we stand and shout, 'No!' Loud enough to rattle heavens. We will not be defeated. We will not allow the basest of traitors to complete their work of death and destruction.

"Now I must go, my fellow citizens, back to the war room to direct the defense of our Earth. To each of you I can only offer my solemn promise that if it takes my last breath, I will see these traitors destroyed…and our world safe."

He paused a moment, waiting until he was sure the camera was off. Then he scooped up a glass hidden behind the podium, and he took a deep drink. It was only water, but it was cold, and it soothed his raw throat. He drained it in two quick gulps and set it down where it had been.

Then he stepped off the stage, a cautious smile on his face. He'd outdone himself, he was sure of it. If any of Taylor's traitors made it out of Siberia, he suspected they would encounter a level of hostility they were ill-prepared to face. And when they were forced to defend themselves against the deluded partisans who would attack them, the word would spread, stories of the invaders firing on the locals, gunning them down. And the massive UNGov propaganda machine would see that these tales spread throughout the world.

Yes, he thought, his grin widening…I do feel optimistic.

It didn't last long. He'd only taken four or five steps before he saw Alexi Drogov standing just inside the door of the studio, looking around for him. As soon as Samovich saw his friend's face he knew. Something was terribly wrong.

* * *

"Half of them destroyed…the rest turned tail and ran?" Samovich roared. "How is that even possible? We had, what, three to one odds? Four?"

"Just over three to one, sir, but the enemy is equipped with ground-based batteries of considerable effectiveness. We've never seen anything like them." General Ahmad stood before the Secretary-General, clearly nervous about having to report that the UNGov forces had been repulsed in the first major battle against Taylor's army. Like all UNGov military Earthside, he was a political appointee, not an experienced soldier. He'd been as confident going into battle as Samovich, sure his forces would prevail with such an advantage in numbers. But fewer than half his aircraft had returned, and most of those that did were badly shot up. UNGov had gambled by sending in its air-power by itself, hoping to catch the AOL still coming through the Portal, with its heavy equipment crated up and vulnerable. Instead they'd handed the enemy a victory, a morale boost that would make those veterans even deadlier in battle. And now it would be weeks, perhaps months before UNGov could hope to launch a similar strike.

"What should I do, General?" Samovich's tone was menace itself. "How should I respond to a level of incompetence that goes well past carelessness…past stupidity? Almost treason, I call it."

The general cringed before Samovich's angry tirade. He looked around, his gaze finding Drogov. But there was no comfort to be found in that killer's cold eyes. If anything, Alexi Drogov was less tolerant of failure than his master.

"Secretary-General, I assure you, I made every effort…took every step to ensure our forces would win the victory."

"And yet, did you lead your air wings from a Dragonfire? From a high-speed flyer?" Samovich started at the quivering officer with an intensity that turned the man to jelly. "No, wait… you didn't. I believe you were here, General, thousands of kilometers from the scene of the fighting. What was it, General

Ahmad? Was it simply cowardice? Laziness? Or was it some-thing more excusable? Perhaps the seats of a Dragonfire are insufficiently comfortable. You should have said something. I would have had a special silk-lined chair installed for you."

Samovich's hand slid slightly to the edge of his desk, his fin-ger pressing firmly on a small button. And instant later, the door opened, and four guards came in. They wore UNGov livery, but they were Samovich's own men, handpicked from his private security force.

"Gentlemen," he said, his voice calm. "General Ahmad is relieved of command. Further, he is hereby judged guilty of treason and cowardice in the face of the enemy. His sentence is death, to be carried out immediately."

"Sir!" the lead guard snapped, gesturing for two of the oth-ers to take hold of the officer. Ahmad stared back at Samovich, his eyes wide with terror. "No, Secretary-General…please!"

Samovich looked back at the general for an instant. Then he turned back to the senior guard. "You have your orders. Take him away…down to the large parade ground. They are setting up the scaffold now."

"No!," the pathetic officer screamed, twisting in vain in an effort to get free of the guards, then collapsing entirely, forc-ing his captors to virtually carry him out of the office. Samov-ich watched as they dragged him out in the hall, still screaming. Then the door closed, and General Mahmoud Ahmad was gone.

"I would have given the fool the slow death he deserves," he said, looking toward Drogov as he did, "but I believe a public hanging will prove far more useful than a private death in the prison levels." He took a breath and sighed. "See that his execu-tion is transmitted live to all military units…especially the ones moving toward Taylor's forces. It is important that they see the price of failure. And I believe this might be a good first assign-ment for some of your Shadow Company recruits, don't you?"

"I concur. I will see it done, Anton."

"And Alexi?"

"Yes?"

"I particularly want all officers to watch. Not just in the

active units, but all those fools down in headquarters who got their fancy uniforms through political favors and bribes. They wanted to be soldiers, so now they will have that chance."

"Yes, Alexi." Drogov nodded, and he turned and slipped through the door.

*   *   *

"They have Tegeri technology, that's the only answer. And it appears the aliens have some capabilities they've never shown us before." Colonel—actually, for the past forty minutes General—Akawa stood before a large screen, displaying the best image available of one of the AOL's anti-aircraft batteries.

"I am inclined to agree with you, General," Samovich said quietly. "Yet to cursory inspection, it looks like a normal vehicle of human manufacture. Taylor and the Tegeri are clever...they aid his army in any way that is not obvious, but they do not join him...or give him weapons that would seem out of place." He gestured toward the screen. "Even if we were to capture one of those, it would have no propaganda value. To the people it just looks like some kind of military vehicle."

"Yes, Secretary-General, I believe you are correct. We will have to rely on your speech to sufficiently...motivate...the people. I do not think either Taylor or the Tegeri will give us anything substantive to add to that."

Samovich nodded, looking down at his desk for a moment. Then he said, "So, General...what would you have me do now? What course of action would you order if yours was the last word. Would you send our ground forces in without air cover... or would you commit what we have that can still fly?"

"That is a difficult question, Secretary-General." Akawa paused, thinking. "If we commit what air assets are currently operational, we will likely be outnumbered, and the enemy will still have their ground batteries as well as their Dragonfires. But if we hold back the flyers and attack only with ground forces, Taylor's army will have total air superiority, which will severely impede our operations."

"Yes, I know it is a difficult question," Samovich said, staring intently at Akawa. "That is why I am asking you, General."

Akawa paused. Then he said, "Permission to speak freely, sir?"

Samovich nodded slowly, a hint of approval in his eyes. Here is a man with some balls, at last...a lion among these sheep. "Permission granted, General."

"Sir, I understand what you have been told, what the general staff has advised you. But I think they are wrong...and if you follow their advice I believe we will simply see an ongoing series of defeats that will attrite our strength and leave us too weak at every point to ever land a crushing blow."

The other officers in the room fidgeted uncomfortably, and there were some sighs and sounds of discontent...and more than one nasty stare toward Akawa.

"Quiet," Samovich said, in a voice that dared any of them to draw so much as an audible breath. "Go on, General. Speak your mind."

"Akawa looked over at his fellow officers, but only for an instant. Then he returned his gaze to Samovich. "Well, sir, ideally I would also be in favor of striking at the enemy position, attacking and destroying them before they are able to disperse and move toward multiple targets. A successful attack in the near term would offer an opportunity to destroy much of the enemy's ordnance before they are able to reassemble it."

"That is what I have heard already, General." Samovich glared at the cluster of officers standing against the far wall. "It is why we have two full divisions already in central Russia...and two more following those."

"Yes, sir...but despite the reasons offered in favor of immediate action, I do not believe we should attack now, not a full scale assault in any event. I said it is what I would do in ideal circumstances. Our situation is far from ideal." Akawa stopped, staring cautiously at the effective ruler of the world, but Samovich nodded for him to continue. "I do not believe we have the capability to launch a strike within the next week, even two. Not one that offers any hope of victory. And I believe those who

have told you we do are either incompetent, or they fear to tell
you the truth."

Another round of mumbled protests came from the other
generals.

"Silence," Samovich roared. "The next one of you that makes
a sound, who so much as breathes in a way I don't like, will find
himself out on the parade ground, next to General Ahmad." He
turned his head. "Please continue, General Akawa."

"Yes, sir. As I was saying, while catching Taylor's army at the
Portal would be desirable, I do not believe we can win that fight.
Not now. His troops are all veterans, and despite his…ah…mis-
guided ambitions, there seems little doubt he is a charismatic
leader who commands the respect and devotion of his men.
Our soldiers, on the other hand, are almost all raw…or they are
police and security forces drafted into the army." He glanced
again over at the cluster of irate generals watching silently from
the other side of the room. "And, with all due respect to my colleagues, our command staff is also inexperienced. They are no
match for Taylor's people. Not one on one. Not even two one
on. We much maneuver and concentrate, and wait until we have
assembled a truly overwhelming army. Wherever we finally fight
his forces we must have a significant advantage in numbers and
ground."

"So you are saying we should just let him march wherever he
wants to go? To occupy any cities or objectives he may target?"

"No, sir…not precisely. Clearly we must fight him, but I suggest we conduct raids, place forces just outside of his reach.
That we set up artillery emplacements and bombard his positions, withdrawing when he moves against them. We must sting
him, threaten his supply lines and rear areas when we have the
opportunity." Akawa paused.

"Please go on, General." Samovich stared at the other officers. "I find this insight fascinating."

"Yes, sir. There are disadvantages to allowing Taylor's forces
to advance, but there are opportunities as well. If we allow them,
they will move toward population centers…and away from their
supply line through the Portal. We may even have a chance to

slip behind them and cut them off entirely. And when they reach towns and cities…and occupy them as you said, what will they find? The people of Earth believe they are murderers, traitors to their own people. By allowing them to advance we force them into confrontations with the civilians, which can only further inflame opinions against them…and which will almost certainly be severely demoralizing to Taylor's troops, who must expect, at least on some level, to be treated as liberators."

"So, you would gather strength, shadow Taylor's forces, harass them when you could, and move against their lines of supply if they give you an opening?"

"Yes, Secretary-General…in essence that is what I would propose. And once we have gathered irresistible forces…either in one location or in many, depending on what Taylor's people do, I would attack, and crush them at all costs."

"Very well, General…do it."

"Sir?"

"I said do it. I am in total agreement with you. So see to it."

Akawa had a confused look on his face. "Do you want me to draw up plans for the general staff? To advise…"

"No," Samovich interrupted. "The general staff consists of a bunch of pompous fools, politicians like me…who are too arrogant to admit they don't know what to do. I need a soldier, one who can appreciate the rewards of victory…wealth, power beyond imagining…a seat on the Secretariat."

He stared at Akawa. "I hereby appoint you Marshal of all Earth armies and supreme commander of the war against General Taylor and his Tegeri allies. Effective immediately, you will take command of all operations."

Samovich looked across the room, his eyes daring the stunned generals to challenge him. He could feel their rage, but none had to courage to argue. He turned to face Akawa. "You may do with this group as you will, Marshal Akawa. Use the ones that are worth something, dismiss the others." A short pause. "And if any of them gives you trouble…" He glared back at the generals. "…you have my authorization to have him summarily executed."

*　*　*

"I want you to expand your Shadow Company, Alexi. At least double its present size, and more if you feel you can use them effectively. I will give you authorization to reassign any UNGov personnel. If anyone gives you a hard time, refer them directly to me." Samovich smiled. "Or, just...handle it...yourself." Samovich was on edge, facing the final struggle, and angry at the reverses his forces had suffered, but he allowed himself a smile thinking about some regional commander, or even an Inquisitor, trying to stand up to Alexi Drogov. UNGov had a lot of arrogant personnel in its ranks, and more than a few cold, hard killers. But Drogov was something different, an incarnation of death itself. Cold-blooded didn't come close to the truth. Indeed, whatever strange liquid flowed through Drogov's veins, Samovich suspected its temperature was near absolute zero.

His oldest colleague—and his only true friend—had an ability to set aside moral concerns, pity, mercy. Drogov wasn't bloodthirsty...he'd as easily allow a foe to live if it served his purposes. But he would also kill...anyone, everyone, who stood in his way, and he would do it without the slightest hesitation or a hint of satisfaction. For all Samovich's ruthless pursuit of power, he'd never seen anyone, including himself, as able to separate emotion from actions. If they hadn't grown up together, he'd have sworn his friend was some kind of robot.

"I anticipated your orders, Anton...and I have already begun. I'm afraid I've left a few stubbed toes and bruised egos, but you know me. Diplomacy is such a waste of time when fear and intimidation are so effective. I came close to shooting one of the Inquisitors, but he backed down just in time." He looked over at Samovich. "I told him I'd come for him if he complained to the Secretariat, but I was only playing around with him. Still, just in case he scrapes up the courage to come crying to you, I wanted you to know."

Samovich smiled again. He didn't believe for an instant Drogov would fail to follow through on a threat, whatever he was saying now. But he also suspected there were few UNGov operatives, even Inquisitors, with the combination of courage and stupidity to truly cross Alexi Drogov. They might as well put a gun in their mouths themselves and save the pain.

"Very well, Alexi. As I said, you have carte blanche on resources and authority. I believe Marshal Akawa will prove to be far more competent than that pack of politically-connected lapdogs he replaced, but I'm still not sure he's a match for Taylor, not to mention the rest of his officers and Supersoldiers."

Samovich felt a surge of amusement at the disgust he felt for the political creatures around him, the men and women who had lied, cheated, and bought their way to power in UNGov. He was the worst political creature of them all, the one who had ascended to the greatest heights of power. But now he looked down on those beneath him, the hoard of backstabbers and liars who would do anything to take a step up the ladder of power. He saw how useless most of them were, at least when challenged by an adversary as capable as Taylor and his people. Sure, they were adept at stepping all over civilians, men and women beaten down for two generations, penned into small neighborhoods, dependent on UNGov rationing. But they were fools nevertheless, not wolves like himself, like Drogov. Like the men and women who had seized power, who had perpetrated the great deceit that had gained them control over a world.

Drogov sat staring at his friend, an odd expression on his face.

"What?" Samovich asked? A few seconds later..."What... what is it with you?"

"I'm just waiting for you to tell me what you really want." Drogov's expression was impassive, perhaps a hint of amusement on his otherwise poker-ready face.

"What I really want?"

"Anton, we have known each other, what, almost fifty years? Yet you never tire of playing these games, of acting as if I don't already known what you want before you ask." Drogov was the only person who characterized the Secretary-General's commands as 'asking.' But despite Samovich's almost limitless power, he and Drogov both realized that everything he sent his friend to do was a request. If they hadn't been lifelong friends, Samovich would tread carefully around the operative, and even fear him. Drogov had never refused his friend, and he'd been instrumental in eliminating political enemies during Samovich's rise...but they both knew he could refuse it he wanted to, would refuse if the Secretary-General ever asked him to do something he didn't want to do.

"It is that obvious? Still, it will not be easy, and there will be great risks involved. But with most of the available nuclear arsenal expended, and the enemy's anti-air defenses so strong, I can't think of anything but black ops."

Drogov sighed, and for a passing instant there was an expression on his face Samovich had never seen, one of doubt. But it only lasted a few seconds. "It will not be easy, Anton. Indeed, it will be the most difficult operation I have ever attempted." He paused. "But I will do it...I will do it for you, my old friend, and because I believe it is where our greatest hope for victory lies." Alexi Drogov stared at his oldest, his only friend, his pale blue eyes betraying a human vulnerability he allowed few to see.

"I will kill Jake Taylor for you."

Chapter 13

Communiqué from Forward Position 3:

This is Major Texera, in command of forward position three.
My lead elements have encountered several small population centers. I have lost contact with several patrols, and have
received reports from others that they have engaged in combat.
Hostiles are not UNGov regulars, they are civilians from the
nearby mining settlements. Repeat, we are being attacked by
civilians...and we have returned fire...

The shot rang out, echoing across the rolling hills...then
another one. Calvin Garth dove to the ground, his instincts taking over instantly. "Down," he shouted, "everybody!" But his
orders, as immediate as they were, came too late. His troops had
already thrown themselves to the ground for cover, their training and experience taking over as automatically—and immediately—as his own.

Garth snapped his head around, his enhanced ears quickly
triangulating on the source of the gunfire. "From the north-
east," he snapped. "I put it two meters west of that copse of
trees." He looked at the area intently, blinking once or twice at
the strange sensation he still felt when his bionic eyes zeroed
in on a small spot and kicked up the magnification. A normal
man wouldn't have seen more than a green blotch of trees, and
a low ridge to their left. But Garth saw much more than that...
he caught movement, leaves rustling...just as another shot rang

out.

"The trees," he snapped. "Target the tress...fire!"

He angled his rifle toward the green area, his finger flipping the switch to semi-auto just before he pulled the trigger. He fired half a dozen times, perhaps twenty shots in all, and his troopers did the same. The trees were riddled with fire, he could see leaves flying around and branches splitting and falling to the ground.

"Cease fire," he snapped, his eyes panning the area slowly, carefully. "Lynch, Eddings...move forward, and scout those woods."

"Sir!" came the almost simultaneous replies. Even as they responded, he could see the two soldiers moving forward, lunging ahead twenty yards and dropping behind whatever cover or folds in the ground they could find. They stopped and waited for enemy fire before pushing on again. But there was none. Finally, they disappeared inside the wall of trees.

"Captain Garth..." It was Eddings on the comlink. "Woods are clear, sir. We've got two bodies...and it looks like two or three more took off north. Should we pursue?"

Garth paused. His instinct was to order his troopers to chase the survivors down...but if there were UNGov forces out there that was a good way to send his two men right into a large enemy force.

"Negative, Corporal. There's no way to know how close their parent unit is." There wasn't supposed to be any enemy activity in this area. All reports indicated the enemy was concentrating in the south. But there was no point in taking any chances.

"Sir, they don't look much like UNGov troops...they seem more like...civilians, sir. Some kind of miners or something like that."

"And how many UNGov soldiers have you seen, Eddings?" Garth paused, thinking. But Eddings is a veteran...he knows what a soldier looks like...

"Very well, Corporal," he added, more or less disregarding what he had just said. "Stay put until we get there." He flipped the comlink to wide channel. "Alright, guys...we're heading to that clump of trees to check things out. I want everybody wide awake and alert…but no happy trigger fingers, okay? You don't fire without my order unless someone is shooting at you…and even then, make damned sure you don't hit any friendlies."

He climbed to his feet and ran out into the field, jogging up the hill toward the woods. There was no sign of enemy activity, but he didn't forget his training. Carelessness gets soldiers killed…he'd been told that a thousand times going all the way back to when Jake Taylor had been his lieutenant so long ago. He ducked down and paused at each bit of decent cover, turning both ways and keeping tabs on the rest of the unit as he did.

He pushed forward, into the cover of the trees, realizing immediately that the wood was considerably larger than it had appeared from down below. The treed area widened considerably as it worked its way north, and it stretched all the way down from the top of the high ground as far as he could see. He slapped his comlink. "Torba, head out to the west, and get a look at north as soon as you're out of the woods." The forest seemed large inside, but Garth knew it didn't extend very far to the east or west along the top of the ridge. He'd seen that much as he'd approached.

"Sir!" came the immediate reply.

Garth walked forward, toward Eddings and Lynch. "Anything new?" he asked as he walked up behind the two men.

"No, sir. I mean, yes…I'm definitely convinced these two were civilians…the poor quality weapons, bad aim, the fact that the rest of them turned tail. And…"

"And what, Corporal?"

"Well, sir, I think these guys are miners."

"And why is that? Inspiration?"

"No, sir…I'm from the west, sir…in old America I mean. My family…they were miners, for four generations. I'd have worked in the mine myself if…if I hadn't gotten in trouble and taken service to avoid a jail term." He paused, leaning down over one of the bodies, grabbing an arm and twisting it. "Look at his hands, sir. See the residue all over them, the gunk under his finger nails? I'd know that anywhere. This guy must have come here straight from a shift." He let go of the arm, and reached down, turning the other body over. "Same thing with this guy, Cap. I'd bet my last clip there's some mining town around here somewhere…and that's were these two came from."

Garth sighed. "Okay, Eddings, let's say you're right. What do we do now? Leave these guys behind us and move forward? Or chase them down and try to get to the bottom of it…and maybe end up in a firefight with a bunch of civilians?"

"I don't know, Cap, but I'm glad it's you with those bars on your shoulders and not me."

Garth nodded, and he turned and looked behind him as the rest of the unit moved up. A few seconds later, Torba came running over.

"Sir, the woods get real wide down there. They swing maybe two klicks to the west, right up to what looks like some kind of river. I saw the civvies, Cap, at least half a dozen. They came out of the woods about a klick ahead. They're heading west, sir." Torba turned back to the west and pointed. "They look like they're slowing down, sir. If you want to catch them, it shouldn't be any problem."

Garth nodded. "Thank you, Corporal." Then he looked down at his feet, kicking a small rock as he did. The idea of chasing after a bunch of civilians—and very possibly having to kill them all if they put up too much of a fight—sickened him. But his people were at the head of the whole army. A few pissed off civvies weren't going to do much damage to the army as a whole—though he reminded himself they were perfectly capable of killing some of his comrades. But what if this was more than that? Some kind of UNGov militia? Maybe there were more of them, with better weapons. They might try to get behind the army, interdict the supplies flowing through the Portal.

No, I can't just move forward without knowing what is going on. We've got to capture one of these guys, find out why they're trying to kill us.

"Alright, let's go. We're going to run these bastards down and find out what the hell is going on." He took a couple steps, and then he stopped and turned back. "We don't kill anybody if we don't have to, you guys got that? If you have to shoot, try to go for the leg...incapacitate them if possible."

His troops replied with a chorus of yessirs, but he knew what he was asking was mostly pointless. His men were armed with heavy assault rifles, weapons designed to kill on the battlefield. A shot to the leg was as likely as not to tear the whole thing off, leaving the victim bleeding to death in agony. Better to take a quick shot to the head then to spend an extra few minutes in pain and hopeless fear.

He shook his head and leapt up, moving swiftly through the trees, in the direction Torba had given them. Maybe they'll give up when we catch them, he thought. But he didn't believe it. And he was beginning to suspect the battle for Earth would be even more bloody and difficult than he'd expected. And a lot more morally ambiguous. He'd signed on to topple corrupt politicians, not gun down a bunch of miners.

*   *   *

"They're coming...they're coming!" Josef Talinn ran through the village, his six companions following close behind. "They can't be more than a few minutes back."

"We're ready, Josef." It was a woman's voice, from the doorway of one of the rickety buildings near the entrance to the town. Nyrob was a small village, just the kind of place that had largely disappeared from the Earth when UNGov relocated the inhabitants of all but essential rural settlements. But it's location in the foothills of the Urals near two producing platinum mines had saved it. It was home to about 300 miners, and their families, along with those providing support services for the tiny community. There was a UNGov supervisor as well, though after he had instructed the people to resist the invaders, he'd hastily fled, claiming he had been called to Geneva for a briefing.

The miners had never liked the supervisor anyway, and they prepared to fight now not because of his order, but because they wanted to strike back at the traitors, the murderers. Nyrob had proudly sent six sons to the war against the Tegeri, and three of them had been on the worlds where the massacres had occurred. They had no idea if they had been killed by Taylor's forces, or even if any of the three had still been alive. But that didn't matter. Their people had bravely faced the Tegeri to protect Earth…and a bunch of filthy traitors had murdered their comrades at least, and possibly them too.

Talinn stumbled into the town, falling to his knees and gasping for air, as did the rest of his people. "They're fast," he rasped out. "Faster than any men I've ever seen." He doubled over and retched, but only a bit of foam came up. Then he forced himself back up again. "No time," he said. "No time."

He stumbled forward a few steps, turning and opening the door to one of the buildings. He paused for a second to look at the makeshift display in the small townsquare, a galley of sorts with three bodies hanging there limply. They'd been in a vehicle when they stopped just outside the town. They had only been out of the transport for a minute when the townspeople came rushing out . The soldiers had left their weapons in the truck, and they yelled to the mob, waving their hands and crying for them to be calm. But there was no calm where traitors and murderers were involved, not to the people of Nyrob. They were on the soldiers in an instant, clawing at them, dragging them to the ground and beating them ferociously. A cursory look at the hanging bodies confirmed the men did not die easily.

But the soldiers coming now were not just three, and they would not be taken by surprise. They'd already killed two of the townspeople, and they had pursued the rest in a murderous rampage. They brought death with them, Talinn knew, but Nyrob would fight them off, kill as many of the traitorous bastards as they could. Or this town with its centuries-long history would at last vanish like its neighbors, and its people would die at the hands of the monsters who had killed 20,000 Earth soldiers.

"Inside, all of you. Get your weapons and go to your places. They are coming!"

Talinn slipped through the door of the dilapidated old shack he called home. He took a deep breath, and he looked around at the house, the place where he had been born. The place where now, he would very likely die.

*   *   *

Garth moved slowly, cautiously. His people had tailed the civilians, driving them hard but staying back far enough that they didn't catch up. He wasn't looking to gun down seven terrified miners in the Russian countryside...he wanted to get back to wherever they had come from, and talk to their leaders, explain that he and his men were here to free them all.

"Hold up," he snapped, pausing behind a large tree just outside the town. He stared down into the small streets of the village. It was quiet, too quiet. Something was wrong.

I hope this town isn't full of homicidal crazies...

Garth sympathized with the townspeople, to a point at least. They'd shot at his people, but they hadn't hit anyone, and that made them a lot easier to forgive than if they'd killed any of his men. But if these villagers attacked his team en masse, he knew his soldiers would fight back. And he knew he would let them.

Farmers and miners might get lucky with a shot or two, but his twenty enhanced Supersoldiers would reduce this town to a smoking pile of rubble in a matter of seconds. If these people started a fight, they were all going to die.

Which means I need to make sure no fight begins.

"Hello," he yelled as loudly as he could. He knew the Tegeri-made attachment to his com unit would translate his words into any Earth language...and do the reverse with any response. "I am Captain Calvin Garth of the Army of Liberation. My men and I do not mean you any harm. We are here to free you all from the unjust rule of UNGov."

He looked down into the town. Still nothing.

"Okay, Torba, Eddings, Lynch...you three with me. Everybody else, grab a spot with good visibility into the town and sit tight. And be ready."

He took a few steps forward, looking back to make sure his companions were with him. They all had their rifles out and ready. Garth didn't want a fight with these people, but he had a bad feeling about the whole thing, and he wasn't about to be caught napping.

It's bad enough we're walking up right in the open…

He looked around, his enhanced eyes giving him a good view of everything in his line of sight. He could see shadowy forms behind the windows, men and women crouched down. He caught the line of a gun in one of their hands.

Damn. They're lying in wait for us.

He knew what he'd do on the battlefield. His people would already be laying waste to the town, obliterating the buildings with mortars and raking the whole are with automatic fire. But this wasn't the battlefield.

At least I hope it's not.

"I can see you hiding in the buildings. You are planning to attack my soldiers, but there is no reason. We mean you no harm. If you come out…"

"Cap!" It was Eddings, and his face had gone as pale as a ghost. His expression was one of horror changing quickly to uncontrollable rage. His arm was extended, pointing toward the town.

Garth took a few steps forward and looked where he was pointing.

My God…

He froze, his eyes fixed on three bodies, dressed in the remains of uniforms. Uniforms from the AOL. Even from here he could see the men had been beaten, hideously mutilated.

One of the infiltration teams…it has to be…

He felt his discipline slam into place, his military instincts trying to exert control, to cut off the rage he could feel surging from the darkest places in his mind. But when the anger came, it was an irresistible force, and it tore right through his feeble control. These filthy townspeople had ambushed one of the army's teams, beat them to death, savaged their broken bodies. He knew he should hold back, call this in to HQ, and wait for orders. But those thoughts were too little too late. All he could think of was his need to avenge his comrades.

He was never sure afterward if he'd fired first or if Eddings had. But the next thing he knew he was blasting away at the town and screaming for the rest of the unit to open up. And by the time they were finished there was nothing left to show Nyrob had ever existed…nothing save ashes and a pile of rotting corpses.

Chapter 14

From the Journal of Jake Taylor:

For more than five years, ever since that fateful day I learned the terrible truth, I have imagined our return to Earth. I envisioned the terrible battle I knew we would face. I saw my soldiers dying, fires raging in Earth's great cities. I saw the people rising up to join us, taking the chance to claim their freedom, to destroy their oppressors...and I saw them dying by the thousands, the brutal cost of freedom.

There were times I wasn't sure we would get here. Standing on the burning sands of Erastus for the last time, staring into the Portal ready to take the first step on the long road home, my doubts threatened to consume me, the need to radiate confidence to my soldiers an almost unbearable burden. Yet I walked into that Portal, and through battles and fire, my soldiers and I continued. We fought many struggles, lost thousands of our comrades. But our message spread, and on a dozen worlds, the UN soldiers, conscripts as we were, flocked to our banners. Our ranks swelled until we had many times the number we started with. And the Tegeri supplied us. The invasion of Earth wouldn't be like the other battles we'd fought on our march, perpetually low on supplies and ordnance. No, thanks to our allies—our former enemies—our depots were overflowing. The battle for Earth would be brutal, but we were a well-supplied, veteran army. I let myself believe we had a chance, that the cataclysm ahead of us might be less terrible than my mind had made it.

I was wrong. Not about our strengths, nor about our chances in a fight. We have met UNGov's air forces, and we have soundly defeated them. And now the army is on the move, the struggle for our homeworld begun. A terrible, difficult war still lies ahead of us, but my soldiers are ready to fight it, to press on until they are victorious.

But my imaginings have also proven dismally, depressingly false. My visions of mobs rising up to join our quest have been replaced with the reality of civilians attacking my troops, of wandering crowds throwing rocks and shouting epithets at our columns as they advance. Of partisans ambushing our forces, taking potshots from the woods at passing patrols. The reports were a mystery to me at first. I knew it would be a challenge to get our message out, to communicate to a world what UNGov had done, how it had seized power. But I hadn't expected the widespread hostility, the resistance we have encountered every time our forces have approached a population center.

Now I know the truth, and I curse myself as a fool. I had considered the campaign from every angle I could envision, and I planned for every contingency. Every contingency but one. For while I knew UNGov would do anything to maintain its power, kill any number of people before it would yield control, it never occurred to me they would repeat the strategy that put them in power initially. A lie, one simple lie...along with a few visual props. They did it again, and it seems to have worked as well as it did forty years ago. And I have no idea how to counter it...before my soldiers are forced to kill thousands of the civilians we came home to free.

"It's the same thing coming in from all over. We've had almost a dozen patrols attacked, fired on by all kinds of weapons...ancient rifles, shotguns. And every time our people return fire, the survivors bolt and run...and the bodies they leave behind all appear to be civilians." Hank Daniels had a frustrated look on his face. He was a decisive man, not afraid to give difficult orders, but now it was clear he didn't know what to do.

"UNGov troops in civilian clothes?" Taylor was shaking his head even as he spoke. He didn't believe that any more than he suspected Daniels would.

"With piece-of-shit shotguns and eighty-year-old hunting rifles? We've been attacked at least ten times, Jake, and all they've managed to do is wound two men. What's the point of UNGov infiltration teams getting to our units if they can't really hurt us?"

Taylor sighed. "Then what, Hank? Any ideas? I'll listen to anything right now." The reports had been coming in for two days. He had scouting parties out in front of the army's advance, mostly his Erastus veterans. They were still moving across the Russian steppe, an area that had been virtually depopulated by UNGov redistribution orders, but every time they got near any of the few population centers they ran into partisans. Taylor had been worried about avoiding any public connection to the Tegeri, and he'd realized there would be enormous confusion when he let it become public, that it would be difficult to educate the people, to explain the terrible truth. But that was supposed to be tomorrow's problem. He hadn't been ready for miners and farmers trying to kill his men every step they took. What the hell was going on?

"I've got nothing, Jake. They've got the people around here roused up against us, but I'll be damned if I know how." He paused. "Maybe…"

"I know how." It was Bear Samuels standing in the doorway to the headquarters shelter. The normally cheerful giant had a stricken look on his face. "You have to see this now." He held up a small data chip. "It's tape of a UNGov broadcast. One of my patrols found it playing on a vid in one of the mining villages they passed." Samuels hesitated, his voice filling with emotion. "My boys had to kill twenty civilians there, Jake. The whole damned place went crazy as soon as they walked up. I'd ordered them to try to contact whoever was in charge, but the second they got within a hundred yards, the villagers started shooting."

"And this explains it?" Daniels walked up and took the chip from Samuels' hand.

"Oh yeah, Hank," Samuels replied in his thick drawl. "You bet it does."

Taylor felt a chill move through his body. Samuels was really upset, and Bear usually took everything in stride. He had no what the broadcast would say, but he knew it would be bad. "Play it, Hank. Let's see what is going on."

Daniels moved over to one of the portable workstations and slid the data chip in the slot. "Play," he said softly.

"Playing," responded the AI.

The three men stood together. Daniels' and Taylor's eyes were fixed, staring at the screen. Samuels looked away, as if he couldn't bear to watch it again.

Taylor watched the man speaking. He was tall, very well dressed...ethnically Russian or Ukrainian, he guessed. He was somber...indeed, he almost looked like he was fighting back tears. Then the screen switched away from him...to a Portal. There was a stream of uniformed men moving slowly from the shimmering device. They were carrying crates of some kind.

No...not crates. Coffins.

Taylor felt his throat go dry as the camera panned back to show the ground around the Portal, a great paved area, and around that a field. And coffins, lined up in perfect rows as far as the eye could see.

What the hell?

"More than twenty-thousand dead." The voice of the man was sad, choked with emotion, but Taylor's instincts were alive. He sensed something else there, below the carefully-constructed facade. Insincerity. Phoniness. "Murdered not by an alien enemy but by human traitors, creatures so utterly detestable, words do them no justice."

Taylor felt his stomach clench, and a wave of red hot rage flooded through him. In one terrible, unimaginable instant he understood. Those coffins bore the soldiers who had declined to join the AOL, those he had left behind unharmed. All of them. They had been murdered, thousands of men, and now their bodies were being paraded before the people of Earth, a propaganda tool designed to...

Designed to turn everyone against us…

Suddenly it was clear, totally, horrifyingly, clear…and in the terrible genius of it he saw shadows of UNGov's original lie forty years before.

"It's the troops we left behind," he said. "On Juno. On the other worlds." Taylor's voice was dead, almost devoid of emotion. "They killed them…they killed them all. And they're blaming us…"

"My God…" It was Daniels. He took a few steps forward and stared at the screen. The image changed back to the man behind the podium as he continued to speak. "Can it be…?"

Taylor's eyes bored into the display. He'd never seen the man before, but he felt his hatred grow, his mind filled with an almost-uncontrollable rage. He wished the man was in front of him, that his genetically-enhanced fingers were even now closing around his neck, choking him…then squeezing harder, the sounds of his neck breaking…

He could hear Samuels behind him, the good-natured country boy turned cyborg-soldier. His friend was fighting back emotion, his eyes glistening with moisture as he stared at the screen, realizing with frightening certainty that it was, in fact true. Over twenty-thousand men had been massacred on at least eight worlds. "I remember some of those soldiers, Jake," Samuels said. "Officers I spoke to, men I told to stay behind if they weren't sure. There was one kid on Juno. He was so damned young and scared…I convinced him not to go with us. Now, he's dead. Now, they're all dead."

Taylor nodded absent-mindedly at his friend's words, but he was too lost in his own thoughts to respond, too gripped by all-consuming anger. He just stared at the screen, listening to the speaker's words, but not really hearing them anymore. It was brilliant, through all the pulsating hatred, he could see the genius of his adversary's plan. Now he understood why normal people, miners, workers were so hostile…why they were risking their own lives to attack his people. UNGov had rallied the world behind it, creating another monster, one he didn't doubt the people would respond to, as they had before. For all UNGov

had stolen their liberty, forced them to survive at barely sustenance levels while the elites lived like sultans...the people of
Earth still wanted to believe their government was there to protect them, and to sustain that faith they would accept everything
they were told.

For an instant, Taylor didn't know what to do, how to proceed. Images of his soldiers gunning down civilians passed
through his mind...men, women, children, lying dead in the
streets of their homes as the soldiers of the AOL—the Army
of Liberation—marched past. For all the planning he'd done
for this day, the endless thoughts about how to hide his Tegeri
backing and explain to the people what his army had come to
do, he'd never imagined something like this. And now he kicked
himself for its obviousness, just another lie, simple, basic, like
the one he'd believed when he'd first stepped through the Portal
to Erastus. He'd come to persuade the people, to speak to them,
lead them. But UNGov knew the people better, that fear was the
way to control them.

Taylor felt movement behind him, Hank Daniels stepping
up to his side. "Those bastards," he said, his voice dripping
with anger. Daniels was perhaps the one person in the AOL
more determined to destroy UNGov than Taylor. "This is why
we're here, Jake. Because this cannot continue. This must be
destroyed, root and branch...and we can show no more mercy
than they do."

Taylor knew how pitiless Daniels was in his attitude toward
UNGov. He realized his friend would massacre everyone related
to the Earth's government, that he would refuse to take prisoners in the field, save for those unfortunates brought to him for
interrogation. Taylor had long told himself he would restrain
his comrade, that he would hold Daniels' back from his worst
instincts. But that was gone now, and in its place was left only a
darkness as frigid as that in Daniels' soul. Taylor would let his
officer do his worst...and now he swore he would be right there
himself, as cold-blooded as Daniels.

He stared at the screen as the address ended and the view
returned to the newscaster. "Secretary-General Anton Samovich

has just finished his historic address. For those of you just joining us, the news this day is grim..."

Taylor stopped listening. He'd heard what he wanted to hear,
what he needed. Anton Samovich, the Secretary-General. The
man responsible for what happened here, I am sure of it.

He was silent for a moment, unmoving, ignoring everything
around him. Then he spoke, and when he did his voice so frozen with hatred that even Daniels turned and looked at him in
shock.

"Before this is done...I will stare into that man's dead face
myself."

* * *

Taylor sat at his desk, struggling to focus on the work in
front of him. He'd never felt rage like he had hours before,
watching the UNGov broadcast. He'd issued the orders he'd
had to...as hateful as they were, he knew he had no choice. His
soldiers were here to risk their lives, to sacrifice themselves to
free a world. He wasn't going to order them to stand down, to
take needless chances with people trying to kill them. No, he'd
authorized all unit commanders of the army to take whatever
actions they deemed necessary to protect their people. He just
hoped they would exercise restraint, that his forces wouldn't
leave behind a trail of burned cities and dead civilians.

He knew he was doing just as Samovich wanted, playing
right into his enemy's hands, but he couldn't think of an alternative. Every dead civilian would push the population farther
away, make it ever more difficult—or impossible—to convince
the people he was there not to harm them but to free them. But
what else could he do? He felt for the people who would die, but
he told himself that was part of the price mankind would pay,
for its foolishness, for its willingness to follow evil leaders and
to believe one lie after another.

He pushed all of that out of his mind again, staring back
down at the tablet in front of him. There was actually some
good news on it. Another Dragonfire squadron was active. That

left only one still to be assembled. And all the anti-aircraft bat-teries were in the field now. That gave him enough to defend his base around the Portal as well as detaching some to cover his troops' advance. The supply situation was positive as well. Tegeri-supplied food, medicines, ammunition…it all continued to flow through the Portal, more than replacing what his sol-diers had used. He'd hesitated before asking T'arza to provide so much in the way of logistics. He had agreed with the Tegeri elder that any overt assistance was likely to be more harmful than helpful, at least until he could get the truth to some of his people. But supplies were different. He knew UNGov officials would realize he couldn't have kept his army so well fed and equipped without the assistance of the aliens. But as long as his allies provided nothing overt, no technology that would seem out of place with his forces, he suspected things would be okay. T'arza had agreed, and while Taylor suspected his friend had not had the easiest time convincing his own people, in the end he'd seen it done. The Tegeri supply line had run day and night, providing everything Taylor's people needed…including dozens of anti-aircraft batteries that looked like Earth-built units but put out five times the firepower.

His head spun around suddenly, his ears picking up the com-motion in the room outside his office. He'd just gotten up and turned to run toward the door when he heard the alarm out-side, a screeching, almost deafening sound. He knew what it was immediately. Air raid.

He burst through the door, his eyes snapping back and forth across the room, feeling almost immediately the barely con-trolled panic around him. "Report," he snapped, his voice loud, demanding.

"General, scanners are detecting incoming missiles approach-ing from the west and south in large numbers. Multiple ICBMs and smaller vehicles as well. Over seventy in total, sir. Perhaps more."

"All ground batteries on full alert…crews are to fire at will at all targets. And scramble the Dragonfires…now!" Taylor turned toward the entrance to the headquarters, his eyes settling on

Hank Daniels and Karl Young as they burst through the door.

"I figured this would come," he said grimly, to himself as much as anyone else. "But this is sooner than I'd expected." He took a deep breath and exhaled hard. Then he looked over at his two friends and senior officers. Young just stared back but Daniels nodded in agreement, and the expression on his face carried the same unspoken message as Taylor's.

Nukes.

Chapter 15

From the Writings of Jinto Akawa:

As recently as several days ago, I had fully expected to retire from UNGov service as a colonel, grateful to have attained a rank that would assure me a sufficient pension and enough privileges to enjoy a comfortable retirement. I was a man without patronage, one with no great political skill, nor with the stomach for the level of backstabbing and deceit success in high government service requires. Yet I manage to obtain my eagles...and avoid posting to one of the Portal planets. And I have always endeavored to maintain a low profile, to avoid being drawn into political disputes...to keep my head down and to draw as little attention to myself as possible.

I have served twenty-five years. I cannot say that in that time I was not called to do things I regret, actions I would have avoided had that been an option. I am not the architect of the way the world functions, and I have done what I must to remain safe, to maintain my position and ensure my family's future. Such has been my place in the world. Until four days ago.

Anton Samovich...the Secretary-General of UNGov and, with the fear he has instilled in the other members of the Secretariat, the effective dictator of Earth. The most powerful man who has ever existed. And now, through life's unpredictable nature, my patron.

I did not seek promotion to the generalship, much less to the top command, to thrust myself toward true power, and the political danger it carries with it. But one does not refuse the

Secretary-General, and for whatever reasons he may have, he has appointed me Marshal, supreme commander of all of Earth's military forces. By fiat, he has placed me in control of all recruits for the planetary armies, all internal security forces, even the Inquisitor Corps. It is more than I could ever have imagined, even if I'd been driven by greater ambition. Though, I must admit, I now better understand the seductive nature of power, the hold it has established on so many, like a terrible drug. But I feel the danger of it too, the terrible consequences of failure. For I stand between those who rule the world and a force come to destroy them. If I do not win the victory quickly, I fear the consequences will be tragic and final. For I face more than the enemy, who will seek to defeat me in battle. I must also watch those around me, the subordinates who look to my position with greedy eyes, who would take any chance to disgrace me in order to take my place.

A life of caution, of modest goals and the pursuit of safe attainable successes. That is how I have lived. All that is gone now, replaced by one of the greatest gambles imaginable. The weeks ahead will decide my fate...fame, a vast fortune, a seat on the Secretariat, the gratitude of the world's rulers. Or disgrace, persecution, death...the bitter rewards of failure.

I have spent my life looking the other way, disregarding the abuses I saw all around me. But now I am forced to embrace the tactics I loathed. I can no longer hide from accountability, tell myself I am merely following orders...and that if I do not, I will be killed and someone else will gladly take my place. No, now I will be giving such orders. I may prevail in this fight, but when it is over I will have to face myself, to reconcile with the great rewards for which I have sold my soul.

"The attack has failed, sir. All missiles were intercepted and destroyed before reaching the detonation points." The officer looked over at Marshal Akawa, his voice edgy, nervous. Reporting bad news to high level UNGov personnel was never a pleasant task. Those accustomed to a lifetime of political clawing and backstabbing had a tendency to blame subordinates when their own plans went awry, setting them up as scapegoats to deflect the blame. But Jinto Akawa wasn't like most of the political officers who ran UNGov forces Earthside, a fact the staff he'd inherited was just beginning to realize.

"Very well, Captain." There was disappointment in Akawa's tone, but no accusation. No bitterness. "I'm not all that surprised. I didn't really expect it to work, but we had to try." That was a bit of a lie…he'd given it about 50/50 odds in his head, which wasn't quite 'not expecting' it to work. Taylor's people didn't have a worldwide detection grid, and Akawa had nursed hopes that his missiles would be discovered too late for the AOL to get its Dragonfires into the air.

Akawa had been in total command of UNGov's forces facing the AOL for only a few days. His first order, after those commanding the arrest of a dozen officers he considered too dangerous to ignore, was to prepare a nuclear strike against the Portal the AOL had used to transit to Earth. With any luck, a well-executed attack would kill thousands of Taylor's soldiers… and very possibly destroy the Portal, stranding any forces still on the other side and cutting the army off from its Tegeri lines of supply. He knew Taylor had strong AA defenses, but a successful strike would virtually end the war then and there. The aftermath might be nasty, a series of bloody fights against Taylor's desperate survivors, but Akawa didn't think even the gifted rebel general could conquer a world without support or supplies, with thousands of his soldiers stranded on the Portal world from which he'd come.

It had been a good plan, one where time was of the essence. Every passing hour was another AA battery Taylor's people put into service, another five hundred of his troops marching through the Portal. Akawa had issued the order without delay, but in the end it had taken two full days to execute. UNGov had dismantled the nuclear arsenals of the old nation-states, more concerned that they could be used by rebels against their new order than that they would have need for them. A small number of weapons had been spared, just in case a need arose, but they were scattered around the planet in different facilities. Samovich had deployed the salted bombs from the reserve arsenals, but there were still some normal warheads left, a few at least. But by the time Akawa had gathered them all together for the strike, Taylor's people had reassembled more of their anti-aircraft batteries, and they proved to be as effective against missiles as they were against flyers. Akawa had launched 82 missiles, all he'd been able to find in immediately usable condition. And Taylor's people had shot every one of them down. First the UNGov air attack had failed, and now the nuclear strike. Akawa realized, as he had suspected, that the war would be won on the ground.

"We will have to look to our main strategy." He looked around the central room of the headquarters. He could feel the fear. Failure would certainly doom Akawa, but he could almost hear the thoughts around him, his aides trying to help him— most of them, at least—but also planning for themselves, holding back enough to escape retribution if the new commander failed.

"I want Green Division to move to the north, to dig in along the enemy's line of advance and prepare to defend." He walked toward the massive display in the middle of the room, staring intently as he did. "Here," he said, his hand slapping down on a spot about one hundred kilometers from Taylor's advance elements. "Here is where they will dig in."

"Marshal, we cannot possibly get reinforcements to that location, not before the enemy is able to engage Green Division." Antonio Bizzetti was a colonel, a skilled soldier who had worked closely alongside Akawa before the latter's sudden promotion. His voice lacked the timidity most of the others had displayed, no doubt the byproduct of his perceived friendship with the new commander-in-chief. "At least let us move Blue Division with them...perhaps the two units together will be able to hold until more forces arrive." His voice suggested he was far from confident.

"No, Colonel." Akawa almost said, "Antonio," and he reminded himself the main HQ was not the place for informality. "A commander as skilled as General Taylor would pin the two divisions and move flanking forces around the south. Our units would be destroyed."

"But Green Division will be destroyed anyway…there is no way they can hold, dug in or not."

"No, Colonel, there isn't. But it will take time…and it will buy us several days to continue concentrating the main army west of the Urals. We must be ready to stop the invaders before they reach Moscow, and Europe beyond…and we need time to do that. If they get past us, to Warsaw or even farther west, they will be in a position to threaten Geneva itself. We will lose all tactical flexibility and be forced into an all-out defense of the capital."

"But what about Blue Division? Surely doubling the force along the line will help us hold longer…"

"Perhaps, Colonel, but I doubt it will make a meaningful difference. And I don't think either unit will hold long against General Taylor's veterans. Two routing divisions are not much more use than one." He paused taking a deep breath. He was beginning to step into his role with more assurance, but he still felt a bit intimidated by the power he now wielded. "Besides, I have other plans for Blue Division."

He stared at the screen, his eyes moving down, to the southernmost positions. There were icons showing the locations of Taylor's troop concentrations, though without any real intel on his order of battle, much of the satellite-obtained data was highly conjectural. Orbital reconnaissance could give accurate information on numbers, at least most of the time. But whether those troops were veterans—or Supersoldiers—he could only guess.

Taylor's soldiers are all veterans. And mine are mostly green. So the only real thing is locating the enhanced units from Erastus…and trying like hell to stay away from them while we strike at his other forces.

His eyes remained locked on the display, looking for a weak spot, any kind of opening. But there wasn't one. *This Taylor knows what he is doing.*

He intended to send Blue Division around the south of Taylor's forces, going around his line entirely and moving against his rear areas. He knew one division wasn't enough to truly outflank the invaders, but if he could get teams all around, individual companies—and in a few key spots, battalions—he might be able to cause enough disruption to slow Taylor's advance. And every day he added to the march was time to get an additional division to his chosen defensive line just east of Moscow. But even in the rear areas, Taylor's army was carefully-deployed, with well-placed pickets supported by what had to be local reaction forces. Anywhere he sent the Blues, Taylor could respond with reinforcements in a matter of hours.

Nevertheless, the plan was still valid. Even if every one of Blue Division's attacks was repulsed, fighting them off would still slow Taylor down...and if the assaults made him nervous enough, he might just call a temporary halt to the army's movement. And that would buy even more time.

"Colonel, open a channel to Blue Division HQ. I want to talk to General O'Reilly myself..."

*   *   *

"Forward, men...there's no point in stopping here. The enemy will just cut you to ribbons. If you want to live then press on...take the position. Or die." It wasn't the encouragement of a heroic officer, perhaps, but it was the best Major Emilio Vargus would manage.

Vargus was crouched down in a small shell hole with six of his soldiers, but most of the battalion was strung out in the open. There was nothing more than a company in front of them, he was sure of that, but they were dug in and well-supplied with heavy machine guns. At least fifty of his men were down, and the others were wavering, their advance slowing to a crawl as the enemy continued to pour fire into them. Some of them dove to the ground on the open plain, and others just froze.

Vargus knew he had to do something, but he wasn't sure what. He wasn't a combat veteran, not really...no more than any of his men were. Internal security duty could be dangerous on occasion, but it carried the unquestionable advantage of massive superiority, in numbers, weapons, tactics. Putting down riots was one thing; charging grim veteran soldiers was another.

He knew he had to push forward himself, lead his troops by example, but the truth was stark. He was afraid. His legs felt frozen. He remembered old missions, breaking up demonstrations. Usually a few shots were enough to put a mob to flight. But not always. More than one group had held firm before his security troops, even rushed at them, often armed with nothing more than clubs or bottles. He tried to put the thoughts out of his mind, to not think about how he'd given the orders for his people to fire. But they were still there, the rioting civilians falling to the ground, racing toward his troops until the last of them went down. He'd always considered them fools, but now he saw something else in those tortured recollections. Courage.

He gritted his teeth and tried to push himself, and then, with a shout, he leapt over the edge of the shell hole and ran toward then enemy lines. "Forward," he shouted, his rifle leveled and firing as he ran. "Follow me, men!"

His legs felt weak, as if the next step would be the one that caused them to collapse…but they endured. He was terrified, and every fiber of his being wanted to turn and run for his life. But he kept moving. And across the field his soldiers followed. Not all of them, but first individuals…and then small groups.

"Forward," he cried again, as he drew closer to the enemy. He could see their trench now, feel projectiles whizzing by. But still he pressed on. Just another few seconds…and his people would be in the trench…

*   *   *

"Pour it into 'em boys!" Aaron Jamison stood between the two heavy autocannons, peering over the trench at the approaching enemy soldiers. He'd thought they were about to break a moment earlier, and for an instant, the advance had stalled. But something had rallied at least part of the battalion. More than half of them were down, and Jamison knew a lot more would fall as they covered the last fifty meters. But if they didn't break, a few of them were going to make it to his line.

"Autocannons, keep firing. Everyone else, prepare to hold the trench." He was surprised at the tenacity of this enemy attack. His people had repelled two other assaults over the past twenty-four hours, but they'd barely had to open up, and the UNGov troops bolted and ran. There was something different about this group.

He turned and walked down the trench, popping his almost-spent cartridge and slamming another home. "Alright, guys. Every one you take down out there is one less you're going to fight in here." His mechanical eyes riveted back and forth, picking out targets and dropping each with a single shot.

His people had the advantage of position, but they'd been heavily outnumbered from the start. The enemy was firing as they advanced, and even with their cover, at least three of his soldiers were lying in the trench. Maybe a half dozen others were wounded, but all but one of them were still on the line.

He'd brought up extra autocannons after the last attack, and he'd positioned them to make it appear his force was larger than it was. But most of his company was deployed off to the left, with a reinforced platoon in reserve. He'd started with forty-one troops in this section of the line...and the enemy had attacked with a full battalion, five hundred strong.

"Here they come!" he shouted, firing once, then again, taking down two enemies just as they reached the edge of the entrenchment. He leapt to the side as one of them fell, splashing him with mud. Then another dozen jumped in, and his men were engaged in hand to hand combat.

He was one of only three Supersoldiers in the platoon, but his men were all veterans, and they made short work of the UNGov troops. Jamison swung to the side, moving toward one of his men who was bracketed between two enemies. He pulled up his rifle and slammed the butt down on one of the soldiers, hearing a sickly crack as his enhanced strength shattered the man's spine. Then he spun around, bringing the weapon to bear and firing off a single shot, dropping another enemy moving up behind him, just before he'd raised his own weapon.

That was close, he thought. You may be a veteran Supersoldier and these guys half-trained bullies, but that doesn't mean one of them can't kill you.

He shook the feeling and snapped his head around, looking both ways down the trench. It looked like every enemy soldier who'd jumped into the trench was dead. He walked slowly down, checking on his men. It looked like he had another KIA, and two more wounded. Not that bad considering they had just repulsed an attack by ten times their number. But they all hurt. The dead man was Colm Randall. Jamison remembered the kid from Juno. He'd been one of the first there to come over to the AOL.

Now he died in the AOL...

He stared down at the UNGov soldiers. He despised them for the enforcers they were, for the civilians they'd intimidated and even killed over the years. He felt hatred for those men, and not a hint of pity. He gave into dark thoughts. It made it easier to gun them down.

Let them all come here, and we will send them to hell. Perhaps their victims will rest better.

But that only worked to a certain extent. He knew the image he crafted in his mind didn't describe all of the soldiers fighting against the AOL. There were recruits in those formations too, eighteen, nineteen, twenty-year olds who'd been destined for the planetary armies fighting the Tegeri. Men like him, like all his people, whether from Erastus or Juno or Capria, but born too late, denied the chance to choose to join the AOL...and shoved forward into the line to oppose it.

"There but for the grace of God go I," Jamison whispered to himself, repeating an old saying his father had often recited. Is this a recruit like I was, he wondered, looking down at one of the corpses, a man so young he seemed little more than a boy. Dragged from home and family to be sent to fight an unjust war? Perhaps...but he found his war closer to home, didn't he? Was my war more defensible? I was lied to, he was lied to. I killed the Machines, slaughtered them for years, yet now the Tegeri bear us no grudge. Indeed, they aid us…while we gun this boy—and his comrades---down. But the result is the same. Death knows no location. A man is no more dead in the blistering sun of Erastus than here in the cold mud of Eurasia.

The man's lifeless eyes were wide open, almost staring back at him. Jamison crouched down, looking at the young soldier. His hatred was gone, drained suddenly from his body. There were men here who had deserved death, no doubt, but not all those who found it this day. His hands moved slowly over the boy's face, feeling his already-cold flesh as he closed the eyelids.

"Captain…"

Jamison turned his head toward the voice. It was Lieutenant Orrin, the commander of the platoon. "Yes, Lieutenant," he said, his voice grim, far away. "What is it?" He stood up slowly, turning to face his second in command.

"We found an enemy major, sir. Dead. We think he was the commander of the attack. He fought well before he went down." There was an odd expression in Orrin's voice, one that Jamison understood immediately. It was pleasing to think of UNGov's forces as inferior, as bully security troopers dressed up as real soldiers. But Jamison knew one thing…if their experiences of going to war had taught his people one thing it was that leaders came in many varieties. These thousands serving UNGov would have their heroes too, their capable and devoted leaders. This one had held his battalion together when the others had run. He'd led them right into the trenches…and if he'd had a regiment instead of a battalion, Jamison knew his lines might well have broken.

"Yes, clearly this unit was better led than the others we've faced so far." He looked over at the lieutenant. "Let us learn from that…we cannot assume the enemy leadership is inferior."

"Yes, sir…I mean no, sir."

"Anything else, Lieutenant?" Jamison could see the officer was concerned.

"Yes, Captain. We've got more enemy forces on the scanner, sir. Looks like another battalion. They're not advancing yet, but they're not far away…and my gut…"

"Your gut tells you they're going to advance on our position. And you're probably right, Lieutenant."

Jamison nodded slowly, his eye catching a red stain on Orrin's uniform, and a torn bit of cloth tied around his arm. It had been shoved under the sleeve—Orrin had clearly tried to hide the fact that he was wounded.

"What is that, Lieutenant?"

"Oh…it's nothing, sir. Just a light wound. Caught a round right before they hit the trenchline."

"You should go back to the aid station. I can handle things up here."

"No, sir…" Orrin paused, realizing his words had come out as if he was defying the captain's order. "I mean, please, sir…I'm fine. I'll get this taken care of after we beat back the next attack." His eyes found Jamison's. "Please, Captain…my men…"

Jamison nodded slowly. "Very well, Lieutenant. See to your platoon." He felt the urge to call up reinforcements. Orrin's people had suffered 20% casualties, and the men in the line had to be close to exhaustion. They'd gotten an ammo resupply, so that was a plus at least. Jamison remembered some of the earlier battles after they'd left Erastus, and the critical supply shortages that had so slowed them…and cost them God only knows how many losses.

He shook his head. No, I can't bring up any reserves yet. I just don't have the numbers, and we've no idea where else they'll hit us.

He'd seen the drone reports…there was an entire UNGov division out there, fifteen thousand troops at full strength. And behind that would be everything a world could muster. And his forces were part of the flank defense. If their lines were breached, the army's entire advance would be stopped dead. And if the lead units had to turn to face a threat from the rear just as the enemy attacked frontally…

No, I have to play the long game. We all do. It's not enough to hold today. We have to hold tomorrow…as long as the campaign goes on…

I'd rotate Orrin's people with the reserve platoon to give

them a rest, but there's no time. He pulled the small tablet from his belt and looked at the scanning display. No, there was no time. Not before the next attack. He'd be doing no one any favors if he allowed the enemy to catch his people while they were withdrawing.

"Okay, Lieutenant, if you're going to stay then by all means, let's get your men ready for the next wave."

*   *   *

Mitchell Klein moved quietly through the camp, glancing quickly to the side as he walked past the familiar gray shelter unit, the unassuming home of the army's supreme commander. He'd contrived to walk by at least ten times over the last week, in the half a dozen different locations that had served as head-quarters while the AOL advanced across the windswept steppe. He'd scouted out the operations shelter too, but that was always busy, far too busy for his intentions.

There was a single guard on duty outside Taylor's quarters, as usual, not a lot of protection for the commander of the entire army. No, Klein thought to himself. General Taylor is more than the leader of the army, he is the beating heart of the crusade. Without him, Klein was sure things would crumble. Taylor's veteran soldiers would be leaderless, confused. They would still fight savagely, he had no doubt about that, but they would fall in the end without their brilliant and beloved leader.

Klein had been planning for over a week now, waiting for the right moment. He'd have to take care of the guard, that much he knew for certain. And though there was only one on duty at any given time, Taylor's Erastus veterans had claimed the job for themselves. It wasn't impossible to kill a Supersoldier, but it certainly wasn't easy. And it was damned sure dangerous as hell. He'd need surprise to have a chance, and if his initial attack failed, he doubted he'd get a second.

He needed more than surprise though. The attack had to be silent, swift. If the guard had a chance to sound an alarm, or even cry out, he knew he would fail. And if he failed he would die. He'd told himself every day he delayed was because the time wasn't right, that a more opportune moment would come. But part of him knew fear was as much to blame. Any way he thought about it, he knew an attempt to assassinate Taylor was dangerous. He had to get past the guard, take the army's commander—a veteran Supersoldier himself—by surprise, and kill him without drawing any attention. If he made any noise, if Taylor shouted out in his death struggle, Klein knew he'd be in deep trouble. If he was caught in the act, even if he managed to kill his target, he knew he'd be dead. He couldn't imagine the ferocity of the soldiers of the AOL, and Taylor's oldest comrades in particular, toward the killer of their beloved general. They'd tear him to pieces, perhaps literally.

Klein had almost given up a number of times, resolved to hide among the other soldiers of the AOL until he had a chance to escape, to sneak off and find his way back to UNGov headquarters. But he'd always been drawn back to his original plan. His mind was in torment, greed and fear fighting to control his actions. He'd let himself imagine the rewards, the power he would gain as the man who'd killed UNGov's worst enemy, and he ached to realize it all. And he was far from sure how he'd be received if he returned to UNGov empty-handed. The government wasn't particularly forgiving of failure, at least not from low-level operatives, and Klein could hear the questions now… why did none of the operatives in the planetary armies do anything to stop Taylor? What did you do, simply hide until you had the chance to flee?

No, running off had its danger too, and without the promise of reward his original plan offered. But if he was going to go through with it, he had to work up the courage. And that was proving to be difficult.

Maybe his quarters aren't the best place, he thought. Taylor was incredibly active, rising early and working throughout the day until late night. He moved all over, from one unit to the next…to the most forward positions to scout. Perhaps there was a better place…

But where? Where?

Chapter 16

From the Journal of Jake Taylor:

The combat strength of the Army of Liberation is just under 70,000. That is far more than I'd dared imagine when our quest began, and yet now, facing the resources of a world, it seems like such a small force. But back then I allowed hope to color my judgment, to cloud my realism. I dared to think of a population that would rally to our cause, of people who would rise up and take the opportunity to cast aside their chains. I knew we couldn't conquer Earth, kilometer by kilometer, nor hold it even if we destroyed every army UNGov threw at us. We are here to free the people, not to subjugate them against their will, simply trading one tyrant for another.

But I have been outmaneuvered, schooled by Anton Samovich in the true artistry of propaganda. I was foolish, naïve, believing truth had its own power. But what good is truth if no one believes it? And are the civilians my people are forced to kill any less dead because they themselves acted on lies?

My soldiers didn't kill the men of the planetary armies, but they have killed civilians. Indeed, the toll mounts hourly as reports come in, scouting parties encountering armed gangs... and defending themselves. And then there is Nyrob...a whole town destroyed, every inhabitant massacred. I recalled the troops involved, and in my initial rage I swore to stand them before a firing squad for what they had done. My soldiers are not barbarians, and I will not tolerate such conduct.

I am grateful they were so far forward, that it took hours to get them back to headquarters, for it gave my temper time to wane. Then I listened to their report...of the men killed, tortured and then hanged in the town square. I cannot approve of what they did, nor can I excuse it. But I understand it. And I'm an old enough soldier to know this will not be the last—or the worst—incident if the people of Earth continue to regard us as butchers and traitors.

I fear now for the safety of the teams I sent out, the men who are even now finding their way to homes...in Russia, in Poland, throughout Europe and China. I even sent a squadron of airships to North America. Perhaps this was a waste—or my own prejudice causing me to send people to my own home, though I myself could not go. But now what would become of those men? They are in grave danger, clearly. Will they be greeted as family, as old friends? Or will they be attacked and murdered before they are even recognized?

I asked myself last night if I would recall them if I could... if I would hold them back were I able to do it all over again? I wanted to say yes, to torture myself with the undoable. But the answer was clearer than I could have imagined, and when I whispered it to myself there was no doubt. No. No, I would not have kept them back. For, though their task has become vastly more dangerous...it is also even more essential. If we are to undo the damage Samovich has done, to expose his horrific lie, it will have to begin with these men, embracing mother and fathers. Telling their stories to brother and sisters and childhood friends.

Anton Samovich controls the media, and his lies begin at the top, and filter down to an entire world. But our truth—the truth—must start at the bottom, at dinner tables and around fireplaces...and it will have to rise slowly, spreading, expanding as it does.

I always considered the teams an important part of our strategy, but now I realize that our entire future, success or failure in this great undertaking, lies with them, on the survival of trust and love between a thousand men and their friends and families. Down to such things, the fate of a world has come to rest.

"General, we're getting reports from all along the left flank. We've got an enemy division hitting our lines." Karl Young stood at attention as he spoke. Like the others who'd been with Taylor since the beginning, he tended toward informality around the AOL's commander, at least until the fighting started. Young's demeanor had tightened in the past two days, 'Generals' replacing 'Jakes,' and his posture improving until it smacked of parade ground precision.

"I know, Karl." Taylor allowed his friend the formalities, though truth be told, he hated it. He endured the revered stares the rest of the army gave him, but Young was like a brother to him, and every crisp salute made him long for the days of firebase Delta, when six young men, as close as friends can be, would gather together and dump out their meager assortment of rations, somehow creating the Erastus equivalent of a feast. He hadn't appreciated those moment enough, he now realized. Gehenna was a hellish place, no doubt, and the fighting there was fierce and dangerous. But now, for all the soldiers following him, for the power he wielded, part of him longed for those simpler days, to watch Bear pull bits and pieces from ration packs and throw together something altogether edible, all the time torturing his buddies with stories about racks of ribs barbecuing on the spit. Or even sitting up late playing poker with homemade cards on nights it was just too hot to sleep. But the past was the past...and the present had urgent need of his attention.

"I saw the scanning reports. The lines will hold. They're well dug in, and the UNGov forces are not experienced in this kind of fighting." He felt a wave of guilt, remembering times he'd been on the lines, facing what had seemed like overwhelming enemy strength, and he wondered what officers had made such pronouncements when he and his friends had been the ones in the shit. "They'll take some losses, but we just can't weaken the main force now. We both know we'll have a big fight on our hands as soon as we clear the mountains. If we detach forces to deal with every distraction, we won't have enough to face their main army."

Young nodded. "Yes, sir." Taylor could tell his friend understood…but also that he was still troubled. He also knew there was nothing to be done about that. He had led these soldiers here to win this war, and that is exactly what he intended to do, no matter what the cost. And his generals would have to deal with it in their own ways, just as he would.

"What about the infiltration teams, Karl? Anything new?" Word had reached HQ of a dozen teams killed or captured, but none of groups reaching their destinations. Their mission had become even more crucial in the aftermath of UNGov's propaganda program, and Taylor was starting to get worried. He hadn't expected immediate results, but with each passing day the silence was growing ominous.

"Nothing, Jake." Young slipped back to his normal informality. "But it hasn't been that long yet. Give it some time."

"Time," Taylor replied. "You're right, of course, Karl. But time is not our ally. Every day that passes means more UNGov troops in the field. Every day is another wave of civilians attacking our patrols…of our men killing misguided townspeople."

Young looked back wordlessly, and Taylor returned the stare. The both knew there was no answer. All they could do was continue according to plan…and wait to see what happened.

* * *

"At least half a dozen ground stations should have detected us, Rod. I'm amazed they haven't sent a squadron up after us yet." Vic Illuri sat at the Dragonfire's controls, his eyes wide open, darting between the cockpit and the scanner displays. "But still…nothing."

"Their air power took it hard, Vic. The battle around the Portal cost them a lot of their strength. Those Tegeri AA batteries are incredible." A pause. "I'm just damned glad they didn't use them against us back on Juno." Rod Charles sat in the commander's seat, though he was a ground pounder, not a Dragonfire jockey. And instead of the normal five man crew, there were a dozen of them crammed on the airship. Between the added weight and the fact that only two of those onboard were experienced flight crew, if they did run into any serious resistance, they could find themselves in trouble very quickly. "Besides," he added hopefully, "we've got some serious Tegeri ECM in this bird, so with any luck we'll slip across the Atlantic like a ghost. We're up here worrying about intermittent signals, but down on the ground they're probably thinking we're weather patterns or some kind of reflection…anything but an airship where they're not expecting one."

"Let's hope. I still don't trust those aliens. I know it was UNGov that did everything we blamed them for, but still…" Dave Neelin's voice came from behind Charles, from the senior gunner's position.

Charles could see several of the others nodding absent-mindedly. He understood their thoughts, even though he knew they weren't really justified. The Tegeri had supplied the AOL with food, weapons, ammunition. They had given the AOL high tech systems like the AA batteries…and the stealth units that gave their Dragonfire a chance to evade detection as it flew almost twenty thousand kilometers. But it was still difficult. Humanity may have been the aggressor, but it was still hard to forget years of war…suffering, hardship, watching friends and comrades die.

"C'mon, Dave," Charles replied. "They've done everything they said they would. And for all you've been through, they endured the same thing. And we started it. Just 'cause most of us didn't know that doesn't make it not true. Focus your anger on UNGov…and put all that angst into convincing the people back home the AOL is here to free them all."

"I'm going to take her up another five thousand meters… okay, Captain?" Illuri was the pilot, but Charles was the highest in rank and the de facto commander of the ship.

"Do whatever you think is best, Vic. This is your thing, not mine." Charles turned his head, looking around the cockpit. There weren't enough chairs, and there were troops sitting on the floor all around. "Just get us there. Get us home."

"Home," Neelin said. "It doesn't even sound real. It's been so long." His voice was soft, distracted.

The airship was silent, only the sound of the engines breaking the calm. Charles knew they were all thinking about what
they would find when—if—they got back home. It had been a
long time for some of them, more than ten years for Charles,
less for some of the others. And more too, at least in the army
as a whole, though Charles knew he was the longest-serving of
those on the ship. Everybody in the AOL knew it had been
eighteen years since General Taylor had left his home, almost
two decades.

There was excitement in the air, but fear too, trepidation at
what they might find. Would loved ones be dead? Would they be
like strangers? Would they look at their long lost sons and brothers and friends and see monsters, as UNGov had indoctrinated
them to do?

*   *   *

"Move it, all of you...they're on to us, and there's no time to
waste." Stan Wickes stood out in front of the building waving
his arms as the rest of the team came running down the street.
The mission had gone well...mostly. The charges were in place,
and in about ten minutes, UNGov was going to get a good idea
just what the Resistance could do. His people had been at it for
hours, planting charges, setting timers, and slipping away to the
next target. But then their luck ran out. A random patrol caught
a pair of his people finishing up with the last set of explosives,
and all hell broke loose.

Wickes and the rest of the rebels moved in to try to save
their comrades, and a confused firefight erupted. The fighters
of the Resistance held their own...until UNGov reserves began
arriving. Things were about to go really bad when the two rebels
trapped inside the building detonated their charges, killing themselves, and most of the UNGov forces positioned just outside.

The rest of the team had frozen in shock, all except Wickes
and his half-century old battle reflexes. He'd screamed and
shouted and harangued his people into making a run for it,
yelling to them that their friends had sacrificed themselves to

give them an escape. He wasn't sure they'd get away, but he was damned determined that they try.

Carson Jones and Devon Bell had brought up the rear, and they ran up and through the door. Wickes took a last look down the street, but he didn't see anyone. That didn't mean a thing, he knew. He suspected he couldn't even count the surveillance devices his people had passed. UNGov's security headquarters would be analyzing input from every camera and spy device in the city, deploying their computer-controlled algorithms.

For the next ten minutes, at least, Wickes thought with a rush of grim satisfaction. Unless they find the bombs before then there won't be a security HQ.

"Down the stairs," he yelled, as he followed Bell and Jones down the hall. "Then through the hole in the cellar wall into the next building."

The Resistance had planned their uprising for years, and they had contingencies and preparations for every eventuality. Wickes would lead the team through the adjacent building and then under the next avenue, using the almost-collapsed subway station there. By the time his people came back up to the street, they'd be two avenues and six streets away, not safe by any means, but a little farther from the hottest spot. From there they'd have a quick run to the waterfront, where their backups were waiting with the underwater gear. Then they'd suit up and swim through the old flooded tunnel to Brooklyn...and one of their rapidly dwindling supply of safe houses.

He ran to the stairs after Bell, closing the rickety old door behind him and barricading it with a heavy timber. Then he reached out, grabbing onto the shards of the wrecked railing and felt his way down into the darkness.

*   *   *

"Captain, I'm picking up something strange." Illuri looked back from the pilot's seat, staring at Charles for an instant before he turned back.

"What is it, Lieutenant?" Charles got up from his seat and

stepped forward, stopping right behind the pilot's chair.

"It looks like some kind of firefight, sir."

"A firefight?" Charles leaned over the pilot's shoulder, looking for himself.

"Do we have troops here, sir? In North America? Another Portal maybe?" Dave Neelin sounded skeptical even as the words escaped his lips, but he stared at the captain expectantly, nevertheless.

"No, we don't have any troops here," he replied. "Another couple of teams like us, but they're all behind us. We're the first ones from the AOL to get here."

"So who is that down there, Captain?" Illuri angled his head, looking up at Charles. "Cause that's southern Manhattan, and there's one hell of a fight going on down there." He paused a few seconds then: "What should I do, Cap?"

Charles just kept staring at the screen. He had no idea what was going on. He knew he should forget what was happening, that he should order Illuri to follow the flight plan, to veer away from New York City and land thirty klicks out as they'd planned. The Dragonfire was probably the stealthiest vehicle in the skies of Earth right now, but that didn't make the thing invisible. Flying over Manhattan would be dangerous. Foolish even. He opened his mouth to order the pilot to follow the original plan. But then the scanners went crazy.

"We've got massive explosions, sir…at multiple location in Manhattan." The pilot's eyes had been locked on his display, but when he looked up he could see everyone on the ship standing, looking through the cockpit. The New York skyline had been barely visible at this range, mandated energy-saving rules having long ago relegated the famous nighttime image to history's scrapbook. But now the city was ablaze with light…explosions, and fires burning fiercely and engulfing at least a dozen buildings.

"Take us closer, Vic," Charles said, his voice soft, half in shock. "We've got to find out what's going on."

* * *

Jones took a deep breath, and tried to steady himself. He was scared, scared shitless. But he was also elated. The sounds of the explosions, the glow of light illuminating the night sky...they had done it. The Resistance had targeted every UNGov installation in the city...offices, security facilities, even troop barracks. He knew they might not win...indeed, the enormity of what they had done almost guaranteed a response so overwhelming, he didn't know if any of them would be alive in a week. But they had taken what chance they had.

He felt a round whip by his head so close he had to put a hand to his cheek to be sure it was still there. A week? I doubt any of us are going to get off this waterfront.

He forced himself to focus, staring down the barrel of the assault rifle. There. A UNGov security trooper, behind a crate... but just a little careless. He closed one eye and stared down the site, bringing the crosshairs onto his target, the back of the man's head. It was only a few centimeters exposed, but Wickes had taught him to shoot...and Stan Wickes learned his marksmanship in the old Marine Corps.

He took another breath and exhaled, remembering everything the old leatherneck had told him. Then slowly, steadily he pulled back on the trigger. Then he felt the kick, heard the crack as the weapon fired. He saw his target fall as the bullet tore of the back of his skull in a shower of gray and red mist. Wickes had told him—he had told them all—that real combat was nothing like they expected, and certainly not the way it was portrayed in any fiction they'd read or watched.

He'd just killed a man, ended a life with the pull of a trigger. It wasn't the first...that had come a few days earlier. And he suspected it wouldn't be the last either, not if his people were going to have any chance of getting away. Jones hated UNGov with a passion, but in the last few days he'd realized Wickes had been right. Killing wasn't easy...no matter the cause.

He snapped his head up toward the night sky. He heard something. For an instant he thought he'd imagined it...and then it came out from behind a row of buildings and flew over the river. A chopper, a gunship...and it was heading right for his position.

*   *   *

"Cap, whoever that is on those docks, they're about to get wiped. I've got a chopper on my screen, sir...the kind they use for crowd suppression. That thing's got dual autocannons... they'll clear those piers in seconds, sir."

Charles stared through the cockpit, looking down on the scene of the fighting. They were close now, close enough to see the muzzle blasts...and the image of the UNGov gunship coming around from the east. It would be in position to fire any second.

"What do we do, sir?" Illuri asked again. "We can't let them waste all those people."

"We don't have any idea who those people are, Lieutenant. And we've got orders..."

"That's a UNGov chopper, sir." The pilot's voice dripped with venom. "I've watched them clear riots, sir. Too many times. I've seen what those rounds do to bodies."

"I've seen it too, Lieutenant." Charles' voice was grim, uncertainty rapidly giving way to anger. He knew what he should do. He even understood it. No group of rioters was more important than getting the twelve men onboard onto the ground, to begin spreading the word of the fight that had just begun. But he couldn't bring himself to issue the order. Those people down there...they were fighting the same struggle, somehow he was sure of it.

"Alright, Lieutenant...bring us around in an attack pattern."

"Yes, sir!"

Charles turned and looked toward the back of the ship. "Sergeant Neelin...you think you can manage that gunner's station?"

"Yes, Captain! I think I can manage it."

"Good...then let's go splash that fucking UNGov gunship."

*   *   *

The chopper moved across the open area along the water-front, its twin guns spreading death and destruction as it passed. Wickes was right along the water's edge, taking cover next to a concrete pier. He'd ordered all his people to take whatever cover they could, but he'd seen at least two of them go down in the hail of gunfire from the chopper. He hadn't had much hope of escape, but now he had none. They were pinned down, with no way to get to the tunnel.

Assuming anyone is still there.

He knew the security forces might have found their con-tacts…and the rebels stationed at the tunnel had orders to run for it if something showed up that they couldn't handle.

And that gunship damned sure qualifies…

He looked up as the chopper climbed, beginning its turn for another run. The Marine in him refused to give up, but he couldn't think of anything to do…nothing but stay here and fight to the death. He reached down and slammed his last clip into place, still staring at the chopper as it came around, heading almost directly for him. He knew the chance of hitting the thing with his rifle was tiny, and even more astronomical to cause enough damage to disable it. But a miserable chance was better than none, and that's exactly what he intended to do.

He climbed up higher on the dock. The concrete pier gave him cover from the UNGov forces on the ground, but we was totally in the open to the chopper. He stared intently, locking his eyes on the fearsome aircraft. He waited, watching, bringing his rifle to bear.

He heard the sounds of the autocannon fire, ripping into the street, tearing away great chunks of pavement. He watched as his death approached, ready to trade his doomed life for one chance in ten thousand of damaging the airship.

Just another few seconds…

He was about to pull the trigger when the gunship fell silent. And then, an instant later he saw it…another aircraft, much larger, looming up behind the UNGov chopper. There was a delay—later he realized it had probably been half a second or less—and then he heard the sound. It was horrible, like death itself, and he saw the UNGov chopper almost disintegrate under the fire of the new ship's four quad autocannons.

He ducked under the concrete piers as flaming wreckage fell from the sky all around. Something caught him in the leg, and he winced from the pain. He ducked his head under his arms and listened as the chunks of metal and plastic slammed into the dock all around him as the big airship, the one that had saved his life zipped by overhead.

For an instant he thought he was finished, but then the rain of flaming debris stopped. He held where he was for a few seconds, pushing himself as far under the pier as he could, but then he took a deep breath and pulled himself back out.

He looked down at his leg. It hurt like hell, and he'd expected to find a terrible wound, but when his eyes settled on it, he exhaled with relief. There was a gash, perhaps ten centimeters long, ugly and bleeding, but not deep. There were a few burns too, but nothing serious. He suspected he could even walk, though he didn't doubt it would be painful. He gritted his teeth and slowly rose to his feet. He stayed low, ducking behind the pier and looking out toward the enemy positions. His leg hurt, but it was bearable, and when he saw what was happening, he almost forgot about it entirely.

The mysterious airship had come about, and now it was making strafing runs against the UNGov security forces. He stared at the craft, his eyes wide with amazement. He knew what it was, he remembered seeing squadrons of monstrous birds like that, firing rockets and providing close support to ground troops. The Corps had fielded hundreds of airships like that, or similar ones at least. The craft he was watching seemed a bit sleeker, more modern than the ones he remembered from fifty years before.

Still, he knew the airship was military. There was no reason for internal security forces to possess something so powerful. Gunning down rioting civilians did not require a massive war machine. And the craft was attacking the UNGov positions, not the rebel ones. Indeed, it had saved his life, and that of the rest of his people hiding along the waterfront.

He stepped up onto the wharf, almost mesmerized by the spectacle he was watching. It was a breach of discipline, the Marine voice inside him cried, carelessness to abandon his cover and stand in the open. But he couldn't stop himself. The security forces weren't firing at his people anymore anyway. They were dead, most of them, and the rest were fleeing in panic, trying to escape the deadly fire of the great airship.

It was all over a moment later, the great open area along the waterfront cleared of UNGov troops. Most of them lay dead, in their original positions or out in the open where they'd run for the cover of the buildings to the north. And the airship swung around one more time, coming back to where he stood. He felt the urge to run, to dive for cover. Perhaps the gunship was simply targeting everyone it found. But something held him in place, a curiosity he could not deny.

He watched as the ship stopped, hovering above a spot perhaps twenty yards from where he stood. His body was frozen, his eyes locked on the flyer as it dropped slowly, setting down right in front of him. He could see its guns were active, tracking any movement on the wharf. But they were silent...and he told himself if whoever was on that ship want his people dead, they'd be dead already.

He stared as the ship stood where it had landed. For a minute, perhaps two, nothing happened. Then a great hatch at the back opened...and Captain Stan Wickes looked on in stunned amazement as he watched half a dozen shadowy figures emerge.

Chapter 17

Communiqué from General Jake Taylor:

I have received your request for reinforcements to support the units defending the lines of communications. I understand the relentless pressure the enemy has placed on you and the great numerical disadvantage you face, but I must regretfully inform you that there are no reserves available to send you. The army will soon be engaged in what may very well be the climactic struggle of the war. I can only offer you my best wishes and beseech you to hold, by whatever means, while the war is decided on the plains before Moscow.

Aaron Jamison ran across the field, turning every few steps to fire a burst behind him. The enemy had thrown two more divisions against the positions defending the AOL's supply lines, and his people had been forced into an extended order, covering more and more ground as the main army advanced farther from the Portal. His people had been reinforced, but only with an extra platoon, and his frontage had been increased tenfold. He could no longer man a continuous line, and he'd been forced to organize his people into a skirmish line of scouts, backed by several response teams, ready to move wherever the enemy threatened to advance. It was a difficult way to defend a large section of territory, especially against an enemy that seemed to have almost unlimited resources, at least compared to the razor-thin line defending the AOL's lines of communications.

"Let's go," he shouted into his comlink, swinging around to the rear as he did and emptying his clip into the pursuing formations. "Faster…back to the fallback line. No stopping to return fire. Just run." He realized the hypocrisy of the order as he held his own rifle, still hot from fire. He slung it over his shoulder, obeying himself, though he didn't actually run as he'd commanded his people to do. His enhanced legs would have greatly outpaced any speed his men could achieve, and he wasn't about to dash forward ahead of them. They would all get back together, or none of them would.

He'd sent out a flight of drones the day before, and their reports confirmed what he had already feared. Fresh enemy forces were heading his way, far more than he could hope to repel from his battered position. He'd detached a third of his soldiers the day before, sending them back half a klick to dig a new defensive line. He'd also sent all his reserve autocannon teams—and half of those deployed on the forward line—to man the new position. He hated retreating, but he knew he had no choice. His old line was a wreck, and the ground in front was torn apart, shattered debris and shell holes providing the advancing enemy with plenty of cover. He'd cleared his plan with the major, who had approved at once. Both men knew there was no other option.

If the enemy had given Jamison another hour, he'd have had his whole force comfortably dug in along the new line, staring out at the untouched and open killing ground in front of them. But the UNGov units hit too soon, and he'd been forced to defend the battered old position with a handpicked rearguard, while the rest of the company pulled back, taking all but one of the autocannons with them.

The tiny group that remained had held, somehow…at least long enough for the others to pull back and bring the new position up to strength. He'd been worried the last attack would overrun the dozen and a half troops he had kept behind with him, that theirs would prove to be a suicide mission. But his people had risen to the task at hand. The two man team on the last autocannon tore a bloody gash in the attacking formation, and the others stood firm, pouring unrelenting fire into the advancing UNGov troops. Dozens fell, perhaps a hundred, and the rest of the green battalion broke, no more than fifty meters from the thinly-held line.

Jamison knew there were more UNGov forces stacked up along his front, and he realized his people had no chance to defeat another assault. So he ordered his battered rearguard to fall back. They spiked the autocannon and grabbed the wounded, abandoning the trench just as the enemy launched yet another attack. His people made it halfway back to the new line by the time the UNGov forces took their abandoned position and pursued. His troops had given into the same impulses he had to turn and fire at the enemy soldiers pursuing them. But all that did was slow them down…and give their enemies—who outnumbered them 30-1—more time to catch them. Worse, the troops waiting in the new line couldn't open up, not while their own comrades were right in their field of fire.

Jamison heard the bullets whizzing by, and more than once he'd have sworn he felt one almost graze him. But his soldier's luck held. He could see the new line ahead of him, the troopers there, shouting, gesturing for their retreating comrades to hurry. He felt the urge to slow down, to stop at the edge of the trench and climb down carefully, but he knew every second counted. He saw the dropoff coming, watched as the startled men in front of him jumped aside as he took one last leap, and slammed into the back wall of the trench.

He fell back, in pain, the wind knocked out of him. But he forced himself up, gritted his teeth against the throbbing of what he suspected were broken ribs. He hobbled back to the front of the trench, trying to keep his grunts of pain as quiet as possible. He climbed up, shoving his head into the open, braving the increasingly heavy enemy fire to confirm that all his people were back. Then, satisfied he'd left no living soldiers behind in no man's land, he shouted two words.

"Open fire!"

* * *

"General Carp reports that the enemy flanks are buckling, sir. He requests three more divisions for the final assault."

Akawa stared back at the aide, suppressing a momentary flash of anger. He wasn't the type to shoot the messenger, but damned if it wasn't tempting sometimes. Lieutenant Holcomb was a satisfactory aide who, despite a lack of experienced had proven to be good at his job. That was a description Akawa would not have extended to General Samson Carp.

"General Carp's definition of buckling does not appear to be the same as mine. He has squandered seven divisions attacking an ever-thinning line of rebel soldiers. He has been reinforced three times, and yet the result is always the same. He pushes the enemy back a few thousand meters, at a cost of thousands of casualties…and he demands yet more reinforcements to feed into the slaughter."

Akawa couldn't understand what the hell Carp was doing out there. He had ten to one superiority in numbers, maybe twenty to one. Admittedly, his raw troops didn't have the staying power of Taylor's veterans, but there was a mathematics in war that asserted itself at some point.

At least when there isn't an imbecile like Carp in the equation…

He'd have sacked the general long ago. Indeed, when he'd accepted the command of all UNGov forces, he'd come in all full of piss and vinegar, ready to purge the officer ranks of polit-ically-connected fools. But then he realized that was virtually all he had. He could have relieved Carp—though there would almost certainly have been some political blowback if he had—but the fool general's replacement would have been no improve-ment, or even worse.

For all his frustration and anger, Akawa would have sent Carp his three divisions…he knew that cutting Taylor's army off from the Portal was the first step to victory. But he couldn't spare the troops, not now, not with perhaps the decisive battle of the war about to take place.

He'd intended to fall back before Taylor's advance, avoid-ing battle, pulling the brilliant rebel leader forward, ever farther from is supply depot at the Portal. He had time, Taylor didn't. The UNGov training depots were pumping out five divisions a week, while Taylor had no source of reinforcement. The new UN troops were raw, their training minimal, and Akawa knew they would die by the thousands in battle with Taylor's veterans. But he wasn't a fool like Carp, and he understood, given enough manpower, he could force the mathematics of war in the battle against the rebels.

It was a brutal calculus. Losses didn't matter to him, at least not in terms of the prospect of final victory. His soldiers were all raw, more or less, just like their replacements. Fifty soldiers he lost could be replaced. On the other hand, every one of Taylor's men who died was an irreplaceable veteran. A war of attrition, even a grossly uneven one, served Akawa's purpose, and despite being conflicted about the brutality of such a war, he'd been determined to wage one. Until Anton Samovich had interfered.

The Secretary-General wasn't a military commander, he didn't understand battle tactics. He saw only one thing…Taylor's forces moving into Europe. He knew once there, the rebel commander would head right toward Geneva. Taylor's reputation had preceded him, and for all the propaganda UNGov spewed forth, it had no immunity from reacting itself to the fear and exaggeration it so frequently weaponized. The political masters, so accustomed to competing with and backstabbing each other now faced something they hadn't seen in forty years. A real physical threat, an army of terrible warriors who would chase them down, kill them in the streets. They were affected by stories of the AOL's legendary commander, of his ruthlessness and grim intelligence. Of the fanatical loyalty displayed by his crack legions.

Samovich had twice urged Akawa to stand and fight Taylor's forces, to stop their advance well short of the great European cities, but the general had merely acknowledged politely and delayed. The third time, Samovich simply ordered the general to engage the enemy before they reached Moscow. Akawa had argued as much as he could, played for time as far as he was going to be able. But he knew what a direct refusal of Samovich's order would mean, and he grimly commanded his forces to suspend their retrograde movements, to prepare to face Taylor and his soldiers in a climactic battle.

He'd walked up to the large display in the center of his headquarters and drawn a line with his finger, connecting two cities...Kirov and Kazan. A little more than four hundred kilometers. That, he decided, was where he would give battle. The cities would protect his flanks...Taylor needed to win the hearts and minds of the people, and attacking population centers wasn't likely to aid him in that uphill fight. And the length of the line would stretch the rebels' lines thin, giving Akawa the chance to exploit any successes, while straining Taylor's reserves.

"General, sir..." Holcomb had been staring silently at the general, hesitant to interrupt the commander when he was clearly deep in thought. But finally, spoke tentatively. "...what should I tell General Carp?"

Tell him to go fuck himself...

"Tell him there are no reserves available now, and he is to do his best with the resources he has."

"Yes, General." Holcomb turned back to his workstation, relaying Akawa's command.

It doesn't matter anyway, Akawa thought, staring at the display. *If Samovich had given me more time, maybe, but not now. Like it or not, it is on this line things will be decided. Kirov-Kazan.*

Chapter 18

From the Journal of Jake Taylor:

The Battle of Kirov-Kazan. The great struggle I had envisioned since that day on Erastus, when T'arza's words began to coalesce in my mind, when my unfocused rage slowly gave way to the drive to strike back, to destroy those who had committed such terrible acts.

There are many routes to victory, or defeat...persuasion, sieges, production. But we humans tend to see the great climactic battle as the ultimate end to a war. And so I knew it would be for our quest. I feared UNGov would play for time, pull my forces farther from our base, deny us the great battle we that needed, and they did not. So I made it obvious we were heading for Geneva, that I sought one thing and one thing only...to chop the head from the snake. For a few tense days I thought they would fail to take the bait, but then I could see it in their moves. They were preparing to fight us.

I knew the battle would be a nightmare, a bloodbath that would claim many thousands of my soldiers. But in our fight with UNGov we are everywhere outclassed...in territory occupied, in production capacity, even in the support of the people. Everywhere save one place, in the maelstrom of battle, where the superiority of my veteran soldiers will give us our best chance at victory.

Had I known I faced an adversary as capable at Jinto Akawa, I might have changed my plans, reconsidered this strategy. But I was blissfully unaware, indeed almost confident that our enemies were led by a political appointee, one who could never match our martial skill. I have providence alone to thank that he complied with my wishes and met us in open battle, and it was only much later I learned he would not have chosen to fight of his own accord, that he'd been compelled to engage by the Secretariat and by Anton Samovich. I perhaps owe gratitude for my army's survival to these politicians, and the egos and fear that made it impossible for them to allow their gifted commander to put his skill to work.

General Akawa's battlefield instincts served him well and, had he been allowed to make his own decisions, they would have led him to the strategy I most feared. For if he'd had his way, he would have fallen back, yielded the Kirov-Kazan line and given up Moscow, blooding us each step of the way before again retreating and further stretching our already long supply lines. And then he would have sent more divisions against our flanks, pounding away until they broke through...and cut us off from the Portal.

I had no counter for such a plan, for to all my military knowledge there was none. The only option would have been to remain in the frozen wastes, huddled around the Portal while UNGov raised more and more troops to face us. I relied on the hysteria of the politicians—rightly—and on the anticipated inability of their general—wrongly—to force a decisive battle, one where the skill of my veterans could prevail and spread panic throughout UNGov...and encourage the people to stand for their own, to join us in defeating their masters and regaining their freedom.

I knew we would be outnumbered, and I realized very well what a gamble I was taking. Defeat meant almost certain destruction, and the continued rule of UNGov. And a battlefield success would only be a step toward total victory. But it was a step we had to take. It was all we had time for. To wait was only to allow UNGov to mobilize greater forces, to send more soldiers against us...tens of thousands, hundreds of thousands, millions...

It was a battle we needed, and one we were ready to fight.

And it was a holocaust beyond my worst imaginings. Over the eight days of sustained combat, I saw men dying by the thousands, veteran officers of ten years' service breaking down and sobbing, even my Erastus Supersoldiers pushed to the very brink of defeat and despair. My oldest comrades and I had always held that Erastus, the sunbaked hell where we were turned into combat veterans, was the truest test of man's endurance. Years later, I added the great battle at Kirov-Kazan to stand alongside Gehenna with that distinction.

And to me, the great struggle at Kirov-Kazan was something else. It was the place I lost another of my oldest companions, a friend who had served at my side since the beginning. And it was there, on that bloody field, amidst the images of hell itself unleashed, staring into the cold dead eyes of a friend, that, on the brink of victory I came closest to defeat, to dropping my weapons, pulling the stars from my collar, and walking off into the wilderness.

Taylor stood atop the rugged hillside, watching his soldiers march out of the mountain pass and onto the great plain below. The location of the Portal had been ideal to allow Taylor to complete the army's transit before they had faced any significant resistance, at least on the ground. But now they'd paid for that with a long march through an almost-uninhabited wilderness. He could not destroy UNGov sitting in the frozen wasteland… he had to take the war to them, to threaten vital population and production centers and force them to fight.

He'd considered moving south, invading the areas that had once been the Chinese Hegemony, but he'd rejected plan that in favor of a westward move. His forces would advance on Europe, toward the centers of world government, but also an area whose inhabitants had once enjoyed considerable personal freedom. If the people were going to rise up and come to his support, he knew it would begin in places that had a history of at least limited liberty, where living memory still recalled a better time. He knew he'd have enough trouble combating UNGov's lies and propaganda, and he wanted every advantage he could get.

That was all true, all part of the thought process that had led to his choice of action. But there was more to it. Taylor had decided to move not just into the old European democracies, but directly toward Geneva. He intended to take the UNGov capital, to end his war by cutting the head off the snake. The destruction of the Secretariat and the central government's headquarters would leave UNGov functionaries still in ruling positions throughout the world. But they would be detached, without the support structure that kept them in power. If Taylor could eliminate the masters, he was confident his people could mop up the lower levels.

The direction of his movement made that intention clear, as he'd intended, and that helped in another way. Fear of his army reaching the capital had compelled UNGov to make a stand sooner rather than later, to meet his forces in battle. Their maneuvers made it clear they had taken the bait. Taylor's aircraft and drones gave him excellent reconnaissance, perhaps not the same as UNGov got from their satellites, but sufficient none-theless, and there was no question about it. There was an army forming in front of his, positioned to block his advance. A big army.

Maybe too big.

He was impressed with the force UNGov had managed to assemble in such a short time. They were waiting, less than a hundred kilometers from his army, 250,000 strong, with more units arriving every day. He looked out at his own men as they continued to march past him. Their morale was excellent, their faith in him only stronger since they'd won the first victory in the air battles that raged over the Portal.

A victory I owe to Tegeri technology, not to any skill of my own.

He had promised to lead his soldiers back to Earth, and now they were there. Taylor knew the worst lay ahead of them all, but to the troops, the men who had followed him from world to world, it felt like they were close to victory. And he would let them believe that, as long as it lasted.

"They look good, don't they, Jake?" Bear Samuels stood next to his commander, the big man towering over Taylor's own, not inconsiderable, height. "How many times have we imagined this day?"

Taylor took a deep breath. "A long time, Bear, a long time. And they do look good. A little tired, perhaps, but otherwise as fit as any army that ever marched to battle, I'd venture."

He knew his people were fatigued. He'd force marched them hard, given them little rest. There had been no choice. He had to move quickly, get through the mountains before UNGov's army was able to advance and catch his people as they were emerging from the narrow passes. And now that they were so close to the massive enemy force, there was no choice, no time to stop. He'd have liked to rest his people before sending them into battle, but he knew it wasn't to be. He'd already given the order, the only order his troops needed. Attack.

"Have you seen the latest drone reports, Jake?" There was a slight hitch in Bear's otherwise confident tone.

"I saw them." Taylor paused, still staring out over the columns of troops. "We always knew we'd be outnumbered, Bear."

"I know, Jake. I know. They've just managed to get more troops together than I expected. I'm sure the boys will get the job done, even outnumbered so badly...but our losses are going to be bad."

Taylor sighed. He agreed completely. His soldiers would get the job done...but they would pay for it in blood.

"Yes, Bear. They're going to be bad."

*   *   *

"I want the 73rd and 74th divisions to move forward now!" Jinto Akawa stood in the battered building he'd chosen as his headquarters. It had been a Russian noble's house one day, he suspected, a lingering vestige of an age long ago, one that had survived world wars and the forced relocation of those who had lived around it. It was broken down more by age than the battle

Akawa's forces were fighting, though the UNGov commander knew that could change any time. The invaders had hit his forward positions hard, and his lead divisions had thrown down their weapons and run. For a while it had looked like nothing would stop Taylor's onslaught, that his entire army would be rolled up and destroyed. But Akawa had raced up to the weakest section of the front, bringing with him one of his strongest units, a group of MBTs he'd found in a UNGov storage facility...and held in reserve for just such a moment.

They were old American tanks, weapons from the last war between Earth's nations, great behemoths that had somehow been stored instead of scrapped after UNGov dissolved the world's military formations. Over one hundred of them had turned out to be functional with a minimal amount of repair, and when Akawa discovered their existence, he requisitioned them at once. He had shipped them to Moscow by train, hidden from surveillance by great tarps, and then he sent them forward to smash into the AOL's lines, stopping the advance cold and buying time for him to pour new divisions into the growing maelstrom.

"Yes, General. Both divisions confirm receipt of your orders. They will be on the move within the hour."

Akawa stared down at the large tablet on the table in front of him. He had every centimeter of the battlefield under satellite surveillance, but his lack of intel on enemy units reduced the effectiveness of his information. He knew all the soldiers he faced were veterans, at least by comparison to his own, mostly unblooded units. But there were considerable differences between Taylor's warriors. The rebel general had his Supersoldiers—veterans of at least ten years' experience, and surgically altered to be stronger, faster, more capable in every way...a force that Akawa viewed with unrestrained terror. Then he had the units from the other Portal worlds, some of those soldiers also seasoned with many years of service, but many relatively recent arrivals.

"I want a status report on the tank division, Lieutenant." Akawa's armor had been a surprise to the enemy. The armies on the Portal worlds had never seen such heavy weapons. It was almost impossible to disassemble an MBT and get it through a Portal. Even Taylor's veterans had proven they weren't immune to fear. They hadn't panicked, but they did fall back in a number of places...everywhere except where the Supersoldiers were positioned. Those grim veterans had held their ground, adjusted their tactics on the fly. They spread out in extended order, surrounded the great tanks, targeting the treads and the rear of the great war machines, where the armor was thinner. One by one they learned how to destroy the great war machines.

"Sir, General Komack has been killed. Colonel Chang is in command. He reports his forces are bogged down, surrounded by cyborg infiltration teams. The regular enemy units have regrouped, and they preparing to counter-attack."

Akawa slammed his fist down on the table. He wasn't one to broadcast his emotions, but he was angry, frustrated. If it hadn't been for the damned Supersoldiers, he might just have broken through the lines, and cut Taylor's army in two. But a few hundred of the cursed cyborgs had stood in the breech... and ground the tanks' attack to a halt. They had paid in blood, there was no doubt...Akawa suspected the Supersoldier units fighting the tanks had suffered losses of fifty percent. That was hundreds of Taylor's best soldiers. But the tanks they were destroying were also irreplaceable, the factories that built them demolished forty years before.

"Lieutenant...the 54th Division is to disengage and turn to the south. They are to advance toward the remnants of the tank division and attack the Supersoldier detachments." Akawa sighed.

That will give those damned cyborgs something to think about besides destroying my tanks...

"Yes, sir."

"And Lieutenant...notify my transport. I'm going back up there to take a closer look myself."

"Yes, General," the aide replied. But Akawa was already half-way through the door.

* * *

"Stay low, dammit. Those things have quad autocannons at the corners." Emmit Finn crouched down in the shell hole, watching as the massive tank halted about thirty meters from his position. He and his platoon had taken out three of the monsters, but he'd be damned if the fool rookie crews weren't learning how to handle those things. He'd started with forty-two men, Supersoldiers all. Now he was down to eighteen, and he'd taken more than half those casualties fighting the last tank.

"We've got a clear shot at the flank treads, Sarge." Emory had always been aggressive, but Finn knew the veteran corporal was letting his rage overrule his good sense.

"No, Corporal." The MBTs were tough even on the flanks. Emory could take a shot, but he had maybe a ten percent chance of disabling the tank with a single rocket from the side. It wasn't just the armor…it was accuracy too. The rocket launchers had been designed as AA weapons, and their hasty conversions to anti-tank use wasn't without its disadvantages. It wasn't hitting the giant tank, it was putting the rocket just where it needed to be.

"But, Sarge…"

"I said no, Emory. I don't need another KIA just because you're fired up to take pot shots. You're a ten year man, for fuck's sake. Act like it."

Finn shook his head. He was proud of his men…they still had a hell of a lot of fight left for an outfit that had suffered almost sixty percent casualties. And most of those were KIAs. He had four wounded, but even a Supersoldier didn't stand much chance when his body had been riddled with dozens of rounds from heavy autocannons.

Finn turned to the right, scoping out the terrain. He had to get his people behind that damned tank…but the thing was stopped, and that mean its crew was cautious, looking around. They'd seen a lot of their comrades taken by infiltration teams, and rookies or not, they were definitely learning. Finn didn't know the specs of the MBTs, as far as he knew, no one in the

AOL did. But he didn't want to underestimate its scanning suite. One wrong move, one careless step, and his whole position would be hosed down with automatic fire. He shuddered to think of how dangerous the tanks had been when they'd been manned fifty years before by trained and experienced crews.

He winced as he turned his head, his hand moving to his shoulder automatically. He'd caught a round himself in the last fight. It could have been worse...one of the autocannon rounds grazed the top of his arm, just under his exos. It tore a significant gash in his flesh, and it had bled badly for a few minutes. It hurt like hell too. But Emory had gotten a quick field dressing on it, and he could feel the familiar tingling feeling as his implants released nanobots into his bloodstream, the miniscule devices working steadily to speed blood clotting and repair the tissue damage. It wasn't a replacement for a trip to the field hospital, but a wounded Supersoldier was enormously better off than a normal trooper.

"Alright...Bern, Estaban...I want you guys to move around to the right. Find a good spot where you've got a shot at the thing from behind."

"Yes, Sergeant," came the replies, almost simultaneously.

"Richter, Santini...you guys too. I want you twenty meters behind Bern and Esteban. Get a clear line of sight and get ready. I'm going to want both teams to fire together, got it?"

"Yes, Sarge."

Finn had just started to turn back toward Emory when the tank opened fire, two of the quad weapons firing in his direction of his troops. He ducked down into the shell hole, his knees digging deeper into the waterlogged mud as he dropped down. He could hear the rounds firing over his head and impacting into the ground in front of the hole.

"Now," he said into the com unit. "Attack teams, around the back now...we'll hold its attention. Fire as soon as you're in position." He took a deep breath and pulled a grenade from his belt. He lurched to the side, away from where the stream of bullets had been. Then he climbed up the front face of the shell hole, peering cautiously as he threw the grenade, diving back down and splashing mud everywhere. A few seconds later, he heard the blast. He knew the grenade wouldn't damage the tank, not even if he'd managed to place it right inside the treads. But a second after the explosion, he realized it had done its job. The tanks guns were firing at his position again, hundreds of rounds slamming into the ground in front and zipping by overhead. The crew was fixated on his location. With any luck Bern and Richter and the others would make it into position.

"Alright, boys," he snapped into the com. "Let's buy the attack teams some cover. Hit that thing with anything you've got. Emory, you can take that shot now…"

"Yes, Sarge."

Finn could hear the predatory sound in the trooper's voice. People handled pain and loss differently, but it was clear it manifested Emory as a need for revenge. He was just about to tell the trooper to be careful when he heard the autocannons firing again. He looked just in time to see the private gunned down, the rocket from his launcher flying up and off to the side, meters wide of the target.

"Emory!" he called. No answer. "Private Emory!" Still nothing.

Finn sighed, angry with himself for not realizing Emory had been too worked up, too angry at the loss of his comrades. He'd thrown his life away. For nothing.

His head snapped around at the sound of a rocket…then another. He saw the fiery trails, and his eye caught the impact… both shots slamming into the rear of the great tank. There were two explosions, and the autocannon fire ceased immediately. Then, a few second later, another blast, louder, greater.

Finn crouched down again as flaming debris came raining down all around him. He flinched as he heard a loud clank. A chunk of hot metal had hit his right exo, bouncing off and dropping into the water at the bottom of the shellhole with a hiss of steam.

He stayed low for a few seconds, and then he straightened up and looked at the tank…or what was left of it. It looked like the two teams had put their rockets almost exactly in the same spot. The first had blown a gash in the armor, and the second had gone right through it, detonating inside…utterly destroying the massive war machine.

He felt a rush of excitement as his two crews came running toward him. Another of the enemy's superweapons gone, good cause for celebration. But his elation didn't last long. His gaze moved to his left, and he climbed out of the shell hole, jogging toward Emory. He knew the hothead private was dead, but he needed to check, to be sure.

He walked over and felt a coldness in his stomach. Emory was indeed dead, almost cut in half by the tank's heavy auto-cannons. And two of his other men were there too, lying in the same ditch. One was in even worse shape than Emory, his body literally torn to pieces by the fire. The other was still alive, though grievously wounded.

He jumped into the ditch and ran to the wounded man. "Higgins," he said, his voice as soothing as he could make it."

The soldier lay almost still, looking up at the sky. Finn could see his head begin to move, slowly, painfully toward him. "Sarge…" The voice was soft, weak. Finn knew it was Higgins' last bit of strength.

"Just stay still, Higgins…we'll get you to the aid station," he lied.

"No, Sarge…" The soldier coughed, gasped for breath. "…I'm done, Sarge." Another pause. "We get it?"

"Yeah, Higgins," Finn said, forcing back the emotion. "We got it."

Higgins' head bobbed slightly, his best attempt at a nod. Then he said, "Good." And instant later he took a deep, rasping breath. Then he fell silent.

Finn looked up, struggling to stay focused, to push away the sadness. He turned, and he saw the two fire teams standing on the edge of the ditch, looking silently at their slain comrades.

"Three good men," Finn said as he rose to his feet. "For one of these monsters." He frowned, and deep down he knew it wasn't a good trade, not the kind of exchange he wanted to make. But he also knew there would be more of them if the

AOL was to win this fight.

"Let's go, boys. There'll be time to mourn later. Right now, we've got a battle to win. And it's up to us whether these men died in vain, for nothing…or if they gave their lives to free mankind."

* * *

"We've got the tanks stopped, Jake. It cost, but the boys figured out how to take the things out. Only a third of them are still active, and they've all halted or started to pull back." Bear's voice was a mix of his usual southern drawl, and the tense edginess it took on in battle. "It cost though," he repeated, his words more subdued as he did.

"How bad?" Taylor was looking at the display, but after a few seconds of silence he turned toward his friend. "C'mon, Bear… how bad? You think I'm not going to find out?"

"Looks like close to two thousand, Jake. Maybe a hundred wounded, but the rest are KIAs. Those things are packed with heavy autocannons." He paused. "At least five hundred of those are Erastus boys."

Taylor took a deep breath and sighed. Another five hundred of his oldest veterans…gone. "There were ten thousand of us once, Bear. You remember that?" Taylor shook his head. "What are we now? Down below three thousand?"

Bear knew his friend didn't really want an answer, but he gave him one anyway. "About twenty-nine fifty still in the field, another two hundred in the field hospitals…but that's just a guess." It was far more than a guess. The enhanced warriors had transponders implanted in their bodies, tiny devices that sent out an encrypted signal…at least until the host was dead. It was possible there were a few troopers out there with damaged transmitters, but Bear knew they'd be lucky if that was four or five. The rest of the men whose signals had vanished were dead.

"We've got to push through in the center, Bear…where the tanks hit us. They're probably weakest there, hoping their secret weapon would get the job done." He paused looking over to the far wall. "Karl, I want you to get up there. Take General Ralfieri and his people with you."

"Yes, Jake. I'm on it."

"Push hard, Karl...we need to break through. Finish off whatever tanks they have left and then rip through whatever they've got behind that. They wanted to split our force in half... so let's return the compliment."

"We'll see it done, Jake." Young snapped off a salute to his old friend and commander. Then he turned and hurried out of the headquarters.

Taylor sighed softly. Hank Daniels was already out on the left flank, trying to get around the city of Kazan and into the enemy's rear areas. And now Karl Young was heading into the hottest part of the battlefield. Taylor hated ordering his friends into battle. It had been different when they shared the dangers together...but now it was by his order they marched off, possibly for the last time.

Of all the pressures of command, it was the one that most affected him...and he had to constantly fight the hesitation, usually accompanied by visions of Tony Black going on the mission that ultimately killed him. The mission Jake Taylor had sent him on.

He wondered how he would deal with more loss...for war was still war, and he knew more good men would die before it was over.

*   *   *

"Alright, I want everybody focused one hundred percent. Our guys on the ground are getting slaughtered. The enemy is feeding in reserve units as quickly as we break their frontline forces. We've got to take out some of these troop trains and get them a break." Colonel MacArthur's eyes were fixed on the display, watching the input from over a hundred drones. The reconnaissance devices were about a hundred klicks ahead of his birds, racing down the rail lines leading to Moscow. His squadrons were taking a huge risk moving this far behind enemy lines. The UNGov air wings had been hit hard in the battle at the Portal, but they still had gunships left…and forces that were inadequate to launch another major offensive were far more dangerous on the defensive, operating from their own bases against enemy squadrons far from their own support. Combined with the UNGov ground defenses, he'd known his people would take losses—and they had, significant losses—but he'd still argued with Taylor, urging the general to approve his plan. UNGov just had too much ability to pour forces into the raging battle, and MacArthur knew victory might depend on interdicting the enemy's convoys of supplies and fresh troops.

After he'd gotten Taylor to approve the strike, he'd had another go around with his commander. He wanted to lead the strike himself. Taylor had started shaking his head even before MacArthur had finished speaking, but in the end the AOL's top general had given in. Jake Taylor understood why MacArthur felt he had to be with his air crews, and in the end, he'd hadn't had it in him to force the colonel to stay behind.

The thirty airships that had taken off on the raid were down to twenty-six, and another ten had peeled off from the formation to engage the UNGov flyers and hold them back. That left sixteen as hunters, each of them following a cloud of drones, looking for troop trains and convoys of transports en route to the front lines.

"All squadrons," MacArthur said into his comlink, "break off. Pursue targets at will. And keep an eye out for AA." He turned toward his pilot. "We've got a contact roughly thirty klicks south, southwest of here. Looks like a troop train. A big one. Let's take it the hell out."

"I've got it on my display, sir." The pilot's voice was tight, tense. "On the way."

MacArthur felt the force as the airship banked hard, heading directly for the designated coordinates. The ship pitched hard to the side—evasive maneuvers against SAMS, he knew—and then the pilot hit the thruster hard.

"We'll be in range in fifty seconds, sir."

MacArthur turned toward the lead gunner. "Prepare ground

attack missiles, Lieutenant. Lock on to target."

A few seconds later: "Missiles armed and locked, sir. Ready to fire on your command."

MacArthur took a deep breath. He stared at the updated scans of the train. It was a kilometer long, at least, and he figured it was carrying three or four thousand troops.

Three or four thousand who aren't going to make it up there to attack our people…

His eyes glanced down to the range on his display. "Ten seconds, Sergeant," he said calmly.

He watched the chronometer click down. Eight…seven…six…

A loud tone screeched from the ship's alarm. MacArthur knew what it meant. All his people did.

"Ground batteries, sir. Dead ahead."

"Stay on target," he snapped.

Just a few more seconds…

He could feel the tension in the ship…he knew he was playing with fire. The ground batteries had been hidden, his scanners hadn't picked them up until they were close.

Close.

"They're firing, sir…"

"Stay on target…"

Three…two…one…

"Launch missiles!" he snapped. An instant later, "Evasive maneuvers!"

He felt the small bumps as the two weapons released from the airship's hardpoints and blasted toward their target. Perhaps a second later he felt the gee forces as the pilot put the ship into a sharp dive, then swung first to the port and then sharply to the starboard, desperately trying to escape from the four missiles chasing the airship.

MacArthur stared down at his screen, his eyes moving back and forth between the tracking plot of his own missiles and the position of the enemy's pursuing the airship. An instant later, his missiles vanished from the plot, first one, and then the other. He read the data coming in, and the video feed from one of the drones that caught the entire thing.

The first missile hit the train in the middle, severing it in half, sending the rear cars off the track, rolling down a steep hillside, trailing a massive fireball. The forward section barreled ahead for another second, and then the second missile slammed directly into the locomotive, blowing it and the first three cars to bits, and sending the rest of the train down the hill, cars careening wildly.

He felt a rush, a wave of satisfaction.

There's a few thousand troops who won't be shooting at our men. Now all we have to do it get out of…

He heard the change in the tone first, the screech deepening in pitch, becoming louder. Then a second later the airship shook hard. A shower of sparks flew across the cockpit from one of the workstations, and he got a sickening feeling in his stomach as the ship began to fall.

"One of the missiles clipped us, Colonel," the pilot snapped. "Bad spot…knocked out the engines…I'm trying to restart now…" The barely disguised panic in the officer's voice didn't suggest he had much hope that would work. A few seconds later: "Nothing, sir. We're going down…"

MacArthur watched the pilot struggling at his controls, trying to direct the ship the best he could, to bring it down for as gentle a crash landing as possible. He could feel the rapid deceleration, and he didn't have to check the display to know they were about to hit ground. He gripped the armrests of his chair tightly and braced for impact.

*   *   *

Klein peered out from behind the tree. He could see the army's makeshift headquarters just down the hillside. It was sparse, perhaps two dozen small shelter units, with a field hospital right next to it. He'd checked out a dozen spots before he'd selected this one. It offered the best vantage point.

Taylor had gone back out to the front a few hours before, but Klein knew he'd be back soon. As much as the general would prefer to stay with his troops in the line, he had a three hundred kilometer front to worry about…and HQ was the only place he could do that effectively.

And when he comes back, I will finish this. I will strike the blow that ends the war.

He reached down and picked up the long rifle he'd lain against the tree. It hadn't been easy to find, indeed he hadn't set out to find it. But when he'd stumbled on the dead sniper in the hills, an idea began to form. All his thoughts had been of killing Taylor at close range, where he would have at best a second or two before the enhanced warrior reacted…and almost certainly killed him. No, that had been foolish. This was sniper's work. And Mitchell Klein was marksman rated.

The rifle was solid, longer and heavier than a normal assault rifle. It was an AI-assisted model. Klein would do the aiming, but the gun itself would adjust for wind and range. If he managed to get the target in the sights, the rifle would hit. And the heavy, exploding rounds were designed to deliver kill shots.

He reached down and grabbed the small bag of cartridges. Each one held ten shots, but Klein knew he only needed one. He had to make one count. The second Taylor went down— or even when a shot missed him—the soldiers all around him would go crazy. They would panic, rush to their stricken commander's side. And when they saw he was dead they would lose their minds. They would fan out, death in their minds and hearts. They would tear apart every shelter, explore every centimeter within range of the headquarters. And if they caught him, if they realized he had killed Taylor, or even attempted to kill him, they would literally tear him into bloody chunks.

No, he couldn't be caught on the hill or with the rifle. He had to be gone the instant the shot was fired. He had to loop around the woods, come back from a different direction and mix in among the others, feign his own rage and pain. And then, while the soldiers of headquarters were seeking Taylor's killer, Klein would slip away. He would head south, away from the battle. He would steal civilian clothes, blend in, make his way to Geneva. And he would collect his due, the reward for the man who killed

Jake Taylor. Who ended the war with one terrible shot.

*   *   *

"It's a victory, Jake...a clear victory." Bear Samuels' voice betrayed his exhaustion, his usually cheerful tone a dull rasp. But there was excitement there too. The battle had raged for a week, but the AOL had broken through in two places. The enemy commander had done everything possible, shifted his forces, plugged every gap, exhorted his rookie soldiers to stand in the line when they looked about to run. Taylor didn't know who was in command of the UNGov army, but he hadn't expected to encounter such a skilled officer.

The transport was almost back to HQ, and it bounced around on the pitted temporary roads Taylor's soldiers had carved out of the semi-wilderness. Taylor leaned back against the inner wall on one side, facing his friend whose long legs took up most of the space between them.

"A costly victory, Bear. Worse than I'd even imagined." That wasn't entirely true. Taylor had let himself envision some truly ghastly losses...though he'd hoped his people might escape the worst. Now he knew they hadn't. "Twenty-three thousand, Bear. A third of the army. Almost half those engaged in the battle. Ten thousand of them dead."

And more would die, he knew. The field hospitals were overflowing with wounded. The Supersoldiers' nanos could buy them time if they were badly wounded, but the regular troops would die in droves, lying on the ground outside the overwhelmed aid stations. The AOL didn't have a large support staff, and certainly not enough surgeons to handle a battle like the one the army had just fought. Taylor was planning to run to the main HQ building for a quick update...then, if everything was under control, he intended to visit the hospitals. He shuddered to think of what he would see, of the horrors that awaited him there. But his soldiers deserved to see him there, and that was the last word.

"Their army is crushed, Jake. At least a hundred thousand dead and wounded. And another hundred thousand prisoners.

The rest are in total rout. I doubt their commander could put twenty thousand in the field in any order. The road into Europe is open." Taylor knew Bear was trying to cheer him up...and he knew the big man hurt just as much for the losses the army had suffered.

"We will see, Bear. They can replace troops, we can't." Taylor leaned over and hit the button, opening the hatch of the transport. "We owe a debt of gratitude to MacArthur and his airship crews..." Taylor's voice trailed off, and he paused for a few seconds. MacArthur was still missing. His bird had crashed two days before, and he hadn't managed to contact HQ since then. That didn't mean he was definitely dead, but it wasn't a good sign...

"You're right, Jake. Best guess, he kept thirty thousand reserves from reaching the field...and a shitload of supplies." Bear spoke softly as he followed Taylor out of the transport, a touch of sadness slipping through despite his obvious efforts. "But he and his crew could have survived. The Dragonfires are durable ships...a crash doesn't mean he's dead."

Taylor just nodded. He didn't know if Bear believed that at all, but his friend had done a decent job of sounding at least a little hopeful.

"I hope so, Bear...I hope so."

*   *   *

Klein had watched the column of vehicles moved into the camp. His eyes locked on the armored transport he knew carried the army's commander-in-chief. His stomach was knotted, and he struggled to breathe normally, fighting the hyperventilation that threatened to overtake him. He was scared, scared shitless. But he knew this was his chance. Perhaps the only one he would get.

He watched as a man climbed out of the command transport, followed a few seconds later by a virtual giant. Klein had been pretty sure the first had been Taylor, but when he saw Bear Samuels, he was certain.

He held the rifle tightly in his hands, staring out at the two men standing in the open as the vehicles moved away. There were at least a dozen other officers and soldiers milling around, moving to Taylor and speaking with the general for a few seconds before continuing on their way. They blocked Klein's line of sight for a few seconds. Then they moved along, giving him an unobstructed view of Taylor.

Now, he thought. Get a grip…focus.

He took a deep breath, completely filling his lungs. He held it for a few seconds and exhaled. Then he did it again.

His hands moved along the rifle, pulling back the small lever to chamber the first round. He punched the tiny red button next to the trigger. The weapon's AI was now on. Klein knew the tiny computer would activate the row of sensors attached to the gun's barrel, reading the wind gusts, humidity…anything that could affect the shot.

Klein stared out, trying to estimate the range. The rifle could have given him an exact figure, but he couldn't risk using the laser rangefinder. It was unobtrusive, but those were Supersoldiers down there, and he wasn't about to gamble on what their enhanced eyes could see.

He brought the rifle up, pointing it down toward his target. He moved his head around, working the rifle into a comfortable place on his shoulder. He leaned against it, bringing his eye down and looking through the sights.

He had a much better view of Taylor through the rifle's scope. The AOL's legendary commander looked shockingly normal as he stood in the quad, speaking to Samuels and two other officers. Taylor was a living legend, but Klein reminded himself he was just a man, that he could be killed as easily as any other.

He adjusted the sights, and then he moved a few millimeters to the right, his eye focused as the crosshairs slipped over Taylor's head.

Klein took one last breath and held it. Then his finger tensed slowly, steadily on the trigger…

*   *   *

"Bear, I think we can get around their flank and bag another twenty-thousand prisoners before they can pull back. I want you to get a message to Hank as soon as..." He turned as his eyes caught sight of one of his aides rushing over.

"General Taylor...I have terrible news. General Ralfieri was hit, sir...just as the Juno forces were pushing through." The aide paused, and it looked like he struggled for a moment to maintain Taylor's gaze. "He's dead, sir."

Taylor paused, just staring at the lieutenant. Finally, he croaked, "Very well, Lieutenant. That will be all." He turned and looked back at Bear. "Ralfieri too..."

Antonio Ralfieri had been Taylor's enemy once, the commander of Force Juno during the desperate struggle on that cursed world. But he'd discovered the truth, as Taylor and his people had years before, and when he did he called an immediate halt to all fighting...in courageous defiance of the UN Inquisitor sent to keep an eye on him. Taylor and Bear had come to accept Ralfieri, despite the losses their people had incurred fighting Force Juno. They understood being lied to, committing terrible acts you believed to be in the right. Jake Taylor was a lot of things, but a hypocrite wasn't one of them. Taylor had taken Ralfieri into his inner circle, just as his soldiers had accepted their comrades from Force Juno. And now he was gone, another friend lost.

"He was a good man." Bear looked down at the ground, moving his foot absent-mindedly through the loose dirt. He paused a few seconds then he said, "Anyway...where do you want Hank..." Bear's head was moving up, his gaze lifting from the ground to look at Taylor. But he paused, froze as he caught a glimpse, a small flash. A reflection?

His response was immediate, his own crack battlefield instincts amplified by his neural implants. He felt the odd but familiar feeling of his artificial eyes changing magnification... and in an instant he saw. A man, crouched partially behind a tree...some kind of rifle in his hand.

Sniper!

He reacted instantly, on pure instinct. He hadn't even had time for a conscious thought, a realization that this was an assassination attempt. His body was already in motion, his huge arms thrusting out, pushing Taylor hard as he leapt in front of his friend.

Bear's eyes snapped around, in time to see the surprise on Taylor's face. "Bear, what the…"

He heard his friend's words, but then his head snapped forward hard. He didn't feel any pain, not really. But when he gasped for air, his mouth filled with blood. He could feel the tingling in his body, the nanos releasing into his bloodstream. They were a potent medical tool, and they had saved thousands of Supersoldiers. But Bear Samuels knew in that instant they weren't going to be enough this time.

His eyes locked for an instant on Taylor's, and he tried to speak, but there was nothing…nothing but a loud gurgling sound and a sheet of blood pouring out of his mouth. He saw the shock on his friend's face, Taylor's mouth moving. But he couldn't hear anything. He felt himself falling, Taylor's arms on him, trying to hold him up.

Then the blackness took him.

* * *

"Bear!" Taylor screamed, tightening his arms, trying to hold the giant man up. "Bear…" His voice trailed off to a miserable whine as realization set in.

He stepped back, lowering Bear gently to the ground, and his eyes went right to the wound. It was grievous—the bullet had entered the back of his friend's neck. It was some kind of explosive round, and there was almost nothing left of Samuels' throat. There was blood everywhere, pumping from the wound, from Bear's mouth. "Medic!" he screamed, but he already knew the wound was mortal.

Taylor felt a wave of despair. "No, Bear…no…not again…" He remembered the terrible feeling of listening to Tony Black die, and now he was crouched down over yet another brother, watching his life force slip away. Bear Samuels had always been larger than life, a man who had managed to maintain his cheerful disposition through whatever hell he'd been forced to walk through. But now he was silent, even the choking attempts to draw breath had ceased. Taylor knew. Bear was dead.

A column of troops had come running over, and they surrounded him, shielding him with their bodies. The officer in charge leaned down. "General, are you hurt, sir?"

Taylor ignored the question, the fear in the man's voice. "Captain," he screamed at the officer, a wave of elemental rage pushing back the horror for a few seconds. "I want that sniper caught. No matter what the cost."

"Sir, we can't leave you…"

"Now," Taylor roared, as if defying anyone to refuse his command. "All of you…go!" He leapt to his feet, and waved his arms. "I'll shoot any man who disobeys." He reached down and pulled out his pistol.

The troops that had surrounded him paused for an instant, hesitant to leave their commander undefended. But none could stand up to Taylor's words, and they pulled away, running toward the hill with their weapons drawn.

Taylor just stood watching. Then his eyes dropped to the motionless body of his friend…and the despair again took control.

Chapter 19

Communiqué from Captain Rod Charles:

Attention all AOL personnel...attention all AOL personnel... this is Captain Rod Charles. If you are receiving this message I request that you abandon your attempts to find your homes and return to your airships. My team has joined forces with a Resistance group in New York City, and we have eliminated most UNGov troops in the city. I urge you to come to New York as quickly as possible, to assist us in maintaining control and defeating any remaining UNGov forces. The Resistance here is able to contact other rebel groups, helping us spread the word much faster than we can do on our own, so it is essential that we are able to hold. Attention all AOL personnel...

Wickes watched as the group from the airship spread out, moving in pairs in different directions. He stayed where he was as two of them walked toward him, weapons drawn. He resisted the urge to turn and run, reminding himself he was a Marine when he felt the fear taking hold of him.

"Don't move. Stay where you are."

He heard the words, stern and demanding, though without anger. In the gloomy darkness of the waterfront he couldn't make out which of the men approaching him was speaking. He just stood where he was, taking care not to move his arms, not to do anything that might appear hostile.

The men were closer now, and he could see it was the one

on the left speaking. They wore some kind of uniforms, vaguely familiar, but definitely not the garb of uniformed UNGov security.

"I have to thank you guys," Wickes said, speaking clearly, his voice steady despite his fear.

"Who are you? What are you doing here? Why was UNGov security attacking you?"

Wickes took a breath. The Marine in him was wary, cautious about supplying information to someone who could yet turn out to be an enemy. But these people had almost certainly saved his life, and while they had mercilessly attacked the UNGov troops, they hadn't touched his people. He figured they deserved an answer.

"I—we—are from the Resistance. There are a couple dozen of my people on this wharf." He paused for an instant, feeling a twinge when he spoke of his people, but he reassured himself with the thought that if these soldiers were some kind of UNGov force, they already knew he was a rebel. Besides, it looked like the others from the gunship were already rounding up the rest of the cell, most of it at least.

"We launched an attack on UNGov facilities in New York tonight. We were trying to get away, but the security forces pinned us down on the waterfront."

"That would explain the fires we saw, Captain." The soldier on the right had turned toward the other one.

"Yes, Sergeant, it would. And if these people really are some kind of resistance organization, we need to talk to their leader as soon as possible."

Wickes listened as two men conversed. They spoke softly, but he could still make out what they were saying. His mind raced. Who were they? Who would have an airship? It didn't sound like they even knew about the Resistance.

The forces that came through the Portal? It must be... but these don't seem like men who murdered 20,000 of their comrades.

Wickes had been suspect of Samovich's speech for the simple reason that he rarely believed anything a representative of

UNGov had to say. But he'd had no idea what the truth was. Now, his mind began to race.

Are these men enemies of UNGov? Almost certainly. Our allies? Perhaps...

The man on the left took a few steps forward, stopping about two meters from Wickes. "We would like to speak with the commander of your resistance movement. If you are opposed to UNGov, we may have much to discuss. Can you take us to him?"

Wickes hesitated, only for an instant. Then he decided to follow his gut instincts. "I think I can manage that, Mr....?"

"Captain Rod Charles, Army of Liberation."

Wickes nodded slowly. "And I am Captain Stan Wickes, USMC, retired. The acting commander of the New York Resistance."

* * *

"The situation in New York is unacceptable!" Samovich slammed his fist down on the table. His eyes glittered with unfocused anger. "I'd order every officer there executed...if the Resistance hadn't killed them all already. How did a group of rebels manage to destroy every UNGov facility in the city...and then kill over fifty security troops sent after them?"

"Sir..." The aide was clearly terrified. In forty years of UNGov rule, no resistance fighters had ever struck with the effectiveness of the New York group. Samovich was already frazzled over the war raging in Russia, and any kind of reaction was possible. That included some very unpleasant options.

Samovich stomped across the room, moving over to the massive wall display. The aide looked cautiously, trying to get a glimpse without drawing any unnecessary attention to himself. There were arrows on the map, right around Moscow, perhaps a dozen. Half of them pointed away from the city, to the west and south...and the others were right behind them, aimed in the same directions.

Defeat. The rumors were true. UNGov's army had suffered a terrible reverse...and it was now in full retreat. He knew

Samovich wouldn't have taken the news from North America well in any case, but now…

"I want them dead, Major Shroeder. Do you understand me? Dead." He turned back from the map. "I will allocate ten squads of security troops…and enough transports to get them to New York." There was something about Samovich's tone, something different than the usual disciplined politician's voice. Something not entirely sane.

Shroeder looked back at Samovich, struggling to hide the tension rising inside him from showing on his expression. He knew what was coming, but all he could do was stand there and listen with growing horror.

"You will command them, Major…and you will see to it there are no further failures. Is that understood?" Samovich's words were a naked threat.

Shroeder opened his mouth. A dozen replies raced through his mind. He could explain he wasn't a combat officer, that he'd been posted to UNGov headquarters his entire career. He could suggest Samovich send someone else. He could beg the Secretary-General to find another officer. But as scared as he was to go, he was more terrified of challenging Samovich, especially now, when the usually ruthless head of UNGov was barely hanging on. One word from the Samovich, and the guards would put a bullet in his head.

"Y-yes, Secretary-General. I will prepare to leave at once."

"Do that."

Samovich turned back to the display, his eyes fixed on the arrows showing the retreat of the remnants of UNGov's army.

Shroeder turned and moved toward the door, anxious to get away, to be anywhere but standing next to the rapidly unraveling despot who ruled the world.

"Shroeder!"

"Yes, sir?" The major stopped, eyes longingly focused on the door just a few meters away.

"I am counting on you, Major." There was a darkness in the words that chilled Shroeder to his core. "Do not fail me. Do not fail me as so many others have…"

*   *   *

Wickes sat quietly, listening with rapt attention as Rod Charles spoke. The story the soldier was telling them was incredible, almost unfathomable. But the old Marine believed every word of it.

His thoughts raced. For four decades he had detested UNGov, hated the self-appointed rulers of the world. He despised them for killing freedom, for the billions who lived in squalor, for the vast numbers who disappeared in the night, never to return. But now he realized things were even worse than he'd dared to believe.

"Are you saying we fought the Tegeri for forty years for no reason? That they were never a threat?" Carson Jones had remained silent for a long time, but now he couldn't hold it back any longer. "That all of this was a fraud. That mankind threw away its freedom over a fucking lie...and sent thousands of its soldiers to die for nothing?"

Charles nodded grimly. "Yes...I'm afraid that is what I'm saying. And my brethren were not only forced to go to war— we killed thousands of the Machines, all the while feeding on a false moral superiority. We saw ourselves as the defenders of our world, when in reality we were just murderers, unwitting tools in a terrible fraud." He paused for an instant, continuing with his voice halting, emotional. "I killed dozens of Machines. I fired at them while they were retreating. I shot them dead in front of me. And now I know they weren't the monsters I thought they were. I was the monster. Even our name for them is misleading. They were living beings...they lived and died just as we do."

Wickes looked at the AOL captain, his sympathy clear in his eyes. He was a warrior too, and he related to Charles in a way the others couldn't. Stan Wickes had suffered in his life...wounds, deprivation, harassment from UNGov. But when he'd gone to war, he'd known the reasons. He'd followed his nation's flag, fought to preserve what little freedom had remained on Earth. He suspected his view was romanticized a bit, that the government that had sent him across the world into battle had been corrupt and deceitful as well. But nothing like the monstrous abomination that replaced it.

He tried to imagine how it would feel to find that nothing he believed was true, that all he'd fought for was a lie. That his motivations had been all wrong, that those he battled against had been in the right, and he and his comrades the aggressors. The murderers.

He looked at his Resistance comrades. "This is all shocking, I know…all that Captain Charles has told us." he said softly. "No less to me than to any of you." He paused. "But, I ask you, should it be? What did you think of UNGov yesterday? Of their totalitarianism, of the luxury they enjoy while people die in the streets, or in the death camps? Would you have imagined them incapable of something like this?" He stopped and looked around the room, glancing briefly toward Charles before turning back to his own people.

"What troubles me the most is my own gullibility. It is easy to condemn those who ran into UNGov's embrace four decades ago, who gave away their freedom, who reacted with fear of the bloodthirsty aliens they were told about with shockingly little evidence. Yet, I have detested our political masters for all that time, plotted and planned in the darkness, seeking to overthrow them. I reckoned myself wiser, stronger, more dedicated to liberty. Yet never have I questioned the essential beliefs about the war. Not once did it occur to me that the Tegeri had come to us in friendship and not as enemies."

"But that is what happened," Charles said softly, getting up and walking toward Wickes as he did. "And that is why we are here. That is why I have followed General Taylor across half a dozen Portals and back to Earth. We are here to right this wrong. To destroy UNGov." Charles paused for a moment, looking around the room at the rebels. Finally, his gaze settled on Wickes. "My team is in New York because we all lived here before we were drafted. In the city, and in the communities surrounding it. UNGov has perpetrated a monstrous lie, told the world that we murdered our comrades, slaughtered thousands of fellow soldiers. Our forces have been attacked by enraged civilians, and everywhere on Earth people have been told we are monsters, no less than the Tegeri themselves."

Charles voice was becoming louder, his anger clearer with every word. "We have come to free Earth, but UNGov's lies have made us hated, despised...they have branded us traitors to our own species. Those lies cannot be allowed to stand. We must find our old friends, our families. We are here to convince them we are not the murderers the government has branded us, and to begin to combat this terrible fraud, one person at a time if need be. It may be slow, it may take years...but the truth must be known." He looked right at Wickes. "Will you help us?"

Wickes stood up, a smile creeping onto his face. He looked around the room, and as he turned toward each of his comrades they nodded and the same grin came over their faces. Then he took a step forward and put his hand on Charles' shoulder. "Yes, Captain Charles," he said. "We will help you." He paused, looking back toward the others. "And I think I have an idea how to do a damned sight better than one person at a time."

Chapter 20

From the Office of the Secretary-General:

By ORDER of Anton Samovich, Secretary-General, UNGov, General Jinto Akawa is hereby removed from command of UN-Gov forces and stripped of all military rank. Ex-General Akawa is to be arrested immediately and delivered to Inquisitor Command in Geneva for interrogation and subsequent disposition for high treason.

MacArthur leaned against the tree, trying to catch his breath. His leg wasn't just broken. It was crushed. He'd been trying to brace it however he could with sticks and strips of cloth from his uniform, but all he'd managed to accomplish so far was tying twigs to his mangled leg.

The crash had been a hard one. The crew had all died on impact, all except for Falk and himself. But the junior gunner didn't last more than a couple hours before trauma and blood loss killed him. Now, MacArthur was alone.

He reached down to the sack at his side, pulling out one of the small injectors. He hadn't managed to take much with him from wreck, just the medkit, a pistol with two reloads, a survival knife, and a sustenance pack. That meant he had six shots each of painkiller and antibiotic cocktail, three days' rations, and two liters of water...and a gun with thirty shots. That was all he had to make it back at least forty klicks through enemy-held territory. That assumed he managed to rig something around his leg that allowed him to walk, or at least hobble around. And that wasn't looking very likely right now.

He jabbed the injector into his thigh, closing his eyes and sighing as the painkiller spread through his bloodstream. It didn't kill the pain, not by a longshot, but it did dull it to the point where it was bearable. He knew he should be going slower with the shots. He only had a few more, and he could already feel the semi-overdose dulling his senses. But the pain was unbearable otherwise.

He didn't know what he would do when the shots ran out. Even if he managed to create a workable splint, he couldn't imagine trying to walk without the painkillers. The slightest movement of his leg caused him agony, and that was just lying against the tree.

His eyes dropped down to the pistol on the ground next to him. He hadn't completely given up hope about getting back, but if he got there, he knew it was an option. He wanted to survive, to return to his comrades. But if the choice was hopeless agony—or capture by UNGov—he knew what he would do.

Okay, he thought. Two doses of painkiller in me...if I can't do this now, I'll never be able to...

He grabbed a fallen branch from the tree and started breaking it into sections of equal length. Then he laid them off to his side and took a deep breath.

He pulled himself back, sitting up straighter against the tree, trying to hold in the yell of pain the best he could. He paused, eyes closed, breathing hard. The pain was bad, even with the drugs. He knew he had to stabilize his leg somehow...if he was going to have any chance of going anywhere.

He leaned forward and put two of the sticks against his leg, gritting his teeth against the pain as he grabbed a strip of cloth and slipped it around. Then he stopped, waiting for the agony to die down before he grabbed another two sticks and repeated the effort.

* * *

Akawa stood alongside the battered, shell-marked road, watching his troops move by.

What's left of them, he thought miserably. He'd always been a very controlled person, able to hide his emotions carefully. But now his rage threatened to burst out. He'd accepted the top command, and he'd developed a plan he still believed could have worked. But then he'd been overridden by his political master, forced to fight before he was ready.

He'd intended to fall back slowly, while detaching as many divisions as he could spare to the flanks of the enemy's line of advance. Even with incompetents like General Carp in command, eventually numbers would have told. He didn't kid himself that he'd have been able to capture the Portal or completely cut Taylor's army off…but he was sure he could have compelled the rebel leader to abandon his advance and fall back to secure his communications. And that would have been the beginning of the end.

He'd tried to explain that to the Secretary-General, but Samovich hadn't listened. All he could see was Taylor and his veterans heading straight for him…and he'd demanded a decisive battle to destroy the invaders immediately. Akawa had argued, as much as one dared with a terrified dictator, but in the end he'd given in. He'd done his best—and for a few days it looked like his people might just manage it—but when the end came, it came quickly.

Taylor's people managed to get around the flanks, despite how thinly spread they were on the enormous front, and Akawa's army collapsed, its rookie units throwing down their arms en masse or surrendering to the advancing enemy. In a matter of hours his forces still in the field had shrunken to fewer than fifty thousand, and the victorious and vengeful soldiers of the AOL were moving relentlessly forward.

How does he inspire his soldiers so? How does he get them to make such superhuman efforts? To sacrifice themselves the way they do?

Akawa had seen too many instances of heroism by Taylor's soldiers to explain in any other way…his men were true believers. And they weren't the traitors and murderers UNGov had branded them as. Akawa had never been a believer of UN propaganda, but now he began to wonder at the depth of the government's dishonesty. Despite his measured cynicism, Akawa had long been a creature of duty, but now he wondered...do Taylor and his people have a legitimate grievance? Are they traitors? Or is their rebellion justified?

He shook his head. None of that mattered now. He only had one duty...and that was to see to his soldiers, do all he could for them in however much time he had left. The Inquisitors were on the way, almost certainly. He had no actual indication that they were coming, but he knew enough about UNGov to be sure he wouldn't. He had failed...failed spectacularly, and he knew he had almost no hope of stopping the enemy before they reached Geneva. Anton Samovich was not a forgiving man under the best of circumstances...and now he was scared, probably on the verge of panic.

It is strange, he thought...staring at one's imminent death. Not like a soldier on the field, in the heat of combat, but just waiting, working, knowing that later today, tomorrow, the next day, men would come and kill him.

If I'm lucky.

There were many ways to die, and Akawa had no desire to experience the worst the UNGov Inquisitor Corps could manage. The thought of suicide passed through his mind. Quick, painless. Indeed, it was almost certainly what one of his ancient ancestors would have done. Though he had to acknowledge it was fear of torture rather than some version of modern samurai honor that drove the thought for him.

Or I could just leave, walk off and not return. I could head toward Taylor's army. At least I might discover the truth...

"No," he said softly to himself. He looked again at the soldiers still in the steadily moving column. They had fought a terrible battle, one they'd been ill-prepared to handle. They had followed his orders, fought hard, and now they clung to the colors, these few good men, despite the disintegration of the rest of the army.

How can I leave them, repay their steadfastness with abandonment?

He knew their reward would be bitter, most likely death in some hopeless stand before Geneva. But he owed them to stay with them, to do whatever he could to save even a few. No matter what.

*   *   *

Taylor stood in the open area, barely a few meters from where Bear had been shot. His friend's body had been taken away, carried back to the field hospital as Taylor had ordered. He knew there was little sense to the urgent order he'd given…there was nothing anyone could do. But he couldn't leave his friend lying in the dirt. He wouldn't.

His aides had begged him to move, to take cover in the headquarters shelter, in case another sniper had managed to get within range. But he'd chased them away with barely restrained rage, screaming at them to get more troops, to send them out into the woods around HQ. To find the man who killed Bear. Whatever it took.

He looked down at his uniform, still wet and sticky with his friend's blood. He felt like he was surrounded, the walls on all sides closing in on him. He remembered the rage he'd felt when T'arza told him what UNGov had done…the instant he'd realized the alien was telling him the truth. The rage…and the determination. Taylor left T'arza that day determined to do whatever it took to destroy UNGov. His anger fueled his drive, and he was alert, aware, his energy almost limitless.

Now he fought the urge to slip down to the ground, to sit in the center of his headquarters and not move. Every action seemed like a tremendous effort, and all he wanted was to be left alone, to empty his mind. He'd thought war against the Tegeri had been hell, but the last four years had been worse. Again and again, he'd faced armies, humans like his people, men who should have been allies and not enemies…all save for UNGov's lies. But he'd killed them all the same, in the thousands. And thousands of his own soldiers died in the wars too. It was a river of blood.

He'd expected nothing less, but it was one thing to set forth on a long quest, swearing victory or death...and another to enduring the cost, the endless pressure and pain. The shadowy dead faces of soldiers, of friends, staring back from his nightmares. Taylor knew he was close, that his forces stood at the verge of final victory. But he didn't know if he had the strength to continue.

He tried to center his thoughts, focus on the next stage of the campaign. But the strength was gone, and there was nothing left but sadness and fatigue.

"General Taylor...sir?"

He heard the sound, calling to him, pulling him back from the dark road in his mind.

"General?"

Taylor turned and looked at the officer calling to him. The man stood in front of half a dozen soldiers. They were holding a prisoner.

"Yes...Phillips...what is it?" Taylor's mind was clearing, and his neural implants had fed him the captain's name.

"Sir, we have him. The sniper who killed General Samuels."

Taylor felt the rush of adrenalin through his body. The fatigue was gone in an instant, replaced by focused rage. He stared at the captive. It was obvious his troops had not been gentle. The man's lip was cut, and his face swollen. There was a nasty gash down one side of his face, and he had a gunshot wound in the arm, one that was still bleeding badly.

He stood almost at attention and glared at the prisoner. He'd expected someone in civilian clothes or a UNGov uniform. But the captive wore the uniform of the AOL. "Are you sure, Captain?"

"Yes, sir!" Phillips replied. We found a sniper's rifle near him. One round had been fired, and it was a match for...for the bullet that killed General Samuels, sir."

The captain's voice cracked as he mentioned Samuels, and then he paused for a few seconds. Bear had been one of the most popular officers in the army. "We scanned the weapon, sir, and matched DNA residue to the prisoner, sir. He's the one." A short pause then: "We got his name out of him, sir. Mitchell Klein."

Taylor felt nauseous. One of his own had tried to kill him. Had killed Bear. He'd known there were UNGov agents in his army, men who'd been sent to spy on the planetary forces. He'd weeded out most of them, but he'd never tried to fool himself into thinking he'd found them all. Now, he suspected, here was one of them, one who had escaped his notice, with tragic consequences.

A coldness flowed through his body, a terrible resolve. He stared at the captive, watching as the miserable creature struggled to return his gaze. "Please," the prisoner said, his voice choked with tears. "Please…"

"You want mercy?" Taylor's voice was like ice. "Were you going to give me mercy? Did my friend, General Samuels, get mercy? You ask for what you were unwilling to give yourself. Having failed in what you had planned, now you would have me take pity on you? But you are nothing but a murderer, a traitor, another UNGov drone drunk on lust for power, and damned the cost to anyone else."

Klein sobbed uncontrollably, his fear completely in charge of his actions. He made a weak attempt to wriggle free of the guards, but they held him like iron.

Taylor stood and stared for another moment, his gaze like death itself. What a miserable creature, he thought…and yet this excuse for a man killed Bear. The cost of war astounded him, though it had been his life for all of his adult years. Taylor had done many terrible things in the name of the quest, and while his resolve had always remained strong, he'd regretted some, and carried the guilt for them. But mistakes in war were one thing, and cold-blooded murder was another. Now, there wasn't a shred of doubt in him, not a gram of pity. There was just cold vengeance.

"Crucify him."

*   *   *

Akawa walked through the sparse woods, his four body-guards positioned, two in front and two behind. He'd almost tried to slip out without them. He needed to be alone, to think about what to do...but he knew most of the army had already moved out. Four guards weren't going to protect him from Taylor's pursuing army, but they'd come in handy if he ran into a couple pickets or scouts.

He had spent his whole life trying to stay out of trouble, to attain a reasonable level of prosperity for his family while avoiding the vicious political rivalries that often made UNGov service dangerous. He'd managed to follow that strategy for a long time...right up until Anton Samovich 'offered' him the top command. It was something he hadn't imagined, but he knew there was no way to refuse. Now things had gone exactly as he'd feared, and he knew it was just a matter of time before he progressed from Samovich's protégé to his scapegoat.

He was doomed if he remained with the army, he was sure of that. He had to decide—now—if he was going to accept his fate, stay in his headquarters and wait for the axe to fall, or if he was going to make a run for it, try to escape, hide...survive somehow.

The guards at least, he knew, would do whatever he told them. They were men who'd served under him for a many years. He'd appointed them almost immediately after he'd been promoted. He'd seen enough betrayal in his years of service, officers done in by hostile operatives in their inner circles.

"Freeze!" One of the forward guards snapped out the command, whipping around and pointing his rifle off to the side. "Don't move," he added.

Akawa accelerated his pace, walking up right behind the two guards. "What is it, Sergeant?" But even before he finished the question, his eyes dropped to the man leaning against a tree about two meters away.

"Who are you?" Akawa asked, as one of the guards stepped up cautiously and picked up a pistol that was lying on the ground next to the man.

The wounded soldier looked up, moving slowly. Akawa saw the man's leg. It was a twisted mess, bent at a grotesque angle, with a sliver of bone sticking out. There were strips of broken branches and some scraps of cloth…he had obviously been trying, unsuccessfully, to make some kind of brace that would allow him to walk. Akawa also saw the uniform. It was a little different than the others he'd seen, but it was definitely AOL. He looked around, but there was no one else, nothing but a heavy burning smell…and a few wisps of smoke coming from just over a small hill.

A pilot. A downed gunship…

"I am Colonel John MacArthur, Army of Liberation." The man's voice was wracked with pain, but there was defiance there too. He stared back at Akawa.

"Your airship crashed?" Akawa's tone was calm, friendly. He had an idea forming in his head, and this wounded officer might play a key role.

"Yes," MacArthur replied, offering no details.

Akawa stepped closer and leaned down next to MacArthur, waving off the guards when they reacted. "I want to talk with you about something."

MacArthur was clearly in pain, and just as obviously trying to hide it. "If you think I am going to give you any information, you're crazy."

"Colonel, I assure you I mean you no harm. And my questions have nothing to do with your army's plans or deployments."

MacArthur turned his head slowly, looking right at Akawa. "Then what do you want?"

"I want to know if it is true." Akawa asked after a short pause, staring down at the wounded officer as he did. "Did your army really kill the soldiers who refused to join you?"

MacArthur looked up at the UNGov general. "No," he snapped back, his outrage overriding his pain for a moment. "I don't know what kind of sick mind thought up that lie, but that is why we are here. Because mankind is ruled by psychopathic monsters." He leaned back and took a deep, ragged breath.

Then he looked back at Akawa, his stare burning with defiance. "We were long gone from those worlds before that atrocity took place."

Akawa thought quietly for a few seconds. Then he said, "I believe you, Colonel. I'm not sure why, but I do."

MacArthur just stared back, saying nothing.

"Why are you here?" Akawa asked bluntly.

"My airship crashed."

"No...why are you here. All of you. Your army. What is the true reason for your invasion of Earth?"

"We are here to destroy UNGov."

"Yes, I understand that. But why?"

"Isn't that obvious? Because it's an oppressive government. Because it has stolen freedom from the people."

Akawa nodded. "Yes, yes...that may all be true. But there is something else. Isn't there?"

MacArthur hesitated, his apprehensive frown giving way to a bewildered look. "Do you really want to know that? You may not like it very much."

"Yes," Akawa said. "I want to know."

MacArthur pulled himself up straighter, grunting from the pain as he did. Then he stared right at Akawa and told him why the AOL had come to Earth. The colonial massacres, the great lie behind the war, the fact that the Tegeri were not hostile to mankind...everything.

Akawa just stared back without a word, trying to process all he had heard. He'd suspected there was more to the AOL than a group of murderous traitors, but he found himself in stunned amazement at the story he'd just heard. And even more shocking, he found he believed it. Every word.

"Colonel," he finally said. "I wish to meet with your General Taylor."

MacArthur shook his head. "If you think I'm going to help you find General Taylor, you're..."

"Just take me to your forces. I surrender to you, Colonel. I am General Jinto Akawa, commander-in-chief of UNGov forces, and I request a meeting with General Taylor."

Chapter 21

Captain Wickes to Devon Bell:

I think it's time you send UNGov your resignation, Dev.

"I wish we had more time to plan this, Captain. Devon Bell was pulling up a pair of suit pants as he spoke. He'd cast aside the filthy rags he'd worn through the last thirty-six hours of non-stop action, and he was trying to make himself look remotely professional. He leaned his head down toward his armpit and took a sniff. "I hope they just take a quick look and don't smell." He looked nervous. No, not nervous...scared to death. But there was something else there too, a determination to overcome his fears, to get the job done, whatever the risk.

"I wish we had more time to plan too, Devon. But UNGov isn't going to leave New York almost devoid of security personnel. They've probably got people on the way right now. Which means we don't have time to waste. This is a fleeting opportunity. It's now or never." Wickes smiled, trying to help boost his friend's confidence. "And you smell fine. Like a spring morning." He reached up, patting down the side of Bell's head, trying to force down a particularly wild tuft of hair.

Bell frowned and nodded, licking his hand and trying to coax some cooperation from the matted rat's nest on his head. He didn't need to look great, just normal enough not to draw attention to himself while he disabled the building's security system.

Wickes looked across the street at the structure, the main

broadcast center for North America. The light from its lobby glowed softly in the predawn darkness. The Resistance had long dreamed of gaining even temporary control of the structure and broadcasting their message live across the entire continent. They'd planned it a dozen times, but it had never been remotely feasible. Not until now. The casualties the UNGov forces had suffered, both in the bombings and the attack by Captain Charles and his gunship, had created a window of opportunity. Wickes doubted there were more than fifty security troopers left in all of Manhattan. They'd already been understrength, half their numbers detached for military training…and probably sent right to the front facing Taylor's army.

There would still be some fighting to do, he knew…the center had its own security force, and whatever field command was still operating would send every trooper they could when they got word the broadcast facility had been compromised.. But Wickes had called out every member of the Resistance who was still alive. He had over a hundred of them gathered, a force he could never had assembled in one place before, not without UNGov security catching wind of it. But the streets were almost devoid of patrols. For once, the rebels would have numbers. It would be the government forces who were hemmed in, outnumbered, hunted down to the last man. It wouldn't last, but on some level, Wickes was drawing considerable satisfaction from it.

"Are you sure you're ready for this, Dev?" he said as he watched Bell shove his arm into the suit jacket. It wasn't a great fit, a little tight and at least two centimeters short in the sleeves, but it was all they could find on short notice. They couldn't take the risk of Bell returning to his home in the Gated Zone to get one of his own suits. Wickes suspected that protecting the enclave where the UNGov personnel and upper classes lived would be a priority for the remaining security, which meant it was the last place he was going to send anyone.

"No, Captain. I'm not sure. But I'm going to do it anyway." He forced a smile of sorts. "Just make damned sure you're all ready. We won't get this chance again."

"We'll be there, Dev. Don't you worry about it."

Bell nodded.

Wickes watched as Bell stared across the street, at the thick glass front of the broadcast center. He knew just what he was asking of his comrade. Bell was a loyal rebel, he didn't doubt that, despite his comrade's position within UNGov. But it was one thing to attend meetings, even to fight in the streets as he had. But once he used his ID to help the rebels gain access to the high-security building, he would be sending a message right to Geneva. I am part of the Resistance. His life as he knew it would be over. He could never return to his apartment. He would leave all his possessions behind. Everything. He would have to hide, and when UNGov forces arrived to retake control of the city, he would have to flee, leave his comfortable life to survive as a fugitive, one of the most hunted men in North America.

Bell turned his head and nodded, pausing as Rod Charles stepped forward, out of the shadows. "I want to thank you again and let you know we've got your back on this. Two of my men are in the gunship, and they'll hit the satellite dish as soon as you're inside. That'll cut the facility off completely from Geneva…but it will also let UNGov know that something is happening. Then the timeclock will really start."

Bell nodded. He looked like he might throw up, but he was holding it together.

"And don't worry about after," Charles said. "You'll come with us…we'll get you out of the city. I've sent a signal to our other groups in North America. With any luck, we'll have half a dozen Dragonfires here by the time UNGov gets reserves to New York in any force."

"Thank you, Captain Charles," Bell said, struggling to sound as confident as he could.

"No, thank you," Charles replied. We thought we'd be hunting through the streets, trying to find relatives, old friends, one at a time. But this will give us a chance to address millions, to challenge UNGov's lies in a meaningful way." He paused. "If we can pull it off, it will be a massive blow toward victory."

Wickes had been standing, shifting his gaze, watching his

comrade and then staring across the street. Finally, he said, "Okay, Dev...it's time."

Bell nodded. He moved his hands down his body, brushing some of the wrinkles from his suit. Then he took a deep breath and walked out into the street. He looked up and down the quiet avenue. It was deserted. He moved across, trying to look calm, relaxed as he walked toward the building.

Bell stepped up to the door, standing in a small lighted vestibule. "Identify," the building AI's voice said sternly. He reached into the pocket of his suit and pulled out his ID card. He could feel his heart pounding in his chest. For two years he had been part of the Resistance, but he'd kept that secret, hidden, living his normal life all the time. But once he swiped his card that was all over. He had no legitimate reason to be here. Regardless of what happened in the hours to come, he knew UNGov's investigations would expose his involvement. Then he would truly be a fugitive. He would spend the rest of his life running, hiding. Or he would die in some Inquisitor's interrogation room.

He stood another few seconds, gathering himself, marshaling his courage.

"Identify," the machine repeated.

He reached out and swiped the card down the reader. Then he waited, a few seconds that seemed like hours, to see if the security system gave him access.

There was a soft click, and the door slid open. He felt a rush of relief, and a wave of fresh stress too. The uncertainty was gone, at least. Until he'd swiped his card, some part of his mind had known he could always change his mind, run and not go through with it. But now he was committed. There was no turning back, and in a way, though he was terrified, that made it easier.

He walked into the marble-floored lobby. There were normally half a dozen guards on duty, but now there was just one sitting at the main desk.

"Good evening, Mr. Bell," the guard said, his eyes darting down to the screen on his desk. "How can I help you, sir?"

"I am here to correct a malfunction on the main network

encryption," Bell said, trying as hard as he could to sound calm.

The guard looked down at his screen again. "I'm sorry, Mr. Bell, I don't have anything on my schedule." He looked up. "Most likely it's just an oversight...with all that's happened tonight that wouldn't be much of a surprise. But I'll have to call it in. If you'll just step into the scanner, I'll send a message to central control to confirm."

Bell nodded. "Thank you." He felt the excitement flowing through his body. It was time...he had to make his move. He couldn't step into the scanner. The pistol under his suit jacket would set off the alarm immediately. And he couldn't allow the guard to send a message either. His comrades needed as much time as they could get before whatever remained of UNGov forces in New York knew what was happening.

"Oh," he said, turning toward the guard, "there is one other thing..." He slipped his hand inside his jacket, pulling the pistol out and firing in one quick motion.

The shot took the stunned guard in the neck. He held himself up for a few seconds, staring back in shock as blood poured from his wound. Then he fell hard to the ground.

Bell recoiled for an instant. The guard had been a UNGov security trooper, which probably meant he had done some nasty things in his career, but he'd seemed so normal, so polite.

And I killed him...

Bell struggled to remember everything. Two shots. That's what Wickes had told him. Two shots...make sure he's dead. He moved around the desk and looked down at the guard. He was still moving, his hands on his throat, pawing at the terrible wound. Bell looked down, trying to force back the pity he felt, the guilt. You have a job to do, he told himself.

He raised his arm, aiming the pistol again. He could see the fear in the dying man's expression, his victim's eyes beseeching him for mercy. But he knew his duty was to his comrades. They were counting on him. And they weren't going to defeat UNGov without killing anyone.

Liberty must be bought with blood...

He pulled the trigger, shooting the guard right in the forehead. The man fell silent, still. Dead.

He felt sick to his stomach, but he ignored it. His comrades were counting on him. He ran back to the guard's workstation, his fingers moving quickly over the keyboard. He disabled the camera feed and scragged the last few minutes of coverage. If someone was watching live, he'd be screwed, but he knew that was unlikely. It wasn't standard practice at 5am in any situation, and he knew UNGov in New York was stretched desperately thin. It was extremely unlikely they had anyone to spare staring at video footage.

He continued punching keys, and an instant later the door popped open. A few seconds after that, Wickes slipped inside, followed by the others. In a minute there were two dozen Resistance fighters standing in the lobby of UNGov's media center. Now they just had to secure the rest of the building...and get on the air before the offsite security forces realized what was happening and cut power to the building.

"Alright," Wickes said looking at the small crowd around him. "Dev got us in, but now it's up to everybody to do their jobs. Stone, Fournier, Giles...get set up down here. Nobody gets in this building, understood?"

The three men nodded.

Wickes looked over at Bell. "Dev, you got the door sealed?"

"Got it, Cap." The former UNGov cryptologist looked up and nodded. Security cams are out, all exterior doors locked, with all security overrides canceled. Whoever wants to get in here is going to have to blast their way in."

"Which they will do, eventually. But hopefully we'll be done by then."

Bell just nodded. Wickes hadn't said anything about how they'd escape after the broadcast, but Bell knew this wasn't a suicide mission. At least not definitely. UNGov just didn't have the forces in New York ready to respond the way they normally would. There was a chance they'd escape. Some chance. Some of them at least.

"The rest of you, let's go. The elevators are too dangerous... we don't want to get caught in there by whatever security is still active in here. So, we've got some stairs to climb."

He ran to the wall, opening the solid metal fire door. Wickes was seventy years old, and his comrades in the Resistance knew him as an old man. But the action of the last few days had invigorated him, awakened a spirit that had long lain dormant. He ran up the stairs, waving one arm for the others to follow...and holding his assault rifle in the other.

The main broadcast center was on the thirty-sixth floor. Wickes bounded up the first ten flights, but then he slowed his pace, looking behind him as he stopped for a moment to catch his breath. Dev Bell and Rod Charles had kept up with him. Carson Jones was just behind them with a few of the others. And the rest were strung out over half a dozen floors.

Wickes stood for perhaps a minute then he started up the stairs again...just as the door above swung open and UNGov security troopers came pouring into the stairwell firing.

*   *   *

Bill Reed rushed down the stairs, firing his assault rifle on full auto. He had four of his men behind him, the entire security contingent for the media center. He was scared to death, but he'd been ordered in no uncertain terms by his commander to stop the rebels, whatever the cost. His choice was clear... wipe out the Resistance fighters and receive a promotion and be showered with rewards. Or fail to do so and, if he somehow survived the defeat, enjoy a one way trip to a reeducation camp. He was scared to fight it out with the Resistance fighters, but his fear of UNGov was greater. He'd seen what happened to those who challenged its power.

He looked down with a start, realizing there were a lot more rebels than the three or four he'd been told to expect. They were strung out along the stairs, which gave his people a chance. Maybe.

He saw one of the Resistance fighters drop...then another. He'd had the advantage of surprise, but it didn't last long. There were two rebels down, but now the return fire was heavy. He heard one of his troopers yell, followed by a thud...and the sound of a body rolling down the stairs.

He kept moving forward, ducking back against the wall, out of the enemy's line of sight. He knew the rebels were just below him...each side pinning the other in place. Whoever moved forward would be right in his enemy's line of fire.

He sucked in a deep breath, feeling the sweat pouring down his back. He was terrified, and he had no idea what to do. He glanced quickly behind him. Two of his people were still with him. Aames and Olsen were crouched down right behind him, covering the stairs just below. Heaton was dead, or at least he looked dead. And Gomez and Dougherty had taken off.

If I get out of here those two are going to die...

He leaned back against the wall, holding his rifle out, covering the section of stairs opposite him. It was a standoff. All he could do was hope help got there and retook the building before the rebels decided to try and force his position.

He was still thinking that when he saw the flash of action from below...and he heard something bouncing around on the floor down a quarter flight from where he sat.

"Grenade!" he yelled, an instant before the explosion. The shockwave slammed him against the wall, and he felt searing pain as bits of hot shrapnel dug into his legs, his midsection. He fell back on the stairs, and his rifle rolled down, out of reach. He was dazed, in pain, grabbing for his pistol when he saw the shadowy figure above him. He looked with a start as he saw the long gray hair, the wrinkled, worn face. It was an old man, not what he'd expected. He was still confused when he saw the gun in the man's hand...pointed toward him.

*　　*　　*

"Are we ready yet?" Rod Charles was nervous, edgy. The firefight in the stairwell had been a surprise, one that cost them three of their comrades, including Carson Jones. He wasn't dead, not yet. But Charles knew the rebel wasn't going to live either, not without a hospital. He'd done all he could to stabilize his new ally, but he didn't see how they were going to get the critically-wounded man the medical assistance he needed.

But the attack meant more than losses...it meant UNGov knew they were there. Wickes had hoped they'd get at least an hour before the UNGov forces realized they'd taken control of the building. But clearly that wasn't going to be. And that made time even more of the essence.

"Just a minute, Captain." Devon Bell was hunched over a workstation, his fingers rapping quickly on the keys. "Go get on the stage. I'll have you live in sixty seconds."

Charles nodded, glancing around the large room before he walked over to the podium his comrades had hastily moved into position. There were about a dozen members of the usual staff, tied up and sitting along the far wall, guarded by two of the Resistance fighters. Another two stood guard over the only entrance to the studio, and Carson Jones was lying on a large sofa, covered with a makeshift blanket and drifting in and out of consciousness. Wickes was next to Charles, and he put his arm on the AOL captain's shoulder. The old Marine had caught a round in the fight on the stairs, but he'd just tied an old rag around his arm and, as well as Charles could tell, he was simply ignoring it.

Wickes had sent rest of the Resistance fighters, fourteen of them, to help defend the building. Four of them were on their way down to the lobby to reinforce the three men already there. With the attack on the stairs it seemed likely they'd face an assault on the building a lot sooner than they'd expected. The others were hunting the rest of the UNGov troops, the ones who'd run...and any others that might be hiding somewhere, planning something.

"Alright, Captain...and Captain...we're ready." Bell motioned toward the podium, and Wickes and Charles walked over, standing next to each other and looking into the small globe that would transmit their broadcast throughout North America.

"Okay, Dev," Wickes said softly. "Let's do this."

The studio had no windows, but Charles knew it was morning now...perhaps not as good a time for a live broadcast as early evening, but millions of UNGov citizens would be watching the morning broadcast. It was usually full of UN propaganda, and people were strongly encouraged to tune in.

"We're connected to all relays. You're live now throughout North America."

Wickes cleared his throat. "My fellow citizens, I am Captain Stanley Wickes, United States Marine Corps, retired. I am also a member of the New York City Resistance, a rebel group struggling to overthrow UNGov. We have taken control of the state media facility in New York so we could broadcast this message to all of you. For too many years we have lived under the iron fist of UNGov control, endured the censorship, the draconian regulations, the poverty and lack of opportunity. We have seen friends and neighbors dragged off in the night…and tried our best to look the other way. For too many years we have done nothing. Those of you who are my age remember something different, freedom, liberty. Your children have never known this wonder…your grandchildren never will. Unless we do something."

Wickes turned and looked at Charles. "And now I wish to introduce Captain Roderick Charles. The captain is an officer of the Army of Liberation. These are our soldiers, men who were conscripted and sent off-world, never to return. They are brave warriors who have been libeled, slandered by UNGov's propaganda machine. They are the friends and brothers and sons many of us thought lost to us forever, sent through the Portals to fight the Tegeri. These brave and honorable soldiers were accused of terrible crimes by UNGov. We were told they murdered their comrades, that they allied with the enemy to enslave mankind. But this is nothing but lies…lies from those who truly enslave mankind, who have done so for forty years. Captain Charles and his comrades have come back to Earth to free its people, to cleanse us of the unclean government that has ruled with brutality and tyranny." Wickes paused and took a breath. "And Captain Charles has something else to say, a truth long hidden, and one all men and women must hear. Listen to what he has to say…and then spread the word, makes sure all know the truth of this war."

Charles looked right at the camera. "Hello, North America. I am Captain Rod Charles. I am one of you, was one of you, at least. Long ago. I was born in New York City, in the Bronx. In the kind of neighborhood some of you would recognize only by description. It was—is—a violent place, an area where people died every day. That is where I was born. It was where I grew up.

"Eleven years ago I was arrested because I was walking home when a food riot broke out. Two federal security troopers were attacked, and in the response, over a hundred civilians were killed. I was wounded, shot in the leg...and I was arrested and charged with assaulting federal officers, though I was nowhere near where the two troopers were attacked. I was given a choice...twenty years at hard labor, or I could 'volunteer' for the off-planet military, and repay my debt to society by helping to defend Earth."

"I agreed to join the military, to do my part to keep Earth... my family, my friends, safe. I went through training, and then I shipped out, stepping through the Portal, leaving the home world I thought I would never see again. I was despondent at leaving my family, but at least I was serving a noble purpose. At least I believed that I was...and it was years before I discovered how terribly wrong I had been. But finally, so many years later, I learned the truth...as I am about to tell all of you..."

Chapter 22

From the Writings of Jinto Akawa:

I will never forgot my first impression of General Taylor. There is something about the man, some inner strength, a power that is irresistible. When I look back on the war his people waged against UNGov I cannot help but wonder at the odds...at the crazy fluke of history that placed a man with his unique abilities at the right place and time. I later learned that the Tegeri had long sought a contact, a man who could lead his people to freedom. As with so many others in his army, I began as his enemy...and now I stand behind him, my loyalty and admiration absolute. I once tried to fight Jake Taylor, to destroy him. Now I would die for him.

"General Akawa, I must confess, I find your proposal surprising coming from a UNGov official of such senior position. I would expect you to be willing to do anything to see us defeated." Taylor sat across the table from Akawa, his best poker face rigidly in place despite the uncertainty and confusion he felt.

"I am not a senior UNGov official, General...or at least I wasn't until three weeks ago when Secretary-General Samovich promoted me from a staff colonel to the supreme command."

"And why would he do that, General?" Taylor was suspicious, but something inside him was telling him Akawa was different. He didn't necessarily trust the general yet, but he wanted to hear what the man had to say.

"I really don't know, General Taylor. If you pressed me for an answer, I'd say that faced with the very real danger of your invasion he didn't trust the political appointees who dominate the high command on Earth. As I said before, I am not a political officer. I am career Earth military, though I had never served in combat before, as you and your soldiers have."

"Why would you surrender to Colonel MacArthur the way you did?"

"Because I believed it was the quickest way I could think of to see you. It would have been difficult to contact you over the com system without our conversation being...overheard. Also, I felt that placing my trust in you that way would be a show of my good faith."

Taylor nodded. "And you want to surrender your entire army?"

"Yes, General. Provided certain conditions are met."

"You're not in a particularly strong bargaining position, General Akawa. You are already my prisoner."

"That is true. You can obviously do with me as you will. But I will not help you capture the rest of my forces, not unless I am satisfied they will be well-treated."

Taylor looked across the table. He found his respect for this UNGov officer growing.

He's concerned about his troops, about their safety...

"I'm afraid there may be little I can offer you in that regard, General. I would be more than willing to guarantee the safety of the conscripts in your force, the men who had been drafted for the planetary armies and then redeployed to face us. But UNGov enforcement units were also assigned to your army. These...soldiers..." He spat the word like it tasted bad. "...have spent their careers abusing civilians, dragging people to reeducation camps. They are part of what we came to destroy, and I have every intention of seeing that done."

Akawa sat silently, looking down at the table. Finally, he nodded and looked back at Taylor. "Will you give me your word than none of my soldiers who were not previously UNGov enforcers will be harmed? And that any who are accused of such will be accorded some kind of due process to ensure no innocents are blamed and punished?"

Taylor returned Akawa's gaze, trying to take his measure of the man. Finally he said, "Yes, General. I will give you my word on that. It has grieved me terribly that so many soldiers were killed in the fighting of the last week. Those conscripts swept up into your army are no different than I am, than any of my soldiers. They are victims, and now twice so for those killed fighting for an unjust cause. I would see them know the truth, be spared any more servitude to unjust masters. Will you help me save them? I have offered you all I can in return."

Akawa nodded. "Yes, General. I will help you. But there is little time. I expect to be relieved any moment now, and we must conclude a surrender before then. I will need to go back, to get to my headquarters to issue the orders. And you will have to have your troops ready...no doubt, some of the UNGov enforcers in the ranks will resist."

Akawa stared at Taylor. "I have trusted you, General, placed myself entirely at your mercy. Now you must decide if you trust me."

*   *   *

Magnus Jarn sat quietly in the back of the transport. He hadn't said more than a few words since the convoy left Geneva. General Volkes sat across from him, but Jarn's single word answers to his questions had shut the general up after a few attempts at conversation. Jarn didn't have the temperament for pointless chatter. He had a job to do, and that's why he was here. He was to apprehend General Akawa, and summarily execute the disgraced general. A simple task. He was clearing the way for Volkes to take command, but he wasn't under the general's authority—he reported directly to Secretary-General Samovich. Which made the relationship between the general and him essentially sharing a ride.

Jarn was a cold man. He'd always been that way, but twenty

years as an Inquisitor had only increased those tendencies. His job was one only a few people could do well. Casual brutality was easy for many, but an Inquisitor had to have complete control. It was the job that always ruled, not pointless cruelty. People looked at Inquisitors and they saw the terror, the shadow of UNGov's most feared enforcers. But the job required thought, patience, intelligence...and a willingness to do whatever was necessary to complete the mission.

The mission, a simple execution, didn't seem like anything that required UNGov's top Inquisitor, but Jarn had been ordered here by the Secretary-General in person. That made it important enough. Jarn had initially planned to bring just two of his people, but Samovich had insisted he take his entire team. There were a dozen transports, filled with over one hundred operatives. All to take one disgraced general out into the woods and shoot him.

"We should be there shortly," General Volkes said, breaking about half an hour of silence Jarn had thoroughly enjoyed.

"Yes," he replied. One word answers had worked so far, and he saw no reason to change his tactics. Besides, Volkes was right. They were almost there...and that meant it was time to prepare himself. It was an easy job, but that didn't mean there was no danger. No doubt, General Akawa had surrounded himself with at least a few loyal soldiers. Jarn had always been surprised how many of the condemned went along without resistance, but some put up a fight. And if Akawa and a few of his officers preferred death in a gunfight to execution, so be it. Jarn and his people would be ready to oblige.

He glanced over at Volkes, the man who would take over the wreckage of the army. Would he do better than Akawa had?

Or will he be my next mission?

*   *   *

Akawa stepped out of the transport, the snow crunching under his boot. He walked toward the shelter that housed his office. At least he thought it was still his. No one had challenged him as he'd driven back into camp, so it seemed like he was still in command.

Good, he thought. That will make things easier.

He glanced back at the column of transports. The makeshift convoy had not been questioned—one of the advantages of having the C in C in the front vehicle. But Akawa knew there were a dozen of Taylor's Supersoldiers in each. He wasn't sure how much they were here to back him up…and how much to make sure he kept his word, but either way, he'd just snuck an enemy force into army headquarters. If the orders for his relief—and likely, his execution too—hadn't been issued yet, this would do the trick, he was sure.

"Major Forbin," he snapped as he leapt from the transport, "I want Colonels Elmsford and Chin to report to my office immediately." Akawa considered the two colonels to be his best officers. There were a dozen other generals in the army, but they were all political officers. People he couldn't trust. People Jake Taylor wouldn't pardon.

"Sir…" The major's voice was soft, distracted. Akawa knew immediately that something was wrong.

"What is it, Major," he snapped.

"Sir, a convoy just arrived…ah…it is…"

"General Jinto Akawa…" Another voice, darker, grimmer. "…I am Inquisitor Magnus Jarn. I hereby inform you that, effective immediately, you are relieved of command. You are further instructed to accompany me." The hulking figure extended an arm, gesturing toward a nearby transport.

Akawa felt a ripple of fear move through him. Just a few more hours, he thought…and we might have pulled this off…

"I'd like to see those orders, Inquisitor." He was playing for time, trying to think of what to do. Anything…"It's not that I don't trust…"

"What you would like is of little account, I'm afraid." The Inquisitor pulled a large pistol from his belt. Akawa could see half a dozen men behind Jarn, all of them armed. "I will repeat myself only once, Mr. Akawa. You are to come with me immediately."

Akawa noted the 'mister,' that the Inquisitor had dropped his military rank.

My former rank…

He nodded, not wanting to risk any escalation. He didn't doubt the Inquisitor was here to kill him, but if he was fated to die, at least he could buy a chance for the men Taylor had sent with him to escape. He understood now, far better than he had before. Taylor's soldiers were Earth's best hope…and most of his own troops belonged at the side of the invaders, not fighting them. If he'd had more time…but there was no point in such thoughts. He didn't have the time. He would go, follow the Inquisitor to whatever place he chose as the execution spot… and he would hope with his last thoughts that Taylor's soldiers escaped…

His head snapped around at the sounds of gunfire, and he stared in stunned surprise. It was the Supersoldiers. They were pouring out of the transports, firing as they did.

Akawa turned back, just as Jarn raised his pistol. For an infinitesimal instant he felt an urge to give up, to allow the Inquisitor to shoot him. But then his spirit rallied. He ducked to the side, just in time, and Jarn's shot went wide. He leapt forward, his hands moving up, grabbing Jarn's arm, pushing forward as they both fell to the ground.

The Inquisitor struggled with him, trying to bring the pistol around for another shot. But Akawa held on, pushing Jarn's arm back, squeezing, trying to force the gun from his hand. He was aware of Jarn's men, at least half a dozen, standing around, waiting for a chance to shoot without endangering their commander. Then they were gone. It was hazy, and it happened quickly. A hail of gunfire, Jarn's men falling to the ground.

Then Jarn was gone too, ripped from his grasp. It took Akawa an instant to regain his sense, but when he did he saw his opponent, standing, gripped in the iron vice of two Supersoldiers. The pistol was on the ground.

Akawa felt hands on him, and he turned with a start. But it was one of Taylor's soldiers, helping him up. He stumbled to his feet, relying more than he wanted to admit on the assist.

"Are you okay, General?" Karl Young stood in front of a row of Supersoldiers, looking toward Akawa with a concerned expression.

"I am fine, General Young," he said. "I didn't know you were in the convoy."

"General Taylor thought it was a good idea. He figured you might need some help." He looked out behind Akawa, to where several dozen of his veterans were fighting with the survivors of Jarn's force. They had already gunned down most of the Inquisitor's troops who'd been in the open, and now they were searching the vehicles and killing any stragglers they found.

"I think we'd better get you to your office, General," Young said tensely. He turned and looked behind him toward the rest of the camp. The fighting had drawn attention and troops were running around, grabbing weapons. "You have to order your troops to stand down, before something...unfortunate... happens."

"Yes, of course," Akawa said, turning back toward Jarn for an instant. "And what of him?"

"General Taylor was very clear about the disposition of UNGov enforcement personnel." From the tone of his voice it was clear Karl Young agreed completely with Taylor's harsh policy.

Akawa nodded. "I will order the army to stand down." He took a last glimpse at Jarn, and then he trotted toward his HQ shelter, half a dozen of Young's men falling in behind him. About halfway to his office he heard a shot from behind him. He didn't need to turn around to know what it was.

* * *

"Sir, the rumors are true. The army has surrendered. General Akawa just broadcast the stand down orders." The commando couldn't keep the surprise from his voice. "It appears that the Secretary-General's order relieving the general was not implemented."

Alexi Drogov sighed softly. Which means Inquisitor Jarn is

dead…

"That is unfortunate." Drogov knew the army was in bad shape, a pathetic remnant of what it had been before it fought a death struggle with Taylor's veterans. But it was also the only thing with any chance of slowing the AOL's advance on Geneva. Drogov knew Anton Samovich would never yield. He wouldn't run either, not with the news from North America. The entire continent was in open rebellion, with widespread riots, and the Resistance in control of at least half a dozen cities. No, abandoning Geneva would be as good as surrendering.

Drogov took a deep breath. He knew what Samovich would do, and for once, even the emotionless, cold-blooded killer that he was felt a shiver of fear.

"Sir, we have our teams in position. We can't stay hidden long. We have to move now."

Drogov looked back at his aide. The Shadow Company was in place, all of it. He had planned and planned, studied every scrap of intelligence, commandeered half of UNGov's satellites to his own purposes. He knew when Jake Taylor got up in the morning, when he ate, when he held his meetings…when he took a dump. All of it, more information that he'd need to plan an invasion. All to kill one man. And now it was time.

And it wasn't time…not anymore. Killing Taylor would have been decisive, if he'd been able to do it before the battle. Or even before Akawa had surrendered the rest of UNGov's military strength. But now it was too late. The war was lost…even without Taylor the AOL would prevail. The secret of UNGov's great lie, the true story of how humanity ended up at war with the Tegeri…it was out, and there was no forcing it back into the bottle. The only way UNGov could maintain power was with massive force, gunning down rebels and protestors, drowning the rebellion in blood. But it didn't have the force to do that, not anymore. Its enforcers had mostly been drafted into the army, and the majority of them were dead on the Russian plains…or prisoners of Taylor's army, which he suspected would ultimately amount to the same thing.

Drogov was an amoral psychopath, at least in his own way.

He'd never been troubled by useless emotions like guilt or fear. But he was rational, as rational as an AI. He was loyal too, though he gave his loyalty rarely. He'd known Anton Samovich since the two of them had been street rats, scavenging for food. He'd helped his friend, been the half of their team in the shadows, while Alexi stood in the public eye, rising through the ranks of UNGov. Anton had given the speeches, connived with the other politicians, crafted the policies and proposals. And Alexi had removed the obstacles in their way, usually burying them in some out of the way location. The two had been a team for as long as he had conscious memory. Anton Samovich was the closest thing he'd ever had to a friend. A brother.

But nothing lasts forever...

He didn't sympathize with Taylor and his people, though he understood their motivations. But above all things, he was a realist. He knew what Samovich would do now, the great bluff he would play with Taylor.

But Taylor will never give in, he will never negotiate with UNGov. He is a zealot, committed in a way Anton could never understand. He will pay whatever price, endure any horror. And that will force Anton's hand. His bluff will be no bluff at all. And in his final desperation, he will do the unthinkable...the bluff will become reality.

Drogov had thought himself immune to pity and the pain of others, but what Samovich would do shook even him to his core. He ached for his friend, and the thought of abandoning him was a difficult one. But he had no choice...

"Sir?" The aide was still standing next to Drogov. "Should I give the order, sir?"

Drogov turned and looked at the man. He paused for an instant and then he said, "No, Lieutenant. No." He sucked in a deep breath. "Pull the men out...get everyone to the rally point."

"Yes, sir..." The lieutenant looked confused.

"Just do it," Drogov said softly. "I will explain later." He turned and began to walk into the woods.

"Sir, where are you going?"

Drogov stopped and looked back. "Do as I ordered, Lieutenant. I have…something to do." He turned back and continued into the woods, walking until the only sound was that of his boots on the snow.

I have to go see General Taylor.

*   *   *

"Get down!" Wickes shoved the last of his people down the stairs, and then he dove after them. Chunks of brick flew around as the autocannons from the UNGov airship fired into the narrow space, the heavy rounds shattering the masonry of the building. The rebels had left three of their number behind, dead in the street, gunned down as they tried to flee. The UNGov reinforcements reached New York just as Wickes and Charles had finished their broadcast. Half the rebels had already pulled out of the media center, but the others got caught by the arriving airships just as they were making a run for it.

The cellar was far from an ideal escape route, but Wickes knew they had no chance at all in the open. At least now, the ships would have to land ground troops and send them after the rebels. They'd be outnumbered, and trapped in the narrow subway tunnels, but that was better than getting gunned down in the street.

At least Captain Charles made it. Or I think he did, at least.

Charles had gone around the back of the media center, off toward where his crew had landed their airship. The UNGov forces had pursued the Resistance fighters, and that gave Charles a chance to slip away.

For whatever good that will do him…

Wickes hadn't known the AOL captain very long, but they had bonded quickly, each recognizing the veteran warrior in the other. And Stan Wickes knew Charles would never abandon his new allies. That meant he would come at the UNGov forces with his airship, do what he could to relieve the Resistance team. But there was a problem with that. UNGov had four airships, newly arrived, and Charles and his crew only one. They might distract the vessels, buy some time for Wickes to save some of his people. But they would likely pay for that with their lives.

Wickes felt the urge to climb back up the stairs, blast away with his assault rifle. Maybe, just maybe, he'd get a lucky shot in, disable one of the UNGov birds. But the thought faded. That scenario was unlikely almost to the point of impossibility...and even if he miraculously succeeded, three airships would still overwhelm and destroy Charles' bird. No, his place was with his fighters, what was left of them. If he went out there and got himself killed, he knew none of them would survive. They needed him.

"Alright, down into the sub-basement, now...and through the tunnel. The subway's our only way out, so let's move!"

He started to follow, but then he stopped abruptly and spun around. Footsteps, and then a shadow, a figure at the door. For an instant he wondered if Charles had followed, but then he saw the uniform, one he'd seen far too many times. UNGov security. His people were out of time.

He whipped up his rifle and fired just as the first trooper moved into the doorway, diving for the cover of a pile of boxes as his victim hit the ground. Then the next came, firing back as he did. And another after that.

Wickes gritted his teeth and flipped his rifle to full auto. "Move, all of you...now!"

I'll try to buy you some time, whatever I can...

And a vicious smile slipped onto his face as another two UNGov thugs went down under his fire.

It's a good day to die...

* * *

Rod Charles stared at the display, watching the four UNGov vessels. One of them was hovering, firing at the ground, most likely at the fleeing rebels. Another had landed in the street, probably deploying a squad of ground troops. But the other two were coming at his bird. One of Colonel MacArthur's crack crews might have managed a two to one fight and prevailed... if luck went their way. But his bird was far from that, just two regular airship crew, and ten others whose primary reason for being there was the fact that they were born within fifty miles of New York. Far from an ideal situation for a desperate, battle against the odds.

"Alright, we've got to take one of them down quick," he said. "Gunners, prepare to fire."

The two UNGov ships were coming on fast, about a thousand meters off the ground, above even the tallest buildings. His flyer was facing them. He wasn't looking to close the distance any faster, so they were just hovering…and waiting. Speed wouldn't be an advantage in this fight, just marksmanship.

"Okay, get ready. We're going to launch the rockets…and then we're going to hit the thrusters and climb. Got it?"

There was a ragged chorus of "yessirs." Charles knew his people were well aware how little chance they had. But there was no panic, no disorder. They were veterans, and they behaved accordingly.

"Fire rockets," he snapped to the makeshift gunners. "Thrusters full now…take us up."

The ship shook slightly as the rockets fired, and then it lurched hard as the thrusters engaged, pushing them higher, in a likely futile effort to gain position on the enemy.

The UNGov ships had launched their own rockets almost at the same time, but the sudden climb confused their guidance systems. Two of them zipped by, impacting into buildings below. The other two swung around, their homing systems pinging hard, seeking a new lock on their target.

Charles stared at the display, hanging onto his chair as he watched the two rockets his ship had launched. If his people were to have any chance, he knew they needed a critical hit. It felt like a punch in the gut when he saw one of the weapons vanish, destroyed by enemy interdictive fire. Then, an instant later, the second one followed, exploding less than a thousand meters from its target.

"Fuck," he muttered under his breath. His eyes darted toward the screen tracking the two enemy rockets still in the air. One of them had reacquired its lock, and it was arcing around to come back at the airship.

"Defensive fire," Charles muttered. But his amateur gunners were already on it. He watched on the screen as the rocket came closer...closer...and then the airship's weapons fired.

The rocket vanished, disintegrated in the concentrated auto-cannon fire. A few seconds later his people took out the last enemy weapon. But by then the enemy ships were closing fast, their autocannons firing at full.

The ship shook hard, and Charles heard the sound as the heavy rounds tore into his bird's hull. He heard a cry, saw a splash of blood against the wall, as one of his people fell, almost torn apart by the autocannon projectiles ripping through the hull. He'd barely turned, jumped from his seat and started toward the stricken crew member when another yelled. Charles turned and saw one of his gunners, the man's arm torn clean off. He turned quickly. The man on the deck was dead, almost certainly. The gunner he could save. If he had time. He suspected all his people would be dead in a minute...

"Sir, we've got a third enemy ship closing."

Charles felt the fight drain away from him. Whatever slim chance they'd had...it was gone.

Then, suddenly, one of the icons on the display disappeared.

He rubbed his eyes and looked again, but the symbol was still gone.

"Captain, we've got incoming Dragonfires, sir. They're firing at the UNGov ships!"

Charles looked back to the display, watching four more icons appear. There was an instant of shock, but then he knew what it was...what it had to be. It was their comrades. The other airships that had come to North America. They had responded to his calls.

Now it was a fight!

Chapter 23

From the Office of the Secretary-General:

I hereby order program omega-99 to be activated at once. All units are to be fully armed and authorized to accept final code.

"Guards!" Samovich screamed, the insanity clear in his voice.

The two soldiers raced through the door, guns drawn. They looked around the room, looking for any threat to the Secretary-General, but there was nothing. Nothing save the body on the floor, one of Samovich's aides. The leader of the world stood behind his desk, staring out the window, pistol still in his hand.

"Sir!" the lead guard snapped uncertainly. "What happ…"

"Get rid of him," said Samovich, the crazed intensity of his scream replaced by an eerie calm. "And get me a new aide, one who understands I have had all the bad news I am prepared to accept."

"Y…yes, sir," the guard responded. He motioned for his comrade to move toward the victim's legs, and he slung his rifle across his back. Then he slipped his hands under the aide's arms. The two security troopers exchanged glances that said one thing…let's get out of here. They hurried through the door, carrying the body as quickly as they could.

Anton Samovich turned and tossed the pistol down on his desk, and he flopped down into his chair. Years…no, more than years. A lifetime. That is how long he had pursued this seat, this office. He'd held it now for almost a year and a half, and when he'd first strode into this room, he'd fancied himself the most powerful man who had ever lived. Secretary-General by unanimous vote. The rest of the Secretariat either his longtime creatures or old enemies, who had seen so many of Samovich's foes die they were too scared to make eye contact with him, much less resist him. His word was law, his slightest whim and edict that all men obeyed.

Now it was slipping away. He could feel it. A few years ago, Taylor and his men were a threat, one that was far away, with a dozen armies between him and Earth. He was a rebel, a madman...but not a real danger, not a power capable of over-throwing UNGov. And now, Taylor's army was moving forward, toward Geneva. Toward Samovich himself. He'd thought about running, about retreating to some city far from the invaders, to regroup and put up a new defense. But North America was in open revolt now, and UNGov's terrible secret was out, spreading all around the world by now, no doubt. In another day, two at most, there would be unrest in every city. There was no place to go, nothing to do but make a final stand...right where he was.

"That traitor, Akawa," he muttered angrily. That was the latest bad news, the dispatch the unfortunate aide had been sent to deliver. Not only did Akawa escape the Inquisitor Samovich had sent to execute him, he'd managed to retain control of the army despite the orders relieving him. And the son of a bitch had surrendered to Taylor...every unit UNGov had left in the field, now prisoners of that accursed rebel. There was noth-ing—nothing—between Taylor's army and Geneva, naught save distance, and each day brought them closer. Samovich had a few days, at best, before the city would come under attack. He had guard battalions in place, but he didn't fool himself that they could stand up to Taylor's veterans.

Alexi, Samovich thought with a smile. Alexi will kill this rebel for me...

Even now he knew his longtime friend and henchmen was out there somewhere, with his elite commandos. The Shadow Company was the best UNGov had left under arms, and Alexi Drogov was the most gifted killer Samovich had ever known.

"And a loyal friend," he muttered to himself. "Not like the rest of these traitors, ready to abandon me at the first sign of trouble." He resented the members of the Secretariat, the other high-ranking officials. He knew their loyalty was based on fear. And they had as much reason to fear Taylor now as they did him. Taylor was a zealot, by all accounts a man dedicated to destroying UNGov root and branch. Samovich supposed the others in UNGov's great headquarters were planning surrenders, deals they would make to preserve as much of their wealth and power as possible. They didn't understand a man like Taylor…they imagined he just sought power for himself, that if they gave him the top position, he would treat with them, offer them a compromise.

Samovich knew better. He was not accustomed to dealing with men like Taylor. UNGov tended to breed a different sort, certainly not the dark hero, ready to die to destroy an evil. People who exhibited such characteristics were rooted out early in UNGov society, sent to reeducation camps…or just shot in filthy UN Security cellars somewhere. But still, he thought he understood Taylor.

"Alexi will kill Taylor. He has never failed me. He will not now."

Drogov and his people knew what they had to do…the assassination that would buy UNGov a chance. Or at least that's how Alexi will explain it to them. But Samovich knew his friend realized, just as he did, that killing Taylor wasn't enough. Not anymore. Things had gone too far. His soldiers would fight on, his officers would take his place. Taylor's genius, his strength had gotten them this far. Now they could go on without him if they had to.

No, Alexi can't do this by himself. The assassination is only part of our salvation. I have to do the rest…

He turned toward his workstation, punching a series of keys and then pressing his thumb against the print scanner.

"Identity confirmed, Secretary-General Samovich." The AI's voice was cold, sterile.

Samovich leaned back in his chair. His eyes were wide open,

glittering with rage.

"Activate Plan Omega-99 immediately. All emplacements to be activated and armed."

"Awaiting final authorization code."

He stood up and turned, looking out over the rolling hills below. But he didn't see any of it, just his imagined images of Taylor and his officers, columns of his soldiers marching through the Polish countryside, into the North European Plain...then down through Germany, into the rugged terrain and foothills leading toward Geneva. He knew the vision was of death itself, a manifestation of hell unleashed. And he would counter hell with another hell, one worse, more terrible even than any vengeance Taylor had conceived.

He turned back toward his desk. "Authorization code delta-nine-nine-seven-three-zero-zero-alpha-omega."

"Plan Omega-99 activated. All emplacements armed and ready for final countdown to detonation."

Samovich turned back toward the window and began laughing.

*   *   *

"I thank you, General Akawa. You did exactly as you promised. I must confess, though I allowed you to go, I didn't really trust you."

"I understand that, General Taylor. And if I had any doubts about that, they were cleared away when I saw that General Young was with us." Akawa looked up at Taylor and offered a weak smile. "I don't suppose I would have been any different in your shoes. And now, I must ask you to honor your assurances that my soldiers will not be harmed."

"We will honor every promise made to you, General. Your recruits, the draftees originally destined for the wars on the Portal worlds will not be harmed. Indeed, they will be offered the chance to join our crusade it they want...though I'm afraid they will have to be split up and placed under the supervision of my own people, at least at first."

"The others?" Akawa had an odd expression on his face, as if he was confused, uncertain about his feelings.

"The ones who were UNGov enforcers? Who abused and killed civilians? Who dragged people away from their families to take them to die in reeducation camps?" Taylor's voice changed completely. It had been informal, comradely, but now it was cold as ice.

"I know, General…but they served under me, they followed my orders. Perhaps we…"

"There is no 'perhaps,' General. The fate of those men was sealed four years ago, when I sat in a Tegeri facility and learned the truth. We are here to free a world, and to do that we must eradicate every trace of the evil that enslaved it." Taylor glared at the former UNGov general. "I was clear about that when we first spoke, General Akawa. You may continue to cooperate with us or you may remain with your soldiers as a prisoner. But you cannot save the men who wielded UNGov's bloody fist. They are as good as dead already. Their executions wait only on positive identification."

Akawa opened his mouth, but he closed it again.

"What is it, General? You may speak freely with me."

Akawa hesitated. Then he said, "It's just that…" His voice was nervous, tentative.

"That?"

"When I first met you, I saw the freedom fighter in you, the man struggling to bring liberty to a world. But when you speak in such absolute, merciless terms…you seem more like those you wish to destroy."

Taylor nodded. "And you were scared to say that to me…but I let you speak, and I have no anger at your words. Ask yourself how Secretary-General Samovich would respond in my shoes."

Akawa looked back silently. Finally, he just nodded.

"And there is one other difference, General," Taylor said. "UNGov seeks to acquire power, to rule over mankind. It does what it does to attain and keep that power. I seek to destroy a great evil. I have no desire to take Samovich's place, no intention of becoming a dictator. Once I have destroyed UNGov, I will…"

"You will what, General?" Akawa interrupted. "You will kill every government official of any significant rank and then walk off into the sunset? Is that what you would bequeath to the world? Anarchy? Brutal power struggles? How long before people start dying by the thousands? The millions? A week? Less? UNGov is evil, I have no argument with that. But are you any better? If you destroy it as thoroughly as you intend to do and you do not put something in its place, you will be responsible for the deaths of more innocents that UNGov has killed in forty years."

Taylor didn't reply. He just sat opposite Akawa, silent. He knew the general only spoke the truth. It was something he'd realized all along but suppressed. A realization he simply could not bear to consider. But now he was close to the victory that had seemed only a dream four years before. He knew he would have to step in, to take control until a legitimate government could be formed to take UNGov's place. The thought of it made him sick to his stomach.

I don't have time for this, not now. He pushed it back, drove the thoughts from his mind.

"I will see that the UNGov personnel among your people get fair trials. Those who have not killed innocent civilians, who have not used their power to terrify and intimidate the people… they will not die. The others will pay for what they have done."

Akawa nodded. "That is fair, General Taylor." He stood up and extended his hand. "I pledge you my continued support… to the end."

Taylor nodded. "I am glad to have you, Gen…"

"Jake!" Hank Daniels burst into the room. "You've got to see this." He hit a switch, turned on the large display in the room.

Anton Samovich filled the screen. He had an odd look, not at all the cool, composed figure Taylor had seen lying about the murders of twenty-thousand Earth soldiers weeks earlier. His expression was distorted and his eyes were wide open, almost glittering in the light. Taylor watched and one thought went through his mind. He is insane.

"You share the guilt in this, all of you," Samovich said. "You have failed to support your government. You have allowed rebels and traitors to threaten the established order. And now you must all pay the price. UNGov is the legitimate government of Earth, and it will never yield to insurrection. And the time has come for drastic measures."

Taylor got a cold feeling in his stomach. He had no idea what Samovich was talking about, but he knew it would be bad. He glanced over at Akawa, silently inquiring if he had an idea, but the former UNGov general just shook his head.

"And now, I have a message for you, General Taylor, as I have no doubt you are watching this broadcast. I am certain you believe you have defeated Earth's legitimate government, that your band of murderers and traitors have prevailed. But UNGov is not so easily vanquished. There is a security program, a resource of last resort, put in place forty years ago against the possibility that a rebellious city could threaten the new world order. That program remains in place.

"Under each of Earth's cities there is a secret chamber, one containing a number of high-yield nuclear warheads. They were placed there to allow the destruction of a city in revolt from spreading its dangerous disorder to other locations. But now I have activated the entire system. In twelve hours, every one of these caches will be detonated, resulting in the complete destruction of every city in the world."

Taylor stared at the screen, his eyes fixed on Samovich, unable to avert his gaze for even a moment. For years he had planned the destruction of UNGov, raged at the evils of Earth's government…but this was beyond anything he'd imagined. His mind raced, seeking for a solution, a way out. But there was nothing. Nothing but the sounds of the madman on the screen.

"Twelve hours, General Taylor. You have twelve hours to surrender your forces, to disarm and submit yourselves to be tried for your crimes. If you do not comply, the deaths of billions will rest with you. Your treason, your refusal to submit, will bring mankind to the verge of extinction."

Taylor felt tightness in his chest. He'd been so focused, so determined. And now he had no idea what to do. And no time...

"And just to prove this is no idle threat, in one hour I will destroy a single city, a demonstration of the power of this final defensive system."

No, Taylor thought...no...

"And to the people of Earth...it is your duty to remain in your homes, to serve your part in this strategy to defeat the invaders. All cities are under surveillance...and any signs of a mass exodus will result in the immediate detonation of a city's explosives. If you flee, you will die. Stand firm, stay put, and serve your government."

Samovich turned and walked away. A few seconds later, the transmission ceased.

Taylor turned and looked around the room, exchanging glances with everyone present. Finally, he locked eyes with Hank Daniels, the most fervent of his inner circle. But Daniels looked as lost as Taylor, shocked by what he had just seen, unsure what to do.

Taylor knew surrender meant death...for him and for all his people. He'd sworn hundreds of times that mankind must pay for its foolishness in allowing UNGov to come to power. But how much of a price could humanity pay? How much could he allow it to pay? He'd realized, in his nightmares if nowhere else, that many would die in the climax of the crusade, perhaps even millions. But billions? Most of the population of the world, blasted out of existence in the fires of nuclear death?

No...I can't.

He felt despair as he had never before imagined. He'd considered the possibility of losing, of being defeated by UNGov. But yielding? Surrendering meekly and allowing Earth's masters to continue to rule. To face execution...or whatever terrible fate awaited him, and to watch his friends and comrades go through the same thing.

Better I had never lived at all, he thought, distraught, miserable. Better if T'arza and his people had killed me that day...

*   *   *

Wickes ejected the spent clip and slammed another in place. Then he opened fire, dashing for the steps as he did. He'd dropped four security troopers, and the others had pulled back, through the door. One of them was at the edge of the doorway, returning his fire from cover.

Stalemate.

His resistance had served its purpose. His people were all down in the subway tunnels by now. It was just a few minutes' head start, but it was something, all he could give them. There was no guarantee, but he'd bought them all a chance…which was more than they had fighting it out in the cellar.

His wounded arm was giving him trouble. He'd ignored it at first, but now it throbbed, and he found it difficult to keep his mind focused. He'd lost blood, not enough to be life-threatening, not yet at least. But he felt his strength slipping away. He'd stayed behind the crates and held his position for as long as he could, but he only had one clip left. If he was going to make a run for it, now was the time.

He considered staying, a last stand, a fight to the death, but the truth was, there was no point. He wouldn't hold long with one clip, and that meant staying was throwing his life away. He'd sacrifice himself if he had to, for victory or to buy his people their escape. But the Marine in him wouldn't let him give up… and sacrificing himself for a few more seconds, making no attempt to get away…that would be giving up.

He jumped down the opening in the floor, grabbing hold of the creaking rail as he leapt half way down the stairs in a single bound. He'd spun his head around as he dropped, taking a last glance at the room. He'd surprised the enemy…none of them had burst into the room yet. But they wouldn't be fooled for more than a few seconds. He had a headstart of his own, but his was measured in seconds, not minutes.

He almost stumbled as he leapt down the wreck of a staircase, feeling the impact of the concrete floor vibrate up his body. His injured arm radiated pain. He felt his legs almost buckle, but he struggled and managed to stay on his feet. He ran toward the half-collapsed wall, jumping over chunks of shattered concrete, crawling through the opening and out into the half-flooded subway tunnel.

He turned instinctively at the sound of shooting behind him, but then he swung around and ran down the tunnel, splashing wildly as he did.

It's over. They're right behind me.

He looked around the tunnel, his eyes seeking anywhere to go but straight. There was some old equipment, now little more than debris. But it was cover of a sort, so he made for it.

He heard the gunfire behind him, louder, more of it.

What the hell are they shooting at?

He ducked behind the broken metal carcass of what looked like a part of a train carriage, and he turned and looked back. Nothing. Just more gunfire, still from inside the passage, muffled now with more distance.

He pulled up his rifle, ready to spend his last shots as well as possible, to take as many of the enemy down with him as he could. But nothing came. Then he saw movement, slow, cautious. His finger tightened.

"Resistance fighters…"

The voice echoed off the walls of the tunnel.

Wickes was surprised. He didn't expect the UNGov security to give the rebels a chance to surrender, not after the losses their comrades had taken. But he had no intention of being taken prisoner…and seeing the inside of a UNGov interrogation chamber.

"Resistance fighters, do not fire," the voice continued. "I am Lieutenant Davis Stevenson, Army of Liberation. We're here to get your people to safety."

Chapter 24

From the Journal of Jake Taylor:

When I embarked on this quest, I swore to myself I would bring all the guilty to justice, that I was sweep the world clean like some avenging angel. And through all the battle, the terrible loss, I never wavered in that resolution. I have sacrificed friends, thousands of my soldiers...I have endured pain and devoted all I have to the fight. And in the end, even my own convictions. For I had refused to deal with UNGov and its corrupt minions...until a deal with the devil became the only way to save four billion human beings.

Drogov stared out from behind the brush, looking out at Taylor's camp. He'd planned the approach for days, taking every detail into account. Evading the AOL's Supersoldiers was a major undertaking, but Alexi Drogov had been a master of covert ops for thirty years. Of course, his preparations had been intended to get him close enough to kill Taylor. Now he planned to get even closer.

He'd snuck as far as he could, and now he was ready for the final tactic of his approach...surrendering. He could have done that kilometers out, but there was no guarantee some sergeant on picket duty or junior officer commanding a patrol would have listened to him and brought him to General Taylor. He would solve that problem by surrendering to Taylor himself. Now.

He saw the general step out of the shelter he used as an

office. It was time. He stepped right out of the woods, his hands extended well above his head. He walked slowly, taking care not to make any sudden moves. Taylor's soldiers were good, and it wouldn't take more than an instant's overreaction for them to gun him down. He wouldn't do anything that could be perceived as threatening.

"General Taylor," he yelled. "I am one of Secretary-General Samovich's chief lieutenants. And I wish to surrender to you."

"Freeze," one of the guards shouted. In an instant, half a dozen rifles were leveled, all pointing right at Samovich. Four soldiers were running toward him.

"I am here to surrender," he repeated, taking care to keep his arms in the air. "I am unarmed." He'd found it difficult to leave his guns behind. Drogov customarily managed to take a weapon with him wherever he went, the shower, a sexual encounter… anywhere. But since he'd decided to parlay with Taylor instead of killing him, he knew the weapons could only get him killed.

A dozen guards ran toward him, grim looks on their faces and weapons at the ready. Two of them grabbed him roughly and forced him to the ground. It took all his restraint not to fight back, to let the natural killer inside him out. But he knew what he had to do.

The guards searched him…twice. Then he felt four hands on him, pulling him back up to his feet. And Jake Taylor was standing two meters from him.

"You wanted to see me? You seem to know who I am…I'm afraid you have the advantage."

"My name is Alexi Drogov, General."

"Well, Alexi Drogov, would you mind telling me why you are in my camp? And how you got here without being spotted?" Taylor's voice wasn't hostile, but Drogov had the sense there was menace there.

Be careful with this man…

"I am here to see you on a matter of extreme urgency. And I was able to get here unseen because…that is what I do."

Taylor shook his head and began to turn around. "I'm sorry, Mr. Drogov, but I'm afraid I have a crisis to deal with and no time for riddles." He turned toward an officer standing next to the guards. "Put him in one of the cells...and..."

"General, your crisis is the reason I am here. To help you with it."

Taylor turned back toward Drogov. "Help me with what?"

"With stopping Anton Samovich from destroying every city on Earth."

Taylor's expression turned deadly serious. "How do you know about that?"

"I have been Secretary-General Samovich's senior operative for thirty years."

The guards tensed, and the ones flanking Drogov moved between him and Taylor.

"It's okay, boys," Taylor said, his eyes locked on Drogov's. "Stand back." To Drogov: "You've been Samovich's henchmen...his murderer...for thirty years, and you think there is any way I would ever trust you?"

Drogov returned Taylor's gaze. "No, I don't expect you to trust me."

"Then what makes you think I'd listen to anything you have to say?"

Drogov stood stone still, his voice deadpan. "Because you have three choices, General. You can surrender...and I assure you if you do, the Secretary-General will show no mercy, not to you nor to any of your people, regardless of any promises he makes to you. You can refuse Anton's demand and watch four billion people die in a matter of minutes." He glared right into Taylor's eyes. "Or you can let me help you stop it all."

* * *

"The trip to Boston is less than forty minutes at full speed. The Resistance there is throwing everything they've got at the UNGov enforcers. But four airships and almost fifty more fighters will make a big difference." Charles was animated, upbeat. New York was as good as liberated from UNGov control. His people had come to link up with family and old acquaintances, to try and work from the ground up. But now they had driven UNGov out of one city, and they were on the way to do the same thing to another. He'd left a few of his people behind in New York at the media center, trying to hijack a UNGov satellite and report back to army headquarters. He knew the AOL had won a victory of some kind, that much he'd been able to glean from media reports and classified UNGov documents his people had found. But as far as he knew, General Taylor had no idea that North America was virtually in open revolt.

Wickes was sitting in the chair next to Charles. He looked tired and in pain, his arm freshly bandaged and held up in a makeshift sling. But there was no mistaking the satisfaction in his voice. "I want to thank you again, Captain. Your people saved my life last night."

"They saved mine too," Charles said, smiling. "A few minutes later and we'd have all been dead." He glanced down at Wickes' arm. "Are you sure you shouldn't have stayed behind, gotten some rest?"

"What, this?" Wickes held his arm up, wincing a bit as he did. "No way," he said, his tone becoming serious. "I'm old, I know that, and I'm beaten up and exhausted. But I've been fighting my whole life for this moment. I'll be with you every step of the way. First New York, then Boston...then all of North America."

Charles smiled and nodded. "Sound like a pl..."

A blinding light flashed through the cockpit. Charles blinked and he jumped up from his chair, moving toward the front of the flyer. "What the hell was that?"

The airship pitched hard to the side, slamming him into the far wall as alarms began sounding. The ship flipped over, Charles and half the other occupants thrown into the wall and the ceiling hard.

Charles felt a sharp pain in his leg, another in his side. He lay on the floor as the ship stopped pitching. "What the fuck was that?" he asked, trying to get up but falling back down again as a sharp pain ripped through his body.

"Holy shit," the pilot said, staring out the cockpit. He was struggling with the controls, trying to keep the flyer steady.

"What?" Charles yelled again, gritting his teeth against the pain as he forced himself up to his feet. He staggered a few steps and fell forward as the ship shook again, grabbing onto the back of the pilot's chair.

"It's New York, sir…" The pilot was clearly shaken, and his voice trembled as he spoke.

"New York, what do you mean…" Charles climbed back up behind the pilot's chair and he held himself up, staring, transfixed. It was on the extreme right of his field of view. New York. Or the rapidly-expanding cloud of smoke and fire that had almost engulfed it. He stood in horror and watched as the massive metropolis they had just left was consumed by thermonuclear fury.

There were millions of people in New York. He'd left a dozen of his own behind, and the rest of Wickes' Resistance fighters were there too.

They're all dead now…

His squinted against the brightness, but he couldn't take his eyes off what he was seeing. He stood, bent over, propping himself against the chair, watching as the last bits of the city vanished in the yellow-white cloud of death. Then he felt as if the floor had dropped away from him. The ship was going down.

"I can't keep her up, Captain," the pilot said, his voice on the verge of panic. His hands gripped the throttle tightly, struggling to maintain control as the ship bounced around wildly.

Charles grabbed onto the back of the chair, leaning forward and looking through the cockpit. The ground was close…and getting closer.

"Everybody hang on," he yelled, dropping low and holding on. "We're going down…"

He could feel the ship falling, his stomach lurching as they plummeted to the ground. And then…impact. A loud crash, the ship rolling…screams of fear and pain…

Charles lost his grip and slammed into the side of the cabin. There were bodies flying around everywhere, creaking sounds as the ship came apart, finally settling

Charles tried to focus, to stay alert. But then he felt the impact, pain across his face...then silence. Nothing. Blackness.

*   *   *

"I'm sorry, General Taylor, but there is no deal without your guarantee. Neither I nor any of my operatives will be held responsible for any acts committed in service of UNGov. I don't care what you do with the Secretariat, the security forces, any UNGov personnel. But you will pardon the Shadow Company and me. Or we can sit here together and listen to the reports come in. It is a simple choice, General. Two hundred of my people...or four billion innocent civilians." There was no arrogance in Drogov's tone, but his resolution was like iron.

Taylor sat still, not saying a word. His mind raced with the horrible things he'd imagined Drogov had done, the murders, the torture, the wreckage and misery he had left in his wake. To let such a man escape justice—escape vengeance—it was anathema to all he had fought for. But he knew Drogov was right. He couldn't surrender his army...he wouldn't. But he couldn't watch billions die either.

"I am willing to commute any death sentences for your people, but..."

"Then there is no deal."

"Mr. Drogov..."

"Jake!" Hank Daniels came rushing into the room. Daniels was the coldest of Taylor's inner circle, the most committed to the quest. His face was white as a sheet. "It's New York, Jake..."

"What?" But Taylor knew.

"It's gone." Daniels' voice was weak, raspy. "The reports are still coming in, but the explosion was massive...hundreds of megatons."

Taylor's stomach lurched, and he felt the bile start to rise from his stomach. He looked at Daniels for a few seconds, and he saw the same horror in his friend's face. Then he turned toward Drogov, and his expression turned to ice.

Drogov met Taylor's gaze. "This is only a preview, General,"

Drogov said, his tone cold, utterly lacking emotion. "No one knows Anton Samovich as I do…and no one else has a chance to stop the cataclysm that is coming in just over ten hours." He paused. "So do we have a deal?"

Taylor turned away, but his eyes caught Hank Daniels' stricken face again. Every fiber in his body wanted to refuse, to throw Alexi Drogov in the deepest, darkest hole he could find. He hated Samovich with a passion, but now he wondered if he wasn't even more disgusted with the turncoat sitting across the table, his hands drenched in three decades of blood. But he knew what he had to do.

"Very well, Mr. Drogov. If—and only if—we successfully prevent Samovich from destroying any more cities…" Taylor paused for a few seconds then forced himself to continue. "… you and your men will be pardoned for all crimes."

Drogov nodded.

"So what is the plan? What do we need?"

"We need my men, General. And two hundred of your very best. And we have to be ready to go in two hours."

Chapter 25

Jake Taylor's Order to Karl Young:

Karl, events continue to defy even my most thoughtful analysis. Of everything I had envisioned, a madman holding the world hostage was not one of them, and even less was trusting one of UNGov's coldest, most unrepentant killers. But I have no choice. Perhaps I walk into a trap, go willingly to my death. But I must follow my instincts, and I must take any chance.

I am taking Hank with me, along with our 200 very best Erastus veterans. They will give me the best chance to survive this mission, a way to resist, even if this is a trap. But just as importantly, I am leaving you behind. If I fail to return, you must take my place, guide the army to its final victory. No matter what happens, how many people die, you must complete the quest we have begun.

If this proves to be my final order to you, go forward with my blessing and my staunchest confidence in your abilities. There is no one I trust more to carry on if I die. And if I do not return, let this be my farewell to you, my friend. My brothers.

"What about Geneva's defenses? What about the detection grid? How can we get this close?" Taylor sat in the airship, staring across the cramped cockpit toward Drogov. His voice was tense, and doubts were creeping into his mind. "I committed most of my air strength to this operation. If you're trying to lead us into some kind of trap, I am telling you now…"

"It is no trap, General." Drogov was hunched over one of the flyer's workstations, his fingers moving frantically over the keys. "Geneva's defensive installations are not what they should be. UNGov never considered a military attack a serious threat, not once they had suppressed the old national military formations. And I have access to what is there." He paused, punching another few keys. Then he turned and looked up at Taylor. "And I have just disabled it all."

"All of it? Weapons? Scanning devices?" Taylor looked disbelieving. "Don't you think that will be suspicious? With the current situation, they will put every installation on alert."

"You don't have to like me, General, but give me more credit as a professional. No system will show any malfunction. The scanners will continue to operate...they will simply provide normal reports, readings that will show nothing of your airships." Drogov paused. "We have been enemies, General, and I realize our cooperation is born of necessity and not choice. But I acknowledge you are an extremely capable soldier. Please accept that I too am skilled at what I do."

Taylor just nodded. He didn't like Drogov, and he hated having no choice but to cooperate with him. But there was no question that Samovich's henchmen was incredibly good at what he did. Just getting as close to headquarters as he had proved that. Besides, Taylor didn't have any alternatives. Four billion people were going to die in a few hours unless Drogov's plan worked.

"Bring us down at the coordinates I just sent you," Drogov said to the pilot. The officer turned and looked toward Taylor, who just nodded.

"And transmit the coordinates to all ships. We need to get on the ground as quickly as possible." The pilot repeated his glance toward Taylor.

"General Taylor," Drogov said, "perhaps you could instruct your people to take my directions. I am the one here with an intimate knowledge of Geneva's layout and defenses."

"Do as Mr. Drogov says," Taylor said, sounding like he'd just tasted something bad.

"Yes, sir." The pilot didn't look happy, but he turned back to the controls.

Taylor turned and stared at Drogov. "There, that's my good faith. Now, you tell me exactly where we're going and what we're going to do right now, or I will turn these fucking ships around, regardless of whatever your insane ex-boss is planning."

Drogov returned the gaze, silently for a few seconds. Then he said, "We're going to a spot where we can land undetected. It's ten klicks out of Geneva, a low spot with a high ridge between it and the city. I've disabled all the detection grids, programmed them to give clear readings. And there's an underground tunnel that leads right into the heart of the city...right to UNGov headquarters."

"A tunnel?"

"It's an escape route, intended for the Secretariat if they had to flee the city. The access point is well hidden, and usually inaccessible from the outside. But I entered the override codes. It should be open by the time we get there."

Taylor sighed. "That sounds like a risky plan. If we get caught there, if someone sees the airships coming and reports them..."

"It is a risk. Everything is a risk. But Geneva is in an uproar... people are running scared, trying to figure out what to do, how to survive, to preserve their wealth and position. There's a good chance we can get in before anyone knows we're there. A very good chance."

"And you know where we need to go to deactivate the doomsday system? To disarm the weapons."

"No," Drogov said. "There is no way to disable the system, not once it has been armed. Not in the time we have."

"Then what is the plan? Why are we here if we can't disarm the weapons?"

Drogov took a breath. "We can't deactivate the system, General Taylor, but we can prevent the final detonation code from being entered."

"How?"

Drogov hesitated, a pained look passing briefly over his emotionless expression. "By killing the one man who possesses those codes. By killing Anton Samovich."

*   *   *

Stan Wickes stared up at the sky. It was dark, hazy, an immense cloud of ash and dust completely blocking the sunlight, creating a bizarre midday dusk. The deep gray of the sky glowed softly, the reflections from the fires consuming New York the only light in the darkness.

He moved to the side, gritting his teeth against the pain. He was hurt, in more places than he wanted to think about. But none of that mattered. He had a stark choice. Get up and on his feet…or lie where he was and wait for death. And Marines didn't give up.

His mind was fuzzy. He remembered crawling from the wreckage. The actual crash was a bit obscure. He remembered the shouts in the airship, strapping in to his seat and bracing for impact. But he couldn't actually recall when they'd hit. The next thing he remembered was lying in the shattered craft, surrounded by chunks of metal and plastic…and bodies.

He struggled up to his feet and staggered back toward the ship. He was dizzy, and he had to concentrate to avoid falling down. But his comrades were in there, and he had to get to them, help them out. He leaned against the broken fuselage and looked around. Nobody. It looked like he was the only one who'd gotten out. He froze when his eyes moved back toward New York. The massive cloud was still there, dissipating a bit, but still hanging over the entire city. He could see the light of a massive firestorm in the gaps in the smoke and dust. He was a groundpounding Marine, no expert in high-yield nuclear weapons. But he couldn't escape an obvious conclusion. Not one person in twenty could still be alive in the ravaged city…and most of them would die in a day or two from radiation poisoning, even if they escaped the rampaging firestorms.

In all his years in the Resistance, all his dreams of rebellion, of freeing the city, and later the world, from UNGov's tyranny, he'd never imagined retribution on such a scale. He found himself frozen, unable to tear his eyes away from the vision of hell before him. Everyone he knew, all the Resistance warriors he'd left behind, friends, comrades...they were all dead now. They had won a great victory, struck a blow toward freeing the world, but their celebration was short-lived. Their struggle had cost them their lives.

No, there's nothing you can do about New York, no way to help your comrades there...

He took a deep breath, steeling himself against the pain, and he pushed his way back into the remains of the airship. It was a nightmare. There were bodies everywhere. His eyes panned around, looking for movement, any sign of survivors. But there was nothing. Nothing but bodies, bloody and mangled.

He stumbled forward, grabbing onto anything he could reach to steady himself. The main body of the ship was at an angle, and a large section of roof had caved in, making it difficult to move around. He looked down at each body, reaching out, checking vainly for a pulse, for any signs of life. But they were all dead.

Finally, he found Charles. The man who had saved his life... twice. The man who had commanded the AOL soldiers who had made the Resistance's victory possible. He knew in his gut as soon as he saw his friend. Charles' was lying on top of a bulkhead, his legs covered in blood. But it was when his gaze fell on the AOL captain's face that he was sure. Charles' head was twisted at an obscene angle, his neck clearly broken.

Wickes knew his comrade was dead, but he reached out and put his fingers to Charles' neck. Nothing.

Wickes felt the strength draining from him. New York destroyed...his home. All his comrades, old and new. He was old, alone, in pain. He felt an almost irresistible urge to give up, to stay where he was, lie down and die next to his comrades. If he hadn't gotten a lethal dose of radiation yet, he knew he would if he stayed put. The effort could end, the pain. Death would bring relief, it would bring peace.

But there were voices in his head, friends long gone...and the men who had trained him so long ago. He could hear the drill sergeants, the officers who had commanded him in battle. He saw images of himself, young, vital, clad in the combat fatigues of the Corps.

Marines don't give up. He'd heard that before, he'd said it. He'd used the phrase to encourage the Marines under his command so many years ago. And the phrase had driven him, provided the strength to drive his Resistance fighters to push themselves to the limit. Could he do less than he had urged so many others to do? Give up when he could press on, even if it was futile…even if he only got a few kilometers before the radiation took him down.

He stared down at Charles for another moment, saying a silent goodbye to a comrade whose impact had been enormous despite such a short acquaintance. Then he turned and stumbled back the way he had come. He stopped next to the twisted remains of the cockpit locker, holding on and kicking open the door. He reached inside, pulling out a survival pack. Then he climbed from the airship, from the wreck he alone had survived.

He turned and looked back toward New York, for just a few seconds. Then he opened the sack he'd brought with him, grabbing one of the two water flasks and taking a deep drink. He hadn't realized how thirsty he had been, not until the water poured over his parched throat. He felt the urge to drain the plastic canister, but he knew he had to ration what he had. He took one more swig and replaced the cap, shoving the bottle back in the sack.

He looked through the survival kit, pulling out two doses of painkillers, tiny injector units. He jabbed one into his thigh and then, without a pause, he injected the second one. He felt the relief almost immediately, and a surge in his energy level as well.

He knew he should eat something, but his stomach was upset. Even the water had made him nauseous. It's the radiation, he thought. He considered trying to force some food down anyway, but even the thought made him retch. He dug through the meds in the kit, pulling out another injector, a stimulant. And he saw another small plastic bag with three of the small injectors inside. It was labeled, 'anti-rad kit.' He ripped it open and pulled out a small scrap of paper with instructions. "One shot every two hours," he said, reading it out loud.

He stood up slowly after he had finished with the meds and repacked the survival kit. He slung the bag over his back and he turned away from New York, and began walking due west. He had no idea where to go, but he knew if he was going to have any chance of surviving the radiation, he had to get some distance from New York. He felt the urge to look behind him, one last glance at the dead city that had been his home. But he wouldn't let himself.

The way is forward, he thought. There is no room for sentiment or weakness, not now...

*   *   *

Taylor moved forward, almost at the head of the column of soldiers. He'd intended to be in the front, but the Supersoldiers had almost revolted on the spot, and he'd finally agreed to allow a dozen scouts to move to the head of the formation.

Hank Daniels was standing right behind Taylor, his position as a general of the AOL currently subordinated to his self-designated responsibility as Taylor's bodyguard. Daniels didn't like Drogov, and he'd argued with Taylor against trusting the UNGov turncoat. There was too much chance it was all a trap, that the AOL's irreplaceable commander was walking into an ambush. Even if Drogov was legit, Daniels knew the mission was a desperate gamble. He'd finally accepted that there was no choice, but he'd begged Taylor to stay behind, to put him in command instead and not risk himself. But Taylor had been adamant. He'd come through four years and a dozen worlds to get to this moment...and he would see it finished. Whatever the risk.

Daniels had known Taylor for a long time, too long to think his friend would back down no matter what he said. He doubted Taylor would have under any circumstances, but having lost Tony Black, and now Bear Samuels, he knew the AOL's commander would never send another friend out while he stayed behind. Jake Taylor was the most loyal person he'd ever met...

and he inspired that same intense dedication in those he led. So, Daniels put his real energy into insisting he come along. If Taylor was going to go on a mission like this, with UNGov's premier murderer at his side, Daniels was determined he would be there too. Taylor had argued, ordering Daniels to stay back with Karl Young, so the two could jointly command the army, lead it on its steady advance to Geneva. But Daniels was as stubborn as his commander, and Taylor finally gave in.

Daniels hadn't been more than two meters from Taylor since…and he didn't intend to get any farther. He made no effort to hide his disdain for their makeshift ally, and the two had almost come to blows twice since they mounted the airships. He had promised the Drogov he'd kill the bastard the instant he decided it was necessary. Daniels knew Drogov was dangerous, but he wasn't scared of the UNGov henchman. Hank Daniels rated himself a match for the worst thug UNGov could throw at him…Supersoldier, veteran, survivor of ten years on Erastus.

"How much farther?" Taylor asked Drogov. The UNGov assassin—at least that's how Daniels saw him—was walking next to Taylor. And Daniels was just behind, ready to carry out his promise at the first sign of treachery.

"Less than a kilometer. We will come up in the sub-cellar of the UNGov headquarters. There is an express elevator that leads to the Secretariat levels, but I don't have the override codes for that. The second we activate it, alarms will go off. And we need to get as close as possible before we're detected."

"Stairs?" Taylor asked.

"Yes. That's the best chance to get up there without being detected. We'll probably run into some intermittent foot traffic, but if we take them out before they can communicate with anybody we should be okay."

"That building is a kilometer in height…that's what, at least three hundred flights of stairs? And there must be some detection devices in there, something that will pick up the sounds of a skirmish or the movement of so many soldiers. So, we'll be fighting our way up at least some portion of it."

"Yes. I suggest we leave forces at various points behind us. If we are detected, we need a rearguard to keep enemy from taking us from behind." Drogov paused. "I'd suggest leaving my men behind, as they will tire more quickly than your enhanced warriors…but I doubt you're prepared to trust me to that extent."

Daniels made a face at the very idea that they would leave his cutthroats and murderers behind them without supervision, but then Taylor said, "I do not trust you at all, Mr. Drogov… but your suggestion makes sense. We will use your men to protect our flank, but you will remain with me until this mission is completed and we have made our escape."

Daniels almost spoke up, but Taylor's last sentence carried a menace with it that reassured him his commander was as untrusting as he was. And he thought he understood his friend's rationale. *We'll be leaving them behind us, but we'll have Drogov…and he doesn't seem like the self-sacrificing type. And the main force will be mostly our men.*

"There," Drogov said, pointing forward. The tunnel widened into a large round room. He ran forward, through the room to a large panel on the far wall. Taylor was startled by the quick movement, and Daniels saw the general's hand drop to the pistol at his side.

"I have disabled the security." Drogov turned and pointed toward the ceiling. "There is the hatch. There should be no alarm when I open it."

"Should be?" Taylor stepped forward after Drogov, his hand moving slowly from his gun.

"Yes, General, should be. Though you do not trust me, I am being very honest with you. I believe I am privy to all security protocols, but it is not impossible that Anton has some safeguards he has kept to himself in case I turned against him."

"In which case…"

"In which case, we'll have a harder fight to get to the top."

Taylor turned and looked back, his eyes meeting Daniels'. "In which case, we will resort to plan B, Mr. Drogov." He waved his arm, beckoning one of his officers to come forward. "Major Quinn…"

"Sir!" The Supersoldier moved up and stopped in front of

Taylor, snapping to attention.

"You are to keep two squads here, Major. You are to activate the device immediately."

"Yes, General."

"Device? What device?" Drogov turned and looked back at Taylor, a confused look on his face.

"As you said yourself, Mr. Drogov, I do not trust you. It is not only treachery that concerns me but even honest failure. Whatever happens, we cannot risk allowing Secretary Samovich to murder billions of innocents. Which is why I have brought a backup plan with me. A nuclear warhead strong enough to vaporize this building, taking Samovich with it." Taylor paused, staring back at Drogov. "Indeed, I would leave it here now, and detonate it remotely if I knew for certain Samovich was in the building. But I cannot take the risk that he is elsewhere, in a bunker or far enough away to survive the blast. If we destroy this building and fail to kill him, he will undoubtedly destroy the cities."

Taylor continued to stare at Drogov. "You seem surprised. I trust it is not my willingness to destroy this whole building, to kill thousands of UNGov personnel, that is the cause of your bewilderment. Why is it that the most brutal and evil of men always seem surprised when their adversaries prove willing to employ their own tactics? Perhaps you view me as some kind of sympathetic creature, one unwilling to do the things you would do."

Taylor walked forward until he was standing right next to Drogov. "So know this, Alexi Drogov. If you do anything—anything at all—that I feel interferes with this mission, I will kill you before you know it is even coming. If destroying Geneva is what I must do to kill Samovich, that is what I will do, with no more thought to its millions of citizens than your former master showed for those in New York."

Taylor stood stone still, glaring at Drogov with an expression that defined cold rage. "I will kill whomever I must, Mr. Drogov, including Secretary Samovich, you, all your men…and every last man, women, and child in this cursed city. You are alive because you are useful to me, and if you wish to stay alive, you will seek to remain so. And know this...if we fail in killing Samovich, if we are defeated by security forces or prevented in any way from completing this mission, Major Quinn and his men will detonate this warhead. So, understand...there is no scenario save total success that offers you the slightest chance of survival. If you want to live long enough to see if I choose to honor my promises, you will stay focused...and do whatever it takes to see your former boss—your former friend—does not survive the next hour."

Drogov just stared back, struggling but failing to keep the surprise off his face.

"Now, Mr. Drogov...you elected to make a deal with the devil...and that is just what you have done." Taylor turned back toward Quinn. "You have your orders, Major. If we do not return or contact you in one hour, you are to detonate the device. If you are discovered and attacked by UNGov security forces, you are to detonate the device. If you feel you are in any way threatened by Mr. Drogov's men, you are to detonate the device." Taylor paused. "I am counting on you, Geoff. We have fought together since the early days on Erastus, and I trust you. I trust you to follow my orders and detonate that device...even if I am still in the building. Even if all of us are still in the building." He paused again. "Even if you and your men are unable to escape."

"Yes, General Taylor. You can count on me, sir."

Taylor nodded. Then he turned back toward Drogov. "Shall we go? Time is not on our side."

Drogov swallowed hard. He was generally unflappable, confident that his abilities exceeded those of his enemies. But there was something about Taylor, something that unnerved him. He'd harbored thoughts of betrayal, of turning on Taylor after Samovich was dead. But now he found himself experiencing feelings he never had. He was afraid of Taylor. More afraid than he'd ever been of anyone or anything.

"Yes, General," he said meekly. "I am ready."

Chapter 26

Excerpt from Preliminary Status Report, New York City:

Preliminary casualty estimate are 3,800,000-4,300,000 dead, with in excess of 1,800,000 critically injured. Over 2,000,000 remain missing. Many of the wounded have been subjected to untreatably lethal radiation doses, with projected survival periods ranging from two to fourteen days. Property damage assessments are as follow: Manhattan, 99.9% total destruction of physical plant; Brooklyn, 96.4% total destruction of physical plant; Queens, 89.3% total destruction of physical plant...

Wickes felt like his insides were coming apart. He was on his hands and knees, retching hard. But there was nothing save a bit of foam, tinged pink now with blood. He'd been on the move for two days, and he hadn't eaten a thing. Just the thought of food make his stomach lurch. All he'd had was two liters of water, and he'd made that last as long as he could. But it was gone now, and his throat was parched, the acid from his stomach making the pain sharper each time he fell to the ground and vomited.

He'd had the usual basic radiation battle procedures training half a century before, and he tried to remember as much as he could. He knew he'd taken a heavy dose, possibly a lethal one, or maybe survivable, at least with treatment. Which he wasn't likely to get. So considering the severity of his symptoms, he settled on effectively lethal.

Still, he kept moving, unwilling to yield to the urge to give up, to lie down on the grass somewhere and wait for death. There didn't seem to be much point to it. He wasn't likely to get anywhere walking through the abandoned New Jersey suburbs. UNGov had herded the millions who'd lived here into New York and the coastal neighborhoods facing it, leaving hundreds of towns eerily empty, most of the abandoned buildings still standing, decaying slowly.

He pushed himself back up to his feet, fighting off the dizziness that almost sent him falling to the ground. The fatigue was almost unbearable, but he pushed forward. He was walking down an old highway. The asphalt was broken up and full of holes, but there was still enough flat area to stumble along.

He walked a bit, perhaps half a kilometer. Then he stopped. There was a sound. At first he couldn't place it, but then he realized it was behind him...coming from above. He turned and looked up at the sky, still dark and obscured by the ash and dust cloud from New York. But he saw something, a tiny dot, moving. Then another.

He stared intently as the figures came closer, until he could see enough to know. They were airships of some kind. And they were heading toward him.

His first thought was hallucination. The radiation sickness... it was affecting his mind. But the ships got closer, and he could hear them now as well as see them. It seemed real, too real.

Then he counted them. There were half a dozen. No, seven. There had only been five AOL craft, and he knew for certain that one of those was twisted wreckage that would never fly again.

UNGov...

It had to be. They'd destroyed New York, and now they were hunting for survivors. He stood and stared as the ships approached. Then he reached down and pulled the pistol from his belt. He had no intention of being captured. And he wasn't going down without a fight either.

He swallowed a deep breath of air, trying to steady the rolling in his stomach. Then gripped the gun tightly, his finger on the trigger.

Just one more fight…and then it will be over…

And I will be with my old comrades…

*   *   *

The fire reverberated through the enclosed space of the stairwell, a cacophony almost deafening to Taylor's enhanced ears. His people had fought three firefights as they climbed the stairs. The first two had been over almost immediately, and the UNGov security personnel had been killed before they could communicate any kind of alarm. The third had just begun, and it looked like it was going to be a much nastier fight.

"We've got more security forces backed up into the hall, Jake." Hank Daniels was standing between Taylor and the enemy, clearly trying to hide the deliberative nature of his positioning. "I think the shit just hit the fan."

"We've got to move then, push them back to the door and take the fight out of the stairwell." Taylor looked at Daniels. "I need you to do it, Hank. Once you drive them off the stairwell, I'll head up and find Samovich." Taylor could see the concern in his friend's face, the horror at the thought of Taylor going on without him. "Hank, I know you're worried about Drogov… but I need you to do this. It's our only chance. That psychotic asshole up there could start destroying cities any minute. There's no time."

"I know, Jake, but…"

"There are no 'buts,' Hank. You've been at my side a long time, old friend. You know I can take care of myself. Now do this, take that landing and push the UNGov forces back onto the floor. It's just a few more flights to the top. I can be up there in a few seconds."

Daniels didn't look happy, but he nodded anyway. "Okay, Jake. I've got this." He turned without another word, waving and yelling to the Supersoldiers at the front of the column. "Let's clear these pieces of shit, boys!"

Daniels lunged forward, firing with his assault rifle as he bounded up the stairs at the head of his troops. The UNGov forces had better cover, and their fire cut into the AOL troopers. Supersoldier mods didn't do much for soldiers packed into a narrow stairwell, rushing up into automatic fire. Daniels' troops fired too, their accuracy almost uncanny, but every UNGov guard they shot down was replaced immediately.

Daniels was right in the front, rushing into the deadly fire. His men were falling around him, two hit...then four. But they kept running.

Daniels leaned down, grabbing a rifle from one of his stricken soldiers, firing now with a gun in each hand as he lunged up to the landing and blasted away through the door.

"Go, Jake," he screamed as he pushed through the door and onto the floor beyond. "Good luck, my friend."

Taylor watched Daniels with admiration and amazement. He'd known Hank Daniels as long as he could remember, but he was still surprised by the strength and courage of his old friend. But there was no time, now, not for admiration...not to worry about Daniels, to respond to the feeling in his gut, the fear that he'd just sent yet another friend to his death.

"Let's go," he yelled, glancing behind him as he did. His soldiers had been running by, following Daniels up the stairs and through the heavy door. Taylor spotted one of his veterans, a man he'd fought with on Erastus, back when they'd both been normal soldiers. "Captain Turren, bring three squads and follow me." He stood where he was and yelled. "Everybody else, follow General Daniels!"

Taylor's eyes snapped to Turren. The officer nodded and said, "Ready, sir!"

Taylor returned the nod. Then he raced up the stairs, ignoring the residual fire still rattling around the stairwell.

Three more flights. Then the final showdown.

Assuming Samovich is there. If he isn't, four billion people will die.

And I will kill Alexi Drogov myself.

*   *   *

Wickes was exhausted, beaten. He knew he was dead. And he was ready. He thought again of New York, of the millions dead, a great city gone, reduced to a few twisted bits of metal, poisoned by radiation. Of friends dead, of men and women who'd followed him. All dead.

He'd felt the elation of victory, the surge of excitement that New York had been freed, that North America was in open rebellion. For an instant, he'd let himself believe it was possible. That UNGov could be defeated. But that hope disappeared in a storm of nuclear fury. New York was gone…and he had no doubt the same fate awaited any other city that threw off the yoke of UNGov.

If it hasn't happened already…is Boston still there? Philadelphia? Chicago?

He hadn't moved. He would stand right where he was, meet the enemy here for the last time. He had no illusions. This was his last battle, and it wouldn't last long. Indeed, the enemy could have blasted him from the air. The fact that they hadn't suggested they wanted to take him prisoner, another victim for their interrogation chambers. Wickes had no intention of being taken alive, but he intended to use whatever opportunities he had to take some of the enemy with him.

The ships were on the ground, and he could see figures emerging. He couldn't make out much in the shadowy gloom, but that didn't matter. Their attempt to take him captive would give him one final gift. A chance to kill his enemies one final time.

He'd had his gun in his hand, but he reholstered it. They had to believe he was surrendering…at least until they were close enough. Then…

He saw them coming, a dozen at least. He knew he couldn't kill them all, not before they took him down. But the numbers didn't matter. What was important was that he die fighting, weapon in hand, true to his cause to the end. Death was inevitable, all he had left of free choice was to determine how he died.

He watched as they came forward.

They should fan out more…they're all clumped together. An easy target. Sloppy.

He squeezed his hand, trying to gather his fleeting strength for the last few seconds, the final battle. He focused on the lead figure, obviously the commander. Just a few more steps…

"Don't move," the soldier in the front said. His voice was firm, demanding. But there was something odd. He'd heard UNGov enforcers for decades, and they shared an arrogance, one he didn't hear now.

No, no distractions…

His hand moved slowly toward his pistol.

Just another step…

"Are you one of Captain Charles' men? Or a member of the New York Resistance?"

Wait…something's not right.

His hand twitched, ready to lunge for the weapon. But something held him back.

"I am Major Arlington, Army of Liberation," the man yelled. "Please, stand where you are. Don't make us shoot you…"

Wickes felt a wave of uncertainty. Was it possible? Or just a trick? The idea of yielding, of being taken by a simple lie was too much to bear. His choice was stark, fight now, and die…or allow himself to be taken. And if these were UNGov soldiers, yielding meant he would lose his chance to die in arms, that his last days would be filled with unimaginable torment.

But they know Captain Charles…if these are General Taylor's soldiers…

He thought, for a second that seemed like an eternity. And then he made his decision.

He held his hands out from his sides, and stood firm, totally still.

"I am Captain Stan Wickes, New York Resistance."

* * *

Taylor burst through the door and lunged forward, his soldiers streaming through behind him. "Where," he screamed. "Where would Samovich be?"

Drogov was right next to Taylor. He took a look around the large open area. "His office is this way." He pointed down the hall, just as a group of guards came running from that direction.

The Supersoldiers behind Taylor spread out and began firing, dropping close to a dozen of the enemy guards before they managed to return fire. By then Taylor and his people had ducked behind the makeshift cover the room offered.

The UNGov guards were mostly in the open, and the deadly fire of the Supersoldiers was gunning them down in clumps. But these weren't normal security troops, they were Secretariat Guards, the most elite soldiers in service to UNGov. They lost perhaps twenty of their number, but then they too dove for cover, and the firefight slowed, became closer to even. Taylor's soldiers had the edge in ability and experience, but they were outnumbered. And worse, they were running out of time.

"How quickly can Samovich destroy the cities?"

Drogov was crouched behind a desk next to Taylor. "He has a series of codes to enter, but once he decides to do it, no more than a few minutes."

"You know him best, Drogov. Will he do it? And when?"

"Normally, he'd wait to see if his security took your people out...especially if he knows you're here. He would want to see if your army fell apart without you if his forces managed to kill you." He paused uncomfortably. "But now, I just don't know. I think he's lost his rationality...and that means he could do anything."

Taylor sighed, and he turned and looked over at his troops. The entire expedition had consisted of the best of the best... long service Erastus men, Supersoldiers all. And Turren had brought the cream of those with him. And Taylor was about to order most of them to die...

"Captain, we've got to break through...now!"

"Yes, sir," Turren replied, not a hint of fear or resentment at Taylor's command. "General Taylor needs us to break through, boys. On my command we go..."

The words cut through Taylor.

Yes…go die for me…

Turren turned back toward Taylor and nodded. "Just give us a few seconds, sir. We'll buy you the time you need."

Taylor just nodded. He knew he should say something, express gratitude or appreciation. But no words came.

Turren lunged forward, leaping over the desk as he yelled, "Charge!"

Taylor watched as the soldiers followed, every one of them. Men who had served at his side for fifteen years or more. Men who were showing him now the true extent of their devotion.

They started dropping immediately. They were charging soldiers armed with automatic weapons. They were slowed, forced to climb over desks and move around chairs and cabinets. But they didn't waver, not for an instant. And they fired as they went, their enhanced eyes and neural implants making their aim deadly, even when running and jumping over obstacles.

About half of them were down by the time they reached the line of desks and overturned tables the UNGov forces were using as cover. But they didn't hesitate…they threw themselves over the barricades, still shooting as they did. Those who had emptied their clips, or dropped their rifles as they jumped, attacked with fists and feet, breaking jaws and ribs with single blows, arms wrapping around the necks of the UNGov soldiers, squeezing, snapping.

Taylor was horrified. He'd seen terrible battles in his life, but it never got easier to watch his soldiers die, especially when he'd sent them on a virtual suicide mission. But one thing would be worse. To allow it all to be in vain.

"Let's go, Drogov." He paused, for just an instant. "And if we don't get Samovich…if my men died in vain, I am going to kill you."

Drogov didn't respond, he just nodded. And then the two lunged over the desk, running toward the Secretary-General's office.

* * *

Wickes was lying on a makeshift cot in the back of the airship. He'd been fading in and out of consciousness since shortly after he'd been rescued. He still couldn't believe it. His pursuers had indeed been AOL soldiers, sent to search for survivors from the crashes. It turned out only two of the four airships heading for Boston had gone down. The others had been shaken up but managed to stay airborne and make forced, but safe, landings. Their crews had just begun to search for survivors from the other two ships when a squadron of new flyers showed up, fresh from AOL headquarters and sent to reinforce the rebels in New York.

Wickes realized his own survival instincts, his drive to press on immediately, had only delayed his rescue. If he'd stayed where we was he would have been found far sooner, and gotten medical treatment two days earlier too. He knew he was in bad shape, but none of that mattered to him. Not anymore. His rescuers had brought him more than an escape…they had carried word with them. The AOL had met UNGov's main army, and they'd crushed it utterly. Even now, they were advancing on Geneva. Wickes was still heartbroken about New York, but the thought that UNGov might fall any day, that the world would regain its freedom—it was almost more than he could process. His friends, the people of New York…they had not died for nothing.

"I see you're awake again, Captain." Lou Vane knelt down next to the improvised bed he'd managed to cobble together to accommodate his patient. "That's good. I think you're responding to the anti-rad agents. It's time for another shot."

Wickes looked back at the medic—Vane wasn't a doctor, just a non-com trained in field triage and first aid. But radiation was a fact of life on the modern battlefield, and Wickes knew he was fortunate his caregiver had both knowledge and meds for treating radiation sickness. Still, Wickes could tell Vane was worried. The sergeant had tried to hide it, unsuccessfully.

"I do feel better, Lou. Thanks for all you've done." He almost didn't add anything, but he found he had no taste for playacting or lies. Not now. "But we both know I'm too far gone for this. You'll buy me a few extra days, but that's all. Not that I don't appreciate it."

"Did they teach you in Marine camp to be so pessimistic?" Vane grabbed Wickes' arm and jabbed in the injector.

Wickes winced. His skin was sensitive, almost sore...another side effect of the radiation sickness. It wasn't the worst symptom by far, but it did make the shots hurt quite a bit. "They taught us realism, Lou."

"Well, you might be right, Captain. Save for one thing. We're on our way back to army headquarters. When General Young heard about what happened in New York, he ordered us to bring you back at once. He wants to meet you...and to be sure you get the medical care you need."

Wickes looked back at the medic, his eyes wide with surprise. "You have trans-continental communications?"

"Yes. That's how we found out what had happened here. We picked up a signal from your broadcast." He paused a moment. Then his voice turned somber. "The one you made with Captain Charles."

A shadow passed over Wickes' face. Rod Charles had been a good man, one who'd become a close friend, even in the few days they'd spent together. It was wrong he hadn't lived to see this.

"Anyway," the medic continued, "that's when General Young sent us here. And we left a trail of airships on station to relay comm traffic back and forth."

Wickes felt a wave of energy...more than he'd had in days. He wasn't sure if it was the meds or the news—probably both—but he picked himself up, raising his head for a few seconds before he dropped back down, overcome by dizziness.

"Just rest, Captain. I know you feel better, but you're still in rough shape. But as soon as we get you back to headquarters, you'll get the treatment you really need. You're going to be fine." He smiled. "Just fine."

Chapter 27

From the Journal of Jake Taylor:

Four years of war. Hell unimaginable. Worlds traversed, friends lost. And for all those lost, the tens of thousands dead, the sacrifice and heroism and courage of legions of soldiers... the fate of Earth came down to a small battle, barely a skirmish by the standards of my army. And to the actions not of an ally, but of an enemy.

Taylor's heart was pounding in his ears, his body slick with sweat. It wasn't the physical danger, nor concern he'd be killed or wounded. No, it was worse than that. He was afraid he'd be too late, that Samovich would have already detonated the warheads. That the blood of four billion people would be on his hands.

Drogov was behind him. The ex-UNGov assassin was experienced and well-trained, in excellent physical condition. But he couldn't keep up with a half-cyborg with more than fifteen years of experience fighting in the worst hells mankind had ever found. Taylor was about two meters ahead. He knew he shouldn't take his eyes off his tenuous new ally, but he had no choice. He'd left his soldiers behind, in two desperate firefights. Those men were dying, many of them at least, to clear the way for him to get to Samovich. And he'd be damned if he would let their sacrifices be for nothing.

He lunged ahead, running down the hall. A guard leapt in

front of him, but he whipped up his rifle and fired, almost instinctively. The soldier's head exploded, and he dropped to the ground, clearly dead. He was the third of Samovich's guards to try and block Taylor...and the third to die.

The door was ahead. It was closed, but Taylor didn't slow down...he pushed harder off his legs, accelerating. Every second could be the one that saved billions. He lunged with one last, herculean push, throwing himself into the door with all the power his enhanced legs could manage.

He felt the impact, the pain from the heavy door in the instant it held against his onslaught...then the cracking, the movement as it gave way. He fell forward, rolling into the room, his head snapping around, scanning his surroundings. The office was large, immense. It was plusher than anything he'd ever seen, with floor to ceiling windows on three sides and furnishings so luxurious, their value was obvious. But his eyes weren't distracted by the view, and his focus settled on the three guards in the room, even now turning toward him, rifles drawn.

He let himself continue forward, using his momentum to bring him back up to his feet, even as the rifle swung around and fired. The first guard fell back, a hole in his forehead and blood pouring down his face. But Taylor didn't hold his gaze to watch. He was already turning, firing on the second.

His enemy was bringing his own rifle around, but he was too late. Taylor's first shot took him hard in the chest, and the next two ripped into his neck. He dropped his gun and fell, his hands grasping at the terrible wounds as he dropped.

Taylor was moving around to the third. But these soldiers were no ordinary UNGov conscripts. They were Secretarial Guard, as well trained as Taylor's own men, or nearly so. They weren't cyborgs, and their capabilities were no match for Taylor's. But they were ready and waiting when he burst in, and there had been three of them. The last one brought his rifle around, and even as Taylor took aim, he fired.

Taylor felt the round slam into his chest. He gasped hard for breath, feeling the pain of the bullet shattering a rib, burying itself in his lung. But he'd been wounded before, and his discipline was absolute. He ignored the pain, set aside the fear of a critical wound. His body was pumped full of stimulants, and he felt the wave of nanobots releasing, rushing through his blood toward the injured area.

It was a bad wound, one that might have instantly killed a normal man. But Taylor was still on his feet, still bringing his weapon around. He pulled the trigger, and the rifle spewed automatic fire, dropping the soldier in a spray of blood.

Taylor staggered forward, bringing his gun toward the man seated behind the desk.

"Stop, General Taylor," said the man, his hand resting on the keyboard of the workstation. "One keystroke and billions die."

Taylor froze.

"At least I assume you are General Taylor. I am Anton Samovich. Pleased to meet you at last." There was a strange tone in Samovich's voice. Taylor recognized insanity. Samovich had lost his mind…and his button was on the deadliest trigger that had ever existed.

"Don't," Taylor said, trying to keep the tension from his voice, but doubting he had succeeded.

"I am tempted to pull the trigger no matter what, General. These people do not appreciate what I, what all of us at UNGov have done for them. They deserve this, no?" Samovich laughed. Then his voice became deeper, more threatening. "Drop the gun, General. Drop it now, or you will kill four billion people."

Taylor stared back for an instant, his eyes gauging the distance between him and Samovich.

Can I make it? Can I get to him before he hits that key?

No, he realized. It was just too far. And his wound would slow him down.

He felt his hands tighten around his rifle, a subconscious protest against the thoughts in his mind. But then he opened his hands, let the weapon drop.

"Very good, General. Now back up. You're a little closer than I'd like considering those cyborg improvements you've got. A gift from me, I might add."

Taylor took a step back.

Samovich nodded. "A bit farther, General." Samovich watched as Taylor stepped back, staggering a bit as he did. "Is that wound getting to you, General? I guess even a Supersoldier smarts when his lung is torn to shreds, eh? Perhaps you have had your final wound. I am tempted to take some time, watch you die slowly."

Samovich turned and glanced over toward the door as another figure entered the room. "Alexi! I was concerned you were dead. Do I have you to thank for bringing this rebel to me?"

Drogov walked into the room. "Yes, Anton. My plan was to assassinate him, but once I knew you had activated the omega protocols, I had another idea, one with a higher probability of success."

"Well done, my friend. With their commander dead and four billion lives in the balance, his troops will have no choice but to surrender." He turned back toward Taylor. "I will offer them clemency, General Taylor, in return for their surrender." A wide smile erupted on his face. "Of course, I will never honor it. Once your men yield, they will learn the price of treason." The tone in his voice turned almost instantly into a dark anger. "Your soldiers in this building will all die, of course. There are far more security troops than they can hope to defeat."

Taylor glared back, struggling to ignore the pain, the wetness of blood in his throat. He felt rage, that his men would all die, that he'd allowed Drogov to trick him. He was a fool, he'd convinced himself to believe…and he'd thrown away victory. Maybe…

He longed to lunge forward, to kill Samovich—or that lying Drogov—with his bare hands. But his slightest move would consign billions to death. He felt lost, empty. There was nothing to do…nothing save remember his last hope. The men at the base of the building…and the weapon they carried with them. He knew he was going to die here, that Hank and the rest of the men he'd brought with him were doomed. But the fight wasn't over. Just a few more moments…

He'd die no matter what, he knew that. The wound was too

grave for his nanos to repair, and he wasn't likely to see a field hospital. But the head of UNGov wouldn't live much longer. The neural implant in Taylor's head told him there was less than fifteen minutes, a quarter of an hour before the entire building, and a good chunk of downtown Geneva, tasted the same kind of nuclear fury New York had. And the war would go on. It would fall to Karl Young's shoulders. The intense man his friends called Frantic would be the last of them, the final survivor of the crew from Firebase Delta who'd gone on to lead a crusade.

As long as one of us lives, the fight goes on…

"Well, General Taylor…" Samovich said, his finger still poised on the keyboard as he pulled his other hand from under the desk, a pistol firmly in its grip. "…I'm afraid we have come to the end."

"Let me, Anton." Drogov stepped forward, an assault rifle gripped tightly in his hand. "It was my job…and you know I hate to fail."

"Of course, Alexi, be my guest."

Taylor held himself up, despite the weakness almost overcoming him. If he had to die, murdered by a traitor who'd made a fool out of him, he was damned well going to die on his feet.

Drogov looked at Taylor, raising the rifle and taking aim. Taylor stood where he was, not willing to give his killer the satisfaction of seeing fear.

Drogov's finger tightened on the trigger. Then he whipped around, moving so quickly he was almost a blur. The rifle cracked loudly, a single shot. And Anton Samovich sat for a moment, a partially-formed look of shock on his face. Then he fell, his face covered in blood from the perfectly-placed head shot.

Drogov leapt over the desk, checking to make sure Samovich was dead. Then he turned toward the workstation screen, punching in a code to disarm the detonation system. He let out a deep breath when he finished, and he turned back toward Taylor. The AOL's commander's strength had failed him, he had dropped to his knees. He was staring, his face a mask of pain and amazement.

"I told you I would do this." Drogov ran around the table, over toward Taylor. He reached out and held on to the general. "Lay back...you're bleeding worse standing up." He pushed slightly then held Taylor as he leaned back down.

"Samovich...dead?" Taylor's voice was weak.

"Yes, he's dead. And the omega program is deactivated."

"Thank you," Taylor said, just as he heard the sound of gunfire outside the door. Then boots clomping hard on the floor, men pouring into the room. For an instant he thought he was dead, that Samovich's guards had come. But then he heard a familiar voice.

"Drogov," it yelled. "Get away from the general." Then, an instant later. "Kill hi..."

"No." Taylor yelled with all the strength he had left.

Daniels held his arm up toward the soldiers flanking him.

"He killed Samovich, disarmed the doomsday device." Taylor's voice gurgled, blood spurting out of his mouth with every word. "He kept his word."

Daniels' eyes flashed toward Drogov for an instant. Then back to Taylor. "Medic," he screamed as he ran over to his friend.

"Jake..." He leaned down, his hand on Taylor's face. "Jake..."

Taylor was slipping in and out of consciousness. His mind reeled, floating, images of the room, of his friend leaning over him, moving in and out of view. He could feel his body, the tingling of the nanobots racing to heel his stricken lung.

I'd be dead already without them. But this is a big lift, even for tech like that.

Was he dying? Would the amazing modifications save his life? Or was his wound too deep...was it mortal, even for a Supersoldier?

He lay back, the voice soft distant...calling to him.

"Jake...Jake?"

Chapter 28

Captain Stan Wickes, Upon Seeing AOL Headquarters:

I feel like I'm dreaming, but God damned if you don't all look like a bunch of silver-eyed Marines!

Taylor was in darkness, lost. Silence.

No, there was something...a sound? His name?

A feeling too...hands on him, a pinprick. Then a surge of energy, of awareness. He could feel the darkness slipping away, like water draining from a sink. Then there was light, above him, bright.

"General?" He could see the face hovering over his. "General Taylor, can you hear me, sir?"

"Hear you..." he rasped, his throat dry, his words barely audible.

Then more clarity, his vision brightening. He felt tugging, his jacket, shirt coming off. Then pressure on his chest, pain. He saw a shadow. The man leaning over him, pressing down on his wound. Then coolness, a fresh dressing. He tried to raise his head, to look around the room.

"General, I need you to lie still until we can get you to a field hospital." It was the soldier leaning over him. And now he saw more familiar faces, standing above, looking down at him. One in particular.

"Hank..."

"Rest, Jake. You got hit bad, but we've got you now. You're

going to be okay." Daniels was trying to hide the worry, but Taylor had known him too long.

"Gunfire," Taylor rasped. He could hear the firing outside the office.

"We hold most of the floor, Jake. The enemy is trying to push their way in, but we've got them held."

Taylor turned his head slowly, painfully. He stared up at his friend. "I've known you too long, Hank. I can tell when you're lying." He paused and gasped for a breath. "Tell me...the truth."

Daniels stared back at Taylor, silent for a moment. Then he said, "We're trapped up here, Jake. We're holding out for now, but there are too many of them. We've got about forty men left up here."

Only forty...

"Turren...the warhead..."

"We got a signal through to him, Jake. I ordered his men to go back the way they came." Daniels paused, as if he was guilty for sending away men they desperately needed. "I didn't think they had a chance of making it up here."

"Did the right thing..."

"General Daniels, they're coming from three directions..." One of the soldiers had rushed through the door. Taylor didn't get a good look at the man's face, but he could see a bandage wrapped around the soldier's leg...just as he noticed a bloody strip of cloth tied around Daniels' arm.

"Pull the men back, Sergeant. Set up a pile of debris along the entry to the corridor. It's narrow there. That's where we'll hold."

"Yes, sir." The soldier turned and ran back out of the room.

Taylor watched the whole exchange, realizing neither one of them believed they could hold out much longer. He felt more alert, the drugs and his nanos combining to help him from his stupor. "How long, Hank?" Taylor looked at his friend. "No bullshit between old comrades...how long?"

"I really don't know, Jake. Ten minutes. Maybe fifteen. Less if they work up the courage to rush us."

Taylor nodded his head forward. "It will all fall to Karl.

Samovich is dead, the UNGov armies destroyed. If we die, at least we die in victory."

Daniels nodded, and he forced a fragile smile. "Yes, Jake... victory. Who would have imagined we would have gotten this far? It could have been a ditch on Eratsus somewhere..." He reached down with his hand, and Taylor lifted his own, grabbing hold of his friend.

"They're coming!" It was a cry from out in the hall, one of the soldiers shouting over the din of gunfire.

Daniels turned and stood in front of Taylor, holding his gun toward the door. Ready to make a last stand. Then he saw a shadow just outside the window. And another...then more. They were coming right toward the building, spreading out. Airships!

*　*　*

"General Taylor...General Daniels...this is Colonel MacArthur. Please respond." MacArthur sat in the flyer's command chair, his face hard and grim, like a statue. "General Taylor, General Daniels...any AOL personnel. Please respond."

Macarthur sighed. He was tense, nervous. He turned toward the pilot. "They're in there somewhere. Captain Turren said they were on the top level. I want the building surrounded, all ships ready to fire on my command."

"Yes, Colonel." The pilot turned to his com and relayed orders to the other ships.

MacArthur flipped the com unit back on. "General Tay..."

"Colonel, this is General Daniels. I'm here with General Taylor. We're trapped in one of the offices, with enemy forces pushing us back. How the hell did you end up here?" There was excitement in his voice.

"Captain Terren, General...he sent word that you might... need some help, sir." MacArthur stared down at his display, punching at the keys on his workstation.

"Well, Captain Terren was absolutely right, Colonel. We're damned glad to see you."

"Stay put, General. We've got your transponder signal, we've got your location. We're coming in blazing."

"Understood."

MacArthur looked back toward the pilot. "Lock in on General Daniels' signal. Transmit their coordinates to all our forces. And order all ships...open fire on the rest of the floor."

MacArthur felt his ship shake, as it opened up on the building. He watched as the heavy polycarbonate of the windows shattered under the impact of thousands of autocannon rounds, intense automatic fire from a range that made point blank seem like a sniper's long-ranged trick shot.

"Keep firing," MacArthur said, his voice feral, almost bloodthirsty. "Keep firing until every gun runs bone dry."

*　　*　　*

"Easy...easy..." Hank Daniels had his hands under Taylor's shoulders, easing his friend into the airship. MacArthur's bird was hovering just outside the window, the top of a desk thrown between its open hatch and the shattered window. It was precarious, even dangerous, but there was no choice. Jake Taylor was a Supersoldier, a hardened veteran of the harshest place men had ever fought...but Daniels knew his friend would die without immediate treatment, care he could only get in a field hospital. And there was no quicker way to get him there than hauling him right onto a Dragonfire and flying him there.

The airship shook slightly, and the makeshift ramp slid to the side. Daniels wobbled a bit, his eyes glancing briefly down, at the kilometer drop below. But he held on, stepping forward, climbing into the airship, and pulling Taylor after him. He took another step back, and the soldier holding Taylor's legs followed.

"Okay, we're in, Lieutenant. Close this hatch and get us back to camp." His eyes dropped to Taylor, his friend's face pale, sweatsoaked. "Full speed. We don't any time to waste."

He looked back at the building as the hatch slid shut. He'd left Major Stamford in command. In command of twenty survivors...plus three dozen troops from MacArthur's ships. Just over fifty men to hold the target of the quest, the building that had been the center of Earth government. He knew he should have stayed behind himself, kept command until reinforcements arrived, but right now he'd didn't give a shit about Earth, about hunting down the survivors of UNGov's security troops…none of it. His only concern was for his friend, for the man responsible for all they had achieved. And he wasn't going to leave Taylor's side. Not for anything.

He felt the ship moving, turning around, repositioning to head back to headquarters. Then he felt the thrust, the flyer blasting hard. He watched the building disappear behind them, and he pushed the concerns from his mind. The top ten floors were shattered wrecks, and most of the UNGov troops below that level had fled. He could see them streaming away from the building, fleeing in panicked rout. There was work left to do, members of the Secretariat and other high-ranking UNGov officials to find, scattered pockets of resistance to stamp out. But he knew the war was almost over. And he had no idea how to proceed. There was only one man who could step into the void, lead humanity from the brink of chaos into the future.

His eyes dropped to Taylor's still form.

"Colonel, is there any way you can get more speed from this thing?"

Chapter 29

From the Journal of Jake Taylor:

Victory. How many times have I imagined it, dreamed about it? How many times have I endured the pain and loss only by telling myself victory would make it all worthwhile? Now that we have it, the taste is bittersweet. Satisfaction, yes, and joy that my soldiers can stop dying, at least for now. But also new burdens, heavy ones. I'd allowed myself to think of the destruction of UNGov as the end, that in bringing liberty to the people of Earth, I too would taste freedom. But alas, it is not to be. I can see nothing in the future, save strife and duty. And more desperate struggles. For Earth is in total disarray, and I fear I will be compelled to replace one totalitarian regime with another, at least for a time. And I can never forget what I alone of my people know, the secret the Tegeri shared with me. The Darkness is coming.

Taylor walked slowly, leaning on a cane. He wasn't supposed to be out, at least not according to the surgeons, but he'd never been one to pay much attention to what he was told to do. Besides, the only one who'd seen him leave was a guard, a private from Juno who stared at him with that horrendous worshipful expression. It drove him fucking crazy, but he had to admit it also had its uses.

Daniels and MacArthur had saved his life at UNGov headquarters, there was no question about that, and perhaps more than anyone, Captain Turren. If the airships hadn't arrived when they had, he knew he'd have died right there on Anton Samovich's floor. That was an end he'd never quite imagined, and one he was grateful to have avoided. He owed Karl Young his thanks too…for violating his orders and responding to Turren's call when Taylor himself had forbidden any offensive moves against UNGov headquarters until further notice.

However the gratitude was partitioned, the surgeons told him he'd been minutes from death when they'd brought him in. They'd gotten him into surgery just in time and removed the projectile…and fixed enough of the damage to allow his nanos to do the rest. And the tiny implants had done just that. It was only three days later now, and he was up and around, even if unofficially and in defiance of his doctors' orders. A normal human being would have been in bed for weeks, probably still in a recuperative coma.

"Jake," Daniels said as he saw his friend and commander walking down the center of the camp. He was standing around with a group of officers—General Young, Colonel MacArthur, General Akawa, a few others he didn't recognize. And a man Taylor never thought he'd welcome in his camp. Alexi Drogov. "Should you be up and around?"

"No, probably not," Taylor said, though it was clear in his voice he didn't give a shit if anyone thought it was a good idea. "But I've been lying in that bed for almost four days, and I'm going to lose my shit if I don't get up and around…at least a little."

He nodded toward the cluster of officers. "Besides, it is past time I do some work and stop dumping my responsibilities on all of you." He turned toward Drogov. "And I don't believe I've thanked you for saving my life…and for killing Anton Samovich. I feel like you did my job for me after I failed to get it done."

Drogov nodded. "I gave you my word, General." He paused. "I doubt we will ever be friends…we are very different people. But I do not lightly make promises. I was loyal to Anton for over thirty years, and my efforts played no small part in his rise. But the man at that desk wasn't my old friend. He had been taken over by madness, broken by the disasters that had befallen him. And though I have employed brutal methods to serve my needs, I am not a monster who would sit by and watch billions killed to no advantage." He paused, looking at the small group of officers. "But there is no place for me in what is to come. I know you could never trust me, and to be honest, I do not share your optimism for democratic government. I respect you for dealing honorably with me, but if you will excuse my bluntness, I find your faith in the population to be a bit naïve. I do not underestimate your abilities, but I think you will be shocked at how little they appreciate you for bringing them freedom and how quickly they will learn to despise you, to blame you for all their failings."

He turned, taking a look at those gathered...and finally at Taylor himself. "So, General, if you honor my pardon, I will retreat to my estate in the Swiss countryside and slip away into comfortable retirement...and interfere no more in your undertakings."

"Your pardon will be honored." Taylor didn't smile, but his look was less than overtly hostile, which was an improvement.

"And my men? There are only fourteen of them left...the rest perished in the fighting."

"And your men. They will all be pardoned." Taylor paused then extended his hand. "And thank you again for what you have done. Whether you believe in our cause or not, you helped bring it about."

Drogov shook Taylor's hand. Then he turned toward the others and said, "Now, if you will all excuse me, I will make my exit...and leave you all to discuss the future of the world." He turned and, with a last nod, he walked away.

Taylor watched him leave, and then he turned back to the others. "So, don't you think it's time you caught me up on things?"

"Well, Jake..." Karl Young sounded nervous, tentative. "...things have been chaotic. There are UNGov remnants hanging on in some areas. I've sent military teams to take care of them." He hesitated.

"What is it, Karl?"

"Well, Jake, we've got other problems too. Some cities are descending into anarchy, others are overrun with criminal elements. Over just the past few days, the number of problem spots has multiplied. Our resources are already stretched thin, and things just keep getting worse. We're trying to govern along the principles we'd agreed upon, but…"

"But?" Taylor's voice was grim, tense. He knew where this was going, what it would push him to do. And all he wanted in the world was to resist.

"But the only way we're able to restore order anywhere is with brute force. Jake, we've got to keep a world in order, and we just don't have the strength to do it. We've lost too many soldiers in the fighting. There just aren't enough."

Taylor sighed. "Well, we can't let the world slip into chaos, can we? We have to make this work, somehow. Maybe if we move up elections…" Taylor let his voice slip away to silence. He knew as well as the rest of his people. Rushed elections, without any safeguards or controls, with no constitutions or guarantees of rights in place…they would only allow the same kind of people to gain positions of power. Taylor had no intention of allowing any vestige of UNGov to remain, but he was just as determined to avoid repetitions of the corrupt, dishonest governments that had preceded it.

But how do we get from here to there?

"Excuse me, General, but if you'll allow me a moment, I might be able to help, at least with regard to manpower if not political nuance."

Taylor turned toward the man standing behind Karl Young. He was old, much older than anyone else in the gathering. He had a few stringy strands of gray hair hanging from his otherwise bald head. His eyes were deep in the sockets, and he looked like death warmed over. But there was something in his stare, an energy, a strength.

"Jake," Young said, "this is Captain Stan Wickes. He was an American Marine back in the day. He was also the head of the New York Resistance."

Taylor nodded, a look of respect replacing one of confusion. "Captain Wickes, it is an honor." Taylor's tone softened. "I don't know what to say about New York, Captain. We all grieve with you."

Wickes nodded, giving himself a few seconds and then wiping the bleak look from his face. "Thank you, General. It is a great honor to meet you, sir. New York was my home, but now all we can do is fight to ensure its sacrifice was not in vain."

"What would you propose, Captain?"

"Well, sir, as I see it, you need trustworthy troops now, to serve as garrisons, to keep order and maintain the peace until a new government can be created. I am old, General..." He gestured toward his head. "...and I look all the more so since the dose of radiation I took as I watched New York consumed in nuclear fire. But your medical personnel saved my life, General. They tell me my hair will even grow back. And I would like to help you. There are more military veterans, sir, not just Americans, but British, German, French, Japanese...from all the old nations. They are all at least sixty, but that doesn't mean they can't serve again, to fill in the breach. And to train the next generation. I say we rally them, call them back to service. And I have contacts with the various Resistance movements too." He looked down for a moment. "My comrades in New York are all gone, but there are hundreds in other cities...no, thousands. Let us reach out to them, form a core of operations for each city around them."

Taylor looked around the group. He could see Young and Daniels both smiling. Clearly, they liked what they were hearing. And it made sense to him as well. "Very well, Captain Wickes," Taylor said. Though we didn't not meet until just now, it appears we have been fighting the same war against the same enemy for a long time. Let us now work together to see that victory is not lost...is not wasted."

He forced a smile. "Captain Stan Wickes, you are hereby appointed Brigadier Wickes, Army of Liberation. Your first orders are to coordinate contact with all Resistance groups. I want you to vet them all, General Wickes...we will have no vigilantes, no local vendettas, no power plays. Groups that wish to join us must be cleared by you, and they must be sworn into the AOL. I want no rogue groups…we will come down hard on anyone pursuing their own agendas."

Taylor took a breath, fighting back a wave of nausea. He didn't like how easily, how naturally, he snapped out political orders…the rigidity, the brutality with which he spoke of suppressing groups that stood in his way. He told himself he was fighting for what was right, that he would stand aside as soon as he could.

The battle cry of every brutal dictator who has ever lived…

"You will also find as many of the old veterans you spoke of as possible, offer them a chance to help us rebuild this world. They must also join the AOL."

Wickes nodded. "Thank you, General. You have my solemn word I will do my best in your service." A short pause. "And thank you. Thank you for everything."

Taylor turned toward another of the officers gathered around him. This one wore a different uniform, one Taylor's people had fought against. "General Akawa, I would also appoint you a general in the Army of Liberation if you will accept."

Akawa nodded. "I would be honored, General."

"And your first order will be to seek out all the UNGov soldiers who were conscripts, men like us, forced into military training and destined for a life of battle on a Portal world somewhere. Their place is with us. But the enforcers, the security troops and the others who had willingly served as UNGov's terroristic thugs…they must pay for what they have done."

"Understood, General. I give you my heartfelt promise, I will see it done."

"Very well, General Akawa. Welcome aboard."

"Jake, there is one last thing." Hank Daniels had a strange expression on his face. Anger, hatred…and a touch of uncertainty. "We have all but two of the Secretariat members under guard. What should we do with them?"

Taylor looked back at his friend. Hank Daniels had been the most aggressive, the angriest of his officers. But now he could see his friend's fatigue. At some point, there is too much death and suffering, even to sate the wildest rage. But some times mercy is just out of reach. He no longer felt the desire to dole out draconian punishments…but there was no choice, and certainly not for those who stood at the top of the machine that killed so many.

"They have to die, Hank. You know that." He looked at the others. "If we are to show mercy, to pardon those we'd never thought to spare during our long marches and bitter struggles, it cannot begin here, not with these self-appointed elites who ruled over the world with lies and brutality. No, they cannot live. They must die. Publically. Sic Semper Tyrannis."

Taylor felt the hypocrisy of his words. What would he and his officers be besides a new elite claiming power for themselves? What was he but a tyrant?

"Yes, Jake," Daniels said, nodding. "You are right, of course. They must die."

*   *   *

"People of the world, I am General Jake Taylor, commander of the Army of Liberation and temporary military governor of Earth." The words sounded unreal to him, like he was listening to someone else, not speaking them himself.

"I will speak to you of much today, of the lies that allowed UNGov to seize worldwide power, of the true nature of the alien Tegeri, of how and why my soldiers and I returned to Earth, to destroy an unclean government and to help mankind move boldly into its future." It had been a week since the climactic fight in Samovich's office, four days since Taylor had checked himself out of the field hospital. He had worked like a madman over that 96 hours, redeploying troop formations, organizing new recruits from the old militaries and Resistance forces, and issuing a blizzard of edicts and laws. He'd embraced his role, his new power, all the while fighting the part of him that screamed from deep within, called him hypocrite, tyrant.

"But first, I must urge you all to remain calm, to wait and allow us to restore order and maintain economic activity. All cities and provinces are under martial law, and they will remain so until further notice. All citizens are instructed to stay home whenever possible, except when working or out obtaining needed supplies. For those needing assistance, AOL teams will be distributing food, medicine, and other necessities." Taylor's voice was firm, commanding. He couldn't show weakness, not in public. He didn't like it, but he realized fear was as powerful a tool as any other, and now he needed everything he could muster.

"The remaining members of the Secretariat were executed this morning, and soon, the last traces of the old government will be gone, wiped clean from the rolls of human history. We begin anew now, all of us, and we commit ourselves to build a new future, one with greater freedom and enlightenment, one offering a better world to our children and grandchildren."

And a new war, one more terrible than any that has come before. They're not ready to hear about that, not yet. But how long can I wait? How much time do we have? It is all well and good to speak of bright futures, but the Tegeri are counting on us. And unless we stand together, we will all be destroyed.

Taylor knew little about the coming Darkness, save that he trusted T'arza, and the wise old Tegeri was clearly scared to death. For all his desires to quickly give up power, he knew that wouldn't happen—couldn't happen, not until this final war was won. But that was a truth he'd save for another day. Now he would worry about feeding people and keeping hospitals open. About sustaining the fragile and moribund UNGov economy and policing the streets.

And already, you are lying to the people, choosing what facts to tell them, and which to keep hidden. They face the worst challenge in history, and you decide they should not know yet, that even your closest aides and friend should not know. You fought, struggled against UNGov. Will you now be different?

He told himself he would be, but deep down he wondered. And that scared him more than any other battlefield.

Epilogue

C'taung stood in the hazy dusk of Ghellusan's twilight. The world was the farthest from Homeworld the Tegeri had yet explored. It was an eerie world, haunted in some way C'taung could feel but not see. It had no strategic value, at least not to his warrior's eyes. But the Council was steeped in the ancient writings and histories, and the words that had been passed down through the millennia said one thing. The Darkness would return, and when they did, it would be here, on Ghellusan.

C'taung wasn't even sure he believed in the Darkness. Was it real? Or some old legend used to scare the young when they refused to sleep? C'taung was a warrior, and he had done his service during the pointless conflict with the humans. He'd chafed for decades, restrained from employing the needed force to sweep the enemy away. But he had held back as ordered, and the war had continued, year after year.

It was over now, and he looked out at the true manifestation of Tegeri might, not the pathetic forces put into the field against the humans. His camp was immense, and as far as he could see there were the tents and shelters of the New Ones, soldiers gathered together in their millions...indeed, tens of millions. And many thousands of Tegeri as well, warriors from the many Clans, come to face the great enemy that had been spoken of for as long as any could remember.

If there is a Darkness out there, we shall be ready for them. They shall not pass us. No, the Tegeri are ready. C'taung turned to walk back to his tent, but he stopped suddenly. There was a breeze, and he felt it in every cell of his being. Not a cool wind, not cold, not even a frigid arctic blast, but the icy numbness of death itself. C'taung had led many warriors, fought many battles, but now he felt fear, a cold panic like nothing he'd ever experienced. He stood transfixed, frozen, and he looked out over his army, watching as the rays of late day light were extinguished, replaced in a few short moments by blackness.

C'taung tried to turn, to run to his headquarters and sound the alarm, but it was too late. He couldn't move. His feet were frozen to the place where he stood.

There was a flash in the sky, a beacon in the darkness, but not the illumination of sun or fire. It was a ghostly light, a cold shimmering that made him feel of death. Then another appeared. And another.

He felt the temperature dropping, the icy coldness coming upon him. And he looked down at the endless rows of shelters, the millions of warriors in his army. They all stood, stone still as he was, in the streets of the camp.

Then he watched as the eerie lights began to descend. There were hundreds of them now, perhaps thousands, and the sky was awash with the cold illumination. They moved quickly, zipping along above the rows of shelters, and the frozen, terrified warriors standing outside them. Then it began.

Beams, great shafts of the deathly light blasted down, slamming into the ground, welling up into massive clouds of fiery death. And they expanded, moving through the rows of troops, through tents and great shelters and lines of massive war vehicles. And where they went, they consumed all, an orgy of death and destruction.

C'taung watched, unable to move, his spirit gripped with a fear so primal it ruled him utterly. All around him, the army died, its millions of warriors consumed, its equipment vaporized... and when it was done, naught remained of the great force save its commander, standing on the hill and looking out at the dark and eerie silence that was all that remained, where tens of millions of soldiers had been moments before.

He stared, both feeling and not feeling his grief and despair. Then he saw the light coming for him, encompassing him. He tried to avert his eyes, but he couldn't move, and he gazed relentlessly on the swirling lights, the horror he knew was his own death. And then he was gone.

And nothing remained on Ghellusan...nothing but the silent emptiness of death...

Portal Worlds: The Darkness
A New Portal Worlds Trilogy
Coming Soon

Also by Jay Allan

Marines (Crimson Worlds I)
The Cost of Victory (Crimson Worlds II)
A Little Rebellion (Crimson Worlds III)
The First Imperium (Crimson Worlds IV)
The Line Must Hold (Crimson Worlds V)
To Hell's Heart (Crimson Worlds VI)
The Shadow Legions (Crimson Worlds VII)
Even Legends Die (Crimson Worlds VIII)
The Fall (Crimson Worlds IX)
Tombstone (A Crimson Worlds Prequel)
Bitter Glory (A Crimson Worlds Prequel)
The Gates of Hell (A Crimson Worlds Prequel)

MERCS (Successors I)
The Prisoner of Eldaron (Successors II)
The Black Flag (Successors III) – June 2016

Into the Darkness (Refugees I)
Shadows of the Gods (Refugees II)
Revenge of the Ancients (Refugees III) – March

Gehenna Dawn (Portal Worlds I)
The Ten Thousand (Portal Wars II)

The Dragon's Banner (Pendragon Chronicles I)

29096076R00199

Made in the USA
Middletown, DE
07 February 2016